The Real Hoodwives of Detroit 2:

Motor City Mayhem

The Real Hoodwives of Detroit 2:

Motor City Mayhem

INDIA

www.urbanbooks.net

Urban Books, LLC
300 Farmingdale Road, NY-Route 109
Farmingdale, NY 11735

The Real Hoodwives of Detroit 2: Motor City Mayhem

ISBN 13: 978-1-64556-407-2
ISBN 10: 1-64556-407-X

First Mass Market Printing January 2023
First Trade Paperback Printing June 2021
Printed in the United States of America

10 9 8 7 6 5 4 3 2 1

Distributed by Kensington Publishing Corp.
Submit Orders to:
Customer Service
400 Hahn Road
Westminster, MD 21157-4627
Phone: 1-800-733-3000
Fax: 1-800-659-2436

Chapter 1

Gucci

I'd arrived home at around 4:00 a.m., and Mario was nowhere to be found. He hadn't called me since he left earlier, and I didn't bother calling his bitch ass because I was tired of fighting with him. Wherever he was he could stay for all I cared. I was extremely exhausted, and the alone time was just what the doctor ordered. Not dancing at the club in a long time really took a toll on my aching body. Muscles hurt in places that I never knew existed, and all I wanted was sleep.

As I reached the top step, I removed all of my clothing, leaving it right where it fell. I dragged myself into the bathroom and cut on the shower. All in all, I was in and out in seven minutes flat. I guess you could say I took a "ho bath." Without bothering to dry off or find a nightgown, I entered my bedroom prepared to fall out. Just as my head hit the silk pillow, the damn doorbell chimed. Immediately, I reached into my nightstand and grabbed the Glock. I thought it might've been Mario ringing the bell because he lost his keys, but I wasn't one for taking chances.

"Who the fuck is it?" I called out with much attitude.

"It's me," the stranger said.

I could see a male figure through the frosted glass, but he was too tall to be my husband. I checked to make sure the safety on the gun was off. Just in case a nigga kicked in the door, I'd be prepared. "Who the fuck is 'me'? Nigga, you better state your name!" I said from behind the door. I kicked myself for not checking the surveillance camera, but I was too tired to go all the way back upstairs.

"It's Cartier."

"Who?" I asked in disbelief.

"Gucci, you heard me."

I snatched open the door with my gun aimed at his chest. "I should blow your chest out just for pulling a dumb-ass stunt like this," I yelled because I was pissed. "What if Mario was home?"

"I'm sorry. I just had to see you." The alcohol on his breath and the look on his face told it all. He was tipsy.

"What do you want?" I asked with my arms folded. The way he was staring at me reminded me that I was completely naked.

"I want you." He stepped up close to me, and I backed away.

"Look, you're drunk. Let me call you a cab." I backed away and tried to make it to the phone in the kitchen, but he picked me up.

"I got a little buzzed, but I'm not wasted. I know what I want, and I came to get it." He licked his sexy-ass lips. "I don't care what your new last name is. You will always be my bitch!"

"Cartier—" I tried to say, but he kept talking.

"That nigga Mario ain't what you want, and you know that. You only fell for the nigga because I wasn't here," he whispered while carrying me over to the marble dinner table. Then he laid me down. "I'm here, Gucci, and from this point forward, I'm not going anywhere."

I stared into his eyes, and every feeling or freaky thought I'd had over the past two months came rushing back all at once. "I can't do this to Mario."

"You don't have to do nothing. Let me do it all." He went to work pleasing my body with his hands, his mouth, and ultimately his penis.

Cartier took me to places I could've only drea-med of. Mario didn't lack any bedroom skills, but he wasn't connected with me emotionally. No matter how freaky our sex was, it was lacking pas-sion. Cartier, on the other hand, connected with me physically, mentally, and emotionally. I was in pure ecstasy, and in that moment, I felt like the old Gucci.

"Gucci, where are you?"

I heard my name, and my eyes snapped open. Like a true hood nigga, Cartier reached for my gun and pointed it in the direction of the voice.

"Who is that?" he whispered.

"That's my friend Mina." I jumped up from the table. I couldn't let her catch me like this, so I flew from the dining room and left Cartier in the darkness.

"I'm right here, girl. Wassup?" I tried to cover my parts. "How did you get in here?"

"The door was open." She pointed to the door, and I caught sight of her bloody hand. "Put your clothes on. We have to go now," she said with panic all over her face.

"Why?" I worried.

"Mario just got shot."

Chapter 2

Nikki

"You slut. I didn't know you had it in you," Anjela teased after I told her about me and Mario. Before I could tell her about Maine, my line clicked.

"Hold on, cuz." I looked at the caller ID and frowned. It said unavailable.

"Hello," I answered with much attitude.

"Is Nikkita Wallace available?" a woman asked.

"Who the fuck is this?" I knew this broad knew better than to play on my phone.

"Nikkita, my name is Jasmine Stevens. I'm an RN here at Henry Ford Hospital. Your husband, Mario Wallace, was brought in and taken to surgery about an hour ago. You were listed as his next of kin." She continued talking, but I zoned out. "Hello?"

"I'm sorry. What was my husband brought in for?" I asked, completely forgetting that I was no longer his wife. Mario must've never updated his medical information.

"Due to HIPAA regulations, I can't give you that information. If you come down here with your identification, someone will speak with you, Mrs. Wallace."

"I'm on the way!" Running to my shoes, I hung up the phone, completely forgetting about Anjela on the other end.

My cell phone rang again. "Hello." I was out of breath.

"Damn, cuz, what happened?"

"Meet me at Henry Ford. Mario is in surgery." I hung up on her again and called Mario's mother. Just as I located my black and pink Nike gym shoes sitting by the front door, Ms. C answered.

"Hey, baby."

"Ms. C," I sighed, finally spotting my keys and purse. "Henry Ford Hospital just called. Mario is in surgery."

"What?" She was in a full-fledged panic now.

"They won't tell me why until I get there, but I think he has been shot." I knew the way Mario lived his life in the streets, so being shot would be the only logical reason he would be at the hospital in surgery.

"Oh, my God." She began to cry.

"Mama, please calm down. I'm on my way to get you."

I pulled into the driveway and stepped from the whip. It was raining cats and dogs, but I didn't worry myself with an umbrella. Ms. C approached the doorway in a tan robe, jogging pants, and Ugg boots. She had Junior with her, and Maria was in her car seat. I took the baby so that she could lock up the house. Going against the grain, I pulled out my cell phone and called Gucci. Regardless of my ill feelings, she deserved to know about her husband.

Her voicemail came on. "You know who you've reached, so leave a message."

"Gucci, this is Nikki. I'm not sure if you know, but Mario is in surgery at Henry Ford Hospital. I don't know any more than what I'm telling you, so there is no need to call me back. Just get to the hospital as soon as you get this. By the way, Ms. C and Maria are with me." I ended the call.

"Nikki, do you think my baby will be okay?" Ms. C was on the verge of passing out.

"Mama, Mario is a fighter!" I reassured her as she began to pray all the way to the hospital.

As I sped into the driveway of the emergency entrance, an ambulance was speeding out. I damn near sideswiped it, but luckily I missed them by about three inches. My nerves were shot, but I had to keep it together. I let Ms. C out and went to park the car. Her nerves were shaky, and I didn't want her to drop Maria or lose Junior, so I kept the kids with me.

Just as I entered the lobby and approached the nurse's desk, Ms. C found me. "We have to go up to the third floor." We briskly walked over to the elevator, and I shifted the weight of Maria's car seat from one arm to the other.

I looked down at the little girl. Her tiny fingers found their way to her mouth, and she licked them. This was my first time seeing her so close. I had to admit that she was simply beautiful. Her jet-black hair was curly, and she had a bow in the center of her head like Pebbles from *The Flintstones*. Her golden skin looked like cornflakes, and the dimple at the bottom of her chin was priceless.

As we stepped onto the elevator, someone called out, "Wait up." It was my cousin.

"Did y'all find out anything yet?" She bent down and picked up Junior. I shook my head, while Claudia said nothing.

"Can I help you ladies?" a redheaded unit clerk asked as we stepped from the elevator and approached her.

"We're looking for Mario Wallace. Is he still in surgery?" I asked. She punched a few buttons on the computer and looked at me.

"Actually, he was just placed in a room. If you would like to go and see him, you can." She smiled and I exhaled. Nothing in her voice was alarming.

"Well, I'll let his mom go first." I patted Ms. C on the back.

"No, Nikki, you go first," she urged. "I don't want to see him if he is messed up. You go first, and let me know what I'm in for."

"Are you sure?" I asked, and she nodded and took Maria. The clerk asked for my identification, then provided me with a visitor's badge and the room number.

Upon entering the dark room, I felt sick to my stomach. Ever since being shot and being in a coma for seven months, I'd dreaded hospitals. Other than the beeping of a machine, the room was silent. I tiptoed over to the curtain to pull it back and jumped from my skin.

"What the hell is wrong with you?" Mario asked after hanging up his cell phone.

"Damn, I didn't expect you to be up." I grabbed my heart. "Honestly, I didn't know what to expect." I wanted to slap his arm but thought against it. The only visible indication of a wound was white gauze wrapped around his head.

"You thought a nigga was dead, didn't you?" He smiled.

"Something like that." I smiled back. "Let me go and get your mother before she has a heart attack." I turned.

"Nah. Let me holla at you right quick." He caught my arm. I took a seat next to the hospital bed.

"What the hell happened to you?" I wanted to know.

"Got into some shit with that bitch-ass nigga you been fuckin'." He grimaced.

"Maine did this to you?" I needed clarification.

"Something like that, but don't worry. I got him too." Mario smiled.

"Got him? What do you mean, Mario?" I paced the floor.

"Look, ma, chill. It doesn't concern you, so relax."

"How can I relax, Rio? You're laid up in this bed, and that nigga could be dead." I shook my head on the verge of tears.

"Well, I'm good, as you can see, so there ain't no need crying for me. And I better not see you shed one tear for that bitch-ass nigga," he threatened.

"Oh, my God, I can't believe this has happened!"

"I'm sorry, baby," Mario apologized. "Please forgive me."

"Rio, you have nothing to be sorry for." I shook my head.

"I'm just apologizing for everything. If I had kept my bond tight with you, we wouldn't be here right now." He spoke of our plans to retire last year before things went astray.

"Ain't nothing we can do about that now," I said softly.

"Nik, I need you. I don't want nobody else." He rubbed my ass. "Pregnancy does a body good." He laughed and I snatched back.

"Ain't nobody pregnant." I closed my blazer.

"Bullshit! I know when you're pregnant, Nik." He laughed again. "Never thought you would be having another nigga's baby though."

I swallowed hard because there was no way I was keeping this child. How could I?

"Mario, you're bleeding." I immediately placed pressure on the wound. He removed his hospital gown and balled it up to soak up the blood. "Is this from the surgery?"

"I didn't get a chance to have the surgery, actually," he explained. "When we got in there, the doctors thought it would be best if I made my own decision before the operation. They closed me up and sent me to recovery. When the meds wore off, they came to ask me what I wanted to do."

"What? Who in the hell stops saving a person's life just to ask their permission?" I was stunned.

"I was shot in my head, Nikki." He looked at me seriously. "They said the bullet is partially lodged into my brain. If they remove it, there is a possibility I may go brain-dead."

"Oh, my God! Are you serious?" I felt my knees wobble. "What happens if you leave the bullet in there?" I hated to ask the question but needed to know the answer.

"If I don't have the bullet removed, it may slip deeper into my brain over time. Either way, the shit doesn't look good." Mario shook his head.

Chapter 3

Gucci

"I'm looking for Mario Wallace," I told the receptionist.

"And you are?"

"Gucci Wallace, his wife." I watched as she scanned the computer screen.

"Ma'am, our records indicate that Mario is in recovery with his wife, Nikkita." She stared at me.

"Which room?" I asked with attitude. Here I was worried sick and feeling guilty about my rendezvous with Cartier while riding down here with Sam and Mina, and this nigga had actually called Nikki in his time of need instead of me.

"Calm down, and wait over there with the other family members. When his wife comes out, we will ask her if you can go back there."

"Bitch!" I hit the desk. "I am his goddamned wife."

"Do I need to call security?" She picked up the phone.

"Whatever!" I snapped and walked past her toward Ms. C. "What room is Mario in?"

"306," was all she said.

Upon entering Mario's room, I could hear him talking to Nikki, so I paused to eavesdrop on the conversation.

"Do you still love me, Nikki?"

I was caught off guard by his question and swallowed hard.

"I realized that I fucked up by marrying her, and I'm sorry, baby."

"Mario, it's a little too late for me and you, don't you think?" Nikki sighed.

I rolled my eyes because I was tired of this conversation already.

"I only married her because I was confused."

"Confused about what?" Nikki asked.

I wanted to know too, because in my opinion there was absolutely nothing to be confused about.

"Gucci had been by my side when you were laid up those months in the hospital. Eventually, we slept together, and I thought I was beginning to have feelings for her. After she got pregnant, I thought I owed her, and I put a ring on her finger." He sighed.

"Okay, I get that! You thought I was dying, so what the hell, right? But what I don't get is why you still married her after I woke up from that coma." Nikki shifted from one leg to the other.

"Because you said that you didn't want me back!" He raised his voice. "What was I supposed to do?"

"You were supposed to be a motherfucking man and fight for what was yours!"

"I'm doing that now," Mario replied. "I love you with every fiber of my being. I don't like the man I am without you. Please say you'll take me back."

"Look, your wife is probably somewhere worried sick about you. Let me give her another call so that she can be here with you." Nikki was about to walk away, but Mario grabbed her hand.

"Nikkita, you will always be my wife. From now until eternity. Don't you remember the vow?" He tried to stand from the bed.

"I will always remember our vow! You were the one who forgot," she cried, and he pulled her in for a passionate kiss.

I bit down hard on my bottom lip as he continued.

"I love you and I want you back. I'm going crazy without you, baby." He slid his hand up her shirt and caressed her breast. "Please take me back, baby. I need you by my side," he begged like some bitch, and she stood still. "Nik, say something," he whispered.

"What about Gucci? She loves you just as much as I do."

"I love her . . ." he started, and I put my head down because I felt a "but" coming. "But I'm not in love with her. I'm in love with you, and I'm ready to come home."

"You love me in spite of this?" She lifted her shirt, and I could've sworn I saw a baby bump.

Mario sighed, then placed his hand over her belly. "I love everything about you, and a baby won't change that. All you have to say is, 'Mario, I take you back.'"

Oh, hell no! I rolled my eyes because it was time to break this shit up.

"Mario, I love you, and I'm willing to take you back." Nikki kissed him like some scene from a movie.

"Just like that it's over, huh?" I stepped out of the shadows into the light.

"G," Mario called out.

"Fuck you and that raggedy bitch! If you couldn't love me the way I loved you, then you should've left my ass alone." I was pissed. "FYI, mother-fucker, I just fucked Cartier in our house on our dining room table, and the shit was good!"

Chapter 4

Chloe

At first, the correction officer was skeptical when I suggested that Lovely should be transported to the hospital. Still believing that I was Sister Mary, she told me that prayer, not a pregnant woman, was my line of work. But after divine intervention kicked in and Lovely's water really broke, we were on our way in no time. Of course, Lovely was cuffed at the wrists and on one ankle. Two officers rode in the ambulance with us, and I held her hand every step of the way.

Just as we arrived at the hospital, I caught a glimpse of Nikki pulling up and barely missing the ambulance we were in. This had to be my lucky day, and I could hardly contain myself. Honestly, what were the chances of running into her at a hospital of all places? As we stepped from the ambulance, I started to walk in Nikki's direction.

"Sister Mary, please don't leave me." Lovely tried to reach for my arm. I could tell that she was scared, but plans had changed.

"I will be back for you," I whispered. Truth be told, I wasn't thinking about her at this moment. I needed to make a break for it before the WVC figured out I pulled a switcheroo with the nun and called the officers here to detain me. I needed to find some cash, change my attire, and make a break for it.

Quietly I looked around the waiting room. There was an older white couple in the corner, and a man standing up against the wall, talking on a cell phone. I also noticed a young woman off in the corner. She was knocked out cold with her mouth open wide. The woman was snoring so loudly that no one had chosen to sit by her, which was perfect for me. Her purse was at her side and mine for the taking. Like a thief in the night, I snatched the purse and was out. The nun costume was really working for me, because no one even raised an eyebrow. I stepped outside and fumbled through the knock-off Coach bag, desperate to find a cell phone, money, and car keys.

"Fuck Nikki and that lying-ass nigga!" I heard someone say, and I put my head down. After years of being in Nikki's circle, I would know Gucci's voice anywhere.

"Calm down, Gucci. Let us take you home. I can't have you out here all upset," Sam consoled her.

I was so excited to see him that I almost peed myself. This day was getting better and better. I silently followed the threesome into the visitors' parking lot and prayed the keys I'd just found belonged to a car over there. Without transportation I was shit out of luck.

Chirp. The horn of a Dodge Avenger went off, indicating that my ride had been found. Everyone was so busy calming Gucci down they didn't notice little old me.

Chapter 5

Gucci

I was pissed off and Mario knew it. I would've taken a cab home, but Sam and Mina insisted on dropping me off. I'd taken Maria with me. As soon as I walked through the door, I remembered that I never activated my alarm system because Cartier was there. Originally I hoped that he would get the hint and leave. The last thing I needed was to get caught with another nigga in my house, but fuck it.

"How is this nigga gon' try to play me like some hood rat?" I cried into my cell phone to Satin, who was barely giving a shit. "If he didn't want me, all he had to do was keep it moving." I placed Maria into her crib and went into the bathroom.

"Gucci, I hate to say I told you so, but I did! You never should've slept with him from the beginning." Her voice boomed through my speakerphone.

"I didn't beg the nigga to fuck me, nor did I ask him to get me pregnant or marry me!" I said. Walking into the walk-in closet, I missed half of what she was saying to me because I was on a mission. I grabbed an armful of his custom suits and ties and came back into the bathroom.

"Gucci, did you hear me?" she called out.

"My bad. What did you say?" I threw the clothes into the tub and reached under the cabinet for the bleach. Twisting the cap, I poured the chemical all over the Valentino, Armani, and Versace custom pieces.

"It doesn't matter because you ain't trying to hear what I'm saying anyway." She smacked her lips.

"You're right! I'll get at you tomorrow." I hung the phone up and went back into the closet. Satin was my girl, but she'd been against me and Mario since day one. I didn't know why I called her anyway.

Reaching onto the wooden shelving, I grabbed several pairs of shoes along with a few pieces of jewelry and headed downstairs. On my way outside, I heard my phone ring, but I figured it was Satin trying to check me for hanging up on her, so I paid it no mind. I slid the patio door back and walked across the deck toward the hot tub. Leaning over the water, I dropped all of the items in and watched them splash. I smiled as the Rolex, Cartier, and Movado watches sank to the bottom. Stepping back into the house for round three, I dashed up the stairs.

"What the fuck did that nigga do to deserve this?" a voice behind me called out, and I nearly passed out in the hallway.

I swung around and came face-to-face with Maine. "What are you doing here?" I backed up.

"Lovely's trial starts in three days, and Mario ain't did shit. I guess he don't value his chick the way I value mine, and that's unfortunate for you." He pointed a gloved finger at me. I wasn't book smart, but I knew enough hood shit to know a gloved intruder wasn't a good thing.

"What you want me for? Nikkita is his prized possession. Didn't you know that?" I smacked my lips.

"Unfortunately for you, Nikki wasn't home, so I'm taking your ass for insurance!"

"Kidnapping me doesn't ensure Meechie won't show up for court," I said honestly. The Feds would have him in court come hell or high water.

"Well, that's a chance I'm willing to take." He pulled a 9 mm handgun from his waistband. Instantly, my mind raced as I thought about what was going down. For once in my life, I felt scared and helpless. Not only was shit about to get real, but my daughter was also in the next room.

"Look, there's another way around this." I raised my hands in surrender.

Shaking his head, my assailant began to speak. "Ain't no other way, Gucci. I need my girl back!

Mario has to deliver Meechie to me personally if he really wants you to live."

I was scared as hell on the inside, but I refused to let a tear shed. I knew Mario would come after me, but I wasn't confident that he would or even could deliver his mom's brother to this man. "Can I at least kiss my baby before I leave?"

"Five seconds and don't get cute." He followed me into Maria's room.

Staring at my precious daughter, I prayed I would see her again one day, hopefully in heaven if not in the flesh. Once I left with this stranger, the chance of me returning was slim. Not only had I seen his face and could identify him, but things also just didn't work like that out here in the streets.

"Hurry the fuck up!" he barked, and Maria jumped in her sleep but didn't fully wake up.

Leaning down to kiss my baby girl, I remembered there was a 9 mm on the top shelf of her closet in case of an emergency such as this. "Can I put an extra blanket on her please?"

"Bitch, hurry up!" he yelled, and I moved slowly to the closet. I stretched my arm and tried to feel for the gun, which caused it to fall to the ground.

Bam! He pistol-whipped me, and I fell to the floor. "I told you not to be cute."

Chapter 6

Chloe

As I followed Sam's vehicle, my thoughts went back to Lovely. I had no intentions of returning to the hospital, so I pulled out the stolen cell phone and dialed the number she'd given me days ago.

"Who is this?" a male's voice boomed.

"No need for names. Just know that your girl has been delivered to Henry Ford Hospital. I got her out of prison, but it's up to you to do the rest. You better get there fast before she has that baby and is taken back into custody." Click. Silently, I prayed for my girl and hoped things worked out for her. I knew we would never see each other again, but I wished her well anyway.

Within half an hour, we had arrived at our destination. Sam punched in a code and entered the gate. I parked on the street and waited ten minutes before getting out of the car. The spacing on the wrought-iron gate was large enough for me to squeeze through, belly and all. With every step I took toward the lavish home, I could feel the fire in my veins. It was so hot that I was sweating. Creeping around to the back of the house, I searched for a window or door left open. Bingo! The kitchen window was cracked open about three inches. Calmly I walked onto the deck and slid over a few pieces of outdoor furniture. Once the stack was tall enough for me to hoist myself up to the window, I removed my shoes and stepped on it. It was a little wobbly, but it did the trick. Just like that, I was inside and one step closer to what I'd come for.

I scanned the gourmet kitchen, and a butcher knife resting on the wooden cutting board caught my attention. I didn't have a gun, so this would have to do. There were no lights on, which was a gift and a curse. Mina wouldn't be able to see me, but I couldn't see her either.

"Looking for this?" Wham.

The bitch actually hit me in the back. I turned to see what her weapon of choice was and laughed when I noticed the frying pan. Thinking quickly, I dodged her next blow and sent one of my own to her thigh. The knife tore through her flesh, and blood squirted everywhere. Mina was startled but unstoppable as she came at me again with the cooking utensil.

"You crazy bitch! Just leave me alone." She swung and caught me on the shoulder.

"Leave you alone?" I looked at her sideways. "You're the one who stole my life." I tried to stab her again, but she blocked me with the pan.

"It was never your life to begin with," she countered.

I was tired of talking, so I jabbed the knife at her face and watched the skin on her cheek separate. The wound caused her to drop her weapon and reach for her face, giving me the advantage. I climbed on top of her, with my left hand around her neck and my right hand clutching the knife. I smiled as Mina gagged and fought for air. Desperately, she tried to reach for the frying pan, which was within an inch of her grasp.

"Chloe, stop!" Sam's voice boomed from the entryway.

"Or what?" I rolled my eyes.

"I will kill you!" He stood trembling with a .38 in his hand. I looked down at Mina, who was practically dead anyway, and decided to turn my attention to Sam.

"Do it then." I walked up to him and he backed away. "You ain't shit but a pussy! Do it!" I yelled.

Bam! A blow to the back of my head made me stumble. I tried to grab on to the wall and hold myself up, but I slipped on Mina's blood and hit the floor.

I came to just as I was being hoisted into the air on a stretcher. I looked down at my hands and ankles to see if I was cuffed. Thank goodness

I wasn't. An officer walked side by side with the medical team as they escorted me to the waiting ambulance. With seconds to make a decision, I grabbed the officer's gun from his holster and shot him twice. Like a madwoman, I removed myself from the stretcher and surveyed the area to see what my next move would be.

"Freeze! Drop the weapon."

I turned to see three policemen with their guns raised. Come hell or high water, I wasn't going back to prison.

"Drop the weapon or I will shoot!"

"Shoot me then! I've seen everything except death anyway," I demanded.

"Drop the weapon, Chloe, please!" Sam begged.

I knew his concern was more for his unborn daughter than for me, so to hell with him. Slowly, I raised the gun toward my face and opened my mouth wide. Everything moved in slow motion as I stared into his pleading eyes. He kept asking for me to stop, but I couldn't go back to prison, and I refused to live my life without him. I squeezed my eyes shut and pulled the trigger.

Boom!

Chapter 7

Lovely

"What's going on here?" I heard someone ask from the doorway. I wanted to sit up and get a closer look, but the handcuffs on my left hand and ankle prevented that.

"She needs an emergency C-section. If we don't get her on the operating table, she may lose that baby," I heard a male voice answer.

My eyes widened because I knew for sure Maine had come to my rescue. At least two hours had gone by since I last saw Chloe. I was unsure if she was able to contact Maine.

"Sir, I need you to uncuff her," a female asked as all three voices entered my dark room.

"If I remove those cuffs, I must be present during the operation. It's policy," the officer explained.

"You can be present wherever you like, but right now I need those cuffs off." The male stared at me. I tried to keep myself from smiling at the sight of my man. He was in full surgery gear, and so was my best friend, Coco, who was acting as a nurse.

The officer scurried around my bed to unlock me. The minute I was free, it was lights out for him. Maine removed a silencer from his waist and sent the officer to the floor with one shot to the chest. Coco unhooked my IV and removed the belly monitors while Maine dragged the officer into the private bathroom. I could tell my man was hurt because his arm was dripping blood, but I had no time for questions.

"Slip this on." Coco handed me a mint green pair of scrubs, the matching top, and a lab coat.

"We have to get out of here," I whispered. The nurse on staff had been making rounds every hour on the hour. The clock on the wall told me we had about fifteen minutes.

Slowly we walked out of my room and briskly past the nurse's desk. There were three nurses all engaged in small talk. Thank God they didn't even bat an eyelash when we passed by. As we approached the end of the hallway, Maine decided we should split up. "Coco, you take the elevator. Lovely and I will take the stairs."

"See you on the other side." Coco squeezed me tight. "I'm glad you're home."

"See you on the other side." I smiled and broke our embrace.

Maine must've forgotten that I was pregnant, as he took the stairs two at a time. "Slow down," I whined.

"Lovely, you need to run like your life depends on it!" he barked, and he was right. My life did depend on it. As we maneuvered down the steps, I thought back to the last time I was at a hospital. Coincidentally, I was breaking out my friend White Girl. Feds were everywhere, and we barely escaped by the hair on our chins, but everything worked out.

We were almost to the second floor when I heard someone enter the stairwell. I didn't know who it was, but I wasn't going to take any chances. "Let's get off on three." I pulled Maine's arm.

He didn't say anything, just turned around so that we could exit. The door opened before we could get to it, and in walked some brown-skinned woman. Immediately, she looked shocked, and so did Maine as he squeezed my arm. Although no words were exchanged between the two of them, their silence and awkward stares spoke volumes. Her eyes were on my stomach, and mine were on hers. It was small, but the fitted shirt beneath her blazer did nothing to conceal the bulge.

"Come on, Lovely." Maine pulled me forward.

"Is this the woman?" I stopped dead in my tracks.

"Girl, let me get you out of here before you start questioning me." He tried laughing, but he knew nothing was funny.

"Are you Nikki?" I asked as she stared like a deer caught in headlights.

"Look, I don't want any mess," she started. "I didn't know that Maine was in a relationship. Please don't be mad."

"Oh, I'm not mad at you. He's the one who needs to explain." I turned my attention to Maine, whose eyes were locked on Nikki's stomach.

"I know it's none of my business, but please don't be mad at him either. Your man did what he thought he had to do in order to get you home."

"Let's go, Lovely," Maine urged and pulled me past Nikki without another word.

Finally, we made it out into the brisk night air, and I cried tears of joys. I'd waited for this moment for so long, and part of me doubted it would ever come.

"Let's ride!" someone called from the corner. I squinted a bit and noticed it was Do It. He and Coco were waiting in an all-black Trailblazer.

"Take us to the spot," Maine instructed, and we took off into the night.

Chapter 8

Nikki

I couldn't believe I ran right into Maine and his woman at the hospital. I could've caused a scene between them, but what good would that have done? He did what he thought was necessary for the love of his life, and I was back with mine, so there was no need to cause problems. At the end of the day, everybody except Gucci won, which was why I asked Anjela to take me over to see her.

"Why are we going over to Gucci's house again?" Anjela rolled her eyes.

"I just want to set things right with her." We turned up into the driveway, and I noticed that the home Mario shared with Gucci was similar to the one he and I had purchased together.

"Cuz, did she come and chat it up with you when she took your man? No, she didn't! Fuck her!" My cousin pressed on the horn.

"Stop that!" I laughed and stepped from the SUV. Approaching the large home, I was aware the lights were all on, so I rang the bell.

"If this bitch comes out shooting, don't say I didn't warn you."

We stood at the door for close to ten minutes and my patience was growing thin. Gucci wanted to be stubborn and leave me outside.

"Let's go," Anjela demanded.

I ignored her and walked around to the side of the house. I wanted to see if I could catch her peeking from a window, but I found the patio door wide open.

"As your attorney, I would have to advise you not to enter this woman's property. Nikki, if you get hurt in there, no judge in Michigan will find her guilty."

"Something's wrong," I exclaimed. "I hear the baby crying." On that note, I flew into the house not caring one bit about what could've been awaiting me. All sorts of things flooded my mind, and at the top of the list was Mario's beef with Maine. I continually called out to Gucci as I made my way around the house, but there was no answer. I followed the sounds of Maria into her bedroom and picked her up. Noticing the gun on the floor, I reached for my cell phone to call Mario. He was still at the hospital under doctors' care.

"Hey, what's up?"

"Rio, I came to your house to talk to Gucci, and she's not here. The patio door was wide open, and Maria was in her crib crying hysterically." I soothed the baby.

"What!" Mario hit the ceiling. "I can't believe she left my baby alone because she is mad at me."

"Rio, Gucci would never leave Maria on purpose. I think she's been abducted."

Chapter 9

Lovely

"Baby, I'm so glad to have you back." Maine smiled as we pulled up to the private jet awaiting our arrival behind Metro Airport. We'd been riding for almost an hour, and neither of us had said a word. Instead, we chose to bask in the glory of my freedom.

"It feels good to be back." I snuggled up next to him. I knew everything would be all right from this point forward. Finally, I could put this bad situation behind me and start over. No more prison brawls or nightmares of giving up custody of my son.

"Let's go, boo." He stepped from the whip and helped me out. "I'm getting you far away from here. Take one last look at Michigan because we ain't ever coming back."

"You promise?" I giggled.

"I have a whole new life set up for us in Mexico." Maine beamed, but at that moment I was saddened. I didn't want a whole new life. I wanted my old life with a few alterations.

"Does that mean I have to say goodbye to Coco and Do It?" I couldn't stand the thought of living without them or my niece, Shawnie, whom I'd been missing so much.

"Shawnie and Coco's boys are already down there with Agent Nichols." Maine smiled. Agent Nichols was now retired from the Feds. She was sort of like the mother I'd always wanted, and I replaced the daughter she'd lost to the streets years ago.

"Are you serious?" I kissed him so hard that my lips turned white. "Coco, are you coming too? What about the salon?" I couldn't believe she would agree to leave her booming business behind.

"We're only coming as an extended vacation, so to speak." She smiled.

"Now get your sexy self on that plane." Maine slapped my butt and turned his attention to our luggage in the trunk.

On my way up to the aircraft with Coco, I paused and overheard Do It. "Yo, what do you want to do about the shorty you got in the warehouse?"

"Let the bitch post up for a few days, and then call her man to come get her," Maine said, then proceeded to join us on the jet.

Chapter 10

Gucci

I was filthy, hungry, and tired as all hell. Two nights inside of a condemned warehouse was starting to get the best of me. My hands were bound to a wooden board behind my back, and the hay beneath my ass was very uncomfortable. My pants were moist from urine, and the smell was beginning to turn my stomach. The only consolation I had was the fact that Mario was combing the streets looking for me by now. I knew with his pulse on the city and ear to the streets, he would find me in no time.

"Yo, little mama, you hungry?" someone asked.

"Forty-eight hours later and now you ask!" I spat.

"Bitch, are you hungry or not?" he asked from the doorway. There were no lights on inside of the warehouse, so it was impossible to see him.

"Yeah, I'm starving." My stomach began to growl right at that very moment. I listened as the man walked over toward me. There was something in the way he dragged his foot that let me know he had a previous injury to his body.

"Eat." He threw a paper bag at me. It was filled with Coney Island. I could tell by the distinct smell.

"Nigga, my hands are tied behind my back." This asshole wasn't playing with a full deck. Reaching up, my assailant turned on the lights, and I blinked rapidly.

"Gucci?" he asked with familiarity. I squinted to see who this nigga was but came up blank. "Aw, shit, my nigga." He began to shake his head profusely, which caused his dreads to sway.

"I can't place you." Honestly, I didn't know this man from a can of paint.

"It's me, Do It." He leaned in closer.

I scanned him again and noted that, without the dreads, minus a few extra pounds and the limp, he was very familiar. For the first time in a long time I smiled, because the man before me was my ace from way back in the day. Me, Mario, Do It, and his girlfriend White Girl used to roll in the streets hot and heavy.

"DeShawn, man, you got to get me out of here." I wasted no time.

"Damn, G! I didn't know Maine was coming after you. I thought he was going after the other chick Mario was fucking with," Do It admitted.

"Well, I guess that plan went sideways."

"Gucci, you're my nigga from the bottom to the top. I swear I didn't know you were back here." He looked apologetic while untying me.

"So you into fucking kidnapping people now?" If I'd had an ounce of strength, I would've tried to beat his ass just on general principle.

"Chill out!" He lent a hand to pull me up. "We did what was needed to get my sister home."

"Yeah, whatever," I retorted, although I would've done the same for one of my peoples.

"Do you need me to call anybody for you?"

"Yeah, my husband. I need to check on my daughter." After a few calls went unanswered, I called Claudia, who informed me Maria was good. She asked me to meet her at the hospital, where Mario still was.

I called Cartier, and he picked me up within fifteen minutes. "You good, ma?" He was concerned.

"Do I look good?" I snapped.

"Where you want me to take you, shorty?" He didn't pay my temper tantrum any mind.

"Take me to the hospital. I have a few choice words for that husband of mine." I folded my arms.

"Gucci, I know you didn't call me to pick you up and take you to see another nigga. If that's the case, you can get out now." He stopped the car in the middle of the road and lit a blunt.

"It ain't like that. I need to tell him that I'm leaving."

Cartier stared at me in disbelief while blowing smoke in my direction.

We pulled up to the hospital, and I begged him to let me handle this on my own. I was sure things would get ugly, and I didn't need that firecracker to make things worse.

"Gucci, we were worried sick about you." Mina ran up and hugged me for dear life. "Sam has been out there looking for you like crazy."

"That's funny." I smirked. "While Sam was combing the streets, where was my bitch-ass husband? Let me guess, laid up with his trick?"

"Gucci, I think you should talk to Mario." She looked sad.

"That's exactly what I plan to do." I laughed sarcastically and barged into his room, prepared to put everybody out.

Chapter 11

Nikki

As we all stood silently surrounding Mario's hospital bed, Gucci burst into the room with an attitude, demanding that everybody leave.

"I'm so glad you're okay, G," Mario said softly.

"No thanks to you, bastard!" she yelled. "You left me out there to die."

"G—" Mario tried to talk, but she cut him off.

"Fuck you and that funky bitch! If you want her, you can have her, because I've moved on." She removed her oversized wedding ring and tossed it to the ground. I had to laugh when she called me funky, because her ass was the one smelling like pee and serious body odor.

Mario tried calming her down. "Gucci, please stop yelling."

"You ain't heard yelling yet, nigga!" she yelled even louder than before.

"Goddammit, shut the fuck up! I don't need to have this shit on my mind before I go under the knife," Rio yelled and immediately grabbed his head. Gucci just stood there looking dumbfounded.

Under the advice of the doctors, Rio had decided to have the surgery. He tried to wait for Sam to find Gucci, but every day that the bullet stayed lodged in his brain, it swelled up and would eventually prove to be deadly. This morning he'd requested that I be present with Junior. Ms. C was there with Maria, and Sam had even shown up with Mina. It was a rainy day, and my stomach was in knots. I didn't know if we were saying goodbye or just "see you later," but it was all too much for me. The only sound in the room was that of the children. Maria giggled as Junior made silly faces at her. They didn't know the seriousness of the situation, and I prayed that their father returned from surgery safe so they would never have to.

After an awkward silence, Mario spoke up. "Feels good to see my family together again."

"I know it does, son." Ms. C rubbed his free hand since the other hand was covered with an IV tube. No one else said a peep. We just hung on to Mario's every word.

"I wanted everyone here today so that I could get a few things straight," he started. "First off, Sam, I'm glad you came back."

"Glad to be back, bro," Sam replied.

"I know you're done with the street life, but if anything happens to me, please make sure H.O.F.

lives forever. You don't have to run it yourself, just find a good replacement for me. A lot of people eat off the money H.O.F. brings in, and it's important to keep it that way. Can you do that?" Mario asked.

"Nothing is going to happen to you, man." Sam waved Mario off.

"I might not come back out here the way I'm going in. I need to know that you can handle what I'm asking," Mario said in a firm tone.

"I got you for sure." Sam appeared sad but held his emotions in check.

"Mina, you better keep my boy happy, you hear me? Sometimes in life you don't get second chances. Now that you have one, you better run with that shit." Mario laughed.

"I'm running down the altar with my second chance." She flashed a rock and I smiled.

"Mama, I . . ." Unexpectedly Rio got choked up, which caused me to tear up.

"Yes, son?"

"Mama, I love you and I'm sorry." He broke down like a baby.

"Sorry for what, son?" Claudia blew her nose.

"I should've chosen a different path for my life. You always told me that if I live by the streets, I will die by the streets. I should've listened." Mario sniffed, and I resisted the urge to wipe the tears rolling down his face.

Ms. C couldn't take anymore. She broke down crying and ran into the private bathroom.

Mario looked at Gucci and began again. "G, you're my best friend, and that shit will never change. You've done more dirt with me and for me than ten niggas put together. The bond we have is irreplaceable. Our daughter is proof of that."

I looked at Gucci, who was on the verge of passing out. I knew the pain of this situation was just as hurtful for her as it was for me. She needed someone to lean on, and I did too, so I grabbed her hand as tight as I could as Mario continued, "I love you, Gucci, but I'm not in love with you. No matter how much we both tried, it just wasn't meant to be. My heart belongs to Nikki, and it always will, but maybe next lifetime there will be another time and another place for you and me." He sniffed. "I heard most gangsters go to heaven, so I'll hold you a spot. In the meantime, tell Cartier to treat you right." Mario sniffed again.

"Why are you talking like you're about to die?" Gucci screamed, but Mario didn't respond.

"Nikki."

At the sound of my name my knees buckled.

"I love you like a fat kid love cake, girl." He laughed. "I'm sorry I fucked this up for us, baby. If I could do this shit differently, I would. If by some miracle I walk out of this shit alive, I want you to be my wife again. I want to start over far away from here with our new bundle of joy."

On that note, everyone looked my way except for Gucci, who was still holding my hand. I cried hard because he truly loved me unconditionally.

"Nik, I love you more than life itself. Anything that is a part of you is a part of me, no matter what." He smiled and I continued sobbing.

Just then the doctor came to roll Mario out for surgery. "Look, if I don't make it, just promise to keep my family together." He finally let out all of the waterworks. "Y'all squash the beef so my kids can grow up together. Keep them as far away from street life as possible so they will have a chance to be something in life."

"I love you, Rio," I called out and ran up to give him a kiss.

"Ay, if shit go sideways in there, tell my new baby his father died a gangster, nothing more, nothing less." He rubbed my belly and winked as the hospital staff rolled him away.

Chapter 12

Nikki

One Week Later

It was a somber day in the city of Detroit. The clouds hung low, and rain was in the forecast. From my bedroom window, I could see the trees swaying from side to side, a telltale sign that a storm was brewing.

"You look pretty, Mommy." Junior lay on my bed playing with toy cars. He looked handsome in the black slacks, white T-shirt, and navy blue Ralph Lauren sweater vest.

"Thank you, little man." I flashed him a half-hearted smile and continued to get dressed. The black spandex dress fit every curve of my size-ten body. My small pregnant belly was barely noticeable. The black hat and funeral veil may have been a tad bit much. However, something was needed to cover the bags beneath my eyes. I'd been crying nonstop. My face was a swollen mess. Typically, I would've chosen sunglasses. They weren't appropriate for such a sad occasion. The mere thought of the funeral I was preparing to attend had me in tears yet again. I grabbed a Kleenex from the box on the dresser. Death is never easy to deal with, especially when you lose someone close to your heart.

"Why are you crying, Mommy?" Junior was concerned, but I had to be strong and put on a brave facade. He didn't need to be burdened with my sorrows.

"I had something in my eye, but I'm okay now."

"Are you sure?" His voice was squeaky and baby-like.

"I'm sure." After reassuring him, I slipped into black slingback pumps and watched my phone dance across the dresser. It was vibrating. "Hello."

"Hey, cuz, how are you holding up?" my cousin, Anjela, asked with genuine concern.

Shrugging my shoulders as if she could see me, I replied, "I'm good, I guess."

"That's good," she sighed. "I really wish I could've been there for you today, but duty calls." She had been hired by the disgruntled husband of a reality star in Los Angeles. He wanted to sue his wife for defamation of character and custody of their children. Anjela met the man at a charity event, and he hired her shortly thereafter. "Anyway, I was calling you on my way to the airport to let you know I love you and I'll be back in a few days."

"Thanks, cuz. Have a safe trip." I ended the call, then placed my phone into the purse on the nightstand. "Ready, little man?"

"Are we going to go play with Daddy?" His eyes were wide with anticipation.

"No, baby, not today."

"Where are we going, Mommy?"

"We're going to a funeral." I knew this would start the game of twenty questions.

"What's a funeral?"

"A funeral is a celebration for someone who has passed away, Junior." I helped him down from the bed, grabbed my purse, and headed down the stairs to the SUV.

"Who passed away?"

He was such an inquisitive kid. Before I could part my lips to respond, my phone started vibrating again. *Thank God for perfect timing!* "Hey, Rio."

"What's up, Nik? What time are you coming up here?" He was so spoiled it was ridiculous. It was only ten o'clock in the morning and he was already calling to see where I was.

His surgery last week was a success. Doctors removed the bullet from his skull. Now he was as good as new! They were keeping him for observation though. Miraculously, he was only left with a visible scar about three inches long on the right side of his head. Mario was pissed that he had to cut his long, curly jet-black hair. It was his signature look. As quiet as it's kept, I actually liked the low-cut Caesar and deep waves better. It gave him a mature, age-appropriate vibe.

"Hello! Did you hear me?"

"My bad. I was strapping Junior into the car seat." I closed the back door, then got into the driver's seat. "I might not make it there today."

"Why not?" Just like a child, he pouted.

"Today is Chloe's funeral. Remember I told you she tried to kill herself with the police officer's gun."

"That rat should've fucking died as a mouse!" Mario scoffed. His disdain for my friend was no shocker. However, it was very disrespectful being that she was deceased.

"Rio, that's no way to talk about dead people!"

"I can't believe you going to that bullshit anyway!" He was on ten right about now.

"She was my friend."

"She was a snitch!" he barked. "Fuck outta here with that my friend shit! Homegirl was a liar, a con artist, and a cop!"

"Everything you said is true. Yet, again, she was my friend." I'd cried with that girl, partied with her, and we'd seen each other through the good and bad times of the game. Mario could think whatever he wanted to think, but Chloe was like my little sister. Yeah, she was on some grimy shit. Still, all in all, she was good people. She didn't deserve to die at six months pregnant, even if it was she who pulled the trigger. Her daughter was in the hospital fighting for her life, and her mother had never laid eyes on her.

Sam called me on the night of the incident and told me to meet him and Mina at Children's Hospital. He explained that Chloe had taken a shot to the face. It caused internal bleeding, which filled her lungs, basically suffocating her. During the process of being rushed to the hospital, she died. In fear of losing the baby, they transported Chloe's body to Children's Hospital, where doctors surgically removed little Chloe from her mother's womb. I was heartbroken about the whole situation: the loss of a friend, the sadness of Sam, and the fact that their daughter would never know her mother.

"Nik, you there?"

"I'm here, but let me call you back later, all right?" I didn't even wait for a response as I ended the call and proceeded to the funeral home.

Chapter 13

Gucci

My ringtone played, "'I'ma be fresh as hell if the Feds watching. I'ma be fresh as hell if the Feds watching.'"

I looked at the caller ID on my cell phone before answering. "What up doe?"

"Gucci, are you okay? Girl, I've been worried sick about you. You haven't been returning my calls or text messages." Mina sounded displeased with me yet relieved that I was okay.

"My bad, girl. I've just been going through it, that's all," I sighed. Ever since Mario's surgery, I'd been missing in action. Part of me didn't want to know the outcome, be it good or bad. My heart couldn't take news of his demise. On the other hand, I didn't wanna find out he made it through surgery and crawled his ass back to Nikki. Either way, Mario would no longer belong to me.

"I understand, but you had me ready to come over there and bust your door down. Don't ever play me like that," she scolded.

"I'm sorry. It won't happen again. I'm just angry."
I didn't want to admit the truth, but it was time to
be set free. Never in a million years could I fathom
losing Mario twice in one lifetime to the same
bitch. All of the rage and jealousy I felt during my
teenage years was back. I still remembered the day
he brought that siditty bitch around. I didn't like
her then, and I don't like her now. There was just
something about Nikki that irritated the fuck out
of me. I realized we consoled one another at the
hospital. However, that was under extenuating
circumstances. If I saw that bitch right now, I
would spit in her face.

"Are you still there?" Mina broke me free of the
trancelike state I was in.

"Yeah, what were you saying?" She had been
talking for over five minutes, and I hadn't heard
one word.

"I said Mario pulled through the surgery and is
just fine." Her words were both a gift and a curse.

"Good." I was relieved yet reluctant because I
didn't know where our relationship stood.

"Well, I just wanted to let you know in case you
were wondering. I'll call you when I leave Chloe's
funeral."

"Why are you going to her funeral?"

"Because it's the right thing to do." Mina was
always being a good Samaritan.

"Bullshit!" It was no secret that I despised Chloe while she was living. Therefore, I damn sure wouldn't be fake about it now. The rat bitch could rest in hell for eternity in my opinion.

"You're a mess," she laughed. "I'll call you later." She ended the call.

I placed my phone down on the nightstand just in time for the doorbell. It was Satin. She was coming over today to watch Maria while I went to handle some business.

Today was the second day of the month, and in all the hoods across America that meant payday. Every government-funded dope fiend depended on social security checks to feed their habits. Those checks came on the first and fifteenth of the month. Therefore, on the second and sixteenth of each month, we collected all the earnings that were received at our spots the previous nights. Mario may have been in the hospital, but I was still about getting my bread. Having him out of the picture meant more moolah for me.

As I pulled the whip up to the gray and black house on Griggs, I put on my game face before stepping onto the gravel in my Prada sneakers. From the expressions on the faces outside, I could tell no one was expecting me.

"What the fuck is all this?" I shouted after emerging from the car. No one said anything, so I continued. "This ain't no muthafuckin' hangout spot!"

There was one nigga standing on the porch, two niggas conversing on the sidewalk, and four niggas playing dice on the side of the house.

"Chill, little mama. My man and them only came through to smoke a blunt with me. As soon as we put it out, they're leaving." The youngster on the front porch had the nerve to speak to me like I was tripping.

"Li'l nigga, don't ever in your life tell me to chill!" I stepped up between his legs. "You and your mans and them can get the fuck on. Go smoke a blunt at your mama's house. I pay your young ass to work, not kick it with your friends."

"Yo, bro, tell ol' girl to calm down." He looked past me, addressing Neo, who was the head of this trap. Neo said nothing. He recognized the young boy had fucked up. With a huge smile on his face, he simply shook his head.

Obviously, the newcomer had no idea who I was. It was time to introduce myself. Whack. I backhanded the shit out of his pathetic face and watched blood squirt from his lip. Carefully, I inspected my diamond to make sure it was still intact.

"What the fuck!" He jumped up, ready to box, but eyed Neo for approval.

"Don't look at him. Look at me! I'm the boss," I yelled for every dude on the block to hear. "Did you know that?"

"I thought Mario ran the H.O.F. organization," he said in a defiant tone. "Ain't you just his side piece?"

There were several pairs of eyes that bucked at the brash remark, including mine. This youngster was trying me. It was time to make an example out of his ass. "Side piece! Did you just call me a fuckin' side piece?" I smirked. "Take this little nigga to the basement," I demanded in a cold voice. Neo did as I instructed. "Everybody else needs to clear out."

After dismissing the gang of young boys outside, I proceeded through the front door of the three-bedroom home. It was a typical trap house, nothing special. There was plastic up to all the windows, a dopefiend nodding on one of the folding chairs, and a girl at the kitchen stove whipping up work. In most traps, the women were always buck-naked, but this girl was fully dressed in a halter top, spandex jeans, and a pair of four-inch heels.

"Hey, Layna." She was Neo's main girl and the mother of his twin boys. They had both worked for us for approximately three years. I thought she was cool.

"What's up, G?" She looked up briefly, then went back to cooking the crack. "I told that little nigga to be easy, but he's hardheaded."

"Well, his ass is going to learn today." As I proceeded toward the basement, I heard a baby crying.

Stopping dead in my tracks, with a frown, I turned on the heels of my feet. "Layna, I know that ain't what I think it is." If this girl had her kids up in the trap, I was going to whoop her ass too.

"No, it's not one of my boys, but Diesel did bring some crackhead and her baby over here last night." She never removed her eyes from the boiling pot. Layna was a pro at whipping up work. "They're in the back."

"What the fuck is this, the Motel 6 or something?" Deciding to put my business in the basement on hold, I headed in the direction of the bedroom where the sound was coming from.

Pushing the door open, I never expected to find a small child standing in the middle of the floor crying while her mom had a train run on her. The young girl, who looked to be no older than 17, was down on her knees, buck-naked. I watched as Diesel slammed into her ass wildly and another nigga palmed the back of her head while she sucked and gagged. Her eyes were closed. It was evident she wasn't enjoying the party.

"Stop this shit now!" I demanded.

"Nah, bitch, you gon' have to let me bust all in that first." Diesel didn't even know it was I who made the announcement.

"It's Gucci and I said stop!"

"My . . . my bad, boss lady," he stuttered, yet he still pumped, trying hard to keep the rhythm.

"If you don't stop right now, I will blow your balls off!"

The mention of his balls being in jeopardy halted him immediately. The other man reluctantly pulled his joint from old girl's mouth and zipped his jeans up.

"All right, boss lady, my bad!" Diesel raised his hands in surrender.

"Sweetheart, how old are you?" I tossed the girl her clothes from the floor.

"I'm twenty," she lied.

"Do you even know where you are or what you're doing?"

"Yes," she admitted shamefully.

"This is no place for you, let alone your daughter." I wanted to remove my belt and beat her ass, but I wasn't her mother. "Do you have somewhere you can go?"

"Yes, ma'am." She was now fully dressed in a dingy yellow top and dirty white bottoms. Her gym shoes had seen better days. I felt bad for the young mother. Sadly, this was life in the trap. Over the years, I'd witnessed some incredibly upsetting events. After a while, you become immune.

Once the girl, her kid, and the other nigga were out of the room, I scolded Diesel. "What in the fuck is wrong with you? First, you are thirty-four years old and have no business messing with that baby. Secondly, your pedophile ass should've known better than to bring her here. And third, since when did you start fucking with crackheads?"

"Gucci, it ain't even like that." He rubbed his bald head.

"So, what is it like then?" I crossed my arms, awaiting his answer.

"She came over yesterday, got two rocks, and told me she would be back after she cashed her check. When she didn't come back, I went looking for her. When I found her, she still didn't have any money. So, I had to teach shorty a lesson."

"Negro, you sound stupid!" I smacked my lips. "Do you know what happens when you fuck crackheads?"

"I know, G." He put his head down.

"Diesel, I'm not your mama, and I can't tell you what to do with your dick. However, I will put a bullet in your ass if I catch you doing that shit in my spot again." I left him standing there, then headed back toward the basement.

Upon entering the midsize room with wooden wall panels and tiled floors, I glanced down at my watch. These niggas and their shenanigans had me late for my next pickup. The youngster was standing against the wall with a scowl. Neo was sitting on a folding chair, texting. "What are you frowned up for? I'm the one who should be pissed off!"

"I didn't even do nothing." He began pleading his case.

"What's your name?" Since Neo was the one in charge of this location, I left all the hiring up to him. Many runners and corner boys came through here looking for work. I didn't have time to get to know everyone.

"Antoine."

"How much money do you make working here, Antoine?"

"'Bout two hundred dollars a day." He did a quick calculation in his head.

"So that's around fourteen hundred dollars a week, right?"

"Yeah, I guess." He shrugged.

"Can you make that kind of money at McDonald's or Burger King?"

"The hell if I know!"

His smart mouth was going to be the death of him. Whack! I backhanded him again and again until his face was a bloody mess. If he weren't a kid, I would've done more damage than that. Had he been a few years older, his ass may not have lived to see tomorrow.

"Tell you what, little nigga." I paused to catch my breath. "You go and work for one of them muthafuckas, then come back and let me know."

"This is some bullshit!" He spoke under his breath while heading toward the basement stairs. "Neo, it's like that?" He turned around, hoping Neo would overturn my decision.

"She's the boss. You need to learn to be more appreciative. Gucci got more stripes out on these streets than most niggas you know. On your way to Burger King, stop somebody and ask about her." Neo and I cracked up laughing.

When the little boy was out of sight, it was time to scold Neo. "You know the way you running this bitch is all wrong, right?" I looked him square in the face. "You got niggas all outside. You got young bitches and babies in the backroom. Man, you are blowing up the spot."

"My fault, boss. Today was just a bad day is all," he sighed. "It won't happen again."

"Better not, or you'll be headed to Burger King too."

Chapter 14

Mina

"Are you sure you don't wanna come in?" I asked Sam from the parking lot of the funeral home on West Grand Boulevard. Although it wasn't the ideal spot to say goodbye to a loved one, it was all we could afford. Since Chloe had no family, Sam and I decided to foot the bill. It was no secret that I wasn't fond of her. Nevertheless, the situation really tugged on my heartstrings. I had never seen death so close. It shook me to the core.

"I'm going to the hospital to be with my daughter." He was dead set against paying his final respects to his baby's mama.

"Suit yourself. Just be back in about an hour." I stepped from the car and closed the door behind me. Sam waited until I was inside before he pulled off.

The place was small and quiet. The only sound I heard was a recording of someone playing the organ.

"May I help you?" An elderly woman dressed in a black pantsuit smiled. She looked like she was close to death herself. The wig she wore was outdated, her makeup was overdone, and her dentures were about a size too big.

"Yes, ma'am. I'm here for the service of Robyn." I couldn't think of her last name right away, but the woman knew who I was referring to.

"Right this way." She escorted me toward a room that was down the hall on the right-hand side.

Upon entering the small room, I was startled at the emptiness. I knew she didn't have any family. However, I did expect to see a few coworkers or friends. Besides myself, there were only Nikki and her son. I didn't know what to do. Therefore, I approached the casket, then stared down at the woman who had tried to kill me. She looked good, if that was a compliment. The funeral makeup was done perfectly. Her hair was styled in a simple wrap, and the yellow skirt suit was nice. I'd picked it up from Burlington Coat Factory along with the costume jewelry she wore.

"Rest in peace, Chloe." I patted her hand, then headed toward Nikki.

"Hi, Mina." She sniffed. There was a tissue box on her lap, and her nose was running.

"Hey, Nikki. How are you holding up?" I took the seat next to her, setting my purse between us. She and I weren't friends. I doubted we would ever be. In spite of this, we always remained cordial whenever in one another's presence. Now that Sam was back hanging with Mario, we would be seeing a lot of each other. Gucci wouldn't like it, but I had no choice.

"I'm good. I just can't believe she's gone, ya know?" She blew her nose.

"Yeah. It's sad how it ended, but she's in a better place now." Although I could've, I steered clear of speaking negatively. Chloe wasn't right in the head. I didn't want to ruin Nikki's memories of who she thought her friend was. "I can't believe we're the only ones here."

"I know, right?" Nikki looked around the room as if something had changed. "Maybe nobody knows."

"They ran the story in the paper," I informed her. "Maybe her street friends didn't want to come for fear of her police friends being here."

"I guess." Nikki shrugged. "How are Sam and the baby?" She hadn't been to the hospital since the baby was born.

"Sam is okay. As a matter of fact, he just went to the hospital to check on Samantha." Sam had decided to name his daughter after him. He was a proud dad, and I was a proud stepmom. For now, we had to pray that she pulled through the next month or so. She was so tiny she could fit in the palm of your hand. Her little body was in an incubator, and she was connected to several different machines. Even so, we were confident she would be fine and couldn't wait to bring her home.

"I'm glad to hear that. I can't wait to visit her again." Nikki shifted Junior, who was asleep across her lap. "I've just been so busy with Rio."

"I heard he pulled through the surgery and is almost as good as new." Since the doctors had wheeled him into surgery, I hadn't been back to visit him at the hospital. Things were very awkward now that he and Gucci were on the outs. Although Sam had visited several times, I was Gucci's friend and more concerned with her well-being.

"Yeah, he's back to getting on my nerves." She laughed and so did I.

Just then, there was a creaking sound coming from the door behind us, causing both Nikki and me to turn. I didn't recognize the chocolate stranger being followed by three kids. Whoever it was had Nikki looking all crazy. "Roscoe, is that you?" She squinted.

"What's up, Nik?" He nodded with watery eyes.

Before he could utter another word, she was up on her feet and in his face. "I thought you were dead!"

"It's a long story. I promise to explain everything. First, please let me and my kids say goodbye to my sister." He stepped past Nikki and went over to the black casket where Chloe lay peacefully.

"Your sister?" Nikki and I both asked at the same time. From what I knew, Chloe had no family.

"Just give me a second, all right?" he snapped.

"Oh, I'll give you a second before I'm on the phone with Mario. Actually, I think I'll let him get to the bottom of this." She retrieved her phone, then proceeded to dial. Before she could punch in the sixth number, he was pulling her toward the back of the room.

Chapter 15

Lovely

Death is a loss that leaves you feeling empty, a feeling that I'd experienced over and over throughout the years. My heart was heavy with grief, and my head hung low with depression. Life had taken its toll on me. I couldn't take anymore. I wondered what it would be like to end it all right here, right now. I questioned myself. There was a 9 mm handgun resting under my pillow. It was locked and loaded. All I had to do was grab it and pull the trigger. The mere thought of leaving Maine saddened me. At least I could be with my family again. Shit didn't work out for us on earth. Perhaps heaven held a new fate for my loved ones. I'd longed for the days to see my mother and father united and happy. I'd missed laughing with my big and little sisters. I wanted to see my son again and nurture him like a mother should. Instead, I was robbed of motherhood. My son was taken from me like he'd been taken by a thief in the night. *That's it!* I wiped away the tears falling from my eyes, then grabbed the gun.

"Lo, are you all right?" Do It stepped into the dark room without knocking, limping over to my bedside.

Immediately, I returned the gun to its hiding spot. Then I balled up into the same fetal position I had been in for the past week. "I'll be all right," I murmured.

"Can I bring you anything?" He desperately wanted to alleviate my pain, but it was useless. Unless he could bring my son back to life, there was nothing he could do for me. As Do It continued to talk, my mind drifted to the night Maine and I fled Detroit. I remembered it like it was yesterday.

We were on the chartered jet heading away from the city that raised me. Something just didn't feel right. I thought it may have been the fear of getting caught. My mind told me not to worry, because the worst was over. The private aircraft had been in the air for two hours already. We were in the clear.

"Maine, I'm not feeling well." I grabbed my stomach to soothe the shooting pains.

"Maybe you should lie back and close your eyes." He held my hand yet continued to gaze out of the small window in deep thought. Part of me wondered what was on his mind. Is it Nikki? I

thought silently but let it go. We were on our way to Mexico, far away from her and any hold she may have had on him. She was no longer a threat to me.

"Baby, are you okay?" I asked.

"I'm just tired." He rubbed his face, then readjusted himself on the cream-colored leather seat.

"Get some rest then. I'm going to the bathroom." The pain in my stomach wouldn't let up. Maybe I needed to do number two and didn't know it.

The second I stood up, my legs became saturated with fluid. Slowly reaching between my thighs, I nearly gasped when I saw the slimy, clear fluid and bloody mixture. "Something is wrong! I need help!"

Instantly, both Maine and Coco were out of their seats and attending me. "Shit! I think your water just broke." Coco dropped to her knees, peering between my legs.

"Oh, my God!" I screamed and doubled over in pain. Something felt as if it was falling outta my vagina.

"Lovely, lie down," Coco instructed, and I did. She lifted the hospital gown above my waist, then went into panic mode. "Maine, we need to land this plane ASAP. She is about to deliver this baby."

"Shit!" Without delay, Maine approached the cockpit. He urged the pilot to land. Unfortunately, we were flying over the Gulf of Mexico, and there

was no landing strip nearby. "Don't worry, baby, just hold on!"

"I can't hold on. He's falling out of me." I wasn't even pushing. The baby kept oozing out.

"Lovely, you'll be okay. I'm going to try to deliver my godson, okay?" Coco smiled and went to work between my legs. I lay there in shock at what was happening. Never did I envision delivering my son on an airplane. In contrast, it sure beat having him in prison. "What's his name going to be?" she asked to divert my mind from what was occurring.

"I want to name him Nazier," I said, which was Maine's middle name. It wasn't an average name and sounded distinguished. I had big dreams for my little prince that didn't involve the street life or dope game. He was going to be a doctor or a lawyer if I had anything to say about it.

A few minutes later, I felt my son make his exit from my body and into the world. I cried. I had done it! He was finally here. After spending my entire pregnancy behind bars and fearing having to give up custody of my son, it was finally over. We were heading into new territory and moving forward with our newfound life. After having endured so much tragedy, with my son and Maine by my side, the sky was the limit.

"Let me hold him." I wiped my tears away.

Closely, Coco held on to my tiny bundle of joy and rocked him slightly. She was crying, and so was Maine. Eventually, I recognized they weren't tears of joy. Both of them were shedding tears of sorrow.

"What's wrong?" I screamed, now noticing that my son hadn't uttered a sound. Weren't babies supposed to cry? "Why isn't he crying?" I yelled.

"I'm so sorry, Lovely." Maine kneeled down and cradled me.

"Sorry for what? Let me see him." I pushed him off of me and fought hard to sit up. Reluctantly, Coco handed the tiny bundle over. I lost my breath.

My son was stillborn. His lifeless body was still connected to mine by the umbilical cord. Frantically, I placed my mouth to his and blew, but it was useless. He was in heaven while I was stuck in hell. I wasn't sure what I'd done to deserve the hand I'd been dealt. One thing was certain: I was tired of losing.

"Lo, did you hear me? I asked if you were all right. Do you need anything?" Do It snapped me out of my miserable mental space.

"I'm fine."

"I brought someone to see you." He went back over to the bedroom door, opening it wider. My niece, Shawnie, was standing there with a huge, snaggle-toothed smile.

"Auntie L, I made you something!" She waltzed her 6-year-old self into the room, then flopped down onto my king-size bed.

"What did you make me, baby?" I sounded more chipper than I actually felt.

"It's a 'get well soon' card." She showed me the card she had created with crayons and construction paper. A few words were misspelled, but it was beautiful, nonetheless.

"Thank you! It's so thoughtful!" I kissed her cheek.

"I just don't want you to be sad anymore." She leaned down, hugging me tightly.

"Auntie L needs some rest. Let's come back and check on her later." Do It pulled Shawnie from the bed, and she reluctantly left.

Chapter 16

Nikki

"Look, Robyn is my sister, my blood sister," Roscoe explained as I tapped my foot impatiently waiting for him to finish the story. "She is much younger than me, so growing up we didn't hang out. I took to the street life. She took the high road and became a police officer."

"So, you knew the bitch was a cop and you still allowed her to infiltrate our organization?"

"By the time she was on the scene, I was behind bars doing that five-year bid. I had no idea, Nikki. I swear to God!" He raised his right hand toward the sky.

"Whatever, nigga!" I smacked my lips, not believing for one second that Roscoe didn't know what his own sister was up to. "Finish the story."

"Anyway, while behind bars, I reached out to her and told her I was ready to clean up my act. In exchange for freedom, she asked for my assistance. At the time, I didn't know she was undercover with y'all. It wasn't until she told me about the shipment Mario was delivering to Zeke that I figured shit out." He paused before continuing. "I'm not going to lie. I had plans to rob that fucking truck."

The mere mention of the truck I was driving when I was shot brought back bad memories. "So, what happened? Why did you send Tonya to do it?" His baby mother was a pain in the ass. If she had not died before I was released from the hospital, I would've killed her my damn self.

"I didn't send Tonya to do it, Nik. Actually, I had no idea she was even in the vicinity when that shit went down." He looked back at his children, who were still standing over Chloe's casket. They were playing a game of rock paper scissors.

"In the vicinity? Nigga, Tonya tried to kill me!" I exclaimed, causing Junior to wiggle in my arms.

"She didn't even pull the trigger," he said, defending ol' girl.

"Somebody shot me, Roscoe! If it wasn't you, and it wasn't Tonya, who was it?" I looked at him sideways when he pointed toward the casket. "What? Are you saying Chloe shot me?"

"That's exactly what I'm saying." He bobbed his head up and down. "I will always have love for my baby sister, but she was dirty. She took me out of the game by staging my murder and putting me in witness protection. She tried to kill you, and she bodied Tonya," he whispered.

"What?" I was stunned with information overload. "How do you know all of this?"

"I found all that shit out after she went to jail for murdering that other cop. All of her secrets fell out of the closet," he sighed.

"Damn!" I didn't know what else to say. I was at a loss for words. More so, I was pissed beyond belief. I would've kicked over that damn casket had it not been morally wrong. How could my "friend" have done me so dirty? All week I'd been shedding tears over this bitch only to learn we were never friends in the first place. Mario was right!

"I only came back here because she's my sister. I also had to see if it was really her in that casket and not one of her tricks." Roscoe looked back at his children, who were now sitting next to Mina, talking her ears off.

"Well, I can attest to the fact that your sister is really dead. She killed herself during a standoff with police," I sighed. "She was six months pregnant with your niece."

"Robyn has a daughter?" I could tell he was elated yet saddened by the news.

"She's at Children's Hospital."

"Wow!" He shook his head. "Do you have a picture or something?"

"As a matter of fact, I do." I scrolled down the photo gallery, then showed him the only picture I'd taken of the miniature baby in the incubator.

"Look at how tiny she is." He stared at the photo.

"Her dad is at the hospital if you want to go visit her for a while."

"No, I only came for the funeral." He handed me back the phone. "I have too many enemies in this city. I can't run the risk of being spotted."

"What happened to the witness protection?"

"After Robyn did what she did, they dropped me and my kids like a bad habit. We're out here on our own, but it's all good. As long as we're together, then we'll be all right." He called out for his children. "Come on, we 'bout to go." They stopped playing and ran over to his side. "It was good seeing you, Nik. Tell the big homie I didn't mean for this to happen."

I hadn't planned on going to visit Mario today. However, after running into Roscoe, I was bursting at the seams to spill the tea.

Upon accessing the private room, I spotted a nurse doing more flirting than actual patient care. She pretended to check Mario's vitals while feeling all over his body. Except for a pair of Hanes boxer briefs, he was lying there with nothing on. Previously, I had appealed to him to please keep the hospital gown on. Saying it cramped his style, he refused. I didn't know what style he was trying to uphold in a hospital, but now I saw.

Mario noticed my presence. "I knew you couldn't stand being away from a nigga for a whole day." His cocky ass looked up with a big smile.

The nurse was obviously upset that I had ruined her play. Who cared? What I had to say was important. "Is this your sister?" the nurse smugly asked to irritate me.

"No, that's my fuckin' wife standing there with my son," Mario barked.

"Oh, I'm sorry. Mrs. Wallace, I'm Brittani. Nice to meet you." She changed her tune so fast I caught whiplash.

"Please excuse us," I demanded.

"Um . . ." She stalled. "I wasn't finished with Mr. Wallace."

"Bitc—"

"Give us ten minutes." Mario cut me off before the rest of the word could leave my lips. She looked as if she wanted to say something but knew better.

"Look at you getting all jealous." Mario smirked after his nurse was out the door.

"Don't flatter yourself, playboy. I only came by to tell you who I saw today." I placed Junior on the bed with Mario.

"You look good in that tight-ass dress." He grabbed his manhood. Even in the hospital, Mario was a horndog. "You should let me get some real quick."

"Seriously, Rio, listen to me!" I stomped my foot.

"I am serious, girl. A nigga is in need."

"If you don't let me talk, I'm leaving."

"After you talk, can I hit it?" He raised his eyebrows multiple times, and I cracked up laughing.

"Anyway, I saw a ghost today. His name is Roscoe."

"Roscoe who?" He was puzzled.

"Your old partner Roscoe. Tonya's baby daddy Roscoe," I reminded him, taking a seat on the chair beside his bed.

"Bullshit!" Mario bellowed.

"Square biz." I smirked.

"Where at?" He turned the television to Disney Channel for Junior, then gave me his undivided attention.

"He showed up at Chloe's funeral."

"How the fuck is a dead nigga gon' show up to a funeral?" Mario asked.

"I said the same thing, but it was him. I even went up and talked to him. Dude had some very interesting things to say."

"Like what?"

"Well, for starters, he told me Chloe was his biological sister, and she placed him in the witness protection program. He also told me she was the one who shot me." I sat back and watched his facial expression change from confused to pissed.

"Are you fucking kidding me?" he yelled so loud I jumped. The monitor attached to his chest began beeping erratically as his heart rate rose. "I swear on my kids, if that bitch weren't already dead, I'd kill her with my bare hands."

"I can't believe it either." Finally processing the facts, I shook my head. I trusted Chloe, treated her like a sister, and the bitch had the nerve to try to body me. It was because of her that I lost my family, almost lost my life, and was left with this limp.

"Where is that nigga Roscoe at now?" Mario reached for his phone.

"What are you doing?" Right away I became alarmed.

"It's time to lay that bitch-ass nigga down for real!" Mario was furious.

"Rio, let him be. He has his children with him, and he's all they've got."

"Fuck that! You think I'm just gon' let a nigga come through and tell you all that shit then live to see tomorrow?"

"Baby, I'm okay. Please let him be. He had no idea Chloe worked for us because he was behind bars at the time."

"Bullshit!" Mario proceeded to dial the numbers on his phone.

"Rio, please just let that man be. He's just a brother wanting to say goodbye to his sister. Chloe was the problem, and she's no longer a threat." Slowly, I placed my hand over his and removed the phone.

"What type of man would I be to let this shit ride?" He rubbed his temples.

"One who trusts me." I smiled. "Baby, not every battle is worth fighting."

"I guess you're right." He placed the phone down on the nightstand near his bed.

"Are you guys finished?" The nurse was back.

I started to tell her hell no, we weren't finished, but I needed to leave anyway. "Yeah, I was just about to go." I grabbed my son from the bed.

"Nik, where are you going?" Rio asked.

"I've got to head home to finish writing my book."

"You really wanna be a writer, huh?" He smirked.

Ever since I came out of my coma, I'd had this compulsion to tell my story. Many people believe the dope game provides the glamorous life without consequences. Sure, I attended the best parties, spent obscene amounts of money, and never went to work a day after I said, "I do." Conversely, constantly worrying over when the police would kick the door in, or when the enemy would catch us slipping, was not a good feeling. If I could prevent one woman from following in my footsteps, then mission accomplished.

Chapter 17

Mina

I couldn't believe all the shit I'd heard while eavesdropping at the funeral. Chloe was something else. I couldn't wait to tell Sam.

"How was the funeral?" he asked after I stepped into the car. His eyes were bloodshot. It was apparent he had been crying.

"Are you okay?"

"I'm good." He nodded, then started the engine.

"Sam, wait." I placed my hand on his to keep him from putting the car in drive. "Let's talk about it."

"I don't wanna talk about it. I just want to get back to the hospital with my daughter." Ignoring my request, he put the car in gear anyway.

"It's okay to be sad about Chloe." I knew exactly what was bothering him. "She was your ex-girlfriend and the mother of your child. It's natural to display emotion."

"I'll be all right. I'm just angry." He gripped the steering wheel and headed into the flow of traffic.

"Why are you angry?" My voice was yielding. I didn't want to come off like an interrogator.

"Look, let's just leave it alone." He brushed me off.

"Sam, if we're going to be married one day, we have to learn how to communicate."

"Fine," he relented. "I'm angry because I felt I should've done more. I also feel guilty because she took the murder rap for what I'd done." For a second, he looked out the window. "Chloe wouldn't be dead if I hadn't killed your husband." His shoulders dropped as if he had been carrying the weight of the world on them.

"So, this is my fault?" I was outdone. Nobody asked him to kill Tre. The murder was entirely his idea.

"Did I say that?" Not once did his eyes make contact with mine.

"You didn't have to." I sighed from annoyance.

"You see, that shit right there is why I didn't want to fuckin' talk in the first place. Females always say they wanna talk, but when a nigga open his mouth and start spittin' that real shit, y'all feelings get hurt." He was upset.

"My feelings aren't hurt," I lied.

"Why are you pouting then?"

"I'm not pouting." I lied again, not wanting him to know how I really felt. In the back of my mind, I was aware that one day he would toss what he did for me back in my face.

"Chloe wasn't perfect, but she didn't deserve that shit," he mumbled.

It was time to shut this Chloe business down. "Her brother attended the funeral today." I let my words linger in the air.

"Her brother? What brother?"

"His name is Roscoe. You might know him. He worked for the H.O.F. organization." I watched as a hint of familiarity came over his face. "He said she was the one who actually tried to kill Nikki."

"Are you sure?" He studied me for any signs of uncertainty.

"I was right there when he confessed to Nikki."

"Ain't this a bitch!" he said more to himself than to me. Feeling satisfied that his bubble had been burst, I reclined in my seat with a smirk.

We rode in silence all the way to Children's Hospital. It wasn't until Sam maneuvered into a parking spot that he broke the deadly silence. "Baby, I'm sorry." He grasped my chin to turn my face toward him. "It's not your fault and it's not mine either. She put the gun to her own head and pulled the trigger."

"It's all good." I grabbed my purse, then stepped from the vehicle. Internally, I was still seething but decided to drop the matter. Little Samantha needed us right now.

Chapter 18

Gucci

"What up, Gucci?" Hassan the Arab gas station attendant said through the triple-thick bulletproof glass. "Muhammad is waiting for you in the back."

"Cool." I grabbed a bag of barbeque Better Made potato chips and a grape Faygo pop before heading through the employee entrance.

The gas station on the corner of Fenkell was one of my favorite traps. It was so low-key that no one would ever guess we pushed pounds of cocaine through the back each month. It was like a workshop, and everything ran smoothly. One of the transporters would deliver precooked crack to the gas station in cleaning supply boxes. Then Muhammad would load the shit into merchandise boxes and distribute them to the other family-owned gas stations. The money would come back the same way. I had no complaints.

After stepping through the employee entrance, I was greeted by an Arab wearing a turban with a gun. "Who the fuck are you?"

"Who the fuck are you?" I had never seen his ass before. It was evident he didn't know the chain of command.

"She's fine, Ishmael." Muhammad placed a cell phone into his back pocket, then greeted me with a hug. "So nice to see you again."

"Muhammad, your boy here almost caught a hot one." While hugging my friend, I mugged Ishmael.

"This is my cousin. He's new. Please forgive him." He smiled. "Come have a seat while I get what you came for." He ushered me over to a computer desk and chair. I took a seat and made small talk while he was getting my bread.

I liked Muhammad. He was cute in his own way. He wasn't your average Arab. He was new school. He dressed in hip-hop gear and wore more chains than some rappers. Had it not been for his crooked nose, stained teeth, and body odor, I would've introduced him to one of the girls from the Doll House.

"Yo, homie, when you gon' take me for a spin in the new Bentley Mulsanne?" While behind the desk, I occasionally glanced at the security monitors. The new car was candy apple red with black rims and a custom black grill.

"You like it?" He poked his head around the wall safe. He was sending the cash through a money machine. I could hear the distinct sound. It was music to my ears.

"Hell yeah. I wish I could get one."

"Boss lady, you can get one without a doubt," he laughed.

"If I got one, the Feds would be all over me." Most Arabs had racks on top of racks. A lot of Arab families owned gas stations, grocery stores, and other establishments. It was nothing for one of them to be riding around in expensive cars. The Feds were too busy watching us to pay any attention to them.

"Do you want to drive it?" he asked, poking his head around the safe again. "The keys are in my drawer."

"No, I'll save it for next time." I twisted the cap off the pop, then took a swig. There was nothing like a cold grape Faygo.

"Where is the boss?"

"You're looking at her." I knew he was referring to Mario, but I had nothing to say about him. Both Muhammad and I laughed.

"Well, here you are, my friend. Three hundred grand in all big bills." He placed the duffle bags on the desk, waiting for me to count it, but I knew it was all good. We'd been doing business with him for over eight years. Never once had his money come up short. Besides that, he was good people.

"'Til next time then." I stood for a hug, then grabbed the heavy bags with all of my might.

Chapter 19

Lovely

I was awakened by the sunlight intruding into my dreams.

"Baby, you have to get up from here."

Maine had pulled the blinds back to reveal the beautiful private beach with crystal-clear blue water. There was also a view of the Mesoamerican Reef in the distance. Regrettably, the scenery did nothing for me. Our secluded property in the Mexican Caribbean was spectacular on every level. Be that as it may, I had no desire to explore beyond this bedroom.

"Maine, please just leave me alone!" I didn't mean to snap, but I was tired of people telling me what to do or how to feel. From the time the plane landed, everyone had given me the "time will heal all wounds" or the "you can't dwell in sorrow" speeches. Until a muthafucka had walked in my shoes, they had no right to tell me shit!

"Baby, I'm not leaving you in here for another day. It's been two weeks already. It's unhealthy for you to stay locked in here like this." He took a seat on the chaise beside the bed.

"What's unhealthy is losing a child!" I snapped.

"You think you're the only one hurting?" His jaw muscles tightened. "He was my son too!"

"You didn't carry him for nine months, Jermaine. I did." I pointed at my chest.

"So that makes my pain less significant?" He stood.

"I'm not saying that!" I snapped again.

"Sounds like it to me." He headed to the door. "This should be a time when we pull together and comfort one another. Instead, you're so wrapped up in your own feelings you're being too selfish to think about my grief!"

"Maine, don't go there." I really didn't want beef between us, but it was what it was. Our relationship had already been tested on too many levels. I realized we couldn't survive too many more blows. All the same, I was feeling confrontational. "Selfish is the last thing anyone should ever call me. Just get the fuck out!"

"Oh, I'll leave, don't worry!" He went into the closet and slipped into a pair of shoes. "When I'm gone, don't try to find me either!"

"I won't!" I screamed. "We need some space any fuckin' way!" I didn't know why I said that. Honestly, there was too much space between us already. Sorrowfully, it was too late to take it back.

"Lovely, in my heart I know you don't mean that. But I don't know what else to do. All I want is for you to be happy." He paused and his shoulders dropped. "If my leaving makes you happy, then so be it. I can't watch you sulk around here day in and day out anyway."

I wanted to stop him. I allowed my pride to get in the way. He was the man of my dreams, and I was letting him walk out of my life like a stranger. Maine had been with me through the loss of both my sisters, my father, my friend, and our son. We'd been on the run from the law more times than I would have liked to recount. Each and every time, he had proven to me he had my back. I didn't know why I was so angry with him. It wasn't his fault our son died.

"I'll be gone for a while. Do It and Shawnie are here if you need them. The rent is paid, and there's money in the safe should you need it. When I come back, I hope it's not too late to save us." He approached the bed for a kiss.

I turned my head in the other direction. "See you later." The words were cold, and I knew it. Silently, I resented him for giving up on me, although I had given up on my damn self.

"Damn, it's like that? You said that shit as if I were running to the store or some shit." He shook his head, then left the room without another word.

Chapter 20

Nikki

Two days after Chloe's funeral, I stepped into Salon 3K for my weekly appointment. All eyes were on me. The attention was nothing new to me, but this was overboard.

"Hey, Nikki," Cynthia, the receptionist, said. She was new to the shop but good at her job. Baby girl could handle the phone lines and appointment book and service the waiting area at the same damn time.

"Hey, girl! What's going on around here?" Nothing went on without her knowing about it. For that reason, I knew she would fill me in.

"Girl, Gucci walked up in here about ten minutes ago. She's in the bathroom," she whispered.

"So why is everyone staring at me?"

"They're wondering if there's gonna be a catfight up in this piece." She stood from her seat, then leaned in closer. "Coco ain't here yet, but I can slide you into the break room before Gucci comes out."

"Girl, ain't nobody scared of her. I'll wait right here. Just let me know when Coco gets here." I walked past two women talking out of the sides of their lips like I couldn't make out what they were saying.

Reaching down to grab one of the *Sister 2 Sister* magazines, I heard the lady to my right whisper, "You know she scared, right?"

"You must not have heard what happened the last time those bitches saw each other. Nikki mollywhopped that ass!" the other lady replied.

"Yeah, but then Gucci made a comeback at the hospital. I heard they was fighting all over Mario's hospital bed," she lied with a straight face. I wan-ted to correct her, but there was no use. People in the hood were always gossiping about someone or something.

When Gucci approached the waiting area, everyone got so quiet you could hear a mouse piss on cotton. I wanted to show these bitches we were better than that. So, I went over and sat next to her. "Hey, Gucci, how are you?"

"Nikkita!" she snapped and looked at me like I had no right to be near her. I was totally caught off guard and embarrassed. Had I known she was going to act like this, I never would've said anything.

"Look, I only came over here to see how you were and to ask about Maria." I stood calmly, trying not to cause a scene.

"Bitch, there's no need for you to be asking about me and mine!" she popped off at the mouth.

I had tried to be grown about the situation, but she blew it. Whap! I slapped her right in the face. "I don't know what your problem is, but you need to get that shit together." I swung with the left hand, but she blocked it, then came with a punch to the stomach. I doubled over to protect my stomach. That's when she came with a knee to my face. Luckily, I saw the move and dodged it.

"Come on, bitch! Don't run now." She followed me toward the receptionist desk. I reached back, grabbed the cordless phone from its cradle, and caught that bitch right in the face.

"That's enough!" Coco was now in between us.

"Fuck that! This bitch thinks she's so tough, let her bang," Gucci barked.

"I've whipped your ass too many times this year. I'm done playing with little girls," I laughed.

"Your man didn't think I was a little girl when he was digging my guts out, did he?" She intended for that to be a low blow. Yet I found it amusing.

"He also didn't think the shit was good. You see who he came back to!"

The crowd burst into laughter.

"Whatever, bitch! Next time, I got a 9 mm with your name on it."

"They didn't stop making guns when they made yours!" I retorted.

"You don't even know how to pop a pistol." She smirked.

"You'd be surprised."

Coco attempted to halt the confrontation. "Come on, Nikki. Let me do your hair."

"Actually, I'll reschedule. Suddenly, I have no need to be in the company of hood rats." The comment was meant for Gucci as well as the crowd of onlookers.

Chapter 21

Gucci

That bitch was back on my shit list! She'd been let off the hook too many times. Sooner or later, I was going to snap, crackle, and pop all over her ass.

"Gucci, are you ready?" my stylist asked after the commotion died down.

"Yeah." I nodded and followed her to the back of the swank salon.

"Girl, that shit was crazy up there." She wrapped a cape around my neck, then led me to the shampoo sink.

"What's crazy is I let her get away with that shit." Just thinking about it pissed me off again.

"Girl, don't trip over that siditty bitch." She smacked her lips. "You got her man and she's mad."

"I'm not with Mario anymore." I didn't miss the whispers and smirks from those around me. They would surely spread the gossip throughout Metro Detroit, but fuck it. "I got a new nigga," I lied. I was as single as a $1 bill, but she didn't need to know it.

"Oh, yeah! Who is this mystery man?" She turned the faucet on, adjusting the water temperature.

"That don't matter. Just know he's a boss!" I placed my head under the water and thought about Cartier. I hadn't heard from him since the day he took me to the hospital to see Mario. He said something came up and he had to make a trip out of town. That was almost two weeks ago.

After my hair was dried and styled, I decided to stop by the Doll House. I hadn't been by the club in a while. It was time to show my face.

"What up, Gucci?" Taz, the bartender, waved. She was a cute girl with dark brown skin, slanted eyes, and a body to die for. Frequently I approached her about working as a dancer. However, she was too shy.

"Hey, girl, let get me a shot of that white Rémy on the rocks." Normally, I liked to mix my white Rémy with Sprite, but today I needed it straight up.

"You can pour your own trouble." She handed me a glass and the bottle of alcohol. It was Monday afternoon. The place wasn't crowded. Therefore, I took a seat atop one of the red barstools.

"You want a drink?" I wasn't one for drinking alone. That was depressing.

"If you don't mind, then I don't mind." She grabbed the Cîroc Red Berry bottle and poured a double shot. "What's on your mind?"

"Why something gotta be on my mind to have a drink?" I tossed the shot back, then poured another.

"Because you're at the bar on a Monday talking to me," she giggled. "Seriously though, what's wrong?"

I looked her over thoroughly and contemplated telling her my business. She was cool and all, but I didn't really know her like that, so I kept it simple.

"Girl, I'm cool. I needed to come here for some paperwork. Might as well have a drink in the process, right?"

"Mm-hmm." Her lips twisted up. "Is it about Mario?"

"What makes you say that?" I downed the second shot, then poured a third.

"Word on the streets is he got back with Nikki." She slowly sipped from her glass.

"Fuck Mario!" I spat. Behind my anger was hurt and resentment. I wanted him to feel my wrath. I just had to wait until the time was right.

"Gucci, I hope I don't offend you with what I'm about to say." She paused.

"Depends on what you're about to say," I laughed.

"The best way to get over one man is to get up under another one," she giggled.

"I'll drink to that." I tossed back the third shot and wiped the excess liquid from my mouth.

The effect of the potent beverage was beginning to take its toll on me. I spent another hour kicking it with Taz before a surprise visitor showed up.

"What up, Gucci? Let me holla at you right quick." Sam tapped me on the shoulder.

"Nigga, whatchu doing here?" My words ran together as I tried to get up from the barstool.

"I was riding past and spotted the pink Charger on twenty-eights." He laughed and helped me get up. I told Taz I would be back and showed Sam into my office.

"So, what's up?" I took a seat behind the desk.

"I got a problem," he sighed.

"Me too!" I smiled but he was serious.

"Man, I need to get put on with the organization again." He took a seat in one of the leather chairs across from me.

"Have you talked to Mario about this?"

"Not yet. Nikki got the hospital sewn up. Ain't no street business coming through there so long as she got anything to do with it."

The mention of her name had me ready to vomit.

"I thought you were done with the dope game. What happened?" Sam was good at what he did. Although he would be an asset to me, I needed to know why he wanted back in.

"I got into some shit, and I need the extra bread." His eyes rested on mine.

For the first time, I noticed how fine he was: tall as hell and covered in tattoos, just the way I liked 'em. "What type of shit?" I took him in from head to toe and couldn't help but wonder how big his dick was. Maybe it was the liquor, but I was suddenly turned on by his presence.

"Something personal, that's all."

"Does Mina know?" I studied his face for a reaction.

"She doesn't need to know everything."

Now it could've been my imagination, but there was something in the delivery of his words that caused me to believe he was talking about more than selling drugs.

"You're right! She doesn't need to know everything." I rose from my seat, then stood in front of the desk.

"So, am I in or what?"

"I can you put back on, no doubt. But you gotta do something for me first." I sat atop the desk and crossed my legs.

"What's that?" He played dumb. I could see the nigga's joint pulsating through the cargo shorts.

"I'm in need of a good fuck! Can you provide that for me?"

"Are you serious?" he stuttered.

"Do I look like I'm joking?" I opened my legs wide enough for him to see the pink thong.

"What about Mario?"

"What about him?" I slid one leg out of my underwear.

"What about Mina?"

"What about her?" I pulled him up close to me. The scent of Armani cologne was mesmerizing.

"Gucci, I can't." He shook his head.

I wanted to tell this boy to stop being a bitch. Instead, I unzipped his pants. His penis was the size of a large Chiquita banana, curve and all.

"I won't tell if you don't." Licking my lips, I watched him ponder my proposition.

"You got a condom?" He pulled my legs up over his shoulders and laid me back. Then he took me places I could only dream of.

Chapter 22

Mina

"Ay, ma, you need a ride or something?" the client I'd just shown a $50,000 fixer-upper asked. We were smack dab in the middle of the hood, somewhere near Finney High School. I was nervous but kept it cool. My whip was in the shop, so I'd been bumming a ride to and from showings with Sam. Normally he stayed with me, but today my clients wanted to see five homes. I told him to drop me off so he could go check on Samantha. He was supposed to be here thirty minutes ago.

"No, thank you. I'm good." I smiled to mask the aggravation I was presently experiencing.

"Are you sure? It gets a little rough out here at night." He didn't have to remind me. I had already removed my jewelry, stuffing the items into my bra. Currently, I wished I could've concealed my purse, but it was entirely too large.

"She said she was sure! Come on, Clyde, damn," Benita, his impatient wife, yelled. She wasn't an easy customer to please. I was happy to see her go. All day, I had to hear about granite countertops this and crown molding that. I wanted to tell that bitch she was ballin' on a budget. Together, the two of them had only managed to snag a $50,000 FHA loan, which wouldn't buy you shit these days but a mediocre house at best. Clyde worked for the Department of Transportation, and Benita was a stay-at-home wife. They wanted to live the lifestyle of the rich and famous on a beer budget.

"I guess we'll call you this weekend." Clyde smiled. "I think the third time is the charm."

"How about the two of you go home and take a look at the website? If you see anything that appeals to you and it's in your budget, call me." I was not about to waste another Saturday with the likes of these two. Casually, I pulled out my cell phone and placed it to my ear.

"I told you we should've hired that other Realtor," I could hear Benita attempting to whisper on the way to the car parked at the end of the driveway. "This bitch doesn't even have a car. How can we expect her to have some class?"

I wanted to let Mrs. Benita know a thing or two but brushed the comment off. Getting Sam on the phone was a more pressing matter than her remark.

"The voicemail you are trying to reach has not yet been set up."

"Damn!" I ended the call, contemplating my next move. There was a gas station a few blocks from here. To get there meant I had to go through the trenches of the hood. Being unfamiliar with my surroundings, I decided to stay put and call Gucci.

"Hey, Mina!" She sounded funny.

"Thank God you picked up! Where are you?" I jumped as a stray cat scurried from the bushes beside me.

"At the club, why?"

"I need a ride from the east side. Sam was supposed to be here a while ago. It's getting dark now, and a bitch is paranoid." I tried to make light of the situation. In all sincerity, I was scared for real.

"Text me your location, and I'll be on the way." She ended the call.

Just as the sun was beginning to set, a gang of men came walking down the street. Instantly, my heart fluttered. I wanted to cross the street, but that would've raised suspicion. As an alternative, I took a seat on the porch, pretending I lived there.

"Ooh wee! Look at what Santa done dropped off in the ghetto." One of the men whistled.

"Christmas must've come early." Another fist bumped the other. "What's your name, baby?"

"My name is Terri." I really wanted to ignore them and pray they passed quickly, but I knew better. There were more of them than of me. Sometimes ignoring them triggered an undesirable reaction.

"Terri, I ain't ever seen you before. Where you from?" The little one came up the walkway. I felt my stomach drop. Why didn't he just keep it moving?

"I'm from Ohio." That part was the truth. "I'm visiting a friend. She'll be here any minute," I rambled.

"Dorothy, you ain't in Kansas no more," he teased. The crowd busted out laughing. "This is Detroit, bitch! Come off them red bottoms. Give me that cell phone, and I want that purse!" he demanded. Out of nowhere, he was brandishing a handgun.

Slowly, I slipped out of my shoes and handed over the purse and cell phone. The young thief took my shit and got ghost.

Chapter 23

Lovely

I lay in bed contemplating my next move. Maine had been gone for almost a day and hadn't bothered to call home. I hadn't called him either, so we were even. It was so peaceful without him I feared I was getting accustomed to it.

Knock, knock. The sound of the door concluded the staring contest I was having with the ceiling.

"Come in." Even though I wasn't up for company, I didn't want to turn Shawnie away if it was her. She'd been down to see me every day. I felt bad about not playing with her.

"Lovely baby, when are you coming out of this room?" Agent Nichols sauntered in wearing a hot pink tracksuit. Her voice was soft and gentle. As a result, it was difficult to snap at her, so I didn't. She was like the mother I never had but always dreamed of. The funny thing about our relationship was she was a retired FBI agent, and I was a fugitive.

"No time soon." I rolled over to look at her.

"Girl, I can't let you lie up in here like this waiting for death to come." She tugged at the covers.

"Death has to be better than this," I groaned.

"Baby, you've got it twisted." Her choice of words put a smile on my face. She was old school, so to hear her talking like the young folks was humorous. "Your life ain't over just because you lost a child. Trust me, I know." She pointed to her chest. Her daughter was killed by my father and his gang back in the eighties. The assassination was solely meant for the daughter's boyfriend. Dreadfully, she was in the wrong place at the wrong time. "My baby was grown. It was too late for me to start over. At least you're young. You've still got time."

"I don't have time." I sat up on the bed, folding my legs Indian style. "When we landed here, Maine rushed me to the local hospital. After they snipped the umbilical cord, examined me, and cleaned me up, a doctor came to see me. He informed me that my uterus was no good. My chances of carrying a baby to term are primarily nonexistent." It felt good to divulge the secret I'd been keeping. I hadn't shared this information with anyone.

"If your uterus is bad, how did you carry a baby for nine months?"

"My son actually died during my second trimester, and I didn't even know it. Regular prenatal checkups would have caught it, but the prison didn't offer extensive medical treatment."

"Lovely, I know doctors are supposed to be smart. Don't ever forget this: the person with the final say-so is Jesus." She pointed toward the ceiling. "Everything is predestined. If it's meant for you to have a child, then the Lord will give you one."

"I guess you're right, but—"

"No buts. You must learn to have faith, sweetheart." She patted my hand.

"I guess I do need to get up from here." Although everyone had said it dozens of times, Nichols was different.

"No, what you need to do is call that man of yours." She handed me the cordless phone she had in the pocket of her jacket, then left me to make the call.

I dialed all ten digits with caution. I didn't know what to say. An apology wouldn't come easy. Still, I would do the best I could.

After four rings, the call was sent to voicemail. "Jermaine, it's me. I want you to come home so we can talk." I paused before ending the call to say, "I love you," but the words wouldn't come out. For some reason, they were stuck in the pit of my stomach. My heart was cold. Love was nothing but a four-letter word. It meant nothing.

Chapter 24

Nikki

"I can't believe I missed all that shit." Anj shook her head in disbelief. I was catching her up about all the latest drama with Gucci. We were having dinner at Benihana, her treat. She had settled the case in Los Angeles out of court for an undisclosed amount. The reality star didn't want the nasty headlines the case was sure to create to prevent her from obtaining future gigs. Anjela flew back in last night with another notch in her belt.

"I'm going to kill that bitch!" I mumbled casually while watching the chef toss my egg into his hat then down onto the sizzling hot grill.

"I'll plan your defense strategy for court," she laughed. "I can't stand that ghetto rat."

"That makes two of us!" Shaking my head, I held the plate out for the chef.

"What's the news with her and Mario?"

"Truthfully, there is no news. Until today, she's been missing in action, and I like it that way." I attempted to use the chopsticks but failed miserably. "Rio is pissed that he hasn't seen Maria, but it's no sweat off my back, especially after what happened earlier."

"Maybe that hood rat will finally get a clue and realize she can't replace you." Checking her phone, Anj replied to a message.

"I guess." I shrugged. "So, besides the case, what's new? I feel like we haven't kicked it in forever." Although Anjela was my first cousin, we were more like sisters. My mother and her father were siblings. They both spent time in the streets, which caused Anj and me to spend a lot of nights with our grandmother back in the day.

"I know, right!" She was still texting on her phone with a smile.

"What in the hell are you smiling so hard for?"

"While I was in Los Angeles, I met a man." She put the phone down. "His name is Carter Jones. He's tall, fine as hell, and pretty well-off." Her phone lit up. She went back to texting. "He's an agent with the FBI."

She beamed as I frowned. Although we were so much alike, our worlds seemed so different at times. Anjela was always into the nerdy, preppy type. Of course, I was into bad boys.

"I see you frowning. He's not that bad."

"I hate the alphabet gang." Anjela understood it was code for the FBI, DEA, ATF, as well as the po-po.

"As long as you ain't doing nothing illegal, then you ain't got nothing to worry about," she laughed.

"Could you imagine what Thanksgiving dinner would be like with him and Mario at the same table?" Just the thought alone had me cracking up.

"Uncomfortable as hell." She continued laughing. "Seriously though, you have to meet him one day. I know you'll like him."

"This sounds pretty serious, cuz."

"I think it is." She beamed. "I haven't met a man who had me this open since Donald."

The mention of her ex-lover had me in tears.

"What's wrong with you?" She looked at me crazy while I was wiping my eyes. He was the goofiest-looking thing I'd ever laid eyes on. His glasses were too big, the suits he wore were too small, and his teeth were too long, but Anjela loved him. That was, until his wife showed up one night at the hotel to claim her property.

"Don't take this the wrong way, but you fuck with some ugly dudes. You're too damn cute for that." My cousin was a bona fide beauty with the brains and body to match.

"Forget you! Those ugly dudes come with big money that's legal." She winked. "You do the ballers, and I'll stick with bankers."

"Now that was cold." I pretended to be offended. "Anyway, when can I meet his ugly self?"

"Keep it up and you won't get to meet him until the wedding," she giggled. "And for your information, my man is not ugly." She grabbed her phone, showing me a picture of him sitting on a sofa reading the *Wall Street Journal* or something.

"Damn." The word escaped my mouth before I could stop it. The brother was fine. I had to give props. For some reason, he looked very familiar.

"Told you he wasn't ugly." She snatched the phone back. "He'll be in town next month. Maybe you can meet him then."

"What's he coming for?" I was being nosy.

"He's looking into some old case files. Trying to tie up a few loose ends before the promotion he wants comes around."

"What kind of case files?" I tossed back the sake. Japanese liquor wasn't the best, but it sure did give you a buzz.

"The hell if I know." She shrugged.

"Well, I hope Mario's name ain't on any of those files." It was meant as a joke, but neither of us laughed.

Chapter 25

Gucci

I pulled down the deserted street bumping French Montana and looking for Mina. She wasn't answering her cell phone. I would've turned around if it weren't for the fact that I had already driven all the way over here. Letting up off the gas, I dropped the car down to a slow speed. The streetlights were on, but it was hard as hell to see anything. I damn near hit a group of niggas who had darted out into the middle of the street. *Damn kids!*

I rode down three more blocks before spotting Mina standing on the porch of a house with a FOR SALE sign out front. She looked scared as hell. I found it amusing.

"What took you so long?" She got in, slamming the door.

"I would've been here sooner if you had answered your cell phone." Whipping the car into a U-turn, I headed back in the direction I'd just come from.

"They took my phone, my shoes, and my cell phone." She sniffed. For the first time, I noticed she was barefoot.

"Who?" I slammed on the brakes.

"Some dudes robbed me about ten minutes ago."

"Mina, are you okay?" I turned on the interior lights to inspect her for injuries.

"He had a gun," she cried. "He could've killed me."

"What did they look like?" There was a 9 mm stashed behind the radio panel. I was prepared to bust a cap in someone's ass.

"I don't know, but there were a bunch of them," she avowed.

"Was one of them wearing a red snapback?" I bet my bottom dollar it was those fuckers I just passed.

"Yeah, how did you know?" She stopped crying. I didn't say anything. Nonchalantly, I put the car back in gear and sped down the block. "Gucci, where are we going?"

"I'm going to get your shit back." I didn't even look at her while I drove. I was on a mission.

A few blocks and several corners later, I pulled up in front of a house on Houston Whittier. "Is that them?"

"Yeah, but don't go up there," she cautioned.

"Girl, I ain't about to let some knuckleheads punk you." Pressing the code on the custom radio, I waited for it to unlock, then grabbed my gun. "Are you coming?"

"No." She shook her head.

"Suit yourself. I'll be back."

The place looked decent with flowers out front and a freshly cut lawn. I knew it wasn't a trap but probably someone's mother's house. "Who dat?" One of the men tried to make me out in the darkness.

"It's Gucci." This might sound conceited as hell but everybody in Detroit either knew me or knew somebody who knew me.

"What are you doing 'round these parts?" Another one of the men stepped down onto the walkway. "You're from the H.O.F. organization, right?" He smiled like we were friends. His lame ass was pretending for his boys.

Wanting to get Mina's shit back, I played it cool. "Yeah, that's me. What's cracking, fam?" I went in for a dap. "My homegirl lost her purse. She says one of y'all found that shit along with her shoes and cell phone."

Instantly, the smile disappeared. It was replaced by nervousness. "Your girl said we found it?" He played dumb. "Fellas, y'all seen anybody purse 'round this bitch?"

Before they could confirm his lie, I lifted my shirt so that he knew I was packing. "Look, homie, I ain't come here for trouble. I just want my girl's shit, and I'm gone."

"Gucci, I don't want it with you." He exhaled noisily, obviously contemplating the consequence of lying to me or snitching on his boy.

"I don't want it with you either. Looks like I got no choice." I shrugged and reached for my cell phone. He thought I was going for the strap and flinched. I pretended to dial a few numbers while resisting the urge to laugh. "Ay, it's Gucci," I said into the phone. "I tried to be cordial and handle shit by my lonesome, but it looks like I'm going to need some reinforcement."

As I spoke his eyes widened. He didn't really want no drama. None of them did. If these were real niggas, they would've pulled the gun they used on Mina on me.

"Just give the bitch her shit," I could hear someone on the porch whisper.

"I would hate to shoot up your mama's house over a handbag. But I've done a lot worse for less."

I watched him process what I said. As if a light bulb came on, homeboy hustled over to the crew. He was back in seconds with a purse, a cell phone, and a pair of red bottoms. "My fault, Gucci. We didn't know she was your girl."

"No harm, no foul. You returned her shit. That's all that matters." I retrieved the items, headed to the car, then swiftly turned around. "One last thing before I leave, homie."

"What's that?" His guard was down.

"Run yo' pockets now, nigga!"

Chapter 26

Mina

It was well past eleven by the time Gucci dropped me off at home. Sam's car was in the driveway. I was seething. The moment I opened the door it was on.

"Hey, baby, I see you got a ride." He waltzed past me with a bowl of ice cream.

"I had to call Gucci after your ass didn't show up." I hung my purse on the coatrack, then bent to remove my shoes only to find they were still in my hand. I hadn't bothered to put them back on.

"My bad. The reception at the hospital is bad. When I called you back, you didn't answer."

"I didn't answer because I didn't have my fucking phone! I was robbed!"

"Robbed?" He looked as if I were making shit up.

"Yes, robbed! As in they took my shit at gunpoint!" Frustrated was beyond what I was feeling.

"Damn, baby, are you okay?" He placed the ice cream down, then grabbed me. The hug was just what I needed at the moment. It didn't exactly stop my anger, but it did feel good. We hadn't been intimate since Chloe died. A sister could use some attention. This wasn't really the attention I had in mind, but it was a good start.

"I'm fine. Gucci came to get me, and she got my shit back. That girl is a beast!"

"Oh." He stiffened up and backed away.

"What's wrong with you? Why are you acting strange?"

"I'm not acting strange." He picked up the bowl and continued eating.

"Anyway, what did the doctors say about Samantha?" I began to undress. It had been a long day. All I wanted was a bath and sleep.

"They said she's coming along just fine. We might get to bring her home in a month or so. They want her up to at least five pounds first."

"Great! I'll start working on the nursery sometime next week."

"Cool." He started to walk away.

"Hey, I wanted to talk to you about the wedding. Do you have time?" With his attitude lately, I'd been ruminating over postponing it.

"What's up?" Sam hesitantly asked.

"I was thinking we should call the wedding off or postpone it, at least until we bring Samantha home and get situated with raising her." After I said it, I wanted to take it back. It was really meant as an attention grabber, but it was too late.

"Actually, I was thinking the same thing." He kissed my cheek.

"So, you don't want to get married?"

"I do want to get married. I don't think right now is a good time." Sam headed up the stairs with me on his trail.

"So, when will you be ready?"

"Mina, chill out. Two seconds ago, you said you wanted to postpone the damn thing. Now you're mad because I agreed with you?"

"I only said it to get your attention. You didn't even protest."

"Are you on your period or something?" He frowned.

I didn't even respond. Storming into the bathroom, I slammed the door.

Chapter 27

Lovely

After being gone for an entire week, Maine seemingly had no intention of coming home. He'd given up on us, thrown in the towel. I didn't even blame him because I'd done the same. There was no use in trying to work shit out. Our relationship had run its course. I was okay with that, or so I told myself. Candidly, it was another letdown, a big disappointment, and a major waste of time. With him out of my life, the yearning to kill myself was overwhelming. There was nothing left to live for. My fight was over. I was ready to lay down my burdens and head into the afterlife.

"Lo, where are you going?" Do It was playing Go Fish with Shawnie at the kitchen table.

"I need some fresh air. I'm going out for a few." I walked over to the table, hugged my brother, and kissed my niece. They had no idea I was never coming back.

"Where are you going?" Do It laid his cards down, then stood. He knew better.

"I'm going to walk along the beach."

"Oooh, can I go?" Shawnie jumped up and down.

"Yeah, let's take a family walk. I could use some fresh air too." His eyes never left mine.

"Not this time, guys. I need to do this alone." I headed toward the door before he could stop me. By the time Do It and Shawnie could slip on shoes, I'd be gone.

I left a note lying on my pillow. It would explain everything. It was my hope they understood my rhyme and reason. Sometime tonight, either Do It or Nichols would find it. When they did, it would be too late. I'd already be well into the afterlife, be it heaven or hell.

I walked down the dirt road for a mile until I saw a sign that read *PLAYA PUBLICA*. It meant "public beach" in Spanish. From a distance, I could see the aqua blue water. Like bathwater, it looked calm and soothing. All I had to do was get in, close my eyes, and submerge myself. The water would fill my lungs and nostrils. In no time, my air supply would be depleted. Then I would drown and float away with the current.

As thoughts of death replayed in my mind, I was distracted by sounds coming from a bar farther down the street. I wasn't familiar with the up-tempo melodies but decided to grab a drink to

calm my nerves. Thankfully, the baggy sweatpants
I borrowed from Maine's side of the closet housed
a Ben Franklin.

Although no one was paying me any mind, I
felt uncomfortable upon crossing the threshold
of the small shack. The bartender was shooting the breeze with a customer. A few people were
in the middle of the floor dancing. Several others
were in booths to themselves.

"Hello, can I get a . . ." I paused. Nothing on the
shelf was familiar.

"*No hablo ingles.*" He shook his head.

"*Obtener la dama un trago de tequila.*" A gentleman approached the bar, then sat beside me. I had
no idea what he'd said, but the bartender smiled,
beginning to pour a drink.

"What did you say?" I asked the handsome
stranger. He was gorgeous with jet-black hair,
tanned skin, and a crooked smile. It was cute in
its own little way.

"I told him to get the lady a shot of tequila." He
winked. There was something about him that made
my heart flutter. Self-consciously, I smoothed
the hair on my head, silently cursing myself for
not looking more presentable. Even though I was
about to die, I didn't have to look busted.

The bartender set a shot glass before me and
one in front of my companion. I nodded my head
in appreciation before taking a sip of the gold
liquid.

"*Como te llamas?*" he asked. When I didn't respond, he translated the question into English. "What's your name?"

"I'm Lovely, and you are?"

"*Me llamo Mauricio.*" He smiled. "Are you from here?"

"No. I'm from the United States."

"Are you on a vacation or something?" He never took a drink. He stared at me. I could've looked into his eyes all night. However, I was on a mission.

"Yeah," I lied, then downed the remainder of my drink.

"Are you here with friends?" He searched the bar for possible acquaintances of mine.

"You sure do ask a lot of questions, Mauricio." I was beginning to feel paranoid. It was time to go. "Thanks for interpreting my order. Have a round on me." I slapped the hundred-dollar bill on the bar top, then stood abruptly.

The effect of the alcohol hit me unexpectedly. My legs felt like cement. I fell over onto Mauricio. Something wasn't right. I attempted to speak, but the only thing coming forth was gibberish. When I noticed the look exchanged between the bartender and Mauricio, I knew what the deal was. They had slipped me a roofie.

Chapter 28

Nikki

"It feels good to be back on the bricks!" Mario looked out the window as we drove down Livernois Avenue. "I never thought I would be so happy to see the streets of Detroit in my life!"

"God is good!" I was not an avid churchgoer, nor was I your average Christian, but I knew enough to give credit when it was due. Ms. Claudia and I had prayed for Mario's life, and He showed us favor. I'd heard once before that He moved mountains if you just trusted and believed. After witnessing what He brought me through, I was a firm believer.

"Amen! God is good." My ex-husband repeated the saying. The streets had damn near killed us both, but here we were alive and well.

"Amen, Daddy," Mario Junior repeated from the back seat. We cracked up laughing. It was good to be a family again. Sorrowfully, I was aware that the good times were nearing an end. It was time to face the reality that Mario was legally married to someone else as well as father to another child. Although Gucci had yet to make an appearance since the beauty shop brawl, she was unquestionably lurking around the corner.

"Where do you want me to take you?" I asked after pulling up to the light.

"Take me to your house."

"Do you think that's a good idea?" I released the brake, putting the SUV back into motion. "You need time to clear your head and decide where you wanna be."

"Nik, I already know where I wanna be, which is exactly where I'm at right now." He looked at me and winked.

"Well, you need to clear the air with Gucci first. I'm not trying to beef with that girl." I was done playing games with her. The next time she came for me would be the last time, and I meant that.

"Oh, please believe I'm going to clear the air," Mario huffed. He was pissed that Gucci hadn't brought Maria to visit him in the hospital. I understood his frustration. Conversely, as a woman, I identified with where she was coming from. She felt betrayed and rightfully so. Mario had played with her like a doll, then placed her back on the shelf. She was hurt and wanted to hurt him just as badly. They were playing the dangerous game of love and war. Consequently, Maria was caught in the crossfire.

"What about the marriage?" The words tasted venomous rolling off my tongue.

"What about it?" he replied indifferently.

"In order for us to move forward, you have to divorce her."

"Knowing her, she probably already filed the paperwork," he laughed. "That broad probably done tore up my shit, bleached my clothes, and burned the house down by now."

"What about the H.O.F. organization? You're done with that, right?" The question had been on my mind daily. I loved Rio but not enough to watch the streets slowly eat him alive, especially after we'd been given chance after chance to leave the street life behind.

"Nik, let's not revisit that shit right now." He brushed the issue under the rug, turning up the bass on the stereo. I decided to give him a break on the subject for a week or two.

Pulling up to the home I purchased after our divorce, I cut the engine off. "You know we need to upgrade, right?" He looked at me. "This place is small."

"Says the nigga who don't even have a house!" I countered while laughing.

"Oh, I have houses, believe that!" He chuckled. "But seriously, we need a bigger spot before the baby comes." He went to rub my stomach, and I swatted his hand. The mention of what was growing inside of me put a bitter taste in my mouth. I shuddered at the thought of having Maine's baby. I barely knew him and never planned on seeing him again. Having his child would only remind me of a poor choice I made in the heat of the moment. Therefore, abortion was the route I wanted to go, but Mario was dead set against the idea. He swore to love the child as his own. Unfortunately, I had my reservations. This was why I hadn't completely written the idea off yet.

"Rio, take it easy!" I changed the subject when he hopped down from my SUV like a man who hadn't just been released from the hospital.

"Girl, I got this!"

"Excuse me, Mario Wallace, may I have a word?" Some white man approached us with a recorder in his hand. Seemingly he had materialized from the thin air.

"Who are you?"

"My name is Michael Jenkins. I'm a reporter with *Detroit Dish* doing a story on crime and our community." He pressed the record button. "Is it true that you are the force behind the Hand Over Fist crime organization?"

"What?" Mario mugged him. "Dude, you got two seconds to get the fuck off my property!"

"Is it true that your organization has made millions of dollars in drug money?"

"One," Mario counted.

"I'm just—"

"Two." Mario reached under the gray Nike T-shirt for a gun that wasn't there. It was a ploy to get the man away from us, and it worked. Homeboy was in his car and speeding off before I knew it.

"I wonder what that was all about." I grabbed Junior from the back seat.

"I don't know, but he's the second dude to approach me about some damn newspaper story." He leaned up against the SUV to get his balance.

"Mario, let me help you." I put Junior down to walk, then went over to assist Mario. The doctor said his sense of balance might be off for a few days.

"Girl, there's nothing wrong with me." He refused my assistance.

"Yeah, Mommy, there's nothing wrong with Daddy." Junior concurred.

"That's right, son, you tell her I'm boss!" He popped the invisible collar on the T-shirt he was wearing with Junior doing the same.

"Whatever."

Just as I unlocked the front door, Mario's cell phone rang. My stomach did a backflip. His phone had been off almost the entire time he was in the hospital. In addition to that, no one was allowed to visit except family and close friends, which kept that street shit far away from us. I knew the minute word spread that he was back on the block the damn phone would be ringing off the hook like crazy.

"What up, fam?" He pressed the speaker button while taking a seat on the couch.

"What's crackin', my nigga! I heard you hit the bricks and shit. How are you feeling, son?"

"I'm one hundred." Mario bent down to untie Junior's shoes.

"That's good." There was a pause. "You up for talking business?"

"I'm listening." Mario looked at me, and I rolled my eyes. He knew I wasn't fond of that life anymore. For him, it was business as usual.

Chapter 29

Gucci

Since my first rendezvous with Sam, he'd been to my hotel several times to put in more work. I felt bad for sneaking behind Mina's back, but a bitch had needs. Sam had a real thick pipe. It was long, too. He knew what he was working with and used the curve well. I rationalized with myself that I wasn't doing my friend real dirty if I didn't fuck him raw or let him give me head. That shit right there just would've been disrespectful.

Buzz. The phone vibrated against the loose change at the bottom of my purse. It was a message from Sam that read: Hey, boss lady! I got some free time tonight. Would you like me to slide through and drop off that package?

I thought about what plans I might have tonight before responding: Yeah, I need that ASAP. See you at eight. We spoke in code to throw Mina for a loop if she ever came across the messages. When she read the word "package," she would relate it to dope.

I dropped the phone back into my purse. It vibrated again. This time it was a call from Mario. "What?"

"For real, G, it's like that?" he asked.

I was holding the cell phone to my ear barely listening. I didn't have time for this nigga and his mood swings today. "Like what, nigga?" I snapped, causing the white salesclerk behind the jewelry counter to stare. "Let me see that right there."

I pointed to a pair of chocolate diamond studs. The money I collected on the second of the month still had a bitch sitting pretty. I had been out splurging on myself and Maria every day. There was something about hitting a nigga in his pockets that did my heart some good. In fact, I thought that was why he was calling, but I was wrong.

"Are you bringing my daughter over here or what?"

"Over where?" He had to be mistaken if he thought I would step within fifty feet of Nikki. "You got me fucked up!"

"Look, you ain't gotta bring her to me. Let me come and get her."

"No."

"What the fuck you mean no? That's my fucking daughter too!"

"I said no. What part didn't you understand, the n or the o?" I placed the earrings up to my ear, admiring them in the oval mirror.

"You been acting really reckless lately, Gucci! Don't let me see you in the streets, 'cause when I do, it won't be pretty."

"I guess I'll have to worry about that when you find me then, huh?" I ended the call. Truthfully, I knew I was on borrowed time, which was why I moved out of the house and into a hotel days ago. When Mario found out I took all the money we made on the second and spent it, he was going to have a fit. But he owed me. We hadn't been married long enough for me to take him to court. Because of that, I collected my shit in the streets.

"I'll take these and the matching necklace, too." I handed the earrings back to the clerk and waited for her to ring me up.

"That'll be $14,247.16." She smiled, pleased with her commission. Reaching into my purse, I was prepared to hand the lady my money when someone handed her a credit card.

I turned to see Cartier standing there. "Where did you come from?" I thought this fool was gone with the wind.

"I didn't follow you I swear." His hand rose toward heaven. "I happened to be shopping over there when I saw you."

"Mm-hmm." I eyed him cautiously. "Where have you been?"

"I had to handle some business in California. Did you miss me?" He retrieved my bag from the sales rep, then handed it to me.

"No, I didn't, but thank you for the gift."

"It's the least I could do for splitting on you like that. My people called and I had to move fast. You could've at least called me though."

"I could've, but I was busy. Besides, the phone works both ways." I dropped the small shopping bag into my purse, then pushed Maria's stroller out of the store.

"I wanted to give you and your man time to work things out." He followed me.

"I told you before, there's nothing to work out." I strolled through Somerset Mall with no destination in mind. Maria and I had just about cleaned the place out already.

"Good." He bent down to retrieve Maria.

"You say that like you got plans for me or something." I smiled.

"I do, Gucci." He eyed me seductively. "I got plans to make you mine again."

"I ain't trying to be tied down anymore." I was only half joking. As fine as Cartier was and as good as his dick was, I wasn't feeling another relationship so soon. I needed some time to do me.

"I know your last nigga hurt you, but he ain't me and I ain't him." He pleaded his case. "Me and you make magic in the streets and in the bedroom. It's only fitting that we team up and take this shit to the next level." The way he cradled my daughter to his chest caused me to wish for a quick second that she was his.

"So, what exactly are you talking about?"

"Gucci, I'm about to take over the world, and I want you riding shotgun." The tone of his voice was serious. "I'm talking about Detroit, Miami, New York, Atlanta, St. Louis, and Las Vegas." He continued to plead his case. "I'm a movement by myself. Together, we're a force to be reckoned with. This thing will bring in more money than you knew existed."

"You know I'm all about the Benjamins." Hearing "more money" was music to my ears.

"Your mouth is saying one thing, but your eyes tell a different story." He was so intuitive. I loved that about him. How many thugs do you know who actually give a damn about a woman's feelings?

"You're right," I affirmed. "Building an organization with you destroys the one I constructed with Mario."

"Let me get this straight. You're sad about putting your baby's daddy out of business?" He laughed hysterically.

"It's not about Mario. It's about the crew I hand-picked and taught the game to. It's about the homies I call my brothers." Regardless of what it looked like on the surface, at the core the H.O.F. organization was a family. "I couldn't care less about shutting Mario down." I smacked my lips.

"Gucci, this game is treacherous. You can't wear your emotions on your sleeve. That shit will get you murked!" Cartier reprimanded. "In this day and age, loyalty ain't shit but a seven-letter word," he scoffed. "I bet you that, for the right price, any one of them niggas you call your family would put your ass in a body bag, real talk."

His words hit me in the pit of my stomach. They were true. I was attached to the organization and every individual associated with it. Sadly, things had changed. Maybe it was time to move on.

"Look, if it makes you feel better, you can bring some of your crew over to our side."

"What would we name the organization?"

"I don't see why it can't still be known as the H.O.F. organization. I mean, you do own half the name," he recommended.

"I guess that's true." In my head, the wheels were turning. I was on a mission to piss Mario off. This would definitely do the trick.

Chapter 30

Mina

As I stepped into the neonatal ward at Children's Hospital, I was greeted by one of Samantha's nurses. "She's doing so well, Mom."

"How much does she weigh now?" I set my purse down, then went over to the sink to scrub my hands. When dealing with sick babies with weakened immune systems, being sterile was the rule.

"She's up to three pounds, eight ounces." She smiled. "I told your husband she should be coming home really soon."

The word "husband" felt like a dagger to my heart. It was a reminder that Sam didn't want to marry me. The fairy tale I thought I was going to have was slowly becoming a nightmare.

"Yeah, we can't wait to bring her home." I smiled, walking over to the incubator.

Baby Samantha was sleeping as usual. She was so medicated, with steroids for her lungs as well as

other medications, that she was rarely ever awake.
I had yet to see her eyes for longer than a minute. I
knew they were pretty though.

"Hey, mama." I slid my finger into one of the
holes to caress her tiny thigh. She was lying there
in a pink cap and diaper. Her face was covered in
tubes. At times it was hard to stomach. "Samantha,
I can't wait for you to come home. I'm gonna paint
your room this weekend. Are you a pink or pur-
ple kind of girl?" I had already decided to use both
colors. Talking to her was soothing to me. It reminded me of when I would talk to my own son.
Sadly, he didn't make it past a year. I felt God had
given me Samantha as a replacement. The funny
thing was that Samantha looked just like Chloe.
That didn't matter. I loved her like she was mine.

"Would you like to hold her?"

I'd forgotten the nurse was still standing there.
"Oh, yes! Please!"

"Of course! Just slip this on over your clothes."
She handed me something similar to a paper surgical outfit. "Okay, now have a seat, and I'll hand
her to you."

I did as instructed, watching her open the incubator like a wrapped present then hand me the gift
inside.

"Here's your mommy."

"Oh, my God, she's so tiny." I blinked back a
few tears. My hands were shaky because I feared I
would drop her. "Will I hurt her?"

"She's strong. You won't hurt her." She stood nearby until I got comfortable enough to sit back.

For over an hour, I held on to baby Samantha for dear life. I talked to her and even hummed a few songs. It felt good to have a child in my arms again. In that moment, I vowed to love her and protect her as if she were my own.

"Ma'am, I hate to disturb you, but when your husband was here earlier, he left his phone." The nurse handed me Sam's phone.

"Thank you! He's always so careless with things like this."

Chapter 31

Lovely

"Where am I?" I blinked rapidly. My vision was cloudy, and I felt disoriented. We were in a car riding down a dirt road. Mauricio was behind the wheel. I was in the passenger seat with both my hands and legs tied.

"I'm taking you to your new home."

His crooked smile no longer appealed to me. Moreover, he looked nothing like the handsome stranger I met in the bar. His brows were now furrowed, and his demeanor was peculiar.

"Why are you doing this?" I tried to break free of the rope around my wrists. It was useless.

"You're just what I needed, Lovely." He spoke without removing his eyes from the road. "My clients are gonna love you."

"What the fuck are you talking about?" At this point, I was more afraid than ever. What in the world had I gotten myself into? A few hours ago, I had plans to kill myself, and now I was being kidnapped in a foreign country by a total stranger. "Answer me dammit!" Most likely, I shouldn't have taken such a tone. I didn't know what this man was capable of, but I wasn't no punk either.

"No questions!" He veered off the road into a private driveway.

The driveway led to a house just beyond a few cornstalks. It sat behind a steel gate ten feet high with the initials S and M on it. The white stucco home was huge. It reminded me of a mansion you might see in a gangster movie. Guards surrounded the property, wearing black suits and dark shades.

"*Bienvenido de nuveo.*" One of the guards opened up Mauricio's car door.

"Take her to the east wing with the others!" Mauricio instructed before walking away.

"What's happening to me? Please help!" I pleaded with the guard, but he said nothing. Lifting me out of my seat, he carried me kicking and screaming inside of the mansion.

"Stop it!" he whispered. His voice wasn't as cold as I guessed it would be. He was a very big guy with a grim expression. I expected his tone to match his appearance. However, there was quite a contrast.

"Please tell me where I am." My whisper matched his. We were alone in the entryway of the well-decorated home. Cameras were pointed at us.

"You are now property of the Mendez brothers: Santiago and Mauricio." He kneeled down to untie my restraints.

"What do you mean property?"

"It means you will remain here until they no longer have use for you." He stood.

"What kind of place is this?"

"This is a whorehouse that caters to the Mexican Cartel. The only way you will ever leave here is in a body bag." He never even blinked while breaking the disheartening news to me.

Chapter 32

Nikki

While Mario and Junior were over at Ms. Claudia's for a visit, I was home catching up on cleaning and writing. The music on my iPod was bumping full blast, and a glass of chardonnay rested next to my laptop. I rationalized that it was okay to have the wine because I was going to get an abortion anyway. I hadn't informed Mario yet. My plan was to get the abortion then tell him I had a miscarriage.

As K. Michelle blared through the sound system, I stroked the keypad with a vengeance. I was in the zone. My novel was only a few chapters short of being complete. Although Mario didn't fully agree with my decision to write an autobiography, he did understand it was my story, and I had every right to tell it. Anjela also thought I was wasting time. Still, she agreed to help me shop the manuscript to various publishing houses. I was determined to not permit their doubts to deter me from my objective nor take up space in my mind. The closer I got to completion, the more excited I became to get it published and into the hands of readers. The content was real and raw! I was convinced it would be well received by the urban community.

After three hours of writing, I needed a break. I grabbed the wine bottle and slid it back into its hiding spot at the bottom of my closet. Next, I picked up my glass, taking it downstairs to wash it out. I couldn't run the risk of being found out by Mario.

Ding-dong.

The doorbell scared me, so I jumped slightly. "Who is it?" I called out on my way to the door.

"It's Maine."

I shook my head as if I'd heard him wrong. What was this fool doing at my house, on my doorstep, like he belonged here?

"I think you should leave." I looked through the peephole. Sure as shit, he was standing there dressed in an all-black ensemble. His haircut was fresh, the gear was fresh, and he looked good. My heart fluttered, and my palms were sweating. Not only hadn't I expected to see him again, but I didn't anticipate having this type of reaction.

"We need to talk." He folded his arms as if he wasn't leaving until we talked.

I sighed, opened the door, then stepped onto the porch. There was no way in hell I could allow

him up in here and have Mario catch us. It was
bad enough I was even entertaining this fool on
the porch. "What do you want?" I stood in front
of the door, watching up and down the street for
Mario.

"I came to see you." He stepped closer to me. "I
missed you."

"Maine, you ain't nothing but a liar. You used
me to get your girl free. Now you have the audacity
to stand here talking about you missed me. Nigga,
please!"

"I know what I did was fucked up, and I apologize. I loved my girl and thought we could work,
but I realize we've grown apart."

"Isn't she pregnant?" I looked at him skeptically.

"We lost our son." He looked away briefly. "He
was stillborn."

"Oh, I'm sorry to hear to that." Instinctively, I
placed a hand on my stomach.

"It's okay. Everything happens for a reason you
know," he responded, somewhat sad. "Me and my
girl have been through a lot. This was the straw
that finally broke the camel's back."

"It's not too late! You can still fix things." I felt
bad for him.

"Our relationship is over. She's given up and I
have too. Sometimes you have to recognize that
when it's over, it's really over." The pain in his eyes
was hard to ignore. He looked as if he needed a

hug. I resisted the urge to do so. "Anyway, I came back here to see if you and I could start fresh."

"So, you're jumping from one relationship into the next?"

"No. I'm not looking for a relationship. I just need a friend." His smile melted my heart like a bag of chocolate candy left out in the sun.

"Maine, how can we be friends? You lied to me and tried to kill my ex-husband." It sounded silly to even be listening to this fool. However, I would be a liar if I didn't acknowledge I still felt something for him. Though it wasn't love, my attraction to him was undeniable.

"I can show you better than I can tell you. Let's start over and let nature take its course." He held out his hand for a truce.

"I'd like that." I placed my hand into his.

"Are you still writing that book of yours?" He leaned up against the banister.

"Actually, I'm almost done." It was refreshing to have someone genuinely take an interest in my book.

"That's good, Nikki. Hopefully, I can get an advance copy."

"Yeah, right! You're not that interested in my life." I smiled coyly.

"You'd be surprised how interested I am in you." The tone of his voice put goose bumps on my neck.

"Maine, it was really nice seeing you, but it's time for you to leave."

Confused, he said, "I thought we just made a truce."

"We did, but Mario is staying with me for a while. He'll be back here any minute."

"Can I at least call you sometimes?"

"Sure. I still have the same number." I was damn near pushing him off the porch.

"What about dinner?" He spoke on his way to the Aston Martin parked in my driveway. It was the very same Aston Martin we'd made love on when I got pregnant.

"Call me." My knees buckled as memories of that night invaded my mental space. Maine was a cold piece of work! Mario had better watch out.

Chapter 33

Gucci

I'd just pulled back up to the hotel and was retrieving bags from the trunk when my cell phone vibrated. "Shit!" I maneuvered a few bags in order to catch the call. "Hello."

"Hey, baby, I'll be there in about an hour." Cartier and I had parted ways at the mall earlier. He had some business to handle. In view of that, we made a date to link up later for drinks and a movie. I was really excited to see him again and explore the new business venture.

"Okay, I'll be ready." I had already dropped Maria off on my way back to the hotel.

"All right, I'll see you in a bit." He ended the call.

I slid the phone into my bra, closed the trunk, and headed inside. The doorman held the door open. I nodded my appreciation. As I passed the receptionist, she flagged me down.

"Miss, you have a visitor waiting over there for you." She pointed toward Mario, and I almost wet my pants. He was pacing the floor with a menacing scowl. I wanted to tell homegirl to call security but played it cool.

Waltzing over to him with a frown of my own, I stopped directly in front of him. "What the fuck are you doing here?"

"Where the fuck is my fucking daughter?"

"She's spending the night out." There was no need to drop Satin's name. Mario would've surely gone over there and banged her door down.

"Bitch, you better quit playing!" He stood, grabbing my face with such force he could've broken something.

"Let me go." I spoke as best I could through clenched teeth.

"Tell me where the fuck my daughter is!" His breathing was heavy.

"You will never see her again if you don't get your filthy paws off me."

"Sir, if you don't remove your hands from this lady, we will be forced to call the police," a security guard informed him as he approached us.

Reluctantly, Mario released me, but not without a mush to the head first.

"Fuck you!" I hawked up a wad of spit and hurled it right into his face. If I had a strap on me, I would've put two bullets right between his eyes.

"Bitch!" He raised his hand to strike me but stopped. "This ain't over! You got until the end of the week to present my daughter," he warned on his way out of the building.

"Are you okay?" the security guard inquired.

"I'm fine."

Retreating upstairs to my hotel suite, a bitch was steaming mad! It took a shot of vodka and two blunts to calm my nerves. *How dare this nigga put his hands on me like some bitch in the streets?* I stepped from the shower and contemplated canceling my date with Cartier. I was in a funky mood, and it wouldn't have been fair to him.

Just as I picked up the phone, there was a knock on the door. My heart skipped three beats. I was fearful it was Mario back for more. Lightly, I crept to the door to see that it was Sam. "Damn!" I had forgotten to cancel our booty call. "Come on in." I opened the door.

"That's what the fuck I'm talking about right there." He looked my naked body over like it was a masterpiece.

"Whoa, killa." I put my hand on his chest. "We can't do this today. I'm sorry."

"What?"

"I had a bad day, and I ain't in the mood." That was the partial truth.

"Believe me, I can make your day much better." He whipped his penis out in one rapid motion.

"You know what, Sam? I was thinking we shouldn't even be doing this. Mina is my girl, and

she's your fiancée. It's wrong." I retrieved a blue
Michael Kors dress and slipped it over my naked-
ness.

"You knew all that shit last week when you kept
calling a nigga over here." He had an attitude.
"Now you wanna have a heart? All of a sudden
develop a conscience?"

"Look, nigga, don't get beside yourself. You need
to be grateful I even let you play in the pussy in the
first place." I grabbed the freshly rolled blunt from
my coffee table, then lit it. Sam had my nerves on
edge again. After lighting the medicinal cigarette, I
tossed a hotel bath towel into the sink, wet it, and
placed it under the door to prevent the smell from
escaping the room.

"Can I get some head then? It's the least you
could do since I drove all the way over here."

"Bye, Sam." I pointed toward the door. He got
the hint. On the way out, he tossed a few obsceni-
ties my way, but fuck him.

Chapter 34

Lovely

"Please help me!" I tried to head for the front door, but the guard swooped me up in one motion.

"What's all the racket for?" A Caucasian woman approached the foyer, wearing a sheer baby-doll gown and four-inch heels.

"Mauricio bagged another one. I was just about to bring her to you." The guard sat me back on the floor. "She's a feisty one."

"Let me go, you clown." I tried shaking free. It was useless because his grip was too tight.

"We haven't had any black pussy since Carmen." The madam strutted down the marble stairs like on *America's Next Top Model*. "What's your name, girl?"

"Why?" I had no intention of becoming chummy with her.

"Listen, little wench!" She grabbed my face with a handful of red nails. "You better learn some manners if you want to live to see tomorrow." She mushed my face away. I would've slugged this broad. Somehow, I knew her threats weren't idle.

"Now I'm going to ask you one more time. What's your name, girl?"

"Lovely."

"Well, isn't that precious?" She smirked. "From now on, you'll be addressed as number forty-two."

"Forty-two?" I repeated.

"Did I stutter?" She looked as if she wanted to hit me. "Phillip, take forty-two around back for branding."

"Branding?" I barely had time to speak the entire word before Phillip tossed me over his shoulder. He carried me through the lavish home and out back.

Once we were outside, he demanded that I remove my clothing and toss everything into a garbage bag. While he plugged in an electric branding iron, I scoped the yard to see if I could break free. Not surprisingly, the place was swarming with security guards and secured by a barbed-wire fence.

"Lie down on your stomach!" He turned on the water hose.

"What?"

"Lie down now!" He hit me with the cold water. It stung so bad my skin felt as though I were being injected with several little needles. It didn't take long for me to get the hint. I had no idea what was about to happen next. Promptly, I dropped to the ground in order to stop the cold-water assault.

"Be still." He pulled out the electric branding iron, then slapped it directly onto my right ass cheek.

"Ahhh!" I screamed out in agony. The pain of being burned with a blazing hot piece of iron was indescribable. The smell of blistering flesh, my flesh, was even worse.

After being branded with the number forty-two on my butt, I was taken back inside the house where the lingerie-wearing white lady waited for me. My body rocked with pain, and my skin was still burning.

"Follow me." She headed up the back entrance of the home until we arrived on the second floor. "This is where you'll sleep until I make room for you with the other whores." She pointed toward a door and waited for me to open it. I was reluctant at first but knew that I had no choice, because she might've turned her goons on me. When I did open the door, I saw that the room was the size of a coat closet.

I turned to look at her. "I can barely fit in there. How am I supposed to sleep in there?"

"Forty-two, please do as I instructed or face the consequences." Her expression was stone cold.

"Lady, I'm not sleeping in no fucking closet." Just as the last word left my tongue, I was hit with a volt of electricity from the pink Taser gun in her hand. The voltage sent me flying into the small closet. I was unable to move and had peed on myself.

The madam couldn't have given two shits about what she'd done. Furthermore, she calmly stepped back, closed the door, and locked it from the outside.

Chapter 35

Mina

I lay in bed just after midnight reading my favorite author's newest novel, titled *Gangstress*, when I heard Sam open the front door. I was about to pretend to be asleep, but he was upstairs before I could even turn the lights off. "Hey." I nodded, then placed the book on the nightstand.

"What's up?" He removed his clothing.

"You left your phone at the hospital. I noticed you had a few missed calls and messages."

"Why are you going through my phone?" He glared at me.

"I didn't go through your phone. I was just making you aware." I was annoyed. If he was that concerned about the phone, then he probably had something to hide. "You think you'd be grateful that you didn't lose the damn thing."

"Thank you for bringing the phone home, baby."

I thought he was about to take a shower, but to my surprise he jumped in bed with me. "What are you doing?"

"Let's make love." He bit on my nipples, then planted slow kisses from my navel down to my sweet spot. The shit was feeling too good. Therefore, I basked in the moment. We hadn't been sexual in a while. In fact, when time permitted, I planned to hold a conversation about where our relationship was headed. For now, I just lay back and watched him work.

We made love for over an hour. I was impressed. He had skills originally, but the passion he brought tonight had not been present in any of our previous sexual encounters. As we lay in the bed side by side trying to catch our breath, I looked into his eyes. Though he was with me physically, he wasn't present mentally. Something had been weighing heavily on his mind, and I was tired of guessing. It was time to ask what was going on. "Sam, do you love me the way you did when you first came back?"

"Why do you ask that?" He looked at me. I didn't miss the fact that he answered my question with a question.

"As of late, your attitude has been shitty. You're rarely home. You haven't mentioned the wedding. And until tonight, we haven't made love in over a month." It felt good to get things off my chest.

"There are some things on my mind, but they have nothing to do with you, so don't worry about it." He kissed my head.

"If something is bothering you, we should talk about it. Maybe I can help."

"Mina, I said it has nothing to do with you, so let's drop it." He got up from the bed and headed for the shower.

The next day, he was gone before seven in the morning. Our conversation, or lack thereof, left me confused. I needed to confide in a friend, so I met Gucci for lunch.

"Hey, girl, what's up?" Gucci sashayed into the Bread Basket Deli on Greenfield, north of Ten Mile Road. It had been a while since we saw one another. I was so busy nursing baby Samantha back to health that my time was null and void. I missed her crazy self though.

"Hey, mama!" I sprung up from the pleather seat with a smile. "Where is Maria?"

"She and Cartier are next door getting ice cream from Baskin-Robbins."

"He's back?"

"Yup!" She smiled.

"You know you're my girl, but you're wrong for keeping Mario from his daughter. Yet you're letting Cartier play Daddy." I shook my head with a giggle.

"Mario can suck a fat one for all I care! In case you need to be reminded too, I run this shit! He'll see her on my terms!" She grabbed half of my corned beef sandwich and ate that shit like it was hers.

"You're cold, girl," I laughed.

"That's my middle name," she laughed. "Enough about me. What's up with you?"

"I'm good, I guess." I shrugged. "I'm thinking about breaking up with Sam."

"What? Why?" She continued to eat my food.

"Ever since Chloe died, he's been acting all strange. We don't spend any time together, and we barely talk anymore. If we do, he always finds a reason to get mad and leave. I was in a bad marriage for too long to deal with Sam and his bullshit. I can do bad all by myself."

"I feel that, girl." She slapped me a high five. "But on a serious note, you and Sam are cute together. He's dealing with a lot becoming a new father and all. Just give him time."

"How much time? That's the question. I feel like I've been patient long enough."

"I can't answer that for you, Mina. Your heart will let you know." She winked.

"So, are you and Cartier serious?" I reversed the attention to her.

"I'm just taking it one day at a time with him."

"What are you gonna do about the marriage to Mario?"

"I'm going to get that shit annulled as soon as I get time. Right now, I'm focused on building a new empire with Cartier."

"So, you're leaving the H.O.F. organization?" The acronym was tatted on her neck. I couldn't believe she was done with it so suddenly.

"Yeah." She looked sad. "Me and Mario will never be what we used to be. And that's not good for business. It's time to move on, ya know?"

"Damn!" I was sad. Although the organization meant nothing to me, I knew what it meant to her. It was her baby, and she was letting it go.

"It's okay. Please believe I will definitely land on top."

"I know you will. You always do."

"The thought of starting over is scary, but I plan to take a few of my workers with me." She finished up the last of my sandwich.

"This will probably initiate a war between you and Mario. You know that, right?"

"I ain't got nothing left for him, Mina. Right now, he's public enemy number one!" She was dead serious.

"You don't think your friendship will ever be salvageable?" The two of them had been best friends since they were 16.

"I don't need no backstabbing friends," she declared.

"He's having a party on Saturday. You should come and bring the baby." I tried to lighten the mood.

"Bitch, please!" She laughed. "If I come through there, it'll be to blow his head off."

"I could take Maria if you want." I glanced past Gucci to see Cartier, who had just walked in.

"Girl, haven't you been listening? He will see her on my time."

"Hey, baby." Cartier handed Maria to her mom, then took a seat.

"You remember my friend Mina, don't you?" Gucci reintroduced us.

"What's good, ma?" He nodded at me, then looked back at Gucci. "You ready?"

"It's time to go already?" Gucci glanced down at her watch. "Mina, we have a meeting to attend. It was good to catch up though. Call me later, and we'll set another date."

"Put this on the bill." Cartier slapped a $50 bill on the table.

"See you later." I watched the couple leave the restaurant and couldn't help but wonder why I felt uneasy about the new man in her life.

Chapter 36

Lovely

Sometime the next day I was released from the closet by the madam, who made no apologies for what she had done. I could tell she was a smug bitch, and I couldn't wait to get in that ass.

"Follow me!" She walked with her nose in the air up the grand staircase. I followed her down the long hallway to the last door on the left. The room filled with women became silent once I arrived. Because she was the head bitch in charge around here, everyone appeared to be frightened of the white woman.

"This is your bunk." She gestured toward the bottom bunk near the door. It was already made up with white sheets and a tan blanket. The room was large and resembled a boot camp facility with several bunk beds strategically placed throughout.

"Do I get my clothes back?" It was a dumb question. Like me, all the other girls were buck-naked.

"Dinner is in an hour." She snobbishly turned around, then headed out the door.

Once she was out of earshot, the chatter among the other women resumed. It wasn't long before one of them introduced herself to me. "Hi, I'm Daphnie." The young white girl smiled.

"What's up?" I nodded.

"Aren't you going to tell me your name?" She made herself comfortable on my bed. I didn't like the fact that her bare coochie was on my bed, but I didn't make any beef about it.

"No offense, Daphnie, but I'm not in the mood to be social."

"I didn't mean anything by it. It just helps to pass the time away," she confessed.

"How did you end up here?" I looked her over from head to toe. Her face was youthful, but her body looked worn out. Her breasts looked as if they had been sucked on one too many times, and her vagina needed a face-lift. I'd never seen someone's clitoris hanging beyond their vaginal lips.

"I was a working girl looking for some quick cash. Mauricio pulled up in an expensive car and offered top dollar for my services. Of course, I jumped into his ride with no hesitation." She looked down at the floor. "He said he was taking me back to his house. Instead, he brought me here."

"How long have you been here?"

"I don't know exactly. I ain't seen a calendar in forever." She smiled with buck teeth. "However, the day I came here was October tenth, the day before my son's birthday."

"That was almost ten months ago." I shook my head in disbelief.

"I think about that day every time I close my eyes." She chewed on her bottom lip. "I wasn't even supposed to be working that day. However, I wanted to buy something special for my boy and needed a little more money."

"That shit is deep."

"So, what's your story?" She lay back and made herself comfortable. Because she had just spilled her guts to me, I decided to spill mine to her.

"I left the house yesterday evening with plans to commit suicide." The expression on her face was one of disbelief. "I headed to the bar for a drink to calm my nerves. Mauricio had the bartender spike it."

"Maybe it's a blessing you ended up here." Her green eyes peered into mine.

"I don't see how being kidnapped is a blessing." This girl was delusional.

"Well, had you not ended up here, you would've been dead by now."

"This shit ain't no better than death!" I replied angrily.

"It's not that bad. They feed us, they put a roof over our heads, and they let us live as long as we obey the rules." She was about as dumb as a box of rocks.

"Girl, this ain't no way to treat people. Are you crazy?"

"Where I came from, I was barely making ends meet. I was on drugs, and my son suffered because of it. This may sound ridiculous, but in a way, they saved my life."

"That does sound ridiculous, especially because you're never gonna get outta here." I rolled my eyes. "Anyway, what actually happens around here?"

"It's basically a high-end brothel. The brothers exclusively cater to the mob. They host parties every other night. We walk the room and mingle. Eventually, someone will pay for sex with you. If you're lucky, one of them will buy you indefinitely." She stood from the bed.

"What does that mean?" I didn't like the sound of that.

"It means they purchase you and take you with them."

"Like slavery?" I frowned.

"Yup. You become the property of whoever purchases you."

Chapter 37

Gucci

After dropping Maria off to Satin, Cartier and I headed to see our potential connect. His name was Bayani. He was straight from the Philippines. Up until recently, I had no idea there was even a drug cartel in their country. Initially, Mario was the one who put me on game. He claimed Bayani was looking to expand his family business to the United States. He wanted to flood the black market with 100 percent, authentic raw white powder and put Colombia and Mexico out of business. In order to do so, he decided to solicit the assistance of Detroit, Miami, and New York. Flying state to state, he met with the highest-selling organizations in each city to determine who he wanted to do business with. Luckily, we had no competition in Detroit during that time. I hoped he wouldn't be upset when he noticed that Mario was not in attendance.

"Is this the place?" Cartier looked at me while I looked at the GPS. We were given an address and a time to be there. It was way out in the boondocks at a warehouse.

"Let's get out and see." I left my purse in the car because my gun was inside of it. I figured Bayani more than likely had a ton of security just waiting for a reason to pop a cap in my ass. I didn't want to alarm them with my piece.

"Right this way." A man in a black suit escorted us toward the door.

Once inside, we had to go through a metal detector and be frisked before meeting with Bayani.

"This is not Mario Wallace!" His voiced elevated two levels, which caused our security escort to draw his weapon.

"I can explain!" I raised my hands. "This is Cartier Jones, and he's with me."

"Where is Mario Wallace?" Bayani frowned.

"He had an accident." Thinking fast, I used Mario's gunshot wound as a quick cover. "He was shot in the head a few weeks ago and is recovering."

"I don't like surprises. You should've come alone." Bayani's tone was now calm. He told the guard to leave, then showed us to the boardroom table in the middle of the wide-open space.

"My apologies, Bayani. It won't happen again."

"It better not," he threatened before getting down to business.

The entire meeting lasted only forty minutes, but we covered a lot during that time. He was very thorough and meticulous, not leaving out one single detail. His family owned a casket business, which they used as a front to smuggle dope into the Unites States. "Everything will ship on the first of every month. The product will be in the lining of caskets."

"I can't wait to get started." I stood from the table.

"One last thing, Gucci." He smiled. "May I have a word in private?"

"Okay." I looked back at Cartier, who nodded.

"My organization is tight-knit. It has never been infiltrated because we've stuck to our own kind. My family was hesitant about this business enterprise. However, I assured them they had nothing to fear. I promised I would handpick each individual, and I have, except for your friend here." He stared at Cartier. "Since you brought him into my circle, you're responsible for his actions."

"I give you my word that Cartier is a stand-up guy."

"Where I come from, your word is all you have, and your life depends on it." The subtle message was not lost on me as I read between the lines. Basically, I was being warned. If Cartier didn't prove to be who I said he was, then it would be the death of me.

Chapter 38

Nikki

All week I had been on pins and needles thinking Maine would call or show up again when Mario was around. Thank goodness he hadn't. Mario had been in a sour mood ever since his run-in with Gucci. He told me he almost laid fists on her but had to catch himself. She was the mother of his child. For that reason, he still had to respect her. I was proud he hadn't let his anger get the best of him. Nevertheless, she was playing with fire. One of these days, he would leave home without any manners and it would be lights out for her.

On the way to Mario's birthday party at the Moët Lounge on Woodward, I noticed he was eerily silent. "What's wrong with you?"

"Something ain't right. I feel it." His leg bounced up and down uncontrollably.

"What do you mean something ain't right?" Subconsciously, I peeped the scene to spot any potential dangers lurking.

"I can't explain it. I haven't been able to hold a civil conversation with Gucci. I haven't been out on the streets like I need to. I feel like I'm losing touch with what's going on around me."

"Rio, you need to let them streets go anyway." Hitting the blinker, I switched to the right lane.

"I am, Nikki, but first I gotta tie up a few loose ends."

"You keep on saying that. Fuck those loose ends!" It was frustrating that he couldn't leave the streets alone. How many more bad things had to happen to us before he would wise up?

The sound of his phone interrupted us. "Speak on it." The call sounded over the car's speakers. Mario's phone was connected to the Bluetooth system.

"Yo, boss, it's dry out here," someone said.

"What you fucking mean it's dry?" Mario sat up in his seat.

"We ain't got no product. I spoke with O, and he said he been blowing up Gucci for the re-up, but she ain't answering."

"So y'all been without work all this time?" Mario was fuming.

"Yup!"

"Let me make some calls. I'll hit you back." He ended the call, then proceeded to make a new one.

"What up, boss?" Omar answered in his usual slow, Southern drawl. He was from Georgia.

"O, what the fuck is going on, bruh?"

"Man, your guh done played us." His pronunciation of the word "girl" always made me laugh. "She took the money on the second and got ghost. I been calling her about the re-up, but she ain't answering. I would've been called you, but I thought she was gon' come through. Then I heard we are being phased out. Niggas on the block getting antsy and shit."

"Fuck you mean, we are being phased out?"

"Word on the streets is a few days ago there was some new nigga on the scene with that killa for the low low."

"How low?" Mario frowned.

I wasn't really into his street dealings, but I knew enough about the H.O.F. organization to know that for years Mario had the lowest prices.

"This new nigga is runnin' BOGO sales, my dog." The caller spoke louder.

"What the fuck is BOGO?" Mario rested his back up against the seat.

"Buy one get one free," Omar replied.

"Are you serious right now?"

"Blood, I'm serious as a heart attack. I didn't wanna tell you this, but these new niggas done already shut down the spots on Piedmont, East Outer Drive, and Flanders."

"Who are these niggas?" Mario sat up in the seat.

"Word roun' the way is it's Gucci and her new ol' man." Omar sounded like he regretted being the bearer of bad news. "They done recruited half of the squad already. When niggas found out they was getting money, they jumped ship."

"That bitch!" he barked. "O, let me hit you back."

"Fa sho."

"She did this," Mario bellowed.

"Did what?" I questioned.

"Before I got shot, there was a deal on the table with my Filipino connect. Gucci knew about it, and the bitch did the deal for that nigga she fuckin'!"

"Baby, calm down." I didn't want his blood pressure to shoot up.

"Do you know how much money I just lost? And now this bitch is puttin' my crew out of business." He hit the dashboard.

"Maybe it's a good thing," I whispered.

Mario looked at me sideways.

"All I'm saying, Mario, is this is your opportunity to leave the game. Wash your hands of that life and start over. It's not like you're broke."

"Fuck that! She crossed the line!" he spat. "I should kill that bitch!"

Chapter 39

Gucci

"'I'ma be fresh as hell if the Feds watching. I'ma be fresh as hell if the Feds watching.'"

The sound of my cell phone startled me awake. "Hello!" I answered with an attitude. First, I wasn't ready to wake up. Secondly, I didn't recognize the phone number.

"It's almost eleven o'clock! What you still doing asleep?" Cartier sounded like he'd been up for hours.

"What the fuck are you doing up?" I rolled my eyes.

"Money never sleeps, baby girl." I heard him flick a lighter in the background. He was probably lighting a blunt. Cartier loved to wake and bake. "Get dressed and meet me down in the lobby in twenty minutes."

"Boy, the only thing I'll be doing in twenty minutes is sleeping." I looked over at Maria, who was knocked out with a pacifier hanging off the tip of

her lips. After my run-in with Mario and taking
the deal with Bayani, it was imperative I move to
another hotel. The only person who knew I was
here was Cartier.

"Come on, I want to take you somewhere!" he
pleaded.

"Cartier, you've been taking me somewhere
every day for a week now. I appreciate all the gen-
erosity, but I'm sleepy," I whined. He had already
taken Maria and me shopping, to breakfast, lunch,
dinner, and to the zoo. I didn't want to sound
ungrateful, but there was nowhere else for us to go.

"Girl, turn those sheets loose. You can sleep
when you die! I'll give you thirty minutes. If you
ain't down here by then, I guess I'll just have to call
the Realtor back and decline. . . ."

"Why didn't you say you were taking me to see a
house?" My ass was out of bed with the quickness.
"See you in thirty." I hung up and headed to the
closet.

The small space was filled with all of the brand-
new things Cartier had purchased for me this week.
He told me to trash everything Mario had bought,
and I did just that. It nearly broke my heart to
dump everything, including my jewelry. However,
I wanted to rid myself of anything that reminded
me of his bitch ass.

Removing the tag from a blue pair of spandex
jeans, I slid them up my bare ass. Wearing panties

was for the birds! I needed my coochie to be free. Furthermore, there was nothing worse than those damn panty lines to kill an outfit. I slipped on a bra and white T-shirt and my gold necklace. It read: TRUST NO NIGGA. I pulled my Filipino weave back into a ponytail and slipped on a Detroit Tigers snapback cap.

When I went to retrieve the blue and orange Nikes from the closet, I noticed Maria was waking up. "Hey there, pretty girl." I planted kisses on her pie face while she giggled. Her curly hair was all over the place, but it was nothing a brush and bow-bows couldn't fix. "Let's get you dressed, little mama." Grabbing one of the OshKosh hangers from the closet, I put Maria in a pink onesie with a white ruffled skirt. I rubbed her down with baby lotion then slipped on her pink booties. We were almost ready to go. I just needed to grab my purse and the diaper bag and place Maria in her car seat/ stroller contraption.

Buzz. Buzz. I grabbed the cell phone and read a message from Sam: What's up? I wasn't in the mood to text, so I called him.

"Hey, Gucci."

"What, Sam? I'm busy!" I rolled my eyes.

"I'm trying to slide though and see what's up between those butterscotch legs of yours."

"Nigga, didn't I tell you I was done fucking with you?"

"What if I ain't done fucking with you?" His voice was more serious now.

"Is that a threat?"

"I'm not a plaything. You don't decide when we're done."

He hung up on me and not a moment too soon. I was just about to hang up on him. Niggas was always catching feelings and getting the game twisted. I needed to keep him away from me, so I sent a text: It's best you go back to work for Mario. I no longer need you on my team. After minutes without a reply, I placed the phone into my pocket, then went back to doing me.

As I pushed the stroller past the mirror, I smiled. Never had I imagined this life for myself. I was always used to living in the fast lane, but I was digging this mommy thing.

"'I'ma be fresh as hell if the Feds watching. I'ma be fresh as hell if the Feds watching.'"

"Cartier, I'm coming." It never occurred to me to check the caller ID.

"It's Mario!" The tone he used signified he was pissed. He probably thought I called him by the wrong name on purpose.

"Oh."

"That's all you gon' say?"

"What do you want me to say?" I smacked my lips, pushing the stroller out of the room.

"You know why the fuck I'm calling!" he snapped. "We need to meet pronto!"

"We ain't got shit to talk about."

"So, you just going to take the deal with the Filipino like that?"

"Straight like that." The coldness in my tone was like a machete to Mario's flesh.

"I don't know what hurts more, the fact that you played me on the connect or that you stole niggas from my organization."

"Mario, let's not talk about what hurts, because I guarantee you'll lose this round." The nerve of this nigga to be acting like he was oblivious to shit he put me through.

"Fuck outta here, Gucci!" he yelled. "You are acting like I was the only one fucking around. Didn't you fuck your man in my crib? Let's not forget the facts, baby girl."

"Look, I gotta go." Hanging up in his face gave me brief satisfaction. I wanted to do some volatile shit to him, but handcuffs didn't look good on me.

"'I'ma be fresh as hell if the Feds watching. I'ma be fresh as hell if the Feds watching.'" I knew it was Mario again, so I turned the phone off. He was not gonna ruin my day with his bullshit.

As I stepped from the elevator, my eyes landed on the finest brown-skinned nigga on this side of Michigan. Cartier sat on the arm of the couch in the lobby talking on his cell phone. As I made my way over to him, I took in the red Cole Haan loafers, black Dickies, and a red button-down. The red and black Detroit hat put a smile on my face. *I guess it's true: great minds do think alike.*

"Pimp, let me call you back. My girl just got down here." He slid the phone into the back pocket of his pants, then stood to greet me. "What's up, sexy?"

"Nothing much." I smiled for no reason at all. Cartier just did that to me. There was something about his swag, his boss-like attitude, and the expensive cologne that had me wet with anticipation of our next romp in the bedroom. The man was gifted between the legs. He put it down like no lover I had ever been with.

"Can a nigga get a hug or something?" He stretched his long arms open wide, and I dove in. Cartier was a safe place for me. He was my first love and my first sexual partner. Had he not been locked up for so long, my life would've turned out much differently. No doubt ya girl would've still been a hustler's wife, but I never would've met Mario or had Maria.

"So where are we going?" I quizzed.

"You'll see." He kneeled down to kiss Maria's forehead. "Now come on and no more questions."

Chapter 40

Mina

"Where are my keys?" Sam yelled from the foyer. I was coming up from the basement with laundry.

"Why are you yelling?" His attitude lately was unnerving.

"Because I'm looking for my keys, and you were the last one with them," he lashed out. "You took my car to show a house yesterday, remember? I told you to leave the keys right here at the front door, but you don't listen."

"Sam, don't speak to me like I'm a fucking kid!"

"Anyway, where the hell are my keys?" His stare mimicked mine.

"When I came home yesterday, I placed the keys right where you told me to. Then you made a run after that, remember? I found the keys in a pair of your jeans I just took to wash." I retrieved the keys from the laundry hamper, tossing them at him. The look on his face was priceless.

"My bad." His apology lacked emotion. "I'm going to holla at Mario. I'll be back in a few."

"I thought you said we were gonna lie in bed and watch movies." All week long we were constantly on the go, ripping, and running. We were barely able to spend time together.

"Not today. I got business to handle."

"What the hell is wrong with you? You've been acting strange, and I don't like it at all." It was time to put my foot down. The tension between us was too thick.

"Ain't nothing up, Mina," he sighed. "I'm going to handle some business. I'll try to make it fast."

"Since when did you rejoin the drug game?" The more time he spent with Mario, the less time he spent with me. I knew he was back in the game but hadn't said anything.

"Some shit came up," was all he said on his way out the door.

I stood there in shock long enough to hear the engine on his car crank up then pull out of the driveway. "Ain't this a bitch!" Resisting the urge to grab the cordless and blow his phone up wasn't easy. However, I did call Gucci.

"Mina, you won't believe this!" she squealed. "Cartier just bought me a mansion!"

"Oh, my God, are you serious?"

"Girl, yes. You have to come and check it out." She went on and on. I didn't want to put a damper on her day. For that reason, I chose not to tell her why I had called.

"Okay, girl, I will. You go ahead and celebrate. I'll get with you later." I ended the call and headed up to my bedroom. I remembered when Sam purchased this home for us and the family we wanted to have. Seemingly, my fairy tale was taking a turn for the worse. I loved Sam and wanted to fight for us. In contrast, it was hard to fight when I didn't know why we were fighting in the first place.

Once upstairs, I dropped the laundry basket onto the bed. I began folding the clothes, stopping midway. Suddenly, I had the urge to go out and listen to music. It was still early. I wanted to be in the company of people in good spirits. Grabbing a pink scoop-neck dress with the back out and a pair of wedges, I quickly slipped them on. My hair was already done. I wasn't into makeup. Therefore, a little dab of Chanel No. 5 behind the ears and I was ready. When I reached the main floor, I gave myself the once-over in the mirror, then grabbed my purse. I armed the alarm and stepped onto the porch.

"Where are you going?" Sam stood there with a smirk.

"I thought you were gone. What happened?" Although startled by his presence, I was happy to see him.

"I came back to apologize for my behavior. There's just been a lot of shit on my mind, and I'm stressed."

"What's wrong, baby? Can I help?" I stepped into his space, embracing him in a hug.

"There are a few things I have to tell you, but not today." He shook his head. "Since you're all dressed up, I'm gonna take you out and make up for lost time."

"Sam, I would much rather know what's going on with you."

"Not right now, ma. Let's just enjoy the moment." He leaned down and kissed the side of my neck, sending shivers down my body.

An hour later, we were seated inside the VIP area in Club Plush. It was the hottest club in Novi that catered to the after-work crowd. All the drinks and food were half off. Party hours were from four to nine. It turned into a regular club after that. Demographics for the average partygoer were a mixture of African Americans and Caucasians, ranging between 25 and 35 in age. Sam wasn't much of a club dude, but he obliged my request to hear some good music.

Currently, they were playing the new Miley Cyrus joint, and all the white girls were twerking, or so they thought. "You want a drink?" He leaned in close to my ear.

"Yeah, I'll take a Sex on the Beach."

"Girl, we can head to the beach right now." He winked then waved the waiter over.

While they conversed, the DJ switched gears, playing hip-hop. Drake and 2 Chainz were now blaring throughout the room. I was up on my feet, headed to the dance floor. It felt good to move and be free. I hadn't been out in a while and was having so much fun. A few younger men even tried to dance with me, which boosted my ego. It was good to know a girl still had it.

On my way back to the table, a woman wearing a fierce Donna Karan minidress bumped into me, causing her drink to spill down the front of my outfit. I would've brushed the shit off, but homegirl didn't even attempt to apologize. She kept walking with her friend like nothing happened. *Oh, hell no!* I followed them, then tapped her on the shoulder.

"What?" She turned around with major attitude.

"You spilled your drink on my dress. The least you could've done was apologize." This young girl was going to learn the importance of manners if I had anything to say about it.

"Bitch, don't nobody give a fuck about that dress you found on the Walmart clearance rack," she laughed. It was my desire to inform her this was no Walmart special, but it wasn't important.

"Mina, what's going on?" Sam approached me with a bottle of Heineken in one hand and my Sex on the Beach in another.

"Not now, baby." Without hesitation, I grabbed the bottle from him and doused her with the beer.

"You bitch!" she screamed as she lunged at me. Quickly stepping aside, I watched her fly into a couple dancing behind me. Now I was the one laughing, until her friend began to speak.

"Sam? What are you doing here?"

"Tynika?" He looked as if he had just seen a ghost.

"How do you two know each other?" I crossed my arms, waiting for Sam to form a sentence.

"I'm his baby's mama." She extended a manicured hand.

"What?" I shrieked.

"Mina, that's what I wanted to talk to you about," he attempted to clarify.

"You must be the woman he left me and his son for," she said over the music.

"His son?" I was stunned and hurt beyond belief.

Most of the ride home was silent. I couldn't believe this nigga had a son and didn't think enough of me to share that information.

"Mina, I know you're mad, but I can explain."

"I'm listening."

"I met Tynika while I was dating Chloe. We messed around, and I got her pregnant. I didn't even know about the baby until after I proposed to you. I was going to tell you, but the timing was off.

You were already being a good sport about baby Samantha."

"How old is the kid?"

"He's one."

"What's his name?" I sighed, relaxing my shoulders. There was no reason to be mad for real. The baby was conceived before he and I were an item. Despite that, my spirit was broken. I wanted desperately to have a baby with him, but now he had two.

"Solomon." His voice was low like he was ashamed that he had brought two babies into this relationship.

"You should've told me, Sam." I shook my head.

"I know, but I also realized the news would hurt you."

"Well, it hurts more to find out from some random bitch in the club."

"Baby, I'm sorry." He pulled into the driveway, turning the engine off. "You've been asking what's wrong with me, and now you have it. I was just so afraid of losing you."

"Sam, for several months I've been feeling pushed away. If you're trying to keep me, you have a mighty funny way of showing it."

"I know. I know." He grasped my face. "I promise on my life I'll do everything I can to make it up to you."

"No more secrets, right?" My heart couldn't take anything else.

"No more secrets." Sam smiled.

Chapter 41

Lovely

Tonight was the first party I would be attending. I was nervous yet curious about the goings-on around here. Sometime after nightfall I could hear guests arriving, as well as the sound of music. It seemed to be a mixture of opera over a Mexican beat. I wanted to peek out the door, but it was locked.

"The madam should be here soon," Daphnie announced seconds before the door opened.

"Okay, ladies, it's show time!" She clapped her hands while everyone stood at attention. Assembled at the door was a single-file line. No one made a sound. "Remember to be on your best behavior." Prior to leading us away from the room and down the staircase, she looked directly at me.

Moments later, we entered a large room. Men lounged around in smoking jackets, puffing cigars and sipping cocktails. At first, it was embarrassing to walk around a roomful of strangers in my birthday suit. I felt like everyone was looking at the number burned on my ass.

"*Vamos a bailar.*" The gentleman with salt-and-pepper hair to my right held out his hand. The dude was clean from head to toe, dressed in Gianni Versace. Two diamond rings rested on his ring and pinky fingers. His shirt was unbuttoned to reveal a mass of chest hair. Although he spoke Spanish, he appeared to be Italian to me.

"Huh?" I didn't know what the hell he was saying.

"Let's dance." His hand was still out, waiting for me to take it. I wanted to tell him this wasn't my kind of music, but I could feel eyes gawking in our direction.

"What the hell? Let's do it." I placed my hand in his and prepared to tango or some shit, but he had other plans.

"My dear, I don't mean dance on the dance floor. I want to take the party to the bedroom." He smiled.

"Okay." I smiled nervously as he escorted me past the other guests and out of the room.

Once inside one of the bedrooms on the main floor, he stood there. "I want you to undress the king."

"No problem, king." Slowly, I undid the last two buttons on his shirt, then made my way to his silk pants. They were pressed to death. The creases were so crisp, I almost cut myself.

"While you're down there, you might as well suck on the prince," he said, referring to his manhood. I was ready to throw up! Seriously, giving up some pussy was one thing, but putting a stranger's dick in my mouth was a whole other situation. Nonetheless, I swallowed hard, closed my eyes, and slid the shriveled-up piece of flesh into my mouth. I didn't know what I expected it to taste like, but it wasn't as bad as I thought.

Slowly, I bobbed my head back and forth until his erection was at its maximum length. "Yeah, that's it," he moaned. When I was finished, I stood from the floor, then headed over to the bed. King, or whatever his name was, took no time grabbing a condom from the nightstand, then diving deep inside the walls of my body. His rhythm was off. He didn't quite hit the spot, but it wasn't the worst. In fact, I was glad my first time was with him. From the looks of some of those other cats, I had snagged the best one.

Knock, knock. "Hurry up in there," someone said through the door. "I just paid for a round with her."

"I'm after you," another person added.

"Looks like you'll be a busy girl tonight." King was smiling, but I wanted to cry. At this rate, my coochie would be looking like Daphnie's in no time.

Chapter 42

Nikki

"Are you ready?" The nurse smiled. She was a skinny woman with brown hair, wearing a black scrub top and matching bottoms. I was at the abortion clinic with Anjela. Today was the day. I was nervous. Mario was out in the streets, and Junior was with his grandmother.

"Are you sure you want to do this, cuz?" Anj looked up from the file she was reading.

"I'm sure." I grabbed my purse, following the nurse.

"Do you want me to come with you?"

"No, I'm good." I headed down the hallway.

She checked my weight first, then my blood pressure, and finally my temperature. While she noted the necessary information on my chart, I couldn't help but stare at the women coming and going to and from each room. The youngest girl I saw was accompanied by her mother. She looked to be no more than 15. The next woman I saw was accompanied by her husband, I presumed. I'd overheard them talking about not being able to feed another mouth and that this was the best choice for their family.

Once inside the room, I was handed a hospital gown and told to wait for the doctor. As I undressed, a feeling of uneasiness came over me. I wasn't sure if this was the right thing to do. I lay back on the table, placing a hand to my stomach. The baby was too small to kick, but just knowing it was alive moved me. There was no way I could go through with this.

Just as the door opened, I sat up abruptly. "Hello, Ms. Wallace. My name is Dorian." The doctor entered the room in full surgical gear.

"Doctor, I'm sorry but I've changed my mind." The tears were flowing uncontrollably.

"Would you like to see a counselor?" He handed me the Kleenex box from the counter.

"No. I just need to leave."

"I understand, Ms. Wallace." He nodded before leaving the room quietly.

Jumping up from the table, I slid on my shit. I never wanted to step foot back in a place like this again. *Who cares who my baby's father is? All that matters is that my child is loved.*

"Anj, let's go." I hurried through the office like a tropical breeze.

"What's wrong?" she inquired as she gathered her work in a rush.

People were looking at me sideways, but I didn't give a damn. Once outside, I took a profound breath. Just minutes ago, I almost killed a precious gift given to me by God. I didn't judge anyone for their choices, but abortion wasn't for me.

"Slow down!" Anjela yelled.

"I'm sorry, cuz. I just had to get up outta there."

"I feel you." She stuffed the papers into her briefcase. "I take it you're going to keep the baby then, right?"

"Yes, I'm going to keep it." Wrapping my arms around myself, I wanted to scream from the rooftop that I was keeping my child.

"Good." She smiled. "Does Mario want another son or another daughter?"

"I don't know," I responded on the way to her car.

"What's wrong? You sound sad. Don't tell me you're second-guessing your decision."

"It's not that." I sighed, sliding into the passenger seat.

"Then what in the hell is it?" She cranked up the vehicle.

"Maine came to see me the other day."

"What?" she screamed. "What did he say?"

"For starters, he apologized. Then he said he wanted to be friends and start fresh."

"How do you feel about that, seeing as how you're trying to work things out with Mario?"

"Honestly, I love Mario, but he loves the streets. I'm not about that life anymore. Maine is more refined. I feel like he and I are on the same page when it comes to life." I never thought I'd choose any man over Mario, but Maine gave me things to think about.

"What do you plan to do?"

"There's nothing wrong with having a friend, right?" I giggled.

"Your ass won't be laughing when Mario finds out." Anjela shook her head, putting the car in gear.

Chapter 43

Gucci

When Cartier said we were going to look at houses, I had no idea what was in store. Unbeknownst to me, he had already purchased a 10,000-square-foot lavish home. "What in the world is going on?" I asked as we pulled into the circular driveway. There were several people outside in various uniforms waving at us.

"Welcome home, baby." Cartier parked the car next to a black and chrome 2014 G550 G-Wagen by Mercedes-Benz. Both the whip and the house were covered in large pink bows.

"Are you kidding me?" I punched him on the arm and jumped out of the car like it was on fire. "This is ours?"

"Yup." He retrieved Maria from the car seat and carried her while I took in the magnificent scenery. "I call it the luxury estate, baby."

"This place is gorgeous!" I squealed. "I can't wait for Satin and Mina to see it."

"Come over here for a second and meet the staff."

"The staff?" I smiled. Living in the lap of luxury wasn't something new for me, but never had I been equipped with staff.

"This is Roseanne, the housekeeper."

"*Buenos dias, senorita.*" She did a curtsy. I didn't know what to say or do, so I curtsied back.

"This is Walter, the resident chef."

"Morning, ma'am. I specialize in gourmet cuisine from all over the world. You name it and I'll make it."

"'Resident' as in he will live here too?" I looked from Walter to Cartier.

"Yes. There are separate living quarters toward the back of the property line for Walter and Sophia."

"Okay, well, nice to meet you, Walter." I smiled at the middle-aged, balding gentleman in blue jeans and a chef's coat.

"Last but not least, this is Sophia, Maria's new nanny." She was a middle-aged, pleasantly plump Filipino woman with black hair and gray temples.

"Nice to meet you, miss." She smiled and instinctively reached for Maria. I thought she would begin to cry in the arms of the unfamiliar, pale woman. To my astonishment, Maria said nothing. Furthermore, she lay on the stranger's shoulder like she didn't have a care in the world.

"Come on, baby, let me show you the rest of the crib." Cartier pulled me past the staff and into the massive house.

There were gold columns, oversized windows with panoramic views, and each room had already been decorated impeccably. More often than not, I would've pitched a bitch about not contributing to the design process. Yet this place was beautiful! There was a formal living and dining area, chef's kitchen, a great room, seven bedrooms, and eight bathrooms. The bonus was the movie theater and two-lane bowling alley in the basement. To date, I had only seen this shit on MTV's show *Cribs*. "Do you like it?"

"Of course I do!" I beamed with excitement.

"To be honest, I was already having this shit built before I returned to Detroit." Cartier took a seat on the spiral staircase.

"Why in the world would you want to live in a big-ass place like this?" I took a seat on the step between his legs.

"This might sound corny, but I knew I would find you and we'd start a family here. At the time, I wasn't aware you had already started a family without me."

"I didn't think you were ever getting out of prison." For some odd reason, I felt the need to explain.

"Yeah, I know." He tugged on my hair playfully. "I hate to sound like an ass, but I'm glad you and homeboy didn't work out."

"We were never truly meant to be. I realize that now." In essence, it hurt to face the truth. Then again, it was what it was. Just because two people love one another doesn't necessarily equate to them being destined to be together.

"Good! Because if you fuck around and go back to that nigga, me and you will have some problems."

"Boy, stop! Mario is the furthest thing from my mind." That was the truth, so help me God.

"What about Maria?"

"What about her?" I turned to face him. "I'll continue to raise her. And when I'm ready for him to see her, we'll make arrangements."

"Gucci, you can't hold her hostage." He laughed. "That's his daughter too."

"Whose side are you on?" The last time Cartier and Mario were in the same place, they fought. Now he was defending his enemy.

"Baby, you never have to question my loyalty. I'm just keeping it one hundred. That's her father, and every little girl needs her daddy. You see how those ratchet bitches on television turned out."

"Are you saying you don't want the responsibility of being in her life?" I snapped, already realizing why. He was telling the truth, but I didn't want to hear it. I was furious with Mario. Cartier wanted me to do the right thing too. Nevertheless, I wasn't feeling it.

"You think I would've moved y'all in here if I didn't want the responsibility of being in her life?" His voice rose. "Needless to say, I would like to be her father, but I'm not, so I respect that."

"The Cartier I know would've said to hell with that nigga!" I laughed. "When did you become so wise?"

"Age will do that to you. Just keep on living." He said it like he was light-years older than me instead of four. "But on a serious note, as long as Mario don't cross you or Maria, we're good."

Chapter 44

Lovely

I'd be lying if I said being in this hellhole had gotten better with time. I'd been fucked by more men than I cared to remember. Some of them were old as dirt with wrinkled penises and sagging balls. They could barely get it up. Still, they wanted me to do all kinds of freaky shit. I was sick to my stomach. Even so, I learned to never complain and pretended to enjoy it. I didn't want to be killed. This week alone, I witnessed two women lose their lives simply for giving bad blow jobs.

"Number forty-two, snap out of it!" The madam snapped her fingers. I'd come to learn that her name was Lucy. After successfully running a prostitution ring in California, she was hired by the brothers. Her clients included tons of A-list celebrities. She'd been in the industry for over ten years. Her business was shut down when the Feds caught on and hit her with charges. They wanted her to give up her clientele in exchange for freedom, but she was no snitch! Homegirl did a five-year bid and never looked back.

"Forty-two, did you hear me? I said it's show time." This time, she pulled the parlor doors open to reveal a roomful of men in casual attire. As usual, the place was smoky and reeked of tequila.

There were twelve women on tonight's shift, twenty of us in total. While we walked around the room in birthday suits, the other eight women stood around in lingerie holding trays and pouring drinks. Because of their menstrual cycle, they were given the night off. Lucky bitches!

I sauntered around the room barefoot, making eye contact with no one except Mauricio. Every time he looked at me, I wanted him to remember what he did to me. I wanted him to know that I hadn't forgotten. If my eyes were daggers, he would've died a thousand times already.

"Forty-Two. I want forty-two."

I turned to see an older Hispanic man dressed in tan trousers and a striped shirt. He was covered in liver spots, wearing triple bifocals, and using a walker with tennis balls on the bottom. I kept walking, trying hard to catch someone's, hell, anyone else's attention.

"You heard him, *puta!*" Mauricio forcefully grabbed my arm, pulling me toward the old man. I'd been around here long enough to learn that *"puta"* meant "whore."

I swallowed hard and mustered a smile. "Come on, daddy. Let me take good care of you." I helped him stand, guided him out of the parlor, and into one of the rooms.

Once inside the bedroom, I closed my eyes and pretended I was still a call girl. In those days, I did what I had to in order to provide for my family. Gradually, I moved my body into an S motion. Next, I played with my nipples, then bent and spread my cheeks. I couldn't tell if he was aroused, but there was a small wet spot on his pants. I wanted to gag in disgust. I didn't know if it was ejaculation or urine. I doubted this man still had sperm. With that in mind, I resolved the wet spot was the latter of the two.

"Are you ready for all of this?" I went over to the bed and lay upside down.

"No sex." He walked over and stopped at my head.

"Oh, you want a blow job?" I watched him unzip his pants, prepared to tea bag me, or so I thought. Nothing could prepare me for what happened next. This old bastard pulled his pants and underwear down, then turned around, spread his ass cheeks, and you know what happened next. He dropped his ass right onto my lips!

Chapter 45

Nikki

The next day, I pulled up to the gate and waited for the security guard to permit me to enter. Anjela owned an upscale condominium in Romulus. Yesterday, she invited me over for lunch and to meet her new beau.

"Here you are, miss." He slapped a visitor sticker on my window, then beckoned me on.

I was familiar with the complex, so finding her unit took no time. Stepping from the car, I grabbed a bottle of merlot, then proceeded to the door. The wind chime hanging from her door swung in the wind as I rang the doorbell.

"One minute," Anjela's voice sang from the inside. I perceived she was in a good mood. Moments later, she stood in the doorway, rocking an oversized business shirt, white biker shorts, and an apron that read, KISS THE COOK.

"What's up, Suzy Homemaker?" Stepping in for a hug, I was greeted with a delicious aroma. There was no way my cousin cooked this meal. She barely knew how to boil minute rice.

"Hey, cuz! Come on in." Taking the bottle from me, she closed the door. "Carter is in the shower. He'll be down in a minute."

"So, he lives here now?" I followed her into the midsized kitchen, taking a seat at the breakfast nook, which was being used as a dinette set.

"It's just temporary." She placed the bottle into the freezer. "He's here so often to work on the case that I figured he could stay with me rather than racking up hotel bills."

"So, what's for dinner?"

"Braised lamb chops, risotto, and a side salad." Like Vanna White, she flourished her hand across the food resting on the stove.

"Sounds good, baby. I'm starving." Carter entered the room with a chuckle. He was wearing a Lakers T-shirt, matching basketball shorts, white socks, and Adidas house shoes. "Hello, I'm Carter. You must be Nikki."

"Yeah, I'm Nikki." While attempting to be discreet, I studied the stranger. There was something so familiar about him. I'd seen him before; I just couldn't place when or where.

"Anjela tells me so much about you." He took a seat at the table.

"I hope it's been all good." I glanced over at my cousin, who was bringing the food to the table.

"Nothing too bad." He laughed. "Seriously, she did tell me you're working on a book manuscript. That's interesting. If you don't mind me asking, what will the book be about?"

"My life." I could tell he was waiting for a more detailed explanation. I didn't offer one. I didn't feel comfortable sharing the intimate details of my life with a fucking federal agent. "So, Carter, where are you from?" It was time to start my own line of questioning.

"I'm originally from Detroit, but I was raised in California by my father." He began putting food on his plate.

"Do you have any siblings?" I noticed the way Anj looked at me with the side-eye.

"I have a brother."

"Carter is a twin." Anjela removed the bottle from the freezer, then poured everyone a glass.

"A twin? Imagine that." I picked up my glass and took a sip.

"Yeah, my brother's name is Cartier. When our parents split up, I went with Dad, and he was raised by our mother."

The mention of Cartier's name nearly caused me to choke. He was the man I saw Gucci hugged up with outside of the hair salon. He and his twin brother were identical. "Where is your brother now? Are the two of you close?" Something fishy was going on around here.

"I don't know where my brother is." The way he shifted his eyes told me he was lying. "He went his own way, and I went mine."

"You're not curious about what he's doing, or at least want to find him?"

"Quite frankly, no." I could discern I had made him uncomfortable. Anjela could tell too.

"No one said if they like the food." She smiled. I wanted to tell her to call the restaurant and thank the chef who prepared it but kicked her under the table instead.

"It's really good. You'll have to share this recipe with me."

"Oh, I will." She kicked me back.

The remainder of the dinner went effortlessly. I wasn't done grilling his ass but decided to let up for now. There was something about him. I just hadn't put my finger on it.

After leaving Anjela, I decided to stop by and visit with my mother-in-law. On the way over, I received a private call. "Hello."

"Hey, beautiful!" Maine's voice was electrifying.

"Hey, yourself!" I blushed for no reason.

"I was calling to see if you wanted to meet me for dinner."

"I just finished dinner about an hour ago." All of a sudden, I lost the compulsion to visit Claudia.

"That's cool. I like dessert better anyway." The way he pronounced the word "dessert" sent chills down my body. "Meet me at the Westin Book Cadillac downtown."

"Right now?" Glancing over my attire, I noted I was underdressed. Typically, a pair of jeans, T-shirt, and gym shoes weren't date attire. However, since we were only friends, I saw no harm.

"I'll be waiting out front." He hung up.

Sure as shit, when I pulled up to the hotel, he was standing there puffing a cigar. The black slacks, black button-down shirt, and royal blue blazer looked good on him. I'd never seen him in anything other than business attire. It was a major turn-on, too. "You look nice!"

"As do you." He put the cigar out and held the door open. I followed him through the lobby and past the restaurant on the main level. I started to ask why we weren't dining there but kept my mouth closed. On the way to the room, I tried to calm my nerves. There was no telling what would happen once we were behind closed doors.

"Do I make you nervous?" His finger grazed my neck, causing the hair on my head to stand up.

"Not at all," I lied, stepping from the elevator.

"Good." He laughed, then slid his key into the door where we were standing.

Crossing the threshold, I was flabbergasted at the sight before me. Several cakes, pies, and Danish were lined along the dining table. There was even a bouquet of pink carnations in the middle of all the desserts. "All of this for me?"

"I forgot to ask what types of dessert you liked, so I had the restaurant send everything on the menu."

"You didn't have to go to this extreme. A cupcake would've been sufficient." I turned around with a giggle.

The look in his eyes spoke volumes. He wanted me and I wanted him. When he leaned in for a kiss, I didn't resist. Somehow, we ended up engrossed in a full-blown sex scene. He ripped my blouse and pulled my jeans down. I removed his shirt and tugged at his jeans. Just when I unfastened the button he stopped.

"What's wrong?" I inquired.

Maine said nothing. Instead, he covered his mouth with his palm, gazing down at my round stomach in disbelief.

"You're pregnant?"

Chapter 46

Gucci

"I can't believe you haven't run into your boy yet."
Cartier spoke from his seat on the toilet as I entered
the bathroom. He was reading the *Detroit Free Press*
with a Glock resting on his lap. I smirked to myself
because my boo was too damn hood for his own good.
Cartier wasn't the type of nigga to get caught slippin',
so he carried a piece of steel everywhere.

"That's not my boy." I rolled my eyes, then went
to brush my teeth at the Jack and Jill double vanity
marble sink. As far as I was concerned, if I never
saw his ass again, it would be too soon. He'd been
blowing my phone up to the degree that I had to
change my number.

Cartier tossed his newspaper into the copper
wastebasket, then wiped his ass.

"I hate that fucker with a passion." I rinsed my
mouth with faucet water.

"You ain't playing, li'l mama, huh?" Cartier stood
from the toilet seat, then stepped straight into the
shower. It was his ritual. Anytime he took a shit at
home, he had to shower afterward.

"Hell no! Not only am I not playing, I won't stop until I see that nigga broke." For nearly two months, Cartier and I had been growing the new empire. My mission was to put Mario's ass out of business for good. So far, the plan was working.

"You look sexy as fuck when you get mad." Cartier stared at me through the clear shower glass. "You should come take a shower with me." The steam crept throughout the custom bathroom. Water dripped from his sculpted body. I was turned on. As I contemplated my man's offer, I heard the doorbell.

"I'll get it." I tightened the belt on my leopard robe, prepared to answer the door, but Cartier stopped me.

"You better act like you have some sense and check that surveillance camera first."

Grabbing the remote control, I turned on the television that was located inside the vanity mirror. There stood Claudia with her arms folded and a scowl on her face.

"Shit!" I cursed. I was not in the mood for her drama today. Ever since our confrontation a few months back when I dog checked her, we'd steered clear of one another. The fact that she was standing on my doorstep was out of the blue. "Baby, it's Maria's grandmother. I'll be back."

"Don't take too long," he called out as I headed down the grand spiral staircase.

As I reached the custom Italian-inspired foyer, the doorbell rang again. I started to make her wait a little longer but decided against it. "Claudia, come in." I put on my best million-dollar smile, batting my eyelashes for dramatic effect.

"Gucci, you look nice." She took in the sight before her. My new house was immaculate, and she was sick about it. Cartier promised to upgrade my life and give me the things I deserved once I became his girl. The mansion he purchased for me was built from the ground up and sat on a half-acre lot. Cartier served it up proper with the house, but he didn't stop there. Every article of clothing, every piece of furniture, and every car in the driveway was brand spanking new and customized just for me. He told me to donate my old shit to charity, and that was exactly what I did.

"No offense, but how do you know where I live? And how did you get past the gate?" I didn't care how rude I may have sounded. I needed some answers.

"Well . . ." she started, a bit taken aback by my bluntness. "Mario gave me the address, and your gate was open."

I wanted to ask her how in the hell Mario knew where I lived. Instead, I asked, "So what brings you by?" I didn't have time for small talk.

"I came over to see my granddaughter. Also, Mario wanted me to come by and see if it would be okay to pick up Maria so he could see her." She paused nervously.

"Tell Mario if he really wanted to see her, then he would've come and picked her up himself."

"Gucci, why are you being so difficult?" She frowned and I lightly chuckled. "He's been trying for a while now to see his daughter."

I smiled. "Listen, I'm not being difficult. I'm keeping it real. Mario won't show up here because he knows I got a real nigga now! That's why his bitch ass sent you. Tell him to come ring this doorbell himself if he wants to see my daughter, and then I'll think about it."

"It's not fair to Maria to keep her away from her father for your own selfish reasons!" Claudia was pissed. Silently, I wanted her to jump stupid. I would've been all over her ass in a Detroit minute.

"Call it what you want, but I'm her mother, and what I say goes."

"He's her father, and he deserves to see her!" she yelled.

Right on cue, Cartier walked down the stairs, holding Maria, who had awakened from her slumber. She was now 8 months old, and her new favorite word was "Daddy." It didn't matter who you were, she just liked to say Daddy. She even called me Daddy sometimes, but I wasn't about to let Claudia in on the secret.

Just as Cartier reached the last step, Maria uttered her favorite word as he cradled her up against his chest like she was his own. Claudia's eyes bugged from her head. "You got my grand-baby calling another man Daddy?"

Chapter 47

Mina

The hospital called last night and informed us that Samantha was ready to come home. We were elated! Her room was prepared and awaiting her arrival. "Are you ready?" I asked Sam, who was running around the house like a crazy person.

"Do we have everything?" He looked at me.

"All we needed to pick up was a car seat," I laughed.

"Did we get it?"

"Of course we did!" Last week we went on a shopping spree for baby Samantha. We had bottles, blankets, clothes, a crib, a car seat, as well as a whole bunch of shit she didn't need. "Baby, let's go already!" I was anxious.

"We forgot to babyproof the house." He looked frantic. "I saw something on television about that shit."

"Sam, she's only an infant. We won't have to babyproof until she starts crawling."

"Well, it's never too soon."

"Boy, stop it! I'm about to leave without you." Opening the door, I jumped at the sight of Mario.

"Hey, Mina." He nodded. "Sam, I'm about two seconds from killing Gucci. I need you to be the voice of reason, dog." He barged inside without an invitation. "My mama went to see Maria, and she said Gucci got my daughter calling her nigga Daddy! Can you believe that shit?"

"Damn, homie!" Sam looked past him toward me. His eyes begged for five minutes. My eyes indicated he only had two before I left.

"I swear I'm gonna have somebody hurt her."

"Don't speak like that, big homie." Sam tried to calm him down, but Mario was all the way turned up.

"I've tried to be the bigger person and let shit slide, but the bitch is dirty! She stole my money, but I let it go. She took my deal with a new connect. I even let that go. Nik been wanting me to leave the game anyway, so I wasn't trippin'! But now she got my baby girl callin' another man Daddy. That's unacceptable!"

It was none of my business, but Mario was right. Gucci had changed the game with this one. It wasn't cool. I felt for him. "Baby, you stay here. I'll go and pick Samantha up myself."

"Are you sure?"

"Yeah, it's fine." I knew his friend needed consoling. It was no problem to pick up the baby. Furthermore, I couldn't wait any longer.

Chapter 48

Nikki

"She said what?" I asked Claudia to repeat what she'd just told me about her visit with Gucci. However, before she had time to, my line clicked. It was Maine. Instantaneously, a smile lit up my face.

"Ms. C, can I call you right back? This is my cousin." I didn't even think I waited for an answer before clicking over. "Hey."

"Hey, baby. What are you doing?" Maine's voice always melted my panties.

"Nothing really, except emailing my cousin the completed manuscript of my novel." The day had finally come. It was finished. Now it was up to Anjela to do her thing and see what happened.

"Congratulations, sweetheart! How's my baby?" After he discovered my secret that night at the hotel, there was no alternative other than to spill the beans. It would've been wrong to lie about it, especially since he just lost a child.

"The baby is fine." I closed the laptop, lying back across the bed. Mario was gone, and Junior was playing on my floor with his toys.

"When is your next appointment? I want to be there." He was excited. However, I wasn't.

"Maine, I haven't told Mario that we've been in contact. Therefore, you just can't be showing up to appointments."

"I thought you said he knew you were carrying my seed."

"He does know, but we had plans to raise the child as ours. I didn't know you would pop back into the picture."

"Well, I'm back, so you can tell dude to step back!"

"Maine," I sighed. *This is where shit gets complicated.*

"What, Nikki? I know you don't expect me to sit back and watch another nigga raise my shorty!" As he spoke, I thought about the current situation Mario was experiencing with Gucci and Cartier. Maine was right. It wouldn't be fair. Now I was between a rock and a hard place.

"I'm not saying that. I'm just asking you to be patient with me."

"All right. I can do that, but my patience is short, so you better expedite this shit."

"Thank you for understanding." Times like this reminded me of why I fell for him in the first place.

"Nik!" Mario called out as he came through the front door.

Shit! I hadn't even heard him pull up. "Maine, I'll call you later!" I hung up the phone, then deleted the call from my log like a scared little kid.

"I'm up here. What's wrong?" I placed the phone on the nightstand just in the nick of time.

"I'm gonna fuck around and murk Gucci's ass."

"Don't talk like that." I slid onto the edge of the bed.

"Do you know what she did?"

"Yes. Your mother told me." I watched him remove his shoes.

"How dare she?" He tossed a shoe across the room.

Junior knew it was time to get out of dodge. He collected his toys, then politely walked across the hallway into his room.

"Mario, calm down. She can't keep Maria from you. Call an attorney." I would've recommended my cousin, but she was no longer a fan of Mario's. After what he did last year, she was left with a bad taste in her mouth.

"I don't want a lawyer all up in our shit like that."

"Have you tried being civil when you call her?" I knew Mario had a bad temper. Most times, it got the best of him.

"Of course I have!" He lay back on the bed. "I wanna do some foul shit to that bitch. But then I think about you and my kids." He leaned over and kissed my stomach. "Some days, y'all are the only ones keeping me sane."

I wanted to tell him about Maine. How could I, particularly after a moment like this?

Chapter 49

Gucci

After my run-in with Claudia earlier, I'd been patiently waiting for my phone to ring. I knew Mario would be calling and going off. Amazingly, the phone hadn't rung all day.

"Gucci, come on," Cartier called up the stairs.

"I'm coming!" I yelled back. "Sophia, please call if Maria gets fussy." I waved goodbye to my baby. She was playing with her nanny as I headed down the stairs.

"'Bout damn time!" Cartier hit the lock on the custom 2014 white and chrome Jeep Commander.

"Why we gotta ride in this? I wanna take the G-Wagen." I smacked my lips. Shit, I was looking fresh to death in a fitted white linen pantsuit, red bra, and red Alexander McQueens. Cartier looked amazing in a pair of white Akoo jeans, white Polo top, and a crisp pair of Nike Air Force Ones. We looked like a million bucks. It was only fitting that our whip matched our appearance.

"Gucci, you should know better!" He frowned.

"What?" I wanted everyone to see me riding around and flexing hard. I needed niggas to know I would be on top with or without Mario.

"First of all, you never take your best shit around your workers." He started the engine.

"Why?" I asked, baffled.

"Because it only reminds them they ain't got what you got. Jealousy will make a nigga bite the hand that feeds him." He pulled a freshly rolled blunt filled with granddaddy purps from behind his ear and lit it. "Second of all, do you realize how stupid it would be to drive a Benz to the trap to pick up drug money?"

"I didn't even think about that," I replied, feeling shamefaced.

Allegedly, overnight my new organization had monopolized the streets. Every dope dealer in Michigan was buying from us. Our prices were so low there was no competition. Mario did his best to remain in the game. Luckily, it was just a matter of time before he folded like a little bitch. It was amusing. I relished the money, power, and respect that accompanied our connection. Conversely, everybody knows more money almost always brings more problems. Our names created jealousy among our enemies. Cartier thought we were untouchable. In contrast, I was constantly watching my back.

As we rode down Telegraph Road, the gaslight came on. Cartier pulled up to the BP station and jumped out. I stayed inside, playing *Candy Crush* on my phone. The game was flat-out addictive.

Tap, tap. I looked toward the window to see a bum standing there with Windex and a roll of paper towel. "I can shine these windows for five dollars." He sprayed the cleaning solution, then began cleaning.

"Look, nigga!" I rolled my window down. "Ain't nothin' wrong with my fuckin' windows. You need to bounce!" In Detroit, everybody had a hustle, even the bums.

"Chill, little mama. I'm just tryin'a get some lunch." He continued wiping the windshield like I hadn't just said to stop.

I rolled the window down farther so I could reach out and shoo his ass away. Shockingly, he reached inside the roll of paper towel and produced a pistol. "Get out with your hands up, bitch! You know what it is!"

"Are you fucking serious?" I was about to laugh. "You don't know who you're fucking with!"

"Bitch, I know who you are. Now give me the jewels." He kept looking back to see if anyone was coming.

"I ain't giving up shit!" I barked. "If you want 'em, you're gonna have to kill me." The look in my eyes dared him to make a move. He apprehensively dwelled on what to do.

"Not a problem. There's a price on your head anyway." He raised the gun to my head, then pulled the trigger. Click. It was jammed. I took the opportunity to jump out of the car, then commenced whooping his ass.

"Who sent you?" I asked after taking his pistol and busting him upside the head with it.

"I ain't no snitch!" He coughed up blood. "Just know your days are numbered!"

"So are yours!" I unjammed the gun, then aimed it directly at his head.

"G, no!" Cartier called from the doorway of the gas station. I looked away for a brief second, which gave the nigga on the ground a chance to get away. "What are you doing?"

"That nigga just tried to kill me!" I screamed, pissed that I let homeboy get away.

"Get in the car. We have to toss the gun." He didn't even bother pumping the gas he had just paid for.

"What about him?" I pointed down the street.

"Fuck him. Don't you hear those sirens?"

Chapter 50

Lovely

Today my heart was heavy with grief. My mind was filled with regret. Had I just stayed my ass home and dealt with my issues, I wouldn't have been in this situation. Because of the suicide note, my family thought I was dead. Accordingly, there was probably no one searching for me.

"Forty-two."

That number was beginning to make me ill. I looked up to see who had spoken them and was shocked to find Santiago standing there.

"Come with me."

Although confused by the request, I stood from the bed right away. He had never spoken to me or even made eye contact the entire time I had been here.

"Where are we going?" I followed him to a part of the house I'd never seen, but I knew it was there. We just weren't allowed to be in that area.

"Rule number one: don't ask any questions," he responded without turning around. I'm not gonna lie. I was terrified. There was something about him that was dark and daring. Perhaps it was the way his thick brows gathered together or the coldness of his eyes. I was positively alerted to the fact that he was the bolder brother compared to Mauricio. He always dressed in suits and never smiled. He kind of reminded me of a young Al Pacino in the movie *Scarface*.

As we entered what appeared to be a study, then walked through to a balcony, I shuddered apprehensively. I didn't know if it was the chill of the night or the possibility of him murdering me.

"Are you cold?" His expression softened.

I was too afraid to respond verbally. Therefore, I nodded. He removed his suit jacket and placed it around my shoulders. "It looks good on you." He traced the outline of the jacket with his index finger. "You're beautiful. Do you know that?"

"Thank you," I mumbled, still trying to figure out where this was going.

"What's your name?" He pulled a cigar from his pocket and lit it. It was a Gurkha His Majesty's Reserve. I recognized the $750 cigar because they were Maine's favorite. Each cigar was infused with Louis XIII cognac. The strong aroma filled my nostrils, reminding me of home.

"My name is Lovely."

"*Encantadora*." He blew smoke out into the night. "That's how you say your name in Spanish. My name is Santiago. Mauricio is my brother." His native tongue was present, but his English was still good. "He did a very bad thing by bringing you here, Lovely." He took another puff, then exhaled. "You see, the house of whores was a place designed for streetwalkers and lowly women. We take them from the gutter and bring them here." Santiago flicked the ashes, reached into his pants pocket, then handed me a piece of paper.

With my hands trembling, I unfolded it to reveal a missing flyer with my picture on it. It was a picture I'd taken on my birthday last year. Tears crept to the sides of my eyes. This confirmed my family was searching for me. They had even put up $10,000 in reward money.

"Lovely, I have to be honest with you." Santiago put out the cigar. "Now that you've seen our faces and know our names as well as what goes on around here, I can't allow you to leave."

"I swear on my life, I won't say one word!" That was the truth, so help me God.

"I'm sorry. I can't. However, I do have a proposal for you." He stepped into my personal space. "I will agree to remove you from the whorehouse if you agree to be my woman."

"Santiago . . ." I paused, shocked to hear what he had just articulated.

"I did my research on you. You're a fugitive from the United States, a drug dealer, and a cold-blooded killer! I like that." He smiled. "With a woman like you by my side, I can take over the world." Picking me up, he sat me atop the cold concrete banister. Gently, he palmed my ass while planting soft kisses all over my body. "Your black skin is so damn sexy."

I didn't know what to say, but I was enjoying the moment. To my astonishment, my body responded well to his. It was the first time I'd had sex willingly in a very long time. I had no idea what I was getting myself into. Right now, it didn't even matter.

Chapter 51

Mina

Ding-dong. Someone pressed the doorbell. I was on a video chat with a potential client looking to purchase a commercial property. "Mr. Wang. I'll get that information right over to you. After you look it over, please contact me if you would like me to make an offer." I smiled.

"Okay, Amina. I'll speak with you sometime tomorrow." He waved goodbye, then clicked off. Mr. Wang owned a large chain of convenience stores across the Midwest. He was looking to bring his business to Michigan. Hilda, my boss, assigned me the project. I didn't want to let her down. Additionally, the commission would be very lucrative.

Ding-dong.

"I'm coming." I scurried to the door to see what the emergency was. To my surprise, Sam's baby's mother, Tynika, was standing there. "Can I help you?"

"We came to see his father." Her arms were folded like she was disappointed to see me.

"Well, his father is out at the moment. What can I do for you?" I folded my arms to mimic her gesture.

"He needs to spend more time with his son." She barged past me and into my house. "Damn, this is how y'all living?"

"Tynika, Solomon can stay, but you need to leave." I pointed toward the door.

"I can't believe this nigga got me staying in the hood and he has your ass laid up in this big ol' house." She ignored my request and continued to walk through my shit.

"Look, that ain't my problem. And again, you need to leave."

"Make me!" She looked at me with a raised eyebrow.

I didn't have time for games, and I wasn't into catfights. Waltzing over to the phone, I was about to dial 911. Lucky for her, Sam walked through the door.

"Tynika, what are you doing here?" He was shocked to see her.

"You haven't seen your son, Sam. What's up with that?"

"What are you talking about? I just picked him up from daycare and brought him to your job the other day." He picked his son up, then hugged him.

"Yeah, but you ain't been by the house to see him." She looked him over seductively. I could feel my temperature rising.

"I can't be kicking it at your crib! I'm about to get married." He pointed to me.

"What she got that I ain't got?" Tynika pouted. "I had your firstborn son. What did she do?"

"Bitch, you got three seconds to bounce!" I was about to snap.

"Tynika, don't come around here with all that shit! When it comes to Solomon, I do what I'm supposed to. But I don't want you!" Sam walked over to the door, holding it open.

"Sam, don't fuck with me, or I will turn you in!"

"I've paid you way more than what you would've gotten in child support court. So, go ahead and turn me in," he dared her.

"Without receipts, you can't prove you paid me a fuckin' dime," she cackled.

"Bitch, you need to leave!" I lunged across the room, but Sam prevented my fist from connecting with her face. I didn't take kindly to threats about my man.

"If you lay one finger on me, I'll send your ass to jail too!"

Chapter 52

Nikki

Finally, my novel, *Memoirs of a Hoodwife: The Autobiography of Nikki Wallace,* had been picked up by a major publishing house. Within days of Anjela shopping it, I had a deal. It hit bookstores nationwide almost immediately. Response from the readers was unreal. One single day after releasing the book, I was on the *New York Times*'s best-seller list. Critics couldn't comprehend why an urban novel was receiving so much attention. What they failed to realize was that my memoir was real, raw, and relatable. In every hood or underprivileged community across America was a hoodwife handling the inner workings of her husband's hustle. It didn't matter if she was the person standing at the stove cooking crack or riding dirty down the highway transporting contraband. A hoodwife knows her position and plays it well. Nevertheless, living the glamorous life comes with incredible sacrifices. It took a bullet and practically losing my life to realize that being a hoodwife didn't exemplify all I thought it would.

"What are you doing, cuz?" Anjela stepped into my bedroom. I was packing for a weekend trip to promote the book in New York as well as reading emails on my phone.

"I'm just packing. What's up?" Not awaiting a response, I continued to read emails.

"I wish I were going with you. Is Mario going?"

"No, he's going to stay behind and watch Junior. Claudia went on a bingo trip. She'll be gone the whole weekend."

"What are you wearing to the signing?" she asked. I didn't respond because I was too engrossed with my email message. "What are you reading? It must be important, because you're certainly ignoring me."

She grabbed my phone, reading the message aloud. "'Dear Nikki, my name is Dee-Dee. I'm twenty-two years old. I'm from Flint, Michigan, but I'm currently locked up at a Virginia State correctional facility for women. I was arrested on my nineteenth birthday for assisting my fiancé with disposing a body. I didn't kill anyone. All I did was drive the car, and for that I'm serving life behind bars.'" Anjela looked at me with widened eyes.

"'Initially, we fled our hometown on some real Bonnie and Clyde type shit. But it didn't take long for the police to find us. My fiancé told me he couldn't do jail and committed suicide on the morning we had agreed to turn ourselves in. Imagine that! Here I was being a ride or die bitch on the run from the law and thinking the shit was cute. Then this mofo takes the easy way out, leaving me alone, scared, and helpless.'" Anjela paused again, and this time her mouth was wide open.

"'Anyway, for three years I sat here angry at him and everybody else. Then I read your book, and it made me think. I'm in this predicament because of me! No one forced me to drive the car. No one forced me to flee the state. Those were all decisions I made as a hoodwife. Girl, if I could've gotten ahold of your book three years ago, my life would undeniably be different. I would've realized ain't no title worth spending the rest of my life in jail for.'" Angela stopped reading, then handed the phone back. Her eyes were moist, and so were mine. "Damn, cuz, that shit was deep!" She sniffed.

"You're telling me!" I had to take a seat on the bed to collect my thoughts.

"All jokes aside, when you said you wanted to write a book, I didn't believe you would actually impact people with your story," she disclosed.

"On a regular basis, I get tons of messages like this."

"Damn, who knew there were so many hoodwives around the world?" she stated.

"There's a secret society of us." I placed the phone down to continue packing, and it rang. It was Maine. "Hello."

"Hey, are you all packed for New York?" He was excited about the invitation I'd extended to him a few days ago.

"Just about." I used as few words as possible. Anjela was all up in my grill.

"Good! I'll see you at the airport in the morning," he reported, then ended the call.

"Who was that?" She reached for the phone, but I was too fast.

"None of your business."

"Mario is going to whip your ass." She shook her head with a giggle.

He walked into the room. "Why is Mario gon' do that?"

"I was showing her my dress for the event tomorrow. Anj said you wouldn't approve." Thinking fast, I removed a black and silver sheer dress with rhinestones from the closet. It wasn't at all what I planned to wear. At the moment, it was the only skimpy dress I could find.

"Hell no, you ain't wearing that without me." He removed the dress from my hand, then placed it back into the closet. "I'll help you find something else."

"Okay, cuz. Have a safe flight, and call me once you land." She collected her items and left the room.

"Here is something more appropriate." Mario stepped out of the closet with a red cocktail dress.

"Thanks, baby, but I had a second option already." I zipped up the luggage and set it on the floor.

"Me and Junior should fly out there for your big event." Mario sat on the bed.

"Huh?" I damn near choked.

"I was thinking about it. I would hate for you to be out there all alone."

"I'm a big girl. I'll be fine." Leaning over, I kissed his lips. "Anyway, it's only for a day."

"I guess you're right." He rubbed my ass.

"So, what will you and Junior get into in my absence?" I sat on top of his lap, straddling him.

"I don't know." He shrugged, lifting me off his lap.

"Where are you going?"

"I have to holla at Gucci." He went into the closet safe and retrieved two guns.

"Mario, please don't do anything stupid."

Chapter 53

Gucci

I was shaken after the run-in at the gas station, but the day had to go on. Cartier thought it was only a bluff from some young nigga trying to flex. I knew better though. Over the years, I'd managed to piss off a lot of people. Therefore, I doubted it was an idle threat. It could've been anybody with a grudge. I intended to discover who it was before they could try me again.

"I shouldn't be long." Cartier got out of the car and ran into the house. It was our last stop for the day, and I was ready to get back home. After about twenty minutes, I stepped from the car to see what the holdup was. That's when I spotted Mario coming up the block. I knew this meant trouble.

The black Hummer was speeding. I didn't have to see his expression behind the tinted windows. I was aware he was beyond pissed. Screech! His tires came to a smoking stop and then he jumped out like a madman. I was standing on the porch with nowhere to run.

"What's up with all that shit you was talking?"

"Mario, you better get away from me with all that shit. Cartier is right inside the house."

"Tell that nigga to come outside. He can get it too!" He beat on his chest like a gorilla. "I'm done fucking with you, bitch! You ain't shit but a dirty, grimy, slime-ass ho!"

"Words don't hurt me, nigga!" I lied. Truthfully, his words stung deeply. I felt like I was being rebuked by my father.

"What the fuck is going on out here?" Cartier stepped onto the porch with a gun.

"Damn, we're pulling pistols now?" Mario reached into his waistband, retrieving two. "I got one for you and one for that bitch!"

"You are talking really reckless for a nigga on my block," Cartier laughed. Mario was outnumbered.

"This might be your block, but I came with my own killas." He pointed toward the street, where four cars of men sat idling.

"Are we gon' hold court in the street or sit down like men?" Cartier asked.

"Dog, I been as much of a man as I'm gon' be. I've been calling Gucci, trying to see my daughter. She on some power trip, and I'm fed up."

"Put the guns away, and let's talk about it." Cartier slid his gun back into the holster.

"My man, we ain't got shit to talk about except when the fuck I'ma see my daughter." Mario didn't drop either of his weapons.

"That can be arranged!" Cartier looked at me.

"Swing by the crib tomorrow. I'll have her ready for you." I smacked my lips.

"I want to see my daughter now!" He folded his arms.

"Obviously, you know where we live. Head on over. I'll call the nanny and tell her to let you in," Cartier avowed.

"What!" Smacking my lips and with my hands on my hips, I shot a disapproving glance his way.

"Cool." Mario turned, then headed back to his vehicle.

"I'm going too!" I headed off the porch.

"Why?" Both Mario and Cartier said in unison.

"I'm not gon' give you the opportunity to kidnap my child."

"You ain't ridin' with me!" Mario shook his head.

"The hell I'm not." Once he unlocked the car, I opened the passenger door and hopped in. "Cartier, I'll grab one of the other cars and be back in an hour."

We were twelve minutes into the ride before Mario broke the silence. "What happened to you?"

"The world!" I retorted.

"That's a shame, G. You were good people. Now you a straight-up bitch!"

"Mario, don't start name-calling, because I have a few names for you."

"Go ahead. Get that shit off your chest. Maybe it'll make you feel better." He turned the music down.

"After everything you put me through, you should be the one talking." I was beyond bothered and trying to keep from socking this man.

"Gucci, I've said I'm sorry dozens of times. If it'll make you feel better, I'll say it once more." He sighed, then glanced at me. "I'm sorry. I never should've led you to believe our relationship could work. We never should've crossed that line. I can see how bad I hurt you, and I wish you knew it was never my intention to do so. I love you, girl." He tried to pat my shoulder, but I moved away.

"You don't love me, so stop lying!" I could feel the tears welling up behind my eye sockets.

"I do love you!" He paused. "I may not love you the same way I love Nikki, but I do love you. You were my ace, my best friend, and my partner. Me and you were like this." He crossed his index and middle finger. "It kills me that we're on different sides now. But I understand and acknowledge it was entirely my fault. I have to take ownership of my shit. That's why I let you slide with taking the money. It's also why I let you live after stealing the deal with Bayani." He turned to face me again. "The only thing I couldn't let you slide with is keeping my daughter away from me. That shit ain't cool!"

"Mario, I knew that was the only way to hurt you. I wasn't gon' keep her from you forever. But I did want you to feel my wrath."

"And you got her calling another man Daddy!" He shook his head.

I wanted to let him in on the secret. Instead, I changed the subject. "How is the organization?" It was a sour subject, but I needed to get the attention off of me.

"Those who chose to remain loyal are good. Them other niggas jumped ship."

"I'm surprised you haven't walked away yet." The tension in the car had diminished slightly.

"I ain't no quitter. I started from the bottom once before, so it's nothing. I got some shit lined up. Once I put my team back on, then I'll leave." He exited the freeway.

"How does Nikki feel about it?"

"We really shouldn't be talking about her." There was a pause before he asked, "How's homeboy treating you?"

"We shouldn't be talking about him either," I giggled. "He treats me good though."

"That's good!" Mario smirked. It was difficult to tell if he was genuinely happy though.

"He's everything I always wanted, so I can't complain."

"I'm glad to hear you're happy, G. All I ask is that you watch your back with him." Mario cut on the blinker and headed down the street leading to my house.

"What's that supposed to mean?"

"I'm just saying something seems shady with him, that's all." Mario pulled up to the gate, which was open. I could've sworn I scolded the guard earlier about this same thing when Claudia came over. "He shows up out of the woodwork, finds you, and starts splurgin' on you like crazy within a meager two months. Did he tell you where his money came from?"

"He has some business dealings in Cali."

"So why did he need your connect if he had his own?" Mario stepped from the vehicle. "If he was doing it on a grand scale in California, why on earth would he ever come back to Detroit? If anything, he would've moved you to his spot."

Mario's words didn't sit well with me. "Whatever! You're just a hater." I unlocked the door.

"Never that!" He shook his head. "I'm just keeping it one hundred."

Chapter 54

Mina

Three days had passed since Tynika dropped Solomon off. She didn't leave him with a diaper bag, so we had to run out to the store. We purchased clothes, diapers, and milk. For the most part he was okay, but today he woke up screaming and wouldn't stop.

"Have you tried calling her again?" I asked Sam while rocking him back and forth.

"Yeah, I've called so much now her fucking phone is going to voicemail." He retrieved the baby from my arms and tried rocking him to give me a break.

"I have a showing today, but I'm going to call one of the other agents to see if she can go on my behalf."

"No, go ahead and go to work. I got this."

"There is no way you can handle two babies, Sam." Shaking my head, I grabbed the phone and proceeded to call the office.

When I came back into the room, Solomon had turned it up a notch. Sam was frustrated, so I took him into my arms, then carried him into Samantha's room. I rummaged through her dresser and retrieved a thermometer. Solomon didn't feel warm, but I had to rule everything out. I took a seat in the rocking chair, placing the stick under his tongue. After a few seconds, the digital reader said 97.1. He didn't have a fever, yet something was undeniably wrong.

I went back into the bedroom and retrieved my cell phone. I googled Solomon's symptoms of a slobbery mouth, not wanting to eat, and consistent crying. The search engine provided websites for teething and constipation. One of the sites recommended Orajel and a frozen teething ring. At present, I didn't have either. In view of that, I hurried into the kitchen to fill a sandwich bag with crushed ice. Once I placed it into his mouth, miraculously the crying stopped. *Thank God!* I took him back upstairs to lie down with his father.

"I'll be back. I'm going to get what he needs for his mouth," I whispered to Sam, who was already dozing off.

On my way to the store, I received a call from Gucci. "What's up, girl? You sound shitty."

"I've been up all morning with a screaming baby," I yawned.

"Samantha?"

"No, bitch, it's Solomon. Sam's son."

"Sam's what?"

"You heard me right."

"When did this shit happen?" She sounded as shocked as I was.

"It's a long story. I'm headed to the store now for some teething stuff. I'll call you later."

"Okay, but I was calling to see if you wanted to go to the movies with me and Satin tonight."

"No, thanks. I'm too damn tired to do anything today. Thanks for the invite though."

"Mina, come on. We haven't gone out in forever," she begged.

"Girl, I have two kids right now. I'm beat! Not all of us have the privilege of hiring a nanny."

"Well, can we at least do breakfast tomorrow? I have a lot to tell you."

"Okay, I'll see you tomorrow. Where do you wanna go?" I pulled into the parking spot and turned the car off.

"Just come to my house. I'll have the chef cook for us while I take you on a tour." She gave me the address, and we ended the call.

Chapter 55

Nikki

The London NYC was a swank hotel smack dab in the middle of New York City. With marble flooring and golden chandeliers, it represented everything elegant. I'd stayed at some upscale places in my lifetime, but this took the cake. The publishing house reserved a standard room for my visit. However, at check-in, Maine decided to upgrade us to the penthouse suite.

The place was absolutely stunning! It measured over 2,500 square feet spread throughout two floors of living space. Both levels were decorated with the poshest furnishings. Even the bathroom was amazing! However, my favorite part of the suite was the 180-degree views of the city from bay windows. I was able to view Central Park, the Hudson River, the George Washington Bridge, as well as the Manhattan skyline.

"It's breathtaking!"

"I thought you would like it." Maine walked up behind me, wrapping his arms around my waist. Casually, I slid from his clutches and went to peer out of one of the windows. "Do I make you nervous?"

"Not really," I lied. Frankly, just the thought of being here with him made me nervous as hell. Although we hadn't done anything since the other night, I felt like I was cheating. I liked Maine but I loved Mario. I felt I at least owed Mario a conversation before kicking things up a notch with Maine.

"So why are you running from me?" He was standing beside me at the window now.

"I'm not running from you. I'm just excited to be here, that's all."

"I'm excited to be here with you, which is why I upgraded our accommodations. I wanted your visit to the Big Apple to be memorable." Slowly, his hand caressed my back.

"Thank you." Relaxing a bit, I permitted my body to give in to his touch.

Bzzzzz.

The cell phone in my pocket broke our embrace. "It's Mario." I placed an index finger to my lip to indicate silence.

"Hey, Rio!" I moved away from Maine, who was still making circles on my back with his finger. "Yeah, I just got here. The place is nice, too. How is my baby?" I didn't miss the look Maine gave me when he thought I was referencing Mario. "Yeah, put him on for me. Hey, Junior, I miss you! You're going to have so much fun with Daddy!" I watched Maine walk away, disappearing into the bedroom. "Oh, your sister is there? That's nice! I love you! I'll see you tomorrow, okay?"

Ending the call, I returned the phone to my pocket. Mario and Gucci must've come to an agreement since Maria was spending the night. Normally, I would've called Claudia for the scoop. However, the sound of bathwater caught my attention.

I walked into the bedroom and gasped. Maine was standing there in his birthday suit. "Boy, what are you doing?" I giggled.

"I saw this large Jacuzzi tub and decided to take a bath. Would you care to join me?"

"Maine, we shouldn't." Guilt was really starting to set in. I believed I was betraying Mario. He was at home with the kids while I was hundreds of miles away in a penthouse with a buck-naked nigga.

"Look, Nikki," he sighed, "I understand you got a man at home, but being here with me has to mean something." Maine stepped up into my face, then bit down on his bottom lip. He slowly unbuttoned my blouse, then released each breast from the cups of my bra. Deliberately, he licked and sucked until they were erect. Next, he removed my belt and unzipped my jeans. Getting on his knees, he pulled my pants to the floor, then began massaging my vagina. A wet spot quickly formed on the pink lace panties. From that point, there was no turning back. That day, we made love until the sun set and then rose in the morning.

The next day it was game time. The PR team had done an excellent job of promoting my event. I half expected no one to show up. Fortunately, the line formed from the door, then spilled down onto the next block. The readers in New York showed me lots of love. I signed books as well as snapped a few pictures. One of the local radio stations, Power 105.1, had even come down to host a live interview. The entire time Maine stayed back and out of the way. He let me do my thing. The independence felt amazing. For the first time in a long time, I was doing something that actually made me proud. No longer was I a mere hoodwife, I was an entrepreneur. I wanted to demonstrate to girls in the ghetto that you didn't need a man to rise above your circumstances. You didn't need to rob for red bottoms. All you had to do was apply your mind.

Chapter 56

Lovely

As I lay in the arms of Santiago, who was snoring loudly and breathing heavily, my thoughts drifted to Maine. I reflected on where he was and how life had been treating him. I wondered if he was thinking of me, or if he even knew I was missing. If life had a rewind button, I would certainly go back and change things. I hated the way I allowed him to leave, and I regretted the things I said. It was too late to make things right. Nevertheless, I truly wished I somehow could just apologize. He needed to know how remorseful I was about the way we ended. Even if he had moved on, I wanted him to understand his love and kindness weren't in vain. He was a good man, and I would forever hold him in my heart.

"*Encantadora,* what's wrong? Why aren't you sleeping?" Santiago yawned.

"Just thinking." I smiled.

"About what?" He sat up, rubbing a hand over his face to wipe sleep from his eyes.

Santiago's facade was rough and ruthless. But within he was a gentle soul. He was my knight in shining armor who rescued me and saved the day. After the night he told me he wanted me for himself, I was removed from the whore roster. He moved me up to his wing of the house and treated me exceptionally well. Mauricio was jealous of our new relationship. Lucy was flat-out panicky. Now that I had free reign of the house, you should've seen her tiptoeing around me.

"Baby, it's my birthday. I want to do something other than be cooped up in here," I whined. Today was not really my birthday, but I was tired of being in the house. Although I was no longer a whore, I remained a prisoner. The only scenery I'd seen since I got here was inside the house and the property outside, which was visible from the back porch. I was no longer permitted to associate with Daphnie. I was bored.

"*Feliz cumpleaños.*" He leaned over, kissing my neck. I could tell by the way he spoke them, the words translated to "happy birthday." "What do you want to do today?"

"I want to go out with you and have some fun. Maybe we can walk on the beach or something," I said, elated that he at least was considering my proposal.

"Do you promise not to do any funny business?" He sat on the side of the bed. He was naked and so was I.

"Santiago, I won't lie. I can't stand being here. On the other hand, I do like being with you." I crawled over to his side of the bed and began kissing his back. I wasn't pretending to like him either. The man was sexy. His body was impeccable. Whenever he spoke Spanish, it sent chills over my body. He was different yet similar to Maine. I felt a connection with him.

"Baby, that feels so good, but I've got an important meeting." He stood from the bed. I watched his tight ass strut across the hardwood floor. His penis swayed like a pendulum from side to side.

"Does that mean I can't get any birthday sex?" I pretended to pout.

"I will give you plenty of that tonight after we come back from our walk on the beach." He smiled.

"Oh, Santiago, thank you so much!" I jumped up on the bed and did a happy dance. Finally, I would be able to leave this house, if only for a little while.

Chapter 57

Gucci

"Girl, where are you?" Satin spoke into my receiver. She and I had a movie date tonight. "I told your ass to be here at eight."

"I'm on the way. I just have to pick up the night deposit from the club." I slid my key into the back-door deadbolt.

"You better hurry the fuck up!" She smacked her lips. "I've been waiting to see this movie all week."

"I'm sorry but duty calls." I closed the door behind me. I was so busy listening to her, it didn't even dawn on me that the alarm hadn't gone off. The club was closed on Monday. Therefore, the alarm should've been set after Raven, the manager, left yesterday evening.

"Whatever, just—"

I never heard what she said because a jolt to my face sent the phone flying across the floor. The blow left me dazed and confused. I stumbled back a few steps, attempting to snap back. Wham! The uppercut sent my body flying across the room just like my phone.

"You think you all that, huh? What about now!" He stumped my rib cage. I heard a crack, then lost my breath shortly thereafter. The assailant punished my body with numerous punches and kicks. I was weak and defenseless.

"What do you want?"

"I want you to pay for what you did!" He kicked me again.

"Please tell me what I did, and I swear I'll make it right!"

"It's too late now! You humiliated me. Now it's time to humiliate you." He unzipped his pants.

"Please don't rape me," I cried.

"Don't nobody want that funk box." He removed his penis from his pants, then pissed all over me. All I could do was lie there and endure it. Thankfully, the ordeal only lasted a couple of minutes, but it felt much longer.

Soon afterward, the masked intruder escaped through the back door, leaving me curled into the fetal position. I'd been beaten to within an inch of my life. My cell phone was too far away for me to reach it. Yelling for help was pointless. I just lay there and prayed someone would find me before it was too late.

Help came in the morning by way of Cartier and Mina. "Oh, my God! She's in here." Mina dropped to the floor, checking me for a pulse.

"Gucci, baby, wake up." Cartier slapped my face. I wanted to tell his ass to stop, but the words wouldn't come. My throat was dry. "Gucci, get up." He shook me until my eyes opened.

"Who did this to you?" Mina asked with tears in her eyes.

"Mario. Please get Mario," I cried. At that moment, he was the only person I wanted to see. He would protect me.

"I'ma kill that nigga!" Cartier roared as he lifted me up. I wanted to tell him I didn't mean that Mario attacked me. But then I would have to explain why I was calling for him.

"I'm going to call Pete and get you home."

"Fuck that. She needs a hospital." Cartier shook his head.

"If there's one thing I know about Gucci, she hates hospitals," Mina declared. "I'm going to call Pete. He'll handle it." Peter Jamison was one of my best clients at the Doll House. As luck would have it, he was also a physician. His specialty was sports medicine. Thus, bruised and broken body parts were in his wheelhouse.

All the way home, tears dangled off the edges of my lashes, but I refused to allow them to fall. The pain was unbearable. I could barely breathe, and the ride was incredibly uncomfortable. My body ached like it never had. I realized bones had been broken.

"Gucci, I swear I'm gonna bust a cap in your boy!" Cartier shouted furiously.

"I don't think it was Mario," Mina said from the back seat.

"Why not? He's been talking big shit about her out in the streets. It's the only thing that makes sense," Cartier rationalized.

"Why would he do that to her after she gave him what he wanted, which was Maria?" She held an ice bag to my face. "Mario would never actually hurt Gucci."

"Mina, for his sake, you better hope you're right! But if the streets don't start talking by tonight, I'm going to handle old boy."

Chapter 58

Mina

I couldn't believe all the shit that had gone down yesterday. Gucci was in pretty bad shape. Pete had stitched her up and given her some painkillers that had her drowsy. I stayed with her last night. Cartier was in no position to care for her. He was too busy trying to plot on Mario. I'd gone downstairs to warm her up some soup the chef had prepared, and I heard him and two goons conversing. They planned to ride by Mario's house and do a drive-by. Although it had nothing to do with me, the shit just didn't sit right in my spirit.

On my way home the next day, I deliberated if I should warn him. Really, it was none of my business, but if there was a war being waged against him, he had the right to know.

Sam met me at the door. "Baby, how is Gucci?"

"She's good. The doctor stitched her up and gave her something for the pain and to help her sleep."

"What happened?" He helped me take my jacket off.

"Somebody jumped her at the Doll House last night. She's pretty banged up."

"Does she know who did it?" He was a little too concerned if you asked me.

"Her jaw is broken, so she really can't talk. However, Cartier seems to think it was Mario."

"He wouldn't do no shit like that." Sam frowned.

"I know. I don't believe it either. But he does look guilty. Especially after all that reckless shit he's been talking."

"He was mad," Sam said, defending his friend.

"I know that, but Cartier was talking about shooting up his house tonight."

"Aww, hell naw!" Sam retrieved the phone from his pocket and proceeded to dial. I really didn't want to be caught up in Gucci and Mario's drama. I decided to let Sam relay the message and went upstairs to check on the children.

As I opened the door, a smile crept over my face. Solomon was sleeping peacefully on the blow-up mattress beside his sister's crib. As of yet, we hadn't purchased a toddler bed for him. However, I planned to get one ASAP. His mother's trifling ass had pulled a disappearing act, but it was all good. I couldn't fathom loving two children I hadn't birthed the way I did. I guessed in a crazy way I viewed them as mine. They'd both been left behind for me to raise.

Tiptoeing over to the white crib with unicorns spinning on the mobile, I leaned over and kissed Samantha. She was knocked out but smiling. My grandmother used to tell me that was what happened when angels talked to babies. Next, I bent down to kiss Solomon's forehead. He was a cute kid.

When I stood back up, Sam was entering the room. "Shit is about to hit the fan! It may be best for you and the kids to get a hotel room for a few days."

Chapter 59

Nikki

On the flight back, I could tell something was up with Maine. "Are you okay?"

"Yeah, I'm good," he stated as he looked out the window.

"It doesn't seem like it."

"I'm cool. Just thinking, that's all."

"Thinking about what?" I didn't think he was going to make me beg for it.

"One of the last times I was on a plane, Lovely was giving birth to my son." He finally looked at me. No tears fell, but the corners of his eyes were moist.

"Have you called to check on her?" He informed me she was a wanted fugitive in the United States, so he took her somewhere she'd be free. Maine didn't give up her exact location, but my guess was Mexico. It was the obvious choice. All fugitives attempted to make it across the border.

"No. I'm done with her." He shook his head. "I left her with family, so I know she's safe. There's no reason to call or go back."

"But you still love her. I thought love was worth fighting for." I should've been applying this lecture to my own situation. My frustration with Mario in the streets was intense, but I did love him. *Maybe I should put my own feelings on the back burner and stick it out.*

"I do love her, Nikki, but I'm not in love with her anymore. It's time to move on and start fresh." Maine placed his hand over my stomach. He must've sensed my apprehension. "Look, ma, I ain't tryin'a marry you or no shit like that. I just like being in your company. You are cool people, and you sexy as fuck. Not to mention the fact that you're carrying my seed. If you and I are meant to be, it'll happen. If we're not, then it won't."

I didn't know what else to say so I chose to say nothing at all. As a substitute, I put on my Beats by Dre headphones, escaping into the music for the duration of the flight.

At the gate, Maine and I parted ways. I promised to text when I got home, and he did the same. After retrieving my suitcase, I headed toward the front door where a gentleman with dreadlocks stood holding a sign with my name on it. I was puzzled because I thought Mario was picking me up himself. After handing the man my luggage, I retrieved my phone to call home. "Damn!" The phone was as dead as a doorknob. I slid onto the back seat and gave the driver my address.

All the way home, I dreaded the conversation Mario and I needed to have. I was nervous. My stomach was in knots. I didn't think he would handle what I had to say very well.

"Miss, I can't go down your street. Should I drop you at the corner or take you somewhere else?" The driver's voice invaded my thoughts.

"Huh?" I didn't comprehend what he was saying. "What do you mean you can't go down the street?"

"The police are everywhere. They have the street blocked off."

At the mention of the police, I opened the car door in full-fledged panic mode. Sure as shit, there were three squad cars and one ambulance blocking the street. To make matters worse, they were right in front of my house. Not caring one bit about my luggage or purse being inside of the Metro Car, I took off down the street.

"What happened?" I asked a neighbor standing on the lawn with two dogs on a leash.

"All I know is I heard rapid gunfire." She shrugged.

"Oh, my God!" I sped up as best I could with my limp.

"Ma'am, you can't cross the tape." An officer held me back.

"My son is in there!" I screamed.

Another cop spoke from the side of my house. "Let her through." As I ran up the porch steps, he stopped me. "Ma'am, that's the wrong house."

"Huh?" I stepped back and looked at the house. It was absolutely my house. What on earth was he talking about? Just as I was about to ask him, I noticed most of the commotion was actually coming from my neighbor's house. She was an older woman in her seventies who lived with her husband. Immediately, I was relieved to know the incident hadn't taken place at my home. Nevertheless, I was still concerned.

I exited the porch, then headed next door. The police officer had already given me permission to enter, so no one tried to stop me. "Mrs. Crooks," I called out. She was a nice lady who I had become very fond of. She was sort of the cool-ass grandmother of the neighborhood.

"I'm in here," she called from the kitchen. When I bent the corner, there was one police officer blocking her back bedroom and two emergency medical technicians attending her. She was sitting on a chair in the kitchen. The burgundy wig was crooked atop her head, and her nightgown was lifted above her waist. A bottle of Hennessy rested in her clutches, and she was smoking a joint. Mrs. Crooks was an old-school gangster for real. You have to have nerve to smoke weed in front of

the cops, medical marijuana card or not. She reminded me a lot of the character Madea, always
saying and doing whatever she wanted because
she knew no one had the balls to stop her.

"What happened? Are you okay?" Blood was
trickling down her leg.

"I'm fine, Nikki. These niggas done fucked
around and shot me in my ass, that's all!" She took
a long, hard pull on her joint, then blew out several small smoke rings.

"You got shot?" It was hard to believe.

"Yeah, girl!" She flicked the funny cigarette into
the ashtray. "I was lying in bed watching the news.
When it went off, I rolled over to go to sleep. A few
minutes later, I heard gunshots and felt a burning
sensation. That's when I knew I'd caught a hot one
in the ass!"

"Oh, wow!" My mouth was wide open. "Do you
need me to call anyone for you?"

"No, sweetie, I'm good. They're gonna stitch me
up. Then I'm going back to bed. I got church in the
morning."

"Actually, Mrs. Crooks, we need to get you to the
hospital," one of the EMTs informed her.

"Ain't nobody got time to be going to the hospital." She shook her head.

"The bullet is still lodged in your flesh. They will
have to take X-rays to see where it is and remove
it."

"Child, please!" She smacked her lips. "It don't even hurt. Just pour some alcohol on it and hand me a Band-Aid.

"Mrs. Crooks, I can't do that," the EMT explained. "Can you please lie down on this stretcher for me? I need to cut your gown."

"The devil is a lie! You ain't cutting nothing I done paid good money for." She shook her head adamantly. I wanted to laugh but held it in. After a few more minutes of debating, Mrs. Crooks eventually surrendered and went to the hospital with her husband. I promised to check on her later, then headed home.

Once inside the house, I could tell no one was home. I went upstairs and plugged up my cell phone. The minute it powered up, it started blowing up.

Chapter 60

Gucci

"'I'ma be fresh as hell if the Feds watching. I'ma
be fresh as hell if the Feds watching.'"

The sound of my phone jolted me from a nap. A
glance at the screen indicated the caller was Mario.
Maybe he'd heard the news and was calling to check
on me, or maybe he was calling to declare his inno-
cence. Either way, I couldn't have answered even if
I wanted to. My face was swollen and hurt like hell.
In view of that, I waited for the call to end, then sent
him a text message: Can't talk. What's up? About
half a second went by before the phone beeped.

Tell that nigga he's a dead man!

I reread the words twice before replying.

What are you talking about?

Don't act like you don't know he tried to shoot up
my fucking house.

By now, my heart was racing. I got ready to
respond, but another message came through.

It was you who said I did it. Just for that, I should
handle you too!

Mario, I had nothing to do with this. I swear!

I slammed the phone down on the nightstand, grabbed a robe, and went to find Cartier.

As I wandered around the palatial estate, my mind raced at a million thoughts per minute. The shit was so disturbing I was beginning to get a headache.

"Ms. Gucci," the housekeeper called from down the hall, "Mr. Cartier is in the sunroom asking for you."

"Okay, thank you," I mumbled with a smile. I continued walking, then stopped. "Which way is the sunroom again?"

It took her a minute to understand what I was asking before she replied. "Keep going down to the end of the hall. It's the first door on the left." She smiled, then returned to complete the task she was performing.

On my way down the spacious hallway, I glanced through the glass at the gardener who was busy spreading mulch. The yard was really coming together. There were dogwood trees, perennials, roses, and lots of greenery. It was absolutely beautiful. I couldn't wait for Maria to start walking so I could take her out there.

Knock, knock. I noticed Cartier sitting on one of the chairs with the phone up to his ear. "Good morning, baby," he said.

"What did you do?" I was furious.

"I handled that shit! That's what I did!"

I wanted to tell this nigga that what he actually did was make a big fucking mess.

Chapter 61

Lovely

About an hour after Santiago left for his meeting, there was a knock on the bedroom door. "Come in." I didn't care who it was. I was just happy to have some company. I was in the bathroom brushing my teeth.

"Lovely, it's me." As Lucy entered, I frowned.

"What can I do for you?" I peeped my head from the bathroom door with my toothbrush in hand. She was standing there dressed in lingerie as usual. I guessed it was her signature look or something.

"Santiago sent me to the store for you." She set two garment bags on the bed along with two shoeboxes.

"I didn't ask for anything from the store." I bent my head toward the sink and rinsed my mouth out. Mexican tap water tasted salty.

"He told me it was your birthday and to buy you something special." I couldn't tell if her smile was sincere, but I let her continue. "Seeing as you two have a date night planned, I thought I'd get you something to wear." She unzipped the first garment bag to reveal a gray strapless Gucci sundress. The second garment bag held the same dress except it was white.

"Lucy, this is very pretty." I favored the white one.

"I didn't know what your taste was. Therefore, I took a shot in the dark," she explained. "I also bought two different pairs of shoes. You look like you wear a size eight. If they don't fit, I'll take them back."

I opened up the first box and saw a beautiful black peep-toe wedge. The second box was a simple gold sandal with rhinestones. Although the wedges were my favorite, I chose the sandals since we were headed to the beach. "Thank you, Lucy. You did a very good job." I smiled, indicating my appreciation.

"I'm glad you like them." She waved goodbye, then closed the door behind her.

It took me two hours to get ready. I hadn't been on a date in so long that I was nervous. Was my hair supposed to be up, or should I let it hang down? Should I put on makeup or just go natural? Finally, I decided to put my hair in a simple bun and apply just a touch of lip gloss. I didn't want to wear the makeup they made us wear when entertaining. It would only serve to remind Santiago of my raunchy past.

At last, Santiago was back, and it was time to go. Hand in hand, we headed out the front door and into a waiting Town Car. Mauricio was shaking his head and yelling at his older brother in Spanish. I recognized by the expression on his face he didn't think our date was a good idea. Santiago paid his brother no mind.

"This means so much to me." I leaned over, planting a kiss on his lips.

"Thank me later." He winked.

The driver took the scenic route toward the beach. Gazing out the window, I marveled at the beautiful sights before me. Mexico was an amazingly beautiful place. It felt as though I were seeing it for the first time. Within twenty minutes, we were approaching familiar territory. Up ahead, I could view the bar I was at when Mauricio drugged me. Farther down was the housing development where Maine's property was located. I tried to keep from getting too excited. I didn't want Santiago to be alarmed.

"There's the beach, baby." He pointed as the driver parked.

"Wow! It's beautiful." I pretended it was new to me.

"Come on, I'll race you to the water." He removed his loafers and got out of the car. I removed my sandals, attempting to catch up with him, but he was too fast.

"You cheated!" I was out of breath. The warm water crept up to our feet, covered our ankles, and then traveled backward.

"Come on. Let's get this walk out of the way before dinner." He grasped my hand as we headed down the beach. We walked for what appeared to be a mile before stopping at a table, two chairs, and a man in a chef's hat. At first, I was confused, but then I understood. Santiago had made reservations for us to have a private dinner on the beach.

"Santiago, this is incredible!" I couldn't stop blushing.

"You deserve it." He pulled my chair out. I took a seat.

Just before the chef could place any food on my plate, something in the distance caught my eye. It was Do It and Shawnie. They were collecting seashells along the beach. The closer they got, the more afraid I became. I didn't know how this was going to play out.

Chapter 62

Mina

Just like I knew it would, a war had been initiated between the two sides. Mario's crew had already retaliated by shooting up a few of Cartier's known hangouts. Luckily, he hadn't been hit. Nonetheless, it was just a matter of time. Had it not been for Maria, Mario would've definitely taken beef to Gucci's front door. He was a killer, but he wasn't crazy. He would never put the life of his daughter in jeopardy. Sam was in and out of the hotel every night. I prayed for his safety but understood he had to do what he had to do.

In order to be with the kids, I'd taken a leave of absence from work. Sam couldn't be with them during this time. I expressed to Hilda that I wanted time to bond with the children. She completely understood. A bitch hated giving up all the potential commissions, but family came first.

Today, I was running a few errands and decided to stop at the nail salon for a pedicure. It didn't matter to me one bit that the kids were with me. Samantha was asleep in the car seat, and Solomon was asleep across my lap. I lay back in the electronic chair, allowing it to massage me until I nearly fell asleep. Unfortunately, my ringing phone not only startled me but interrupted the relaxing time I was enjoying. "Hello."

"Hey, girl." It was Gucci. "Did you hear about what happened?" Her mouth was still messed up. Therefore, it was difficult to understand what she was saying.

"Gucci, Pete said you shouldn't be talking until your jaw heals," I reminded her, pulling back Solomon, who was sliding down my thigh. He was sleeping so well he was drooling all over me.

"Fuck what Pete said!" she snapped. "Cartier done fucked around and got us into some shit!"

"I know. He was wrong for attempting to shoot up Mario's house. What if the baby had been hurt?" People did dumb shit for the sake of retaliation. They never stopped to think of the consequences of their actions. "And you know he shot up the wrong house, don't you?" I wasn't one to gossip, but she needed to know the facts. "He shot up the neighbor's house. That seventy-something lady was asleep in her bed, minding her business!" Sam had given me the scoop.

"What?" she gasped.

"That shit has been all over the news. They were soliciting businesses in or around the community to assist the homeowners with repairing damages to both the exterior and interior that were a result of AK-47 bullets." The nail tech was filing my pinky toe too hard. Moving the phone away from my mouth, I gave her a piece of my mind, then rejoined the conversation with Gucci. "Mario said he would foot the bill for the damages because he felt bad."

"Man, I can't believe . . ." Gucci's sentence was left unheard. From my seat, I witnessed two chicks enter the nail salon. One of them was Tynika.

"Let me call you back." I didn't even wait for a response before I disconnected the call. Sliding the phone into my pocket, I picked up Solomon, and headed over to his mother. "You can't answer the phone, you can't check on your child, but you can come and get your nails done?" I had a straight attitude.

"He was with his father. He's cool." She dismissed the issue like it was nothing. Had the boy not been in my arms, it would've been on.

"What kind of mother are you, Tynika? He's a one-year-old baby! You're okay with just dropping him off and never looking back?"

"Mina, I ain't got time for no lectures." She smacked her lips. "Since he's a problem, give him back, and I'll take him."

"Bitch, the only way you're going to get him back is through court." I held on to Solomon for dear life. "He's not a problem! You're the problem!" I snapped. These young girls killed me, having babies and treating them like a fashion accessory. "Solomon is not a purse or a pair of shoes. You can't just pick him up and put him down when you get ready." I was on the verge of tears only because I'd lost a child, and here she was unappreciative of the blessing God bestowed upon her.

"Fine! Keep him. He was cramping my style anyway."

Chapter 63

Nikki

The night Mrs. Crooks' house was shot up, Mario informed me the hit was meant for him. He explained everything, then instructed me to head over to Anjela's house. She was expecting me. He had already dropped Junior off. Mario had tried to catch me on the phone before I left the airport, but my phone was dead. Needless to say, I packed an overnight bag and got the fuck out of dodge.

"This shit is crazy!" Anjela was in the kitchen reading the newspaper. Junior was asleep on the couch next to me.

"What?"

"The beef Mario is involved in is making head-lines." She rolled the newspaper up and tossed it at me. Sure as shit, on the front page of the paper was an article about the H.O.F. organization. The media reported the incident as a drug war. They also estimated the number of casualties to be somewhere around ten. The article went on to say that the mayor didn't take kindly to thugs destroying his city. He was working with the city police to regain control of the situation and bring the responsible parties to justice. At the bottom of the article, there was a picture of the reporter. He was the same man who approached us when I brought Mario home from the hospital.

I laid the paper down across my stomach. I felt nauseated. This was bound to get much worse, real soon. Not only was Mario's life in jeopardy, but his freedom was, too. "I'm done with this shit!" I stood from the couch. "It's always something."

"What's going on out here?" Carter stepped into the living room, fully dressed and holding a briefcase. He placed the briefcase down on the table to adjust his tie.

"Girl stuff." Anjela kissed him on the cheek, then handed him a titanium cup filled with coffee. She was loyal to me and hadn't ratted Mario out. Furthermore, it was none of his fucking business.

"Well, you ladies have a great day and be safe. Things are getting crazy. Have you two seen the news?" He sipped from the cup. When he wasn't looking, I rolled my eyes. There was more to him than he was letting on.

"Yeah, we've seen the news. Have a good day." Anjela ushered him out the front door. Once he was gone, she looked at me. I was watching her with my lips twisted. "What?"

"Something ain't right with your man. That nigga is up to something."

"Up to what, Nikki?" She blew out an audible breath.

"Let's find out." I walked over to the briefcase, but she stopped me before I could even touch it.

"Don't go in his stuff!"

"Girl, bye!" I shrugged her off, then returned to the metal contraption. It was some high-end, top-of-the-line type shit with a finger scanner.

"Put it down!" She popped my hand and not a moment too soon. The front door opened, and there appeared Carter.

"I would've knocked, but the door was still unlocked," he proclaimed. "I forgot my briefcase."

"Nikki just noticed it. As a matter of fact, we were about to call you." She grabbed the heavy object from the table and handed it to him.

This time, I locked the door after he left. "We need to find out what his deal is."

"I don't need to find out a damn thing. All my shit is on the up-and-up, and yours is too." She took a seat on the love seat.

"But what about Mario?"

"Fuck him!" she snapped. "You need to stop being so concerned with him. One minute you're ready to go, then the next you want to be a ride or die bitch. Damn, pick a side and stay there!"

"You're right!" I nodded. "But I know it's no co-incidence that both Carter and Cartier showed up outta nowhere." After I met Carter, I'd informed Anj that his brother was Gucci's boyfriend. She didn't seem bothered one bit and decided not to tell him that she knew.

"My man said he had no idea what happened to his twin brother, and I believe him. I mean, who would lie about that?"

"Anjela, put that Harvard education to use!" I stomped my foot. "Your boy is a fucking Fed. He could find Santa Claus if he really wanted to."

"Whatever, girl! It's time for me to do some work. I'll be in my office if you need me." She waltzed down the hall.

I was about to call Mario, but my phone buzzed. It was a text from Maine asking if he could see me. After quick consideration, I texted back Anj's address.

Chapter 64

Gucci

"What it does, Eddie. It's time to collect." I stepped into the small barbershop in Highland Park. Other than two other barbers, a lady, and two children, the place was just about empty. One child stood at the vending machine checking the slot for loose change. The other boy was in the chair with his eyes closed tightly.

"Give me two seconds and I got you." He brushed the small child's head to remove the excess hair, then wiped him down with alcohol. After Eddie sprayed the little boy's head with oil sheen, he jumped down and ran over to his mother. The heavyset woman reached into her bra, handing her son a twenty. He ran back over to Eddie, then placed the money in his palm. Eddie slapped him a low five, then told him goodbye.

Once the customers were gone, Eddie removed his smock. "It's in the back. Are you coming?" He gestured for me to follow him, but I didn't move.

"You go ahead. I'll be out front." Although my team was right outside, I didn't know Eddie that well to be in close quarters with him. He had only been on my list of distributors for a month. I had to get to know him before I felt more comfortable.

"No problem. I'll be right back." His raspy voice reminded me of Fred Sanford.

When I stepped outside, the crew was posted up and down the street. I felt like Obama or somebody with all the protection.

"Yo, who the fuck is that?" My little homie Mondo pointed toward the red Nissan speeding down the block. Without delay, all my niggas reached for their guns, which were concealed underneath their shirts. My shit was also clutched tightly. Today was payday, and everybody was on edge. Cartier wanted me to stay home because I wasn't really in a position to be out and about yet. However, I refused! I never missed the opportunity to collect money.

When the car approached us, it slowed down slightly but soon passed us like nothing was up. The minute everyone relaxed, we heard a commotion from inside the shop. Pop! Pop! Boom! The gunfire seemed to come from everywhere. From my vantage point, I watched mirrors break and blood splatter. These niggas had attacked us from the back, using the red car as a distraction.

"Fuck!" I heard Mondo scream. He'd been hit in the arm, but it didn't stop him from shooting back. Pow! Pow! I watched two men wearing bandanas drop. A third bandana-wearing man was carrying the duffle bag I was there to collect. Not one to lose money, I aimed my pistol, letting loose several shots.

"Fuck!" I had missed. The thief ducked and dodged several more bullets until he was able to escape through the back door. I wanted badly to run after him and reclaim my shit. However, the sirens told me to take it as a loss and get the hell away from here.

Chapter 65

Lovely

As Do It and Shawnie approached us, I saw his expression change from casual to shock then betrayal. Shawnie hadn't even paid any attention to me. If she had, the operation would've been blown. I tried not to make eye contact, but it was hard. For weeks, I didn't believe I would see my family again. Now that they were a few yards away from me, I was conflicted. On one hand, I wanted to jump up from the table and run toward them. Then again, I didn't want to piss Santiago off.

"I bought a bottle of Ace of Spades for your special day. It's my understanding that it's a very popular drink among the wealthy in America." He pulled the metallic gold champagne bottle from the black box and sat it on the table. "Almost five hundred dollars for one bottle is ridiculous," he stated as he chuckled.

I wanted to remind him that his cigar hobby wasn't cheap. Instead, I smiled. "Thank you, you didn't have to do that though. I won't be having a drink tonight."

"Why not?" He looked offended. "It's your birthday. I thought you wanted to celebrate."

"I do want to celebrate, but after your brother spiked my drink, I won't ever be drinking again." I looked into his eyes, hoping he would understand I wasn't being ungrateful or disrespectful. I simply had a new respect for being sober.

"Okay fine." He placed the bottle back into the box. Rising from the table, he stated, "I'll go to the car and get your gift instead."

"What gift? You already bought me what I'm wearing."

"Well, you didn't have any clothes." He smiled. "Your real gift is in the car. I'll be right back."

The second his back was turned, Do It told Shawnie to run along and made his way over to me. "What the fuck is up, Lo? I thought you was fucking dead!" He was furious.

"I was drugged and kidnapped by some Mexican brothers, Santiago and Mauricio. They've been holding me hostage in their prostitution house a few miles from here." I tried to cram all of my words together for the sake of time. The car was a little ways away, but Santiago ran fast.

"Let's go!" Do It urged.

"No." I shook my head. "He's with the mafia. If I get up and we're caught, he will kill us. Please leave and get Shawnie out of here."

"What about you?" He looked conflicted. "Fuck the mafia! I can't just leave you here."

"Do It, me and you ain't big enough to battle the mafia, especially not on their turf and in their country. I'll be fine. Just go!"

My brother looked as if he wanted to say something else before he walked away. I sat there with a tear in the corner of my eye. Had I just made a big mistake by letting my only opportunity slip away?

"Who was that, and why was he talking to you?" Santiago took his seat at the table. The tenderness he left with was gone. He sat before me now wearing a scowl and breathing hard.

"Oh." I was trying to think fast. "He explained to me that his daughter was collecting shells, and he asked if he could have the big one by my foot." I bent down and picked up the large seashell shaped like a horn.

"What did you say?"

"I told him no, obviously." I giggled. "This is our first date. I wanted to keep the seashell as a souvenir." I laid it on thick, and he devoured every ounce of it.

Chapter 66

Nikki

Maine stepped into Anjela's condo smelling good and looking even better. The ash gray suit was tailor-made, and his loafers were Italian. The man exuded class every time I saw him. "What's up, sexy?" He winked.

"Nothing much. What's up with you?" I blushed, closing the door.

"I just left a meeting, nothing major." As he scanned the living room, he noticed my son. He walked over and sat beside him. "What's up, little man? I like your cars."

"Thank you." Junior continued to play with his toys.

"I have one of these. Maybe I can show it to you one day." He pointed to a motorcycle. "Would you like that?"

"Yes." Junior smiled. Maine patted his head, then turned back toward me.

"So, what brings you by?" I asked, still standing.

"Two things," he sighed. "The first reason is I wanted to see you. Secondly, I'm leaving for Mexico tonight."

"What?" I frowned. "So, you're going back to her?" I knew things were too good to be true.

"My ex got into some trouble. Her family called me for help." He stood. "Baby, it's not what you think it is." He tried to kiss me, but I moved away out of respect for my son.

"Whatever!"

"Really, it's not like you should care anyway. You're still lying up with your ex-husband, remember?" He backed away from me.

"You came into my world, turned it upside down, and now you're leaving." I couldn't believe how gullible I was.

"Nikki, I swear I'll come back!"

"No, you won't, Maine, so just cut the bullshit! I was just someone you used to kill time with while you and that bitch sorted things out."

"Baby, come here." He pulled me close. "I'm only going to help a friend. But if you give me a reason to stay, I won't get on that plane." The look in his eyes was sincere.

Knock, knock! The sound of the door captured my attention. I pushed away from Maine, then went to check the peephole. Right then and there I wanted to faint. Standing on the other side of the door was Mario.

"Oh, shit!" I grabbed my stomach.

"What's wrong?" Maine came to my aid. I couldn't even speak. He got the hint, then checked the peephole as well.

Knock, knock! This time the knock was harder, louder, and raised the hair on the back of my neck.

"Why aren't you answering the door? It's Mario. Security called, I told him to let him through." Anjela stepped into the living room and stopped dead in her tracks. "Oh, shit!" She looked from Maine to me.

"I'm not about to hide behind this door like a bitch." Maine walked past me, taking the liberty of letting Mario in.

"What took so lo . . ." He stopped midway through the sentence. "Nigga, whatchu doing here?" Gritting his teeth, he sized Maine up.

"You need to be addressing your girl." Maine tossed me under the bus.

"Mario, I've been meaning to talk to you about something. Now is as good a time as any." I motioned for Anj to remove Junior from the room. She looked at me as if she hated to miss the drama.

"You fuckin' this muthafucka?" The ferocious tone in Mario's voice made me jump.

"Mario, calm down please."

"Look, Nikki, I'm gonna give you and him privacy to talk. Call me later. My flight is scheduled to leave at nine." Maine kissed my forehead, then left.

"Were you leaving with him?" Mario looked devastated.

"No!" I shook my head. "Baby, please calm down."

"Nikkita, I expected some foul shit from Gucci, but not you." He spoke as if the wind had been knocked out of him.

"Rio, it's not like that."

"Well, tell me why I come over here to see you, and you're entertaining your baby's daddy!" He took a seat on the sofa.

"Maine came back in town a while ago. Yes, we've spent some time together—"

"You love him?"

"I love you, but I can no longer sit back and watch the streets take you from me. I've begged and I've begged you to leave the game. You keep brushing me off, and I'm tired. I want to grow old with you, but you're making it impossible. As much as I hate to say it, it's me or the streets."

I held my breath. Mario sat silent for a second, then stood. He walked over to me and tongued me down. Without a word, he pulled his lips away from mine, then walked right out Anjela's door.

I was devastated. Once again, he had chosen the streets over me. As I broke down crying, Anjela stepped from the room with Junior by her side. Her mouth was wide open.

"Cuz, are you okay?"

"Just give me a few minutes. I'll be all right." I sniffed.

Buzz. Buzz. My phone slid across the sofa. It was a message from Mario. The streets don't mean shit if I ain't got you. Grab your shit, and let's get our family outta here!

Chapter 67

Mina

I couldn't believe Tynika's trifling ass had the nerve to give her son up without a second thought. Solomon was such a wonderful child. He deserved so much better.

"Hello," Sam said into the phone. He was probably in a bad area, because there was a little static in the background.

"You won't believe this shit." I was sitting in the car at the parking lot of the nail salon. Resisting the urge to sucker punch that bitch wasn't easy. Therefore, I packed up the kids and left without finishing my pedicure.

"What happened?"

"I finally ran into your baby's mother. I checked her about being at the nail salon but not having time to check on her son."

"What did she say?" Sam was all ears.

"Basically, she told me she didn't want him." I paused. "Her exact words were, 'He's cramping my style anyway.'"

"What type of monkey shit is that!" Sam was upset.

"I know." I shook my head as if he could see me. "I was outdone!"

"I'm about to come over there and talk with that ho. What's the address?"

"Baby, there is no need to come up here. If she doesn't want him, it's her loss and our gain." I looked through the rearview. Both of the kids were silent but awake. "First thing next Monday morning, you need to contact the court for full custody." Legally, I wanted the shit on record. "Tynika should not have the opportunity or the right to simply have a change of heart, then decide she wants to be a mother again when it's convenient for her to do so."

"Mina, we just brought home one child. Do you really think we can handle two?"

"Sam, that's not even a question! He didn't ask to be brought into this world! It's not his fault his mammy is a deadbeat!"

"You're right."

"Between the two of us, these children will be loved, spoiled, and raised the right way." I started the car.

"See, that's why I love you. I've never had someone like you in my life. You always see the positive in every situation, and you prove daily how down you are for a nigga."

"One day, I'm going to be your wife, and it's a role I plan to take seriously. I love you, and I'll always be here no matter what obstacles come our way."

"Mina, the Bible says a man who finds a wife finds a good thing." He paused. "I don't want to let my good thing get away from me."

"I'm not going anywhere." I pulled out into traffic and proceeded back to the hotel.

"Just to be sure, let's get married next week."

His words brought tears to my eyes.

Chapter 68

Gucci

After the shooting at the barbershop, Cartier put me on house arrest. Within twenty-four hours I was tired of sitting in the house. I decided to take Maria out for ice cream. On the way out, I grabbed the mail and flipped through the stack. There were a bunch of bills with my name on them.

"What the hell?" I opened the first one. It was from the mortgage company. The second was from the car company, and the third one was a credit card statement. Everything Cartier had purchased for me was in my name. Perplexed, I pulled out my cell phone and called him as soon as I got into the car. His voicemail came on. How in the hell did he get my social security number, and why would he put shit he purchased with drug money in my name?

About ten minutes later, I pulled into a parking space near the door of Cold Stone Creamery and called Cartier again. Still no answer. Disconcerted, I needed an explanation. I slammed the phone down on the passenger seat, then got out to retrieve Maria. That's when I noticed Cartier and that chick Anjela leaving the Chinese restaurant next door. They were holding hands and laughing like old friends.

I slammed my car door, then ran over to the happy couple. "What the fuck is this, nigga? Are you two-timing me with her?"

"I beg your pardon." Anjela placed a hand to her chest. "My man wouldn't touch your ghetto ass with a ten-foot pole."

"Bitch! That's not your man. He's my man! You better tell her, Cartier."

"His name is Carter." She pointed to the dude with the suit and tie on.

"Look, there's obviously some big misunderstanding here." He smiled. It was then that I realized that, although he looked like Cartier, he was slightly taller and a little more toned. "My name is Carter Jones." He extended his hand.

"My man is a federal agent, not some hoodlum like yours." Anjela's revelation was startling.

"Well, uh . . ." Carter pulled nervously on his tie.

"Tell her, baby," Anjela prodded him, but the man said nothing. "His twin brother is your man. They were separated as kids."

Something didn't feel right. I began to back away. Running to the car, I hopped in and put that bitch in gear. Fear enveloped my heart as I dialed Cartier one last time.

"Hello."

"You bastard! You set me up!"

"What?" He played dumb.

"Your brother is a Fed! The jig is up." While driving back home, I began to put two and two together. When Cartier turned himself in all those years ago, he was facing life. When I asked how he got out so early, he said it was because some evidence came up missing. In reality, Cartier had been released from prison with the help of his brother, but not without a price. The H.O.F. organization had been on the FBI's radar for years. Fortunately, they could never build a case against us. I'd been in the streets long enough to know that Cartier cut a deal with Carter to set us up in exchange for freedom. "You put all those expensive items in my name to build a case against me, you bastard."

"That's the game, Gucci." He didn't even sound remorseful. "I told you loyalty ain't shit but a seven-letter word."

"Rot in hell, you bastard!" I hung up the phone and pulled onto my street.

By now, the place was swarming with Feds. Carter realized the case was blown and had probably called every cop in the area to search for me. I reversed down the block like a bat out of hell. There was no way I would turn myself in.

I looked in the back seat at Maria and broke down crying. I didn't know what to do or where to go. I had less than $1,000 on my person. For the first time in a long time, I was scared.

Chapter 69

Nikki

I left Anjela's condo that day with Junior on one hip and my overnight bag on the other. Mario promised he was done with the game. On the ride home, I tried to apologize for how I had been sneaking around with Maine. Mario said it was done and we would never speak of it again. I was elated he had forgiven me. I guess there's something to the saying "Love conquers all."

Anyway, the minute we hit the front door, he grabbed a hat and tossed destination ideas into it. Whichever one we picked was where we were headed. Among the list were Rio de Janeiro, Tahiti, and Paris. Any of those would've been swell, but Paris was what Junior picked out. That night, I booked our first-class tickets and could barely contain myself. Just the thought of finally leaving Detroit had me antsy. I couldn't wait to start life anew. Little did I know what lay in store.

They say joy comes in the morning. However, on this morning, I was awakened by Mrs. Crooks' dog. He was barking up a storm. Therefore, I was unable to go back to sleep. Getting up from bed, I walked across the hall toward the fourth bedroom. If he kept it up, that dog was going to wake up the neighborhood. I lifted the blind to see what was going on. That was when I spotted the task-force van parked in the alley. This wasn't a good sign. Fearing the worst, I ran back across the hall and tried to wake Rio.

"Nik, let me sleep. The flight isn't until noon," he moaned.

"Get up. The police are downstairs about to kick the door in." I was petrified, and Mario hadn't heard anything I said. "Get up!" I slapped his face, jolting him awake.

"What the fuck you hit me for?"

"The police are about to kick the door in." I spoke calmly, although I was anything but calm.

"What?" He was now out of bed and on his feet.

"Go look out the back window. The van is parked in the alley." I pointed.

"Ain't no time for that. Just go in the room with Junior." He headed down the stairs.

"Where are you going?" I whispered.

"Ain't no sense in letting them tear the door off the hinges. I'ma open it and wait for them on the porch."

"Rio, I'm scared!" No matter how many times this had happened over the years, I was never prepared for it.

"No need to be scared. You know how this shit is going to play out. Just don't let my son see them take me away in handcuffs." He headed down the stairs and opened the front door. I knew my instructions were to go in the room with Junior. On the contrary, I had to make sure Mario was going to be okay.

Inching my way down the steps, I could hear walkie-talkies on the side of the house. "The suspect is on the front porch. I repeat, the suspect is on the front porch."

I made my way toward the front door just in time to see Mario lie down with both hands behind his back. He had on a pair of Nike basketball shorts and a wife beater.

"Can I at least give him a shirt and some shoes?" I ran outside as they read him his rights.

"Mrs. Wallace, my name is Daniel Townsend. I'm with the Federal Bureau of Investigation. You're under arrest with your husband under the RICO Act." Forcefully, he grabbed me and placed cuffs on my wrists.

"What?" I couldn't believe this shit.

"We can talk down at the station." He pulled me off the porch in my nightgown toward one of the waiting squad cars.

"Don't say nothing, Nik!" Mario yelled before getting into the back of a police vehicle.

"Officer, my son is sleeping in the house. Can I please call his grandmother?" My heart pounded.

I had watched Mario be arrested numerous times. However, never had I gone to jail with him.

"What's the number?" He looked annoyed. I gave him Ms. Claudia's number, praying like hell she answered.

"Hello." She was sleeping.

"Ms. C, it's me. Mario and I are being arrested. Please come over to the house and get Junior now."

"Oh, no, Nikki!" She was obviously upset. "Baby, I'm on my way right now!"

"Call Mario's attorney," I attempted to say before the officer ended the call.

"Let's go." He escorted me in the direction of the car. My heart stopped when I heard my son screaming from the porch.

"Mommy!" he cried hysterically. A female officer in a blue coat with yellow letters tried to console him.

"Junior, Granny is on the way. Mommy will be right back, I promise." My voice was strong and believable. Conversely, I felt helpless. By now, all of my neighbors were in the windows or on their porches, looking and whispering. The whole scene was like something out of a movie.

Once downtown at the FBI office, I was placed in a small conference room and given a blanket. Then I was left alone for over an hour. My nerves were all over the place. I was jittery. I hadn't done anything to be arrested. Sometimes we were simply guilty by association.

A blonde female with blue eyes stepped into the room. "Mrs. Wallace, my name is Perri Kensington." I wasn't fooled one bit by the fake smile. This was part of the game.

"I want a lawyer." There was no need in going any further. Once I dropped the L word, there was nothing she could do.

"I can call one for you, but that won't be necessary." She sat down across from me at the table. "Mrs. Wallace, I want to apologize on behalf of the FBI for arresting you in error. We're actually looking for Gucci Wallace, Mario's current wife."

"Am I free to go then?"

"Yes, you are. I've arranged for an agent to take you home. Do you mind answering a few questions first?"

"I can't help you." I stood from the seat and headed for the door.

"Do you know where we can find Gucci?"

She was only asking to see if the ex-wife would turn on the current wife. Her case files probably documented our disdain for one another. Even so, she was barking up the wrong tree. I was no snitch. No matter how much I disliked Gucci, I wasn't going to make finding her easy.

Chapter 70

Lovely

The remainder of my date with Santiago went smoothly that evening. He was a perfect gentleman. The beachside dinner was awesome. We even went dancing afterward. I learned a lot about him, such as how he and Mauricio ended up in the prostitution business.

As we were heading to the car after dancing, he said, "We were born and raised in Mexico City, Mexico. Our family consisted of my mother, my brother, my grandmother, and me. We were poor, very poor." The blank stare into the distance revealed he was replaying childhood memories in his mind. "When I was about fourteen, I began working for Conseco Alverez, a known kingpin with the cartel. As a kid, my duties were never anything serious, but I was with him all the time. I learned that he liked women, a variety of women." He smirked.

"Mr. Alverez didn't care who they were or where they came from. He would rent rooms for hours just to have sex with everyone except his wife. As time went on, I noticed this was the way most of the cartel men operated. The only downside was some of the females became attached or started running their mouths around town. No matter how much a man like Mr. Alverez cheated on his wife, he loved her. Therefore, he would kill someone dead before they had the chance to inform her of his infidelities. Needless to say, a lot of bodies turned up for that reason. It was a mess. But I had a solution."

He looked at me. "I decided to save enough money to buy a house, my first house, and turn it into a place the cartel could come and relax. They wouldn't have to worry about their secrets and fetishes being exposed because my girls never left the premises. I left it up to my brother to acquire the women. Before we knew it, business was thriving."

"Wow! That's something to be proud of." I was being sarcastic.

"Come on, it's no different from selling drugs and murdering people." He used the terms to strike a chord that I wasn't perfect. There were skeletons in my closet as well.

"I did what I had to do for my family."

"And I did what I had to do for mine!" His voice elevated. "Look, let's not ruin your birthday with this nonsense." He held the car door open, and then we headed home. Overall, the date was nice, and I did have fun. Santiago was different but I liked him. I honestly wished we had met under different circumstances.

For days following the date, my thoughts often traveled to seeing Do It. I partly expected him to bust down the doors at any moment. If I knew him, he had more than likely called Maine and tried to devise a plan. In all probability, Maine didn't care one bit what happened to me. Without Maine, Do It didn't stand a chance.

"What are you doing down here?" Lucy asked when I approached the kitchen. She was standing at the sink, looking out the window.

"I came to get something to drink. Is that okay?" Opening the refrigerator, I glanced over my choices of milk, water, orange or apple juice, and pop.

"There is a party in the front. You need to get whatever you're looking for and make your way upstairs." Her eyes never left the window.

Casually, I grabbed some orange juice, then walked over to see what she was looking at. My stomach turned when I saw a girl being held down and branded with the electric brander. She was fighting and screaming just as I had. I turned away from the window. The image had me sick to my stomach.

I grabbed a cup, poured my drink, and headed back up to my room. However, rather than taking the servants' hallway, I chose to pass the parlor where the guests were and go up the main staircase. I could hear soft music and laughter. Easing the parlor door open slightly, I sneaked a peek. The smell of smoke filled my nostrils.

Mauricio approached me. "What are you doing?"

"I was looking for Santiago," I lied.

"He's busy." Mauricio attempted to close the door in my face, but I wasn't having it. I forced the door back open, scanning the room for Santiago. For some reason, thoughts of him and a whore crept into my head. I was slightly jealous.

"*Encantadora,* what's wrong?"

Santiago was not in the parlor. He was coming from the study with a black man. The familiar face hadn't changed one bit. In reality, having not seen it in so long actually made it look better.

"I had something to tell you, but it can wait." I nervously dropped my glass.

"Let me get that for you, miss." The familiar face kneeled down to retrieve my glass. He was wearing a Tom Ford exclusive and smoking a Gurkha His Majesty's Reserve.

"Honey, this is Maine. Maine, this is *Encantadora,* my future wife," Santiago said.

I could've died right there on the spot. I could tell Maine was bothered by my new title but didn't let on.

"Doesn't that mean 'Lovely' in English?" he asked Santiago, never removing his eyes from me.

"Actually, it does." I extended my hand, and he kissed it. Santiago frowned.

"We're in the middle of doing business. Go back to the room. I'll send for you later," he interjected.

"Actually, I think I found what I'm looking for." Maine turned to Santiago. "How much for her?"

Santiago was taken aback. "She's not for sale, my friend." He laughed nervously. "Come into the parlor. I'll show you my lineup."

"I want her." Maine hit him with a stone-cold stare. "How much?"

"I said she's not for sale. You can choose someone else, or you can be escorted out." Santiago opened the parlor door, beckoning for two security guards.

"I don't like my options," Maine retorted. "How about I take the girl and let you live?"

"Let me live? Are you insane? There's only one of you and fifteen of us, not to mention the members of the cartel." Santiago was beet red in the face.

"Suit yourself."

Maine pulled a silver gun attached to a silencer from the waist of his pants, then sent four bullets into Santiago's body. I watched in slow motion as his body flew backward into the security guards. I had no idea how Maine planned to get us out of this, but I prayed like hell it worked.

Chapter 71

Gucci

I'd been on the run for nearly two days. Maria and I had only managed to get to Lima, Ohio. It was only two hours away from Michigan, but it was the best I could do. While we were on the road, two of my tires blew, and I had to get towed to the nearest town. The local mechanic was working on it and said it would be done today. I still didn't have a destination in mind. Even so, we had to keep it moving. With the tire situation, my funds had taken a hit. But there was still $800 left.

I sat up on the bed in the motel and rubbed my head. The severity of my situation was weighing heavily on my mind. Buzz. Buzz. The phone vibrated. I checked the screen to see a private number. I knew it was the Feds trying to track my whereabouts, so I didn't answer. Then the motel phone rang. The sound frightened me so badly that I held on to my heart to keep it from leaping from my chest. Initially, I wasn't going to answer it.

Then I remembered I told the mechanic I was staying here and to notify me when the car was ready.

"Hello."

"Gucci." The voice belonged to Bayani. I cringed. "I told you once that your life depends on your word." He paused. "Now that we know your word doesn't mean shit, I guess your life doesn't either."

"Bayani, I had no idea what Cartier was up to." Until now, I had completely forgotten about the Filipino Mafia.

"That's not my problem. You vouched for him, and now you owe me." His voice was cold.

"I'm on the run myself. I don't have anything to give you at the moment." I stood and instinctively walked over to the blinds. There were several cars in the parking lot of the cheap motel. However, the only one that appeared to be out of place was the white Lexus. I could barely see the driver behind the tinted windows. Eerily, his lips moved in conjunction to the words Bayani was speaking into the phone. It had to be him.

"You will pay me in blood!"

He hung up. My stomach rumbled. With him in the parking lot, at any moment he could've kicked in the door. It was time to get out of here. Foremost, I had to think about my daughter. Thinking fast, I dialed the last person on earth I expected assistance from.

"Hello."

"Nikki, it's Gucci. Don't hang up!" I paused. "I'm in trouble. I need your help."

"Are you okay? Where is Maria?" To my surprise she was concerned.

"We're okay but not for long." I walked over to the window and peeked through the blinds again. The Lexus was still there. "I'm at a place called the Wolfe Motel in Lima, Ohio. It's right off I-75."

"That's two hours away from here, right?"

"Yeah, it is. I need you to come and get Maria for me. I can't keep going strong with her on my hip." I looked at my baby girl, blinking away the tears. It was going to kill me to part ways with her, but it was in her best interest. As much as I hated to admit it, Nikki was my saving grace.

"Okay, I'm leaving as soon as I get Junior dressed." I could hear dresser drawers slamming.

"You might want to leave him with his father." Bringing him wasn't a good idea.

"Mario is in jail, Gucci." Her words hit me all at once, but I dared not ask questions on the phone. "I'll call you when I get there."

Chapter 72

Mina

I couldn't believe it was my wedding day and no one was there to bear witness except Sam's children, the pastor, and his assistant. Gucci had gone AWOL, and I had no other family. I looked at myself in the dresser mirror and smiled. For the first time in a long time, I was genuinely happy. Everything we'd been through lately had somehow made our relationship stronger.

Tap, tap. Sam opened the bedroom door. I ran into the closet to hide. "It's bad luck to see the bride before the wedding, fool."

"I need to talk to you." His voice concerned me.

"What is it?" I stepped from behind the closet door to see my man standing there in a button-down shirt and a pair of jeans. "Where are the kids?"

"The kids are in their rooms." He took a seat on the bed, patting the spot beside him.

"What is it, Sam? You're scaring me!"

"Amina, I love you more than life. You've proven your love for me through and through. Many women would've given up on me after all I put you through. But you didn't, and that means the world to me. You love my children, and they love you. In my wildest imagination, never could I have dreamed I'd be blessed with such a wonderful woman. To be honest, I don't deserve you."

"What are talking about?" I lifted his chin, which was buried in his chest.

"We vowed to have no more secrets, but I've been keeping something from you."

"It better not be another child!" I stood.

"No. It's nothing like that." He stood with me.

"Well, spit it out." I couldn't believe this boy and all his fucking secrets.

"This secret has been burning a hole in my heart, and I wanted you to know before you said, 'I do.'"

"Depending on what it is, I may not be saying, 'I do.'" I backed away, folding my arms.

"Me and Gucci messed around a few times, but it was nothing."

"What do you mean it was nothing?" I screamed. He grabbed my arms to prevent me from swinging at him. "You fucked my friend?" Tears gathered in the corners of my eyes.

"Mina baby, I'm sorry. I was going through some shit."

"That's no excuse, Sam!" I pushed him off of me. "I was calling her for relationship advice, and you guys were screwing! Here I am standing by your side like a real bitch, and you're sneaking around with my friend?" Wiping my face, I ruined my makeup. "I was thinking I wasn't good enough for you when, in fact, I'm too damn good for your wack ass!" I took my ring off, then hurled it across the room. "Fuck you, Sam! I'm done."

Chapter 73

Nikki

It was a little after ten when I exited the freeway and called Gucci's motel room. She told me to pull around back and meet her at the back door of the shabby motel. When I pulled up, I saw her standing there with Maria in a car seat. I left the car idling while I ran inside.

"Thank you so much for coming." She hugged me, then handed the baby over.

"What are you going to do?" I felt bad for her. She looked as if she hadn't slept a wink in days. Her clothes were wrinkled, and her hair was a mess.

"I'm going to keep running until they find me, I guess." She shrugged. "Was there a white Lexus parked out front?"

"Yes." I did recall passing the vehicle on my way through the parking lot.

"Shit!"

"Why? Who is that?"

"Cartier and I did a deal with him a while back. He found out that Cartier was a rat. Now he's gunning for me because I vouched for him." She shook her head.

"That shit has been all over the news. They've arrested twelve other people including Mario on drug trafficking for the H.O.F. organization. You and he are also being charged under the RICO Act." I'd come to learn that RICO stood for Racketeer Influenced and Corrupt Organizations. It was a United States federal law that allowed for harsher punishment and even civil charges resulting from organized crime. Under RICO, whoever ordered criminal acts could be tried alongside those who executed them. "Gucci, they have pictures, receipts, and even you on tape during a meeting with the Filipino." I wanted her to know what she was dealing with. "It's not looking too good."

"Nikki, I didn't mean to get Mario in trouble," she sighed. "Cartier set me up. He had me split up H.O.F., purchased that expensive shit in my name, and put my life on the line with the Filipino Mafia."

"Gucci, your best bet might be to turn yourself in." At least being inside under police protection was safer than being out here all alone.

"Hell no! The mafia has connections everywhere. The minute I'm in custody, I'll be a sitting duck waiting for Bayani's people to kill me. My odds are better if I stay on the run."

"Suit yourself." I couldn't force her to do anything. She was a grown-ass woman who had gotten herself into this mess. I was sure she would figure out how to get out of it. "It's about to rain, so we better get out of here."

"Bye, Maria. I love you!" Gucci bent down to kiss her daughter.

My heart ached for her. As a mother, I could only imagine what she was experiencing. I waved goodbye to Gucci, who stood in the doorway. After strapping Maria in, I closed the door and got into the driver's seat. I wanted to drive away, but I couldn't leave her alone. I exited the car again, then ran back up to the building.

"I can't leave you here. Come on!" By now the rain was coming down hard.

"I can't put you in danger." She shook her head.

"Just get in the trunk. I'll drop you off at the Greyhound station." My heart would be more at peace knowing I got her to safety.

"Okay," she said after a few moments of contemplation. She ran out into the rain, and I lifted the trunk. She got in quickly, and then I closed the trunk behind her. Once again, I got into the driver's seat, and I pulled away from the motel. The white Lexus was still parked out front as I drove by.

The Greyhound station was a mere two miles away. I surveyed the area before letting her out.

"Did anyone follow you?"

"No, it's all good." I reached into my purse, then handed her two large stacks of money. When she called earlier, I hit the closet safe and withdrew it just in case. It was a total of $5,000. Although the Feds had raided my house, they couldn't take any of my property because Mario and I were legally divorced. His name wasn't on the deed. Furthermore, I had legit money from my book sales. "Take this." I shoved it into her hand.

"Thank you, Nikki!" She looked as if she wanted to cry.

"Now go ahead and get a ticket on the next thing smoking. When you reach a destination, grab a minute phone and keep in touch."

"Thank you again!" She made a mad dash toward the bus station.

I didn't know what was going to become of the situation, but my prayers were with her. I hopped into the driver's seat, then put the car in gear. It was time to get back home.

Being out in the rain in the middle of nowhere had a bitch on edge. To calm my nerves, I turned on Tamar Braxton's CD. Hearing her talk about "Love and War" gave me a lot to ponder. *Should I purchase another flight ticket, or should I stay in Michigan for Rio?* He needed me now more than ever. Either way, I was done being a hoodwife and could actually use the time away from him to go my separate way. So many thoughts flooded my mind as I merged onto the highway.

Beep! Beep! The horn on the car behind me was distracting. The driver must've been in a hurry. I sped up to allow him to pass. Beep! Beep! Now they were riding my bumper with the high beams on. I couldn't see shit. Therefore, I merged into the passing lane in an attempt to shake him. That was when I realized it was the same white Lexus from the motel.

"Oh, shit!" I mumbled. I didn't want to alarm the kids, but I was scared. Speeding down the highway, I grabbed my phone, then dialed 911.

"What's the emergency?" the operator asked.

"I'm being followed by an aggressive driver on I-75 North!" I switched back to the middle lane, and the white car did the same. This time he bumped the back of my SUV. "Please help me. I have two children in the car, and I'm pregnant!"

"What's your exact location on I-75 North, ma'am? Can you see a mile marker?"

I was driving too fast to see any of that. "Please, ma'am! Just use the GPS tracker on my cell phone!" I screamed. By now the children were both crying.

Pop! A shot was fired into my back tire, causing my vehicle to sway from side to side. The shot might've slowed me down, but I was not stopping. Boom! Another shot entered the window, shattering the glass.

"Please get us help now!" My car was now rolling on the rim, which meant it was about to stop. Sparks were flying everywhere. I maneuvered the whip as best I could, except one final shot to the other back tire sent us spiraling out of control. Then the driver of the other vehicle slammed his car into mine.

I went flying into a ditch at almost ninety miles per hour. Crash! The SUV only stopped when it connected with a tree. My body was hurled through the windshield and catapulted on the hood among shards of glass.

I couldn't move my body, but at least I wasn't dead yet. I could hear three things distinctively. The first was the sound of footsteps coming in my direction. The second were cries of the kids, who sounded far away, as if they had been tossed from the truck also. The last thing I heard was the 911 operator. I still had the phone in my hand.

"Ma'am, help is on the way!"

Chapter 74

Gucci

As I sat inside the funky Greyhound station, my mind raced nonstop. I was in a fucked-up situation indeed. On one hand, I wanted to return home and face the wrath awaiting me. On the other hand, I was too much of a thoroughbred to just lie down and die. Both the Feds and the Filipino Mafia could kiss my fat ass! These niggas would have to work hard to catch me, because I wasn't going out like no bitch!

"Excuse me." Some overweight white woman tapped my shoulder.

"What?" I barked. The bitch was interrupting my thoughts.

"Are you going to use the phone or are you going to just stand there? I need to call my ride." The woman shifted her weight from the right to the left side. There was only one pay phone in the entire place, and I was blocking it. Truthfully, I hadn't done that on purpose. I just couldn't think of anyone to call.

"Make it quick," I snapped before stepping aside and allowing her to make the call. She looked as if she wanted to say something else, but the look on my face told her not to. I was the wrong bitch to fuck with on a day like today.

Taking a seat on a nearby vacant chair, I placed my head into the palms of my hands and closed my eyes. "Think, Gucci, think." As popular as I was, I couldn't believe I had no one to call. My friends were all in Detroit, and most of my family was too. I did have some people in Alabama, but we hadn't spoken in so long I doubted they would even recognize me.

"I'm done!" the white woman said before walking away.

I sat there a moment longer before acknowledging that my only option was to call down South. Approaching the phone, I dropped some change into the machine and dialed the number I knew by heart. My aunt Lucy and cousin Rhythm had had the same phone number since I was in the sixth grade. Aunt Lucy was my mother's sister. My dad let me visit Alabama to see them every summer when I was kid. Rhythm and I used to be besties. We talked almost every day for years until I turned 16. That's when I hit those streets and grew up fast. By then Rhythm and I were living in totally different worlds and had nothing in common.

"Hello."

"Hey, Rhythm. It's Gucci." Butterflies fluttered in my stomach.

"Gucci?" She sounded shocked. "My cousin?"

"Yes, girl." I laughed lightly while looking over my shoulder.

"Long time no hear from, stranger."

"I know. I know." I sighed. "Look, cuz, I was thinking about coming your way for a little vacation if that's okay."

"When?"

"Tonight." Once again, I looked over my shoulder.

"Gucci, are you in trouble?" The tone of her voice changed.

I could've lied, but I never wanted to put my family in danger. She needed to know what I was up against before allowing me into her home. "The short answer is yes, I am in trouble, but I have nowhere to go, Rhythm. I need to come there just for a few days. I swear I won't be there more than a week."

Rhythm sighed. "I'll tell Mama you're coming."

"Thank you, cuz. I'm at the Greyhound station. I'll call you at the last stop before Birmingham, okay?"

"Okay, Gucci. Please be safe. I love you." Rhythm closed the call, leaving me in awe by the way she said "I love you" so effortlessly, although she hadn't spoken to me in forever. Her words touched my heart in a big way. All my life I'd encountered snakes and rats. It was good to feel genuine love from someone.

After placing the phone on the cradle, I headed to the cashier and purchased a one-way ticket. Thankfully, Nikki left me with some cash. "That'll be $125.98."

"How long before the next bus leaves?" I asked while handing her two Franklins.

"You've got about twenty minutes."

"Cool." I grabbed my change and took another seat.

The place was semi-crowded with people from all walks of life. An Amish couple sat nearby with four children and a baby. She was a chubby baby with rosy cheeks. Her head was covered with a black bonnet, but I could tell her hair was red by the edges. Looking at the little girl made me miss my daughter tremendously. She was my world, my everything. I hated to leave her, but I knew it was best. Besides, I knew the safest place for Maria to be was with Nikki. For once I was thankful that Nikki was removed from this hood shit. She didn't have the occupational hazards of Mario and me. Therefore, I didn't have to worry about my daughter being in harm's way.

"The bus to Birmingham, Alabama, will be arriving in ten minutes." The announcement came over the loudspeaker. People started gathering their bags and belongings. I had nothing except my purse, so I used the time to use the bathroom.

Normally public bathrooms weren't my thing, but the ride was almost nineteen hours long.

As soon I entered the women's restroom, a stench like nothing I'd ever smelled filled the air. "Goddamn!" I choked. It smelled like old salmon and shit on a stick. Naturally my first reaction was to turn and leave but I had to relieve myself. While holding my nose and mouth closed, I flew into the stall and did my business. I could see two pairs of feet in the other stall. One belonged to the nostril offender and the other to her small son. His Spider-Man gym shoes paced the small space, and I couldn't help but feel bad for the kid. Lord knew the smell was strong enough already. I could only imagine what it was like up close and personal.

"You stank, Mommy." His little voice emerged from the stall. I couldn't help but laugh before flushing and heading to the sink.

"Hush up, Vonte," she scolded him.

"Girl, you know that baby telling the truth!" I had to say something. It was a damn shame the way her insides smelled. "You better make a fuckin' appointment as soon as you leave this place. Your pussy is rotten!" I left her on that note with words of wisdom, then washed my hands and went to catch my bus.

Chapter 75

Lovely

I watched in silence as the man I'd come to love lost his battle with life at the hands of the man I used to love.

"Lovely, let's go!" Maine grabbed my wrists and pulled me toward the door. Part of me yearned to run back to Santiago's side, but I knew it was too late.

"Shoot him!" Mauricio yelled at the guards while simultaneously tending to his brother. Pop! Pop! Pop! Several bullets from multiple-caliber weapons flew in our directions. Luckily for us, we weren't far from the door.

"Wait! We can't go that way." I hesitantly pulled back. "There are more men outside." I knew we were facing certain death.

"Don't worry. I got it handled." Maine opened the door as more bullets ripped our way. Shards of glass and wall fragments exploded just as they did on movies. I felt like I was on the set of some action-packed motion-picture thriller as Maine and I escaped within inches of our lives. Sitting out front in a dingy red Jeep was none other than Do It.

"Let's ride!" He smiled from ear to ear as we hopped inside and pulled off. Looking back at my old residence one last time, I said a little prayer for Santiago.

"Welcome back, sis!" My brother was happy to see me, but I couldn't say the same.

"Why did y'all do that?" Nothing good could come of going against the Mexican Cartel. My stomach cringed at the thought alone. They were known to dismember bodies and shit.

"Sounds like you're mad that we saved your life." Maine looked at me sideways.

"Who said my life needed saving?" I smacked my lips. "I was just fine where I was."

"Damn, Lo, what's up?" Do It peered at me through the rearview mirror while speeding down the streets of Mexico.

"Nothing." I didn't know what else to say, because honestly, I had no idea why I was mad.

"If you want to go back there, I will have him stop this fucking car right now and take your ungrateful ass back. We didn't have to risk our lives to save yours." Maine was pissed.

"Maine, stop acting like you fucking care anyway," I hissed.

"What are you talking about? I've always cared about you."

"Yeah, you cared so much you left!"

"Don't jump down my throat. You're the one who gave up on us, not me, remember?" Although Maine concealed it well, I could tell his feelings were hurt.

"In life, situations change, and people grow apart. Shit happens." I sighed while simultaneously looking out the back window to see if we were being followed. Thank God we were not.

"Ain't nobody growing apart, so let's cut the bullshit. You know you still love that nigga." Do It tried to lighten the mood, but it didn't work.

"Don't worry, bro. Maybe she's right. Shit does happen," Maine interjected while shrugging his shoulders. "Lovely, I'll get you to a safe place in a day or two. Then I'll be out of your hair for good!"

"Come on, fam. We can fix this, right?" Do It looked from me to Maine.

"I didn't mean it like that." I tried to clean it up. Maine had done a lot for me over the years. I didn't want him to feel like I played him. However, after losing my entire family and then my son, I'd reached my breaking point with everything and everybody. This was the reason I'd tried to commit suicide in the first place. If Mauricio hadn't kidnapped me and taken me to the whorehouse, I would've been dead with no more cares or worries. Although I was still alive, I knew deep down inside that the old Lovely Brown died on the jet the night I lost my son.

Chapter 76

Nikki

"Ma'am, are you there?" the 911 operator asked.

"Help me please," I whispered as the sound of footsteps drew closer. My hands were trembling uncontrollably as I slid the phone into my pocket, and my head was pounding, too. Although I was in pretty bad shape, I willed myself to slide down off the car and find the kids. Once on my feet, it took a few seconds to get my bearings. Things were spinning, and I could barely see, partly because it was dark but mostly because the blood pouring from my head was like a steady stream down my face.

"Mommy." I could hear Junior screaming for me. It killed me not to answer, but I didn't want to notify the gunman of my whereabouts. While remaining silent, I wiped my face, then went to find the kids.

After a brief search of the area, I realized the children were still in the car, safely strapped into their seats. Quickly, I unstrapped them and ran for dear life. In the distance I could see a house and a barn. All the lights were off, and it looked like something out of a horror movie. Still, I pressed forward.

"Mommy, what happened?" Junior asked as I practically dragged him down the wooded hill toward the barn.

"Shh," I whispered. "Mommy needs you to be very quiet, okay?" I knew my son was scared, but I needed him to stay strong. This was indeed a matter of life and death.

Within minutes we made it to the barn. Thankfully, the door slid open with ease. Carefully I carried the children inside and closed the door behind us. The place smelled like the zoo. Therefore, I knew some kind of animals were in there with us.

"Are you okay, baby?"

"My arm hurts." Junior sounded like he wanted to cry.

"Let me see." Using the light on my cell phone, I could see that my baby was bleeding. I could also see a huge shard of glass protruding through his skin. It looked bad, but I didn't want Junior to freak out, so I played it cool. "You'll be okay as soon as help gets here," I whispered before placing the phone up to my ear. "Hello, are you still there?"

Beep. Beep. Beep. All I could hear was a dial tone indicating that I'd lost the call and the only chance of help I had.

"Fuck!" I wanted to cry, but I was a survivor, no doubt. There was no way I would let anything happen to these babies. The thought alone replaced fear with determination. I was going to get us out of there.

Again, using the light on my phone, I checked Maria over. She was doing fine at the moment. Her eyes were wide and alert, but she remained silent as if she knew how important keeping quiet was. Next, I used my light to survey the area inside the barn. As suspected, there were a few horses in the stable. I saw a pile of hay behind me and an old, rusted Ford truck resting near the door. There was also a crack in the bottom of the barn door. I used it to see what was going on outside, which surprisingly was nothing at all. Maybe the driver of the other car decided to get out of dodge before the police showed up.

Just when I let out a sigh of relief, I could feel something hard pointed to my head. "You better state your fuckin' business before I blow your goddamn head off."

"Please don't shoot me. I have children in here." I nearly shit myself while begging for my life. Click! The sound of his flashlight sounded like the pull of a trigger. I thought I was dead.

"You and them young'uns look beat up pretty bad. What in tarnation happened?" The stranger's voice was now filled with concern.

"We were in a very bad accident up the road. I saw your barn and decided to come for help." I chose not to disclose the entire story for fear that he would put us out.

"Jesus Christ." The blond man with pale skin stared down at us. "Come on in the house, and let's call you some help." He extended his hand and helped me off the ground.

I grabbed Junior's hand and cradled Maria before following him out through the back of the barn and into the side of his home.

"Sorry if I scared ya." The man set the shotgun down in his mudroom, then continued into the house. "We get all kinds of crazy people snooping around my barn. I have a few racehorses out there," he explained.

"I understand," I mumbled.

"John, what happened out there?" A woman's voice came from deeper inside the house.

"Betty, grab the phone and call the life squad. This little lady and her kids done been in a wreck." John turned on the light in the kitchen and pulled out a chair for me to take a seat.

"Thank you so much." Although I was scared shitless, I felt safe with John. Between all the religious statues around the kitchen and the humongous Bible resting on the table, I knew I was in a good place.

"Would you like something to drink? Do you think the kids would like some cookies?" John grabbed a box of Girl Scout cookies from the pantry and came back over to the table. He noticed the glass sticking out of Junior's arm but knew not to make a fuss just like I hadn't.

"Oh, my. What do we have here?" A thin white woman with washed-out highlights entered the kitchen to join us. "Honey, get me some towels from the wash."

"I'm sorry about the mess." I looked down at the blood I'd leaked all over their cluttered kitchen.

"Nonsense." Betty smiled before John returned with the towels. She applied a few to my wound while John wrapped Junior's arm.

Boom! Boom! Boom! The banging on the door damn near gave me a heart attack.

"I just got off the phone with 911. That was quick. They must've been nearby." Betty looked from me to John.

I wanted to tell them it wasn't the police, but I couldn't. The words were stuck. Instead, I watched in slow motion as John went to answer his door. Betty tried to make small talk, but I couldn't comprehend anything she was saying because I knew what was about to happen.

"What in the hell?" John hollered.

Instantly Betty was up on her feet. "Stay here, dear. Let me see what the problem is."

Seconds felt like minutes before the sound of guns blasting filled the air. Thinking fast, I grabbed two sets of keys from the table, snatched up the children, and ran like our lives depended on it. We had to get out of here quickly if we wanted to see tomorrow.

Chapter 77

Mina

"Baby, please don't leave." Sam followed me around our bedroom as I packed my shit.

"I can't do this anymore. I'm done!" It hurt like hell to leave the only family I had left, but it was what it was.

"Please let me make it up to you. I swear I'm a changed man." Sam tried to block my path to the closet.

"I've changed too." I stopped and mustered a smile. "The old me would've stayed and tried to make it work, but the new me is tired of being fucked over. I'm done." Pushing past him, I made my way to the closet and began snatching a few of my favorite items from their hangers.

"What can I do to prove my love?" Sam asked, and I looked at him briefly.

"Love in my book doesn't mean shit without loyalty." I wanted to cry, but the tears wouldn't even form. "While I stood by your side, taking care of these babies who aren't even mine, you went and fucked my friend. There ain't no coming back from that!"

"She wasn't your friend!" Sam barked as if he were really saying something.

"And you wasn't my nigga!" After reaching up on the shelf and grabbing my new Chanel bag, I barged past Sam and headed for the bedroom door. Of course, Sam tried again to stop me, but the look I gave him told his ass to fall back.

As soon as I stepped into the hallway, there was a loud banging sound at the door. "Police. Open up!"

"What else did you do?" I looked back at Sam, who was just as surprised as I was.

"I didn't do shit!" He flew past me then down the stairs to open the door. I was hot on his heels.

"Are you Samuel?" a large white male in uniform asked once Sam opened the door.

"Yes, I am. May I ask what this is about?" Sam frowned. My heart was beating so loud I thought everyone in the room could hear it.

"Turn around please."

"For what?" Sam was turned up.

"You're under arrest for participation in the distribution of narcotics. You have the right to remain silent. Anything you say or do can and will be held against you in a court of law." The officer turned Sam around and slapped handcuffs on him so fast that my head spun.

"Wait, Officer, please don't take him," I begged, but the officer completely ignored me while forcefully shoving Sam out the door.

"Call Nikki and get me the fuck out, Mina. I can't do jail!" Sam hollered.

On cue, both the children started crying upstairs. "Fuck!" I screamed, then hit the back of the door. My shit was in shambles. As much as I wanted to leave Sam right now, I couldn't. Who would care for the kids in his absence? There was no telling how long he'd be gone, especially with the charges he had.

"Excuse me," a man said behind me after clearing his throat. I turned and looked at the reverend and his secretary, who were still waiting in the living room. "The love offering for this service is nonrefundable."

"Reverend, get the fuck out!" I snapped, then pointed toward the door *Martin* style, the same way he did when he told Pam, Tommy, and Cole to get to stepping.

Chapter 78

Nikki

Thank God I was able to make it to the garage and unlock the white Mercury before our location was found by the gunman.

"Mommy, I'm scared." Junior looked at me with tears in his eyes.

"Me too." I couldn't lie. A bitch was about to pee on herself. I didn't know what the fuck was going on, but I knew I had to get these kids to safety. "Get inside and put your seat belt on," I whispered while putting Maria in the passenger seat. I didn't have time to strap her in. Therefore, I used my right hand to hold her in place and prayed like hell we didn't have another accident.

"Where the fuck is the garage opener!" Frantically I searched the car but came up empty. "Goddammit!" Briefly I placed my head down into the palms of my hands and exhaled loudly. That's when I spotted the opener on the floor beneath my feet. Without hesitation I reached down and clicked it. After starting the engine, I put the pedal to the metal and gunned it full throttle. I was prepared to take out anything or anyone in my way.

Surprisingly, the coast was clear! For as far as I could see there was no one was in sight. I wasn't sure if that was a good or bad thing.

"Mommy, call Daddy," Junior hollered. "He handles the bad guys. I'm scared." Now my baby was crying hysterically. "Please call my daddy."

"Daddy is away right now, Junior, but we will be okay. I promise." Although I sounded tough, the tears falling down my face proved otherwise. Junior was right! For most of my life Mario handled all my issues. I never feared nothing or no one when he was around because I knew he would take care of it. Even when we were divorced, I still had a sense of security, but now I was on my own completely. The reality that Mario would be doing hard time had me shaken to the core, but what could I do? They say there are only two places a man in the streets can end up: the cemetery or a jail cell. If those were his only options, I'd easily take the latter. Naturally, I didn't want to lose Rio at all, but I would gladly visit the prison every week for a million years versus spending five seconds at a cemetery crying over his headstone.

"Are we still going to Paris?" Junior wiped his eyes, and I did the same. Right now, we were supposed to be thousands of feet in the air flying into our new life. Instead, there we were, running for our lives.

"Yeah, baby," I lied with a sniff. The severity of the situation hurt way more than the injuries I sustained while being thrown from the car. I didn't know what to do or where to go from here, so I just drove in silence.

After being lost for thirty minutes, I finally saw a sign directing me back to I-75 North. Before I could pull onto the freeway, there were flashing red and blue lights in my rearview. I knew things were about to go from bad to worse in the stolen car of two murder victims, so I pulled over and awaited fate.

"License and registration please?" a black officer in a sheriff's uniform asked after tapping on the window. Nervously I rolled it down and looked up at him before swallowing hard.

"Sir, this car is stolen." I began to cry. "My car was run off the road by some crazy person. I ran to the nearest house for help. Those nice people invited us in, and someone came to the door shooting. I grabbed my kids and the keys to this car." I wiped my eyes. "Please don't take me to jail."

"This is Officer Kendall requesting assistance on Route 2 and Maine," the man said into his walkie-talkie, and I knew my ass was done! On top of all that, I knew he was going to add child endangerment to my tab since neither of the kids were properly secured.

"Can I please call their grandmother before you take me in?" I looked up at him with pleading eyes.

"Calm down, miss. You are not being arrested." The officer's face softened. "When we responded to the 911 call, Betty Florest told us what happened."

"She's alive?" My eyes widened. "Thank God! What about John?"

"Unfortunately, Mr. Florest didn't make it. The perp shot him dead in the doorway." The officer looked down at the ground briefly before another squad car pulled behind his. "We're going to take you and the kids to the county hospital to be checked out, and then we have some questions for you to answer."

I wanted to decline, but we all needed to be looked at by a doctor. Junior still had glass in his arm, and my body felt like it had been hit by a Mack truck. Hopefully, my unborn child was okay, but at this moment that was the least of my concerns. "Can you at least keep us all together?" I requested.

"Yes, ma'am," Officer Kendall agreed, then proceeded to help me out of the car.

Chapter 79

Lovely

"Auntie Lovely, is that you?" My niece DeShawna practically ran me over when I walked into the house Maine purchased when we first moved to Mexico. Although I used to call it home not long ago, it now felt unfamiliar.

"Hey, pumpkin." I squeezed her tight while looking around. Things were practically the same as when I left, but it still didn't feel like home. Maybe it was because the house held some of my darkest memories, or maybe because it felt like a prison. Whatever it was had me feeling uneasy.

"Why did you leave us? Where did you go?" DeShawna looked up just as curious as always.

I looked back at Do It and Maine before responding. "I took a vacation." It was the best thing I could come up with.

"Where to?"

"A friend's house," I replied.

"I didn't know you had friends here."

"That makes two of us, Shawnie." Maine patted her head before passing us in the foyer. Although I continued talking with my niece, my eyes watched until he reached the back of the house. I hated to be in such an awkward place with Maine. He didn't deserve my coldness. Even if things were over between us, it was time I made things right.

"Baby, let me go talk to your uncle for a minute. I promise you can tell me everything I missed while we play dolls later, all right?"

"Okay." Shawnie was upset at first, but then her dad told her she could get some ice cream, and quickly she was over it.

"I don't know how long you plan on staying, but it does feel good to have you back." Do It pulled me in for a hug, and I nodded.

"I missed you too, bro." Blood couldn't have made Do It and me any closer. It really was good being back in his company if only for a little while. Gently I pulled back and headed off down the hall behind Maine.

I found him in his office sitting behind the cherry-oak desk. There was a small stack of money resting near his left hand and a half-filled glass of cognac resting near his right. He was about to light up his favorite cigar, Gurkha His Majesty's Reserve.

"Can I come in?" I asked after knocking. Maine set the cigar and lighter down, then nodded his approval for me to enter. "What's the money for?" I asked, not really wanting to know but making conversation.

"It's yours, Lovely." Maine looked from the money to me.

"Mine?" I frowned.

"After the shit that happened today, we all need to get the fuck out of dodge. That's just a little something to get you wherever it is you're going." Maine picked up the cognac glass and took a drink.

"Where are you going?" I asked softly.

"I might take a visit to Dubai or head back to the States for business. I don't know yet." He sat back in the leather chair and stared at me.

"The States, huh?" I smirked. "You gon' marry the new bitch?"

"Does it matter?" Maine questioned nonchalantly.

"Yes, it fucking matters!" I snapped. Out of nowhere tears formed in my eyes, and feelings I thought were dead hit me all at once.

"Why would it matter when you said you didn't love me anymore? Why would it matter when you were all too eager to be the next man's ho? Why would it matter when you just fucking told me that shit happens?" Maine was so angry the vein in his neck popped out.

"It matters because she's having your goddamn baby, and I lost mine!" I smacked the money off the desk and sent it flying across the room like someone making it rain at the strip club. "She is giving you the one I couldn't, Maine! That's why it fucking matters." I began sobbing uncontrollably, to the point where I scared myself. "I've lost everybody. They should've just let me die."

"Lovely, you haven't lost me yet. I'm still right here. In case you haven't noticed, I'm still fighting for us." Maine stood from the desk and wrapped his arms around my shoulders. I could tell that my outburst really touched him. "I don't have a father or mother either. My grandmother died when I was young, remember? I was alone until I found you. Together we can get through this rough patch, but only if you want to."

"Maine—"

"All you have to do is tell me you want this, and I will try my damnedest to fix it." His eyes peered down at me, and my entire body trembled. "Just say the word, and I will do whatever I have to to get us back on track."

"I love you too. I never stopped." With tears falling from my face, I wrapped my arms around him and held on for dear life.

Chapter 80

Gucci

As you may have guessed, the long-ass ride to the South was some bullshit! First off, the bus was crowded damn near to Birmingham. Niggas was packed on that bitch like sardines. Of course, I had to sit next to the fattest lady for ten hours. She took up half of my seat and hers. When she got off, I thought I was in the clear until this funky-ass Mexican plopped down beside me. He smelled as if he'd been cutting onions, which caused my eyes to tear up. Silently I wished I could've traded him for big mama again. At least she smelled good.

After riding all night to the sound of people coughing, sneezing, passing gas, and babies crying, I was finally less than an hour from Birmingham. The driver pulled into the Flying J station and announced we were taking a fifteen-minute break to switch buses. I thought it was stupid to stop so close to the final destination. However, I was

so happy to get a break from the smell of onions,
I didn't say a word.

Hopping up from my seat, I practically fell
over myself trying to get off the bus. My legs were
cramped, and my stomach growled. I needed to
eat, but the first thing on my list was to make a call.

"Gucci?" This time it was Aunt Lucy.

"Yes, ma'am, it's me." Inwardly I groaned.

"What kind of trouble your ass done got into
now? And why you wanna bring that shit this
way?" She was not a happy camper about my visit.
Truthfully, I never thought my aunt cared for me
because she never hid her disdain for my city ways.

"Aunt Lucy, can I speak to Rhythm?" I tried to be
polite, but after all I'd been through in the past few
days, she was really testing my limits.

"Yeah, you can after you answer my damn question. What kind of drama are you bringing into my
home, Gucci?"

"I'll explain everything when I get there, I promise. Please tell Rhythm I'll be at the Birmingham
station in fifty minutes." Lightly I placed the
phone on the hook.

As soon as I stepped in line at the Subway
counter, I realized my purse was missing. "Shit!"
Frantically I tried to remember where I could've
left it. It had been around my neck the entire
ride except when I took it off to use it as a pillow.
"Fuck!" In my haste to vacate the bus, I'd left my

purse in the seat. Running like a track star, I flew back outside.

"Where is the bus?" I asked the Amish lady who had been on board with me since Detroit.

"It just pulled off, but there is the new one pulling up." She pointed.

"Fuck my life!" I cursed, unwilling to believe I'd just let $4,000 and some change walk away from me.

"Is everything okay?" a fine, light-skinned nigga with dark, deep waves and dimples asked. He was wearing a black T-shirt, red belt, black denim jeans, and a pair of red Rockports. There was a duffle bag resting on his shoulder.

"Yeah. I left my purse on the bus with my money in it," I replied, embarrassed that I managed to make such a big mistake.

"Would you like for me to grab you a sandwich or something?" He reached into his pocket and retrieved a stack of money so big it couldn't fold.

"Thanks, but I'll be all right. My transfer bus just arrived." I pointed over to the bus with BIRMINGHAM on the front sign.

"I just left Birmingham a few weeks ago." He slid the money back into his pocket. "It's a cool place."

"Where are you headed now?" I asked flirtatiously.

"I'm a drifter, ma. I go wherever the wind blows me." He smiled, exposing his dimples.

"A drifter, huh?" I smiled back. "Is that Southern slang for a d-boy?"

"Excuse me?" The new stranger was now uncomfortable. I could tell by the way he shifted nervously.

"Relax, baby, I ain't no rat." I raised my hands midair. "I've been in the game so long that I can spot a dope dealer with my eyes closed," I whispered. "My name is Gucci. If you ever 'drift' into Detroit, just ask about me." I winked and walked away. Of course, I had to make a show with my ass in the process.

"What gave me away?" the stranger called out.

With a smirk I turned and walked back over to him. "For starters, nobody with the amount of money you just pulled from your pocket would be on the Greyhound. Secondly, you might want to zip that bag up." I pointed to the semi-exposed brick in his duffle bag.

"Damn, I'm slipping." Quickly he zipped his bag, then laughed. "You got a number, Gucci?"

"You got a name?" I said, reminding him that he had yet to drop it.

"My friends call me Majesty." He extended his hand I shook it. "Can I have your number? I'd like to call you sometime."

"Can I have yours instead?" I didn't have a number for him to call, but I did want to keep in touch.

He was just my type of nigga. Once the dust settled and I landed on my feet, I would surely hit him up.

"You got a man or something?" Majesty then looked down at the rock on my ring finger and frowned.

"This is the last call for Birmingham," the driver announced.

I looked back at the bus, then returned my focus to Majesty. "It's complicated, but if you give me your number, I promise to call when I get where I'm going."

Majesty grabbed a pen from his pocket, then reached for my arm and wrote his digits down. "Don't forget to call me, all right?"

"Scout's honor," I said with a smile before making a beeline for the bus. I was salty about losing my money and ID, but it was what it was, and there was nothing I could do. Once I got where I was going, I would figure out how to recoup my losses.

Chapter 81

Mina

I'd been up for nearly twenty-four hours waiting by the phone for Sam to call, but he never did. My heart was racing just as fast as my mind, and I didn't know what to do. Nikki wasn't answering her phone, and I dared not call that two-timing bitch Gucci.

"Fuck!" I shouted, then hit the counter in the kitchen. I was trying to calm my nerves by fixing myself some breakfast, but it was no use. I'd burned the bacon, scorched the toast, put shells in the eggs, and let the grits splatter all over the stove. As if this weren't enough, on cue both Solomon and Samantha started crying.

For just one brief moment I wanted to put on my shoes, grab my purse, and walk out the door, leaving Sam, the babies, and all the bullshit behind. "Here I come," I hollered before grabbing two premade bottles from the fridge and warming them up. After testing the temperature, I headed

to get my babies. Yes, I said "my babies" because
they belonged to me. It wasn't their fault they had
fuckups for parents. Therefore, I loved them a
little harder.

"Hi, pooh." First, I grabbed Samantha. "Hey, big
man." Next, I grabbed Solomon. With both babies
in my arms, I sat down on the recliner in my room
and fed them quietly.

As soon as the babies were done eating, it was
time to change their diapers. Gently I sat them
down on my bed, then went to retrieve wipes,
diapers, and some baby powder from the nursery.
On my way down the hall, I caught a glimpse of
myself in the mirror hanging on the wall. A bitch
looked like a zombie. I needed sleep, but since the
babies were up, I didn't count on catching a nap
anytime soon.

Ringggg! Ringggg! The phone blared. Quickly,
I made a mad dash back to my bedroom and
grabbed it on the third ring. "Hello."

"You have a collect call from—"

"Mina, it's me." Although I was mad, I was still
relieved to hear Sam's voice.

"Press one to accept."

"Can you believe they are just now giving me a
goddamn phone call?" Sam barked as soon as I ac-
cepted the call.

"What are they saying? When can you come
home?"

"I don't know yet. I haven't had a bail hearing. Have you talked to Nikki?"

"No. She isn't answering her phone." I hated to give him bad news, but it was what it was.

"Can you do me a favor please?" Sam sighed. "Can you please reach out to Gucci?"

"Are you fucking serious?" I knew this nigga had lost his rabbit-ass mind.

"I'm facing a ten-to-fifteen-year bid for this shit!" he hollered. "I know it's asking a lot, but I need to put a pulse on the situation, Mina," Sam begged.

"Fuck you!" I shouted, then stared at the phone in disbelief. Every time I wanted to believe he cared for me and loved me as much as he said he did, he would always manage to prove the complete opposite.

"I'm going crazy in here. At least get me a lawyer," he pleaded just before hearing a click, indicating that I'd ended the call.

With tears running down my face, I cried hard! Never had I been so insulted in my life. How could he even fix his lips to mention Gucci's name after telling me he fucked her? What did he take me for?

Ringgg! The phone rang again, and I contemplated not answering until I saw the name of the mortgage company I worked for on the caller ID. "Hello."

"Hey, Amina, it's Jamison. I just saw the news about your boyfriend and his crew. Are you okay?

Do you and the kids need anything?" Jamison was a very dear colleague of mine.

"What news?" My heart sank as I grabbed the remote control.

"The story is on every news channel this side of the world, sweetie." Jamison cleared his throat.

"I'm turning it on now. Hold on." I hit the volume and watched in silence.

"This is Eva Evans, reporting live in front of Thirty-sixth District Court, where members of the H.O.F. drug cartel are supposed to be arraigned on Monday morning. They were arrested in a massive sweep that took place yesterday. Nearly two hundred members have been taken into custody. Among them are the head of this cartel, Mario Wallace. His partner in crime and wife, Gucci Wallace, has yet to be apprehended. More on this story to come. Back to you in the studio."

"I can't believe this." I sighed, trying to process all of it.

"My sister is a defense attorney if you need one," Jamison chimed in.

"This is all too much!" Again, I started to cry. "Can I call you back?"

"Mina, you can't handle this alone. I'll swing by later when I leave the office." Jamison was a single father who understood my plight when it came to the babies. His baby mother had chosen to chase some basketball player shortly after giving birth rather than be a mother to her only daughter. The little girl was now 5.

"Okay. I'll see you soon. Thank you." I wiped the tears from my eyes, then returned the phone to the cradle. I didn't know what was going to happen from here, but it did feel good to have someone in my corner.

Chapter 82

Nikki

After being taken to the hospital yesterday, we were examined and held for a twenty-four observation. This morning, the doctor on call cleared us to go home since we hadn't sustained any major injuries. Maria was okay, and Junior only received two stitches, thank God! I was treated for bruised ribs along with a fractured wrist and a few minor scrapes, but all in all I was good. The baby looked good too. However, I was told to follow up with my obstetrician in a day or two to be sure.

Almost two hours ago I'd called Ms. Claudia to pick us up. While we waited, Officer Kendall continued the line of questioning he'd started yesterday until the nurse had him leave. Not one to miss a beat, he was back first thing this morning with a cup of coffee and a slew of questions.

"Why would someone run you off the road and then hunt you down to kill you?" Officer Kendall asked for the hundredth time.

"Look, man, I've already told you. I don't know!" I paced the hospital floor while periodically checking the window to see if my mother-in-law was outside. The small county hospital had only three floors.

"Mrs. Wallace, I've done a little research." Officer Kendall sat up in the seat he was occupying. "Your husband is the kingpin of a well-known drug ring. In my book that explains a lot." He gave me the once-over.

"What the fuck is wrong with you?" I snapped. "Don't be saying no shit like that in front of my kids." I looked over to Junior, who was sitting in my hospital bed, coloring. Maria was asleep in the car seat the hospital provided us since we lost ours in the accident.

"I'm sorry." He raised his hands. "It's my job to uncover the truth. I'm just trying to figure out what happened, that's all."

"Well, while you were digging up my past, you should have seen that I've been divorced from my ex-husband for nearly a year! That part of my life is over." I shook my head and lied as best I could. This wasn't my first time being interrogated, and I was sure it wasn't going to be the last.

"I didn't know that." Officer Kendall swallowed hard.

"No, you didn't, because you didn't bother to look. All you saw in my files was the association to Mario Wallace, whose name is all over the goddamn place right now, and decided to make your own speculation! While you're sitting here babysitting me you could be trying to find the person responsible!" Last night while watching the news, I found out the assailant was still at large.

"Mrs. Wallace, do you think this was—" Officer Kendall was cut off by the transportation tech.

"Mrs. Wallace, your ride is downstairs." A young girl wearing a green shirt and khaki pants smiled. She was standing there with a wheelchair.

"Who is that for?" I looked at her suspiciously.

"It's for you. The hospital has a policy to transport all patients by wheelchair to the front door."

"Girl, bye." I shook my head. "I'm good but thank you, sweetheart." In one swift motion I helped Junior from the bed and grabbed Maria's car seat. Immediately I doubled over in pain and grabbed my side.

"Are you okay?" Officer Kendall and the tech asked in unison.

"I'm fine. My ribs hurt like hell, that's all." With a deep breath, I regained my composure and stood. The tech pushed the chair closer, and grudgingly, I took a seat. Officer Kendall grabbed Maria's car seat and lifted Junior into his arms.

Once in the lobby, we were greeted by Claudia, Mario's mother. "Grandma." Junior damn near leaped from Officer Kendall's arms when he saw her.

"Hey, big boy." She smiled wearily. I could tell she had seen better days. Her eyes were red, and her face was puffy.

"Thank you." Slowly I stood from the chair. The tech made sure I was okay before strolling away.

"Mrs. Wallace, I'll be in touch as the investigation continues." Officer Kendall placed Junior on the ground, then reached into his pocket and produced a card. "Take my number and call me if anything jogs your memory. Also, may we run ballistics on your vehicle?" They'd recovered it from the scene of the wreck.

"Suit yourself." I took the card and shrugged. "Good day, Officer." I grabbed Junior's hand and made my way outside. Ms. Claudia carried Maria to the car, then strapped her in. Without a word she got into the driver's seat but didn't start the engine.

"What's wrong?" I looked over to see her head down.

"Nikki." She sniffed. "What is happening to my family? I'm scared to death." Her hands were shaking uncontrollably. Even though my entire body was rocked by pain, I willed myself to reach over and embrace her. "Look at you. Look at my grandbabies. Look at my son, Nikki." She pulled back, then wiped her eyes. "I'm petrified."

"I know you are, Ms. C, but it will be okay." I tried my best to reassure her, but it wasn't working. "We've been in hot water before. We'll be all right." Although I spoke with confidence, I wasn't certain about a damn thing. This was by far the hottest water we'd ever been in.

Chapter 83

Gucci

"Cousin Gucci, over here!" Rhythm waved from her parking spot in front of the bus station. She was holding a damn sign with my name on it like I didn't know who she was.

"Girl, why do your crazy ass have that billboard?" I ran up to her. "You think I wouldn't recognize my favorite cousin?" The girl was still tall and skinny just like back in the day. The only differences were that her dookie braids and pimples were traded for crochet braids and a small nose ring. Her tits and ass had filled out nicely, too.

"Look at you, city girl." Rhythm smiled, exposing the gold fronts on her bottom teeth. It must've been a Southern thing, because nearly everyone working inside the Birmingham bus terminal had them.

"You got a grill!" I smiled.

"It's removable." She pulled them off for me to see. "I wear them on the weekend or when Mama ain't around."

"Aunt Lucy is still a trip, huh?" I shook my head. "Your mother is nuttier than a fruitcake."

"I love my mama, but sometimes she is a little too overprotective." Rhythm laughed.

"Girl, overprotective is something you are with a child. Your ass is in your thirties. She needs to let it go." Raising my hand, I blocked the sun from my eyes. The temperature was in the mid-eighties.

"Mama ain't letting nothing go until I'm married, and even then, she's liable to move in with us."

"Speaking of marriage, do you see that in your future?" I raised a brow.

"One day, cousin Gucci." Rhythm looked away briefly. "Enough about me. What brings you my way? Where is your husband, and where is your baby?"

The mention of my daughter made me sad, but I didn't let on. Leaving her with Nikki was the hardest thing in the world for me to do. "May I see your phone?"

"Sure." Rhythm reached into her pocket and handed me the oldest phone I'd seen in a long time. It actually had real buttons to press instead of the flat screen, but who was I to complain when I didn't even have one? Quickly I dialed Nikki, but the phone went straight to voicemail.

"Hey, Nikki, it's me. Call me back on this number as soon as you get this." After ending the call, I handed the phone back to my cousin.

"So, are you going to tell me why you came all the way down here?"

"I got into something in Detroit." I sighed.

"Something like what?" Rhythm frowned.

"The less you know, the better off you are. Until I can get a handle on it, I need to lie low."

"Mama is gonna need more than that before she lets you stay with us." Rhythm shook her head.

"I'll just tell her that I'm having domestic issues with my husband, and she'll believe me." My aunt Lucy was cold, but she wasn't the ice queen.

"Are you sure this won't come back to bite us in the ass?" Rhythm asked skeptically, and rightfully so. As children I always kept us in deep shit.

"I promise, cuz." With a smile I wrapped my arms around her tiny waist.

"All right. Well, let's go then." Rhythm hit the lock on her two-door maroon Mazda, and we jumped in. "First stop, the mall!" She was excited, but I had to burst her bubble.

"Nah, cuz! I don't have no money for shopping," I admitted as she reversed from the parking space.

"What?" Rhythm frowned. "Since when are you broke?"

"I'm not broke. My funds are just tied up at the moment." Even thinking about it caused a lump to form in my throat. It was crazy how things could change in the blink of an eye. I needed to come up fast!

"We can still go. I got you," Rhythm offered. "Forever 21 is having a big sale!" she added while driving down the street.

"Girl, I don't shop at no goddamn Forever 21! Neiman Marcus and Nordstrom are more like it." I laughed hard, but after realizing I had offended her, I quickly changed my tune. "Look, I didn't mean it like that. I'm sorry."

"I know it's not Hermès, Louie, or anything like that. I just wanted to do something nice for you, that's all." Rhythm laid it on thick, making me feel like more of an ass than I already did.

"I appreciate your effort, cuz, I really do. You know I just say shit as it pops in my head, but I need to work on that," I admitted.

"It's all good, cuz." Rhythm smiled, although I could tell she was still tight. "I guess I'll take you to the house then."

"Hold up!" I hollered. "Pull up in this strip mall."

"Why?" Rhythm asked while swerving into the driveway, nearly sideswiping the car beside us. "What's over here?"

"The pawn shop," I replied while grabbing the diamond necklace around my neck. It was a gift from Mario. Looking at it now made me depressed. I would be lying if I said my thoughts and prayers weren't with him. As much as I wanted to hurt him, I didn't ever want to do it like this. He was sitting in jail because of me. The pain was a hard pill to swallow. "Come on," I said, beckoning my cousin to follow me.

"Welcome to Will's Place. Can I help you ladies?" a fat white lady with dirty blond hair asked from her seat behind the counter. The place smelled of sour mop water and stale bread, but they had a nice setup. It reminded me of Zeidman's back home.

"I would like to see how much I can get for this necklace." With a frown I removed the jewelry from my neck and handed it over. Instantly I wanted to snatch it back.

"This is nice," the woman said while inspecting it carefully. "About two carats, right?" She looked up at me.

"Three and a half," I replied, and her eyes bucked. "I'll be right back."

"Cuz, are you sure you want to part with such a pretty piece?" Rhythm asked once we were alone. "I'm sure that set you back a mint!" She whistled.

"Actually, it was a push gift from my husband when I had our daughter." I smiled momentarily.

"Hello, ladies. I'm Will." An older white man approached us. He was now the one carrying the necklace.

"Will, I'm Gucci and this is Rhythm."

"Those are some creative names." Will chuckled. When neither of us joined the conversation, he continued. "So, I hear you're looking to get some money for this here necklace. I have a couple of questions first." He looked from me to Rhythm. "Is it stolen?"

"Absolutely not!" I was offended.

"That's good." Again, Will chuckled. "My next question would be, are you looking to sell it or pawn it?"

"What's the difference?" I hadn't pawned anything a day in my life. All I knew was people took their shit in and came out with money. A few of the crackheads I used to serve did it all the time.

"Selling means just that, and pawning it means we're just holding it for you. We give you a lump sum and then a repayment schedule. Once you've repaid your loan, we'll give you the necklace back."

"How much will you give me if I sold it outright, and how much if I pawn it?" I asked as this was the determining factor.

"Two thousand cash right now if you sell it, and nine hundred if you pawn it." Will shifted his stance.

"You are out of your fucking mind!" I snapped. "The necklace cost almost fifteen grand!"

"Sweetheart, I don't know where you think you're at, but this is the best you're going to get from Will's Place!" he said as a matter of fact. "Do you want the deal or not?"

"Make it five thousand if I sell it and you've got a deal." I was still getting the shitty end of the stick, but I needed cash in my hand pronto.

"Make it three thousand and you're in business."

"How about you hand me my shit and I'll go elsewhere?" I extended my hand.

"Fine, five thousand it is," Will relented. "I don't keep that much money in the store. Can I give you fifteen hundred now and write you a check for the rest?" Will asked while walking over to the cash register.

"Fine." I shrugged. Even though I would have liked all my money up-front, I was happy to at least have something.

After counting my cash and telling him to make the check out to my cousin, I stepped outside to call Nikki again. "Come on," I said. Just like the last time though, I ended up getting the voicemail. "Nikki, it's me. Please call me back and let me know that everything is okay."

Chapter 84

Lovely

"It feels good to hear you say you love me again." Maine smiled. "I never thought we could get back here."

"Me either, but I have terms and conditions before we go any further."

"Name them," he replied eagerly.

"First, I need to know if you love me. I mean, really love me," I said while looking him in the eyes.

"Of course I do!"

"Do you love her too?" I raised a brow and watched him get uncomfortable.

"Who?" Maine wasn't stupid. He was buying time.

"The woman who's carrying your child!" I tried not to get irritated.

"No." He turned away from me and stared out the massive picture window.

"So, she means nothing?" I walked over and stood beside him.

"Nothing at all," he replied nonchalantly.

"Are you sure?"

"What the fuck is up with the goddamn questions?" he barked. "Get to the fucking point, because I'm beginning to lose interest."

"Why are you so hostile?"

"Lovely, I feel like you're playing with me, and I'm not with it! You said you love me. I said I love you. I say let's work on things, and you say you got terms and conditions. I love you to death, but I'm not some circus animal! I don't jump through hoops for nobody. Either cut to the chase, or let's be done with this."

He looked me over with a glare that got my panties wet. I hadn't seen him in this light in a very long time.

"Spit it out, Lovely. Tell me what you want me to do to fix us." Maine crossed his arms, then leaned up against the window.

Instantly I was all over him like a fly on shit. He smelled and looked so good that I couldn't control myself. Passionately I began to kiss him on the lips then the neck. Before I knew it, his shirt was off and his pants were down to his ankles. With lust in my eyes, I dropped down to my knees and took his dick so far into my mouth I almost threw up.

"Fuck!" he moaned as his erection thickened within the limits of my jowls. Up and down, I bobbed and slobbered on his manhood until spit was dripping down my chin. "Shit!" Maine palmed the window for dear life as I attempted to swallow him whole. Just when he was about to climax, DeShawna could be heard in close proximity down the hallway. The office door was open, which meant I had to stop.

"Wait!" Maine mumbled. "Where are you going?"

"We'll finish this conversation later."

"Can you at least tell me the terms and conditions?" Maine asked while fastening his pants.

"I want you to go back to Detroit and be with Nikki until she delivers."

"Why? For what?" he asked cautiously.

"Once the baby is born, I want you to bring it to me for us to raise." I watched as Maine's face turned from stunned to flat-out bewildered.

"Are you serious?"

"As a heart attack!" I replied without so much as a second thought. I knew exactly what my life needed, and Nikki had it. Her baby was the missing piece of my puzzle.

"Come on, D." I grabbed my niece's hand as she approached the doorway, and we set off down to the hall to her bedroom.

"Auntie L, why did you leave us?" DeShawna asked once we were in her room with the door closed.

I answered as best I could. "Sometimes grown-ups need time alone to think things out." The baby didn't need to know that I really had intentions to commit suicide.

"My daddy said you had to find yourself," DeShawna said with a serious giggle.

"What's so funny?" I asked, thinking I'd completely missed the joke.

"Think about it, Auntie L. How can you find yourself?" DeShawna giggled again. "You're always with yourself, so you can never get lost from yourself. I don't think Daddy knows what he was talking about." DeShawna slapped her knees and laughed again.

This time I did too. "For a six-year-old, you are way too smart."

"I'm almost seven!" DeShawna corrected me.

"That's right!" I smiled. "Your birthday is in, what, two weeks?"

"Yup!" DeShawna went over to the desk in her room and grabbed a pink notebook covered in rhinestones and pink fur. "This is my birthday list." She handed me the notebook and patiently waited for me to skim the pages.

"'Number one, a dog named Scooter,'" I read aloud. "'Number two, a birthday party with all my friends. Number three, I want Auntie Lovely to come home.'" It took a lot for me not to cry. Her words touched me tremendously.

"I got my third gift. Do you think I'll get the others?" DeShawna asked with hope in her eyes.

"It depends on if you've been good." Quickly I dabbed at the tear dangling on the tip of my eyelash. I didn't want her to see me crying.

"I'm always good," DeShawna stated as a matter of fact.

"Well, then I don't see why you wouldn't get those other things." After closing the book, I handed it back to her.

"Auntie L, I'm glad you came back." With a smile, DeShawna wrapped her little arms around me, and I practically melted. It felt good to be missed. Maybe I needed to stop focusing on what I didn't have and learn to appreciate what I did have.

Chapter 85

Nikki

As soon as we pulled into my driveway, Mrs. Crooks flew down her porch steps. She was wearing a beige slip and house shoes. Her wig was slightly crooked, and she had a joint in her hand as usual. "Hey!" she hollered while waving me down.

"Mrs. Crooks, what's wrong?" I asked after rolling down the window.

"Nikki, can you step over to my house for a minute?" she said with a half-hearted smile while making eye contact with Claudia.

"It's been a long day. Can I come by tomorrow?" I was sure whatever she wanted could wait.

"I really need to talk to you now." This time she spoke from the side of her mouth the way old people did when they tried to whisper. "It will only take a second, I promise."

"Okay," I relented. "Ma, please take the kids inside with your spare key. I'll be inside shortly." With a sigh, I opened the door and slid from the seat as best I could without hurting myself further.

"You okay, baby? What happened?" Mrs. Crooks tried to assist me across her lawn.

"I was in an accident. I'll be okay." There was no need to run down all the details of what happened, so I kept it plain and simple.

"How is Mario?" She was outside along with the entire neighborhood the night we were arrested.

"Honestly, I don't know. I haven't been able to speak with him. My phone was lost in the wreck."

"He's been all over the news. They're saying he'll go away for a very long time if convicted." Mrs. Crooks stopped in front of her porch and placed a hand on her hip. "Anyway, I couldn't care less about any of that." She put the joint up to her mouth and took a puff. "The reason I brought you over here is because I seen some men let themselves into your house last night." Mrs. Crooks took another pull while looking from side to side. "They were wearing them alphabet jackets."

"The fucking DEA I bet!" I smacked my lips. The Drug Enforcement Agency was known to be dirty at times. "They had no business in my home, at night, without permission."

"I don't know what they were doing in there, but it only took them twenty minutes to do it. They parked in the alley and never turned on a light inside. The shit seemed foul as hell, which is why I wanted you to know." Mrs. Crooks was the neighborhood watch all by her lonely. I appreciated the information.

"They were probably bugging my shit!" Shaking my head, I began contemplating my next move.

"Well, if you ever need to use the phone or something, feel free to use mine." With that, Mrs. Crooks gave me a hug, adjusted her wig, and marched up the stairs back into her house.

Once I was inside my own house, an uneasy feeling came over me. On top of the place being bugged with listening devices, I felt as though someone was watching me, too. The DEA had probably planted video surveillance as well. This was their way of obtaining illegal evidence for the case they were trying to build on Mario.

"You know, Ms. C, I think I'm going to take the kids to a hotel for a while. If you like, you can come too."

"A hotel?" Ms. C frowned. "Girl, that's nonsense. Y'all can come back to my house. There is no need in spending money, especially right now."

"Let me grab a few things and I'll be ready." Slowly I took the stairs with ease until I finally reached the top. Immediately my heart stopped when I noticed the dirty footprints on my beige carpet. It was a telltale sign that someone had surely been in my house. For a second I froze, but I didn't want to look suspicious in case I was being watched, so I continued throughout the house like nothing was up.

One by one I entered each room and grabbed clothes for myself and Junior. I also hit the safe on the floor in my closet and grabbed a few bundles of money. Thank God they hadn't touched it. As soon as I zipped the bag and lifted it over my shoulders, the house phone began to ring. My heart nearly jumped from my chest as I contemplated answering it.

"Hello," I said finally.

"This a collect call from—"

"Nik, it's me!" Mario replied.

"Press one to accept."

"Hello." I tried to sound normal.

"Where the fuck you been? I been calling you and—"

"Mario, please don't call here anymore," I said with attitude. "Your sneaky ass brought drama to my door again, and now I have to deal with it! I'm sick of listening to your lies and watching this bullshit unfold! My attorney will contact you soon, but I'm leaving and taking your offspring with me!" I paused briefly, then asked, "Do you understand?"

With a smirk, I took a seat on the bed. Although I used to think talking in code words was stupid, I was thankful Mario taught me how to speak them back in the day. He knew by reading between the lines that I was telling him not to call the house anymore because someone snuck in and was listening and watching. I told him I would contact him through an attorney as soon as I could and that I had both the kids. I used the word "offspring" instead of saying "your kids" because I didn't want the agents to know I had met up with Gucci, who was a fugitive.

"I understand you loud and clear." With those words Mario ended the call.

Chapter 86

Gucci

As soon as we pulled in front of my aunt Lucy's house, I could see her peeking through the front window. My stomach tensed up, and I hesitated momentarily. "Come on and get it over with," Rhythm urged while taking out her gold teeth.

"I'm coming," I said while simultaneously exiting the car and swatting one of those biting flies at the same time. The South was notorious for those fuckers!

"Gucci Robinson, is that you or are my eyes deceiving me?" Aunt Lucy met us at the door of the enclosed add-on porch that was connected to the rear of her house. She was wearing an expression that I couldn't quite get a read on.

"If you're in a good mood, then yes, it's me. If you're not in a good mood, then it's someone else." I smiled.

"Oh, child, hush!" Aunt Lucy smiled. "I'm always in a good mood when my kinfolk come to visit, even if it has been forever since they been here." She walked up to me and wrapped her arms around my waist.

"I know it's been a long time, but you know how life is," I said while hugging her back. Regardless of how long it had been since I'd seen my cousin and aunt, it was still a good feeling to be in the presence of family.

"I was just fixing to clean us some chitterlings for supper. Come on in and tell me what mess you done got yourself into now."

"I hate chitterlings. Do you have some chicken?" I frowned while following her inside the small two-bedroom house. It still looked the way it did back in the day.

"You eat what you get, and you don't throw a fit!" Aunt Lucy recited her saying from when we were kids. "Anyway, what happened up there in Detroit that sent you hightailing it down here?"

"I got into a situation with my husband." I danced around the truth.

"What kind of a situation?" Aunt Lucy wanted details. Lucky for me, her phone started ringing and she got distracted.

"Come on." Rhythm pulled me to the back where her room was. "I have to be at work in a few. You can come with me or you can stay here," she said as she switched into a work shirt with her name on it.

"Where do you work?"

"At the general store down the road," Rhythm replied, and I frowned.

"Nah, I'm good." Staying with Aunt Lucy and her chitterlings was much better than sitting outside in the Alabama heat waiting for Rhythm's shift to be over. Besides, what the fuck was a general store anyway?

"Suit yourself. I'll cash your check on my way to work and bring the money back tonight." Just then Rhythm's phone started ringing. "I think this 313 phone number is for you." She handed me the phone.

"Nikki?" I said, knowing she was the only person I'd called. However, the number on the screen was unfamiliar.

"Hey, Gucci." She sounded drained. "I just got your messages off my old phone. Lock this new number in."

"Okay, I will, but why did you get a new number?"

"I think the DEA might've tapped the other one," she responded nonchalantly. "Did you make it to your destination?

"Yeah, I'm in Alabama with my aunt and cousin. How are things your way?" I could tell something was wrong.

"Someone ran us off the road after I dropped you off. It was that white car in the parking lot of your hotel. They tried to kill us, Gucci."

"Is everyone okay?" I wanted to specifically ask about Maria, but that would have been selfish.

"I'm banged up, but I'll survive. Junior had some glass in his arm, but Maria is all good, not a scratch on her."

"Thank God!" I sighed. "Thank you, Nikki, for being there for my daughter."

"She's family." Nikki sighed. "As much as I hate to admit it, you are family too, Gucci! We are in this together."

"You're right." I nodded as if she could see me. Nikki and I had almost always had an underlying beef with one another since day one, but that was dead now. How could I hate the woman who was caring for my daughter? "Have you spoken to Mario?"

"Briefly. He's still locked up. They have an arraignment on Monday. Hopefully, he makes bail." In the background Maria started to cry. Nikki put me on hold to comfort her, then returned shortly thereafter. "Say something to her, Gucci, so she can hear your voice."

"Hey, mama. I love you. Mommy will be home soon, I promise." With a grin I wiped my eyes. I missed my baby girl tremendously.

"Okay, let me put her down for a nap. You stay safe out there, and I'll be in touch, all right?"

"Later," I said, then handed the cell back to Rhythm.

Chapter 87

Mina

Just as I put the kids down for the night, there was a knock at the door. A quick glance through the peephole indicated that it was Jamison. Although he told me he would stop by earlier, I had completely forgotten. Not only was my house a mess, but my hair was, too. Usually, I handled pressure well and kept things under control. However, today was not a good day. I wanted to tell him to come back, but I knew he wouldn't leave, so I decided to let him in.

"Everything is a mess in here just so you know." I opened the door with a smile and an apology.

"These are for you." Jamison stood there looking finer than ever in a black pinstriped suit. He was holding a carryout bag and a dozen orange carnations. "I figured you had a long day and could use the food." He smiled.

"What are the flowers for?" I raised a brow.

"Just because it's Sunday." He shrugged before stepping inside.

"Thanks. Let me put these in water. I'll be right back. Please make yourself comfortable," I said while heading toward the kitchen.

When I returned, Jamison had removed his suit jacket and was folding some of the kids' laundry I'd left on the sofa. I was so embarrassed. "You don't have to do that."

"Mina, you need a break, so let me help you," Jamison demanded. "I'll do this while you eat."

"Where is Dominique?" His 5-year-old was usually attached to his hip when he wasn't in the office.

"I paid the babysitter for three additional hours so I could swing by and see how you were doing."

"I'm fine I guess." I shrugged while popping the lid on the food container. The food was still hot.

"That's not an answer. How do you really feel?" Jamison stared at me.

"I don't know how to feel, honestly. I mean, Sam is no saint. I knew this day would come, I guess." Forever I'd been urging him to open a restaurant like he always dreamed, but for some reason he couldn't leave Mario and the H.O.F. alone.

"Have you thought about what you would do in the event he goes to jail?" Jamison was asking some really tough questions tonight. He was forcing me to tackle this issue head-on.

"I haven't thought that far out yet," I replied honestly.

"Well, I was talking to my sister. She said the likelihood of your man serving some time is real." With a sigh Jamison looked at me. "Mina, you have to get your business in order." He was speaking to me as if we were planning a funeral or something. However, the only thing dying around here was the relationship between Sam and me.

"May I get you a glass of wine?" I decided to change the subject.

"Yes, if you have red, I'll take it." He continued folding the clothes, and I headed back into the kitchen for two glasses and a bottle of Lindeman's. It was resting in the wine chiller.

For the duration of the night we talked about work, laughed at some of our clients, and finished two bottles of wine. He had to leave when his babysitter called to remind him that he was two hours over the three additional hours he'd paid for. I hated to see him go, but I was thankful he had stopped by. Not only was he good company, but he had also helped me get my house back in order and listened out for the babies while I showered. Before leaving, he placed his sister's card on the table and said she was on standby for the arraignment tomorrow if I needed her. Jamison was a great friend and just what the doctor ordered to get my mind off things with Sam. I had a lot of thinking to do in terms of our relationship, but for now all I needed was to close my eyes and get some rest.

Boom! Boom! The sound of the door woke me from my sleep. With one eye open, I noticed the clock on the nightstand read 5:45 a.m. With an attitude, I stepped into the hallway and peeped in on the babies. Thankfully, they were still knocked out.

"Who the fuck is it?" I hollered once I was down the stairs. Naturally, the person didn't respond, so I crept up to the peephole. "Fuck!" I spat while gripping my chest. Boom! Boom! The knocks came again, urging me to open the door. "Yes, can I help you?"

"We have a warrant to search the premises," a man said before shoving a document in my face and barging past me with a team of men behind him. I was then escorted into the living room by another officer who was instructed to stand there and watch me closely. I felt helpless as the men went in and out of every room in my house. Although I couldn't see what they were doing, I could hear things being thrown around and crashing to the floor.

"What the fuck!" I hollered as one of them pulled a switchblade from his pocket, then poked it into the pillows on the sofa and commenced tearing my shit up.

Reaching over to the cordless phone, I grabbed it and tried to call the number on the card Jamison had left for me. However, when one of the agents saw what I was doing, he went over and snatched the cord from the wall. I was no genius, but my gut was telling me this wasn't right.

"Make another move like that and you will go down with your boyfriend!" the officer barked. I wasn't sure if they could legally charge me with anything, so I didn't protest. Instead, I sat there like a bump on a log while these agents destroyed my home. Naturally when they made it upstairs, they woke the kids up with all the noise. Both babies were crying hysterically, and I couldn't do anything about it.

Finally, after a gruesome forty minutes, the place was empty. They had all but removed my door from the hinges. The cereal and everything in the pantry had been dumped out. The mattresses had been flipped, and almost all of my upholstered furniture had been sliced and diced, along with my carpet. The worst part about the whole thing was that these bastards walked away empty-handed.

"All this for nothing!" I mumbled while grabbing the babies who had both cried so long, they were now shaking. "It's okay. I got you now." I rocked them while assessing the damage done to their nursery. The blinds were on the ground, and all their stuffed animals were ripped to shreds. "I guess this is what I get for loving a street soldier, huh?" I cried to the babies as if they understood me. In this very moment I was reminded of the flip side of the game everyone always talked about. Nothing was safe when it came to love and the dope game, not even the place you laid your head.

Chapter 88

Lovely

It was just after eight o'clock in the morning when Maine finally came into the bedroom. He had fallen asleep on the sofa in the den last night, and I didn't want to disturb him. Quietly he moved around the room, removing his clothing and then slipping beneath the covers. He thought I was asleep and tried hard not to wake me. However, before he could get too comfortable, I hit the light on the nightstand and sat straight up.

"Did you think about my proposal?" We hadn't addressed it at all after I mentioned it the other day.

"Can we talk about this in the morning?" He tried to brush me off.

"It is morning!" I reminded him. "I need to know how bad you want this relationship back the way it used to be, and I need to know now!"

"Why does it have to be her baby?" Maine sat up in the bed beside me.

"Why not her fucking baby?" I rolled my eyes.

"There are plenty of adoptable children in this world, Lovely. Hell, we can go out and get three or four of them if it's babies you want." Maine smirked.

"If I can't carry our baby on my own, then the next best thing would be to raise one that your sperm created with that bitch." I was being cynical, but the facts were the facts.

"Why do you keep bringing that shit up?" Maine was getting irritated.

"Why do you keep acting like it's nothing?" I raised a brow.

"Because it is nothing! She's nothing!" Maine flung the covers back and slid to the side of the bed. "Look." He sighed. "I've been trying to make this work for way too long. Maybe it's best that we just leave it be." He stood, then turned back toward me. "I don't know how many times I have to say it to make you understand. You're the only woman for me, and the love we have is real."

"You say your love for me is real, so prove it," I dared him.

"I've been proving shit the whole time you been my girl!" Maine barked, causing the veins in his neck to protrude again.

"No matter what, I'm taking that baby! Either you're in or you're out. It's just like that!" Although there was some truth in his words, I was done being passive. I knew what I wanted, and that was that.

"She's in Detroit. You're a fugitive in Mexico. How in hell are you going to work your plan?" he asked smugly.

"When my sisters and I didn't have a pot to piss in or a window to throw it out of, I got in the streets and hustled. Not only did I sell dope, I changed the fucking game!" I spat. "When my sister was murdered, I killed the nigga who I thought was responsible without so much as batting an eyelash. Need I remind you I'd never pulled a trigger a day before that one." I paused with a smirk. "And you're right. I'm on the FBI's Most Wanted list and still managed to break out of prison. If you haven't learned by now, I always get shit done!"

For nearly three minutes Maine stared me down as I returned the gesture. Neither of us appeared to be backing down. The line in the sand had been drawn. Maybe this was it for him and me for real. "All right, I'll handle it like I do everything else." He nodded, then left the room just as fast as he'd entered.

I wanted to chase after him and work out the details of our plan but decided to let him be. Truth was, I was just happy he was on board.

With a huge grin, I slid back under the covers and closed my eyes. When I opened them again the clock said 2:30 p.m.

"Damn," I cursed while stretching. I didn't mean to sleep so late, but the rest did feel good. Standing from the bed, I took a quick peek out the window toward the beach, then headed for the shower. Everything was just the way I'd left it, including my old toothbrush. My robe still hung behind the door, and my slippers rested beneath the vanity. After turning on the bathroom light, I began to undress and check myself out in the mirror. Aside from three new gray hairs, everything was the same.

"Hmm, I think I'll take a bubble bath," I said while reaching beneath the sink to grab a bottle of lavender soap. It was one of my favorite scents. As soon as I bent over, my ass was met by the presence of Maine. I didn't know where he'd come from, but the heat generating between his legs was electric.

"You scared me." I stood up, but he bent me back over. Gently he rubbed my back then up and down my thighs. When he got to my ass, he paused abruptly.

"What's wrong? Why did you stop?" I looked up at him through the mirror, and that was when I saw it.

"They did this to you?" Maine's finger traced the number 42 that had been branded on my ass at the whorehouse with a hot branding iron. Immediately I stood and tried to reach for my robe. "Baby, I'm sorry I wasn't there to protect you." He pulled me into his massive arms.

"You're here now, and we'll have our little family soon. That's all that matters." I wrapped my arms around him and squeezed tight. I'm not going to lie. Although my body was here with Maine, my thoughts quickly drifted to Santiago. Part of me wished he was the one holding me right now. We hadn't known each other long, but our chemistry was real.

"Take your bath, get dressed, and meet me downstairs in about an hour. My surprise should be here by then." Maine pulled back from me and glanced at his Cartier wristwatch.

"What's the surprise?" I smiled.

"If I told you, then it wouldn't be one." He shook his head and backed out of the door. "See you in an hour."

Chapter 89

Nikki

Shortly after both kids fell asleep, I slipped back into my shoes and tiptoed out of the bedroom into the living area of the hotel suite. Ms. C was on the couch watching the news. Earlier I'd informed her about the bug in my house and told her they had probably bugged hers too. She agreed to join me and the kids at the hotel until we knew exactly what it was.

"They said Mario could get life behind this," she said while shaking her leg uncontrollably. It was something she did out of nervousness. "Nikki, how can he get life when he hasn't even been charged with murder?" Ms. C looked up at me with tears in her eyes.

I wanted to explain how the RICO charge covered everything from racketeering to murder, but she didn't need to know the logistics. Some things were better left unsaid. If she knew how dirty her son's hands really were, she would've been sick about it.

"Ma, you need to stop watching the news." I casually grabbed the remote and switched the station to Bravo. Hopefully, there was a *Housewives* show on to hold her attention.

"That's my baby." Claudia blew her nose into the tissue she pulled from her bra. "I tried to get that boy to do right. I swear I did." She sniffed. "Despite my efforts, he turned out just like his father."

"Ms. C, don't beat yourself up. You did the best that you could as a single mother. Mario knew right from wrong, and unfortunately he chose the latter." Taking a seat beside my ex-mother-in-law, I rubbed her back. Mentally she was going through a lot. I knew she was on the verge of a breakdown. We all were.

"He never even knew his father, so tell me how he turned out so much like him?" Ms. Claudia looked to me for the answer she knew I didn't have. I remained silent. We never talked about Mario's dad. Honestly, the only thing I knew about him was that he was a stick-up boy in the late seventies. In '83, he was shot dead while trying to rob a pastor on his way to Bible study. Mario was born two months later.

"Ms. C, don't get yourself worked up. Mario will get through this just like every other thing in his life." I stood from the couch. "I have a meeting with his attorney. I'll be back in a few hours."

"Nikki, please be careful." Ms. C warned as her cell phone starting ringing. "Hello. Hey, Anjela. I'm doing okay and you?"

"Hang up," I whispered.

Ms. C paused for a minute, then did as I instructed. "That was your cousin. I'm sure she was just checking on Mario," Ms. C responded, completely confused about why I had her hang up the phone.

"Don't talk to anyone on your phone about Mario until I speak with the attorney. I'll call her on my new phone." With that I grabbed the keys and headed out the door.

Once in the hallway I called my cousin back. "Who is this?" she asked because she didn't recognize the number.

"It's Nikki," I replied with an attitude. Honestly, this bitch was the last person I wanted to have a conversation with. She and her boyfriend Carter were number one on my shit list.

"Where have you been? I've been calling you like crazy."

"Ask your nigga where I'm at. I'm sure he got a LoJack on my ass." I smacked my lips. "Anyway, what did you want?"

"Nikki, don't be like that."

"Be like what?" I hollered. "I asked you flat out if your boy was building a case against Mario, and you said no!"

"Cousin, right hand to God I had no idea about the case. You have to believe me," Anjela pleaded. "Y'all my family. I would never willingly allow anyone to build a case!"

"Well, he did, and now Mario is going to jail!" I stepped onto the stairwell and screamed at the top of my lungs. Tears fell down my face like raindrops. I'd held them back and tried to be tough for so long, but reality was finally setting in. "My son will never remember his father if he goes away now." I wiped my eyes. "Do you know Mario will fuckin' die in jail?" The thought alone was killing me.

"Cousin, don't speak that into existence." Anjela tried to run that "think positive" shit I'd been running on everyone else, but it was useless.

"Look, I gotta go." I wiped my eyes and exited the stairwell.

"Can we meet for dinner?" Her voice softened.

"I'll call you when I leave the attorney's office." I ended the call without another word.

Chapter 90

Gucci

For several long hours, me and Aunt Lucy sat on her porch and chopped it up while waiting for Rhythm to return from work. I filled her in on most of my life after turning 16, and she shared memories of my mother.

"Gwendolyn was not only my little sister, but she was also my best friend." Aunt Lucy laughed. "She was the prettiest thing you ever did see. All the boys liked her."

"Yeah, she was pretty." I recalled the few pictures I'd seen of her.

"That girl was something else, too. She was always fascinated with fancy cars, jewelry, and clothes. That's how you got your name." Aunt Lucy smiled. "I remember we was sitting out in the field reading magazines one day. She saw a Gucci ad and told me that was what she was going to name her daughter when she had one. Needless to say, she was a woman of her word."

"How did she end up in Detroit?" My father had already told me the story, but I wanted to hear it again.

"We were at Sandy's nightclub one night. That's where all the teenagers hung back then, ya know." Aunt Lucy took a sip from her mason jar filled with sweet tea, then continued. "Me and your mama were sitting in the booth when this tall, lanky, baby-faced nigga with processed hair approached us. He was wearing a silk suit and a thick herringbone chain. He kissed your mom's hand, then asked her if she was tired. Gwen said, 'No. Why do you ask?' Your father replied, 'Because you've been running through my mind all day.'" Aunt Lucy cracked up laughing.

"Chile, his game was wack, but he had your mom open. He escorted her to the dance floor for just two songs, but, honey, when Gwen came back, she was in love. Next thing I know she told us she was leaving." Aunt Lucy stopped laughing. "My sister left and never come back though, Gucci."

The conversation had taken a gloomy turn to the left as Aunt Lucy began to mourn her dead sister. I sat there in awkward silence because I didn't have as much pain as she did. I was a baby when my mother died from cancer. I didn't know her at all, but I often wished I did.

"Well, that's enough storytelling for tonight. I'm going inside. Are you coming?"

"No. I'm going to wait out here for Rhythm." I shook my head.

The time alone was supposed to provide me with peace of mind. Instead, my thoughts consumed me, and before I knew it, I was crying. The tears were not due to sadness but anger. All I wanted was to beat the fuck out of Cartier right now. How could he jeopardize my freedom and put me in such a fucked-up situation? I thought he loved me.

"Never confuse love with loyalty, Gucci." Although I was alone, I could hear Mario's voice loud and clear.

"Loyalty ain't shit but a seven-letter word." I could hear Cartier's warning just the same. This nigga was telling me then that he wasn't shit. I was just too blinded by what I thought I wanted to pay attention.

"Fuck!" I stomped my feet. I hated feeling helpless. I hated being out of my element, and I hated having to sit on my fucking hands.

Just as I stood to go in the house, I saw Rhythm's car come down the dirt road. She didn't look happy.

"What's wrong? Did you have a bad day?" I asked when she stepped out of her car.

"Gucci, you better sit down." She proceeded up to the porch with caution.

"Why?" I questioned.

"I took the check to the bank. When I tried to cash it, they told me it was bogus. The account he wrote the check from is closed." Rhythm handed me the paperwork.

"So, this motherfucker played me?" I hollered.

"Maybe it's a misunderstanding," Rhythm whispered so as not to alarm her mother. "We can go back tomorrow."

"This ain't no goddamn misunderstanding." I paced the porch. In Detroit, niggas would never attempt to play me. In Birmingham, nobody knew my gangster. It was time to show these Alabama folks who exactly the fuck I was!

Chapter 91

Mina

There was no time to even attempt to clean up the mess left by the DEA before I had to get myself and the babies dressed and out the door. "Shit!" I cursed upon noticing these muthafuckas had tossed all of my panties and bras around the bedroom. Angrily I grabbed them piece by piece and stuffed them back into my drawer. The picture frames from my dresser had also been trashed. Among them was a photo of my son who died of SIDS: sudden infant death syndrome. Of all the things that could've pissed me off, this one took the cake.

"How could they do this to you, son?" I talked to the picture while carefully trying not to cut myself on the broken glass covering my baby's face. "I love you and I always will. Mommy is so sorry they disrespected you." After wiping a tear from my face, I took a seat on the bed. With a deep sigh I tried hard to collect my sanity. What was I doing here? How did I end up in this predicament? These thoughts and many other things invaded my space as I pondered my relationship with Sam. Stupid, betrayed, and taken for granted were a few things that described how I was feeling. Here I was being faithful and loyal to a muthafucka who probably couldn't even spell those words if I paid him.

Looking around the distressed bedroom, I quickly contemplated my exit. Now was the time to pack my shit and get the fuck out of dodge! I needed to start anew somewhere else where nobody knew my name. However, before I could even muster the strength to get up from the bed, I suddenly remembered why I'd chosen to stay the last time. In all honesty, it had nothing to do with love or loyalty. It also had nothing to do with his children, whom I adored. The only reason I was still by Sam's side was because I owed him for killing my abusive husband, who was also an undercover police officer. Not only had Sam freed me from that bad situation, but he'd also literally put his life on the line to save mine. Even though it was an unspoken thing in our house, we both knew we were bonded by this secret 'til eternity. I couldn't go anywhere even though I wanted to.

Almost forty minutes later, the kids and I arrived at Happy Places, a daycare center I used from time to time. It was closer to the city, which was quite a way from my house, but the owner Hannah was such a sweetheart. Her place was clean, and her staff was amazing, too. They loved their jobs and treated all the children well.

"Hello, Ms. Mina." Hannah smiled from behind the desk at the front door.

"Hi, Hannah. Thank you so much for taking Solomon and Samantha on short notice." Quickly I signed them in and paid the five-hour daycare fee.

"It's not a problem at all." With a smile she grabbed Samantha from my arm, then called into the office for someone to come out and get Solomon. "This is my new employee, Tynika. Tynika, this is Amina."

"Oh, my God," I replied before I even realized it. "What are you doing here?" I asked with an attitude.

"I work here. Didn't you hear her?" Tynika replied with a smile, but I didn't miss the roll of her eyes.

"Do you two know each other?" Hannah was perplexed.

"I'm Solomon's mother," she said casually while reaching for him.

"I'm Solomon's mother. Don't get it twisted," I replied while snatching him back. "Hannah, I don't have time to deal with this now, but she"—I pointed—"is not, I repeat, she is not allowed to touch my children."

"I can touch whatever I gave birth to!" Tynika snapped back.

"Hannah, I'm serious." I tried hard to ignore Tynika, but the bitch was jumping all over my last nerve. "I don't want her anywhere near my children."

"Mina, hush, girl. We both know ain't none of these babies yours." Tynika laughed. "Your old ass probably don't have any eggs left," she mumbled.

"Bitch, don't get fucked up today," I snapped. She had me completely out of my zone. "They may not have come from between my legs, but I'm more of a goddamn mother than you will ever be!" I was ready to collect my kids and storm out. However, I didn't have anywhere else to go.

"Okay, ladies, that's enough," Hannah intervened. "I don't know what is going on, but this is not the place for powwows and power trips." She wiped sweat from her brow. This poor white lady had probably never seen confrontation this up close and personal. Had this been a black daycare, the owner probably would have picked a side and joined in.

"Tynika, you have a job to do. Please remain professional and go do it." Hannah looked on as Tynika grudgingly headed down the hallway, before returning her attention to me. "I'm sure you have somewhere to be too, right?" She reached over and grabbed Solomon. "Don't worry. I'll keep them with me. Your kids are in good hands. Go ahead and handle your business." She smiled, which comforted me.

"Thank you," I said before kissing the kids and waving goodbye. To say that I was angry with Tynika for choosing employment at the one day-care I used was an understatement. Beneath the anger was an underlying fear that she would take Solomon and get missing. Then I remembered she didn't want him in the first place. It was her choice to give him up, so I probably had nothing to fear.

After saying a quick prayer, I started up the engine and headed downtown to tackle the next task at hand. During the short drive I wondered what may have been going through Sam's mind. I knew he was scared, and rightfully so. I was petrified for him. This hearing could change life as we knew it.

Buzzzzzzzz. Buzzzzzzzz. I answered the vibrating cell phone in my lap. "Hello."

"Hey, it's me. How are you?" Jamison's voice was rich and smooth, almost like a late-night radio host's.

"I've had better days, but this too shall pass. How are you?"

"You're right, this too shall pass. I've been in a few storms myself, and the one thing I know for sure is the sun almost always comes after the rain." He paused to let his words sink in. "Hey, I'm not going to hold you, but I was wondering if you wanted to swing by my spot for dinner tonight. I'm making my famous five-meat lasagna."

"I don't think I can tonight, but I will definitely take you up on that offer one day." I smiled lightly. Jamison was a good man. I knew he'd make some man very happy one day. That's right, I said "man." Recently he'd confided in me his feelings toward the same sex.

"I understand." He sounded discouraged. "Well, keep your head up, and we'll talk soon."

"Okay. I'll call you when I get out of court." I ended the call.

After circling a few blocks to find a decent parking spot, I finally gave up and paid the hefty $25 parking lot fee. The lot was close enough that I didn't think twice about walking in the four-inch heels. Inside, I went through the metal detector, then went in search of the courtroom Sam would have his hearing in. Once I found it, I stood against the wall and scanned the crowd for Carla. She arrived almost three minutes later.

"Thank you so much for coming down here on such short notice," I said after recognizing her face from a picture on Jamison's desk. She was a petite lady with ebony skin. Carla wasn't bad looking, but the semi-rimless glasses and church-lady wig made her appear older than I knew she was. Her suit was sleek and up to date, but the black loafers on her feet threw the entire outfit off. I wanted badly to make over my new acquaintance, but today was not that kind of day.

"No problem," she said while shaking my hand. "Jamie filled me in on the case, but is there anything I should know before I step into the courtroom?"

"No." I shook my head while dodging a man trying to get past me. The court building was packed, and everyone seemed to be in a rush. "Do you think Sam will do time?"

"This is just an arraignment," Carla replied while going through her briefcase.

"What's an arraignment?" I asked. "This is all new to me." I felt the need to explain my lack of court knowledge.

"It's the first part of the process, if you will." Carla pushed her glasses up her nose. "The judge will explain to Sam what he has been charged with, and he will be expected to make a plea of guilty, not guilty or no contest."

"What's no contest?" I asked with a raised brow just as Nikki and another lady entered the courthouse. They were in line to go through the metal detectors.

"That means Sam will not plead guilty, but he doesn't dispute the charges." Carla looked down at her watch. "I'm going to go inside and prepare. Are you coming?"

"Yeah, but give me a minute," I said as Nikki and her companion approached us. "Hey, Nikki." I spoke with a nod.

"Hey, girl. How are you?" Nikki smiled and embraced me with a tight hug. I was shocked but returned the gesture, nonetheless.

"I'm good, I guess." With a shrug I asked, "How are you?"

"I'll be all right once this is over." She smiled halfheartedly.

"I know that's right."

"How are the babies doing?"

"They're doing well. How is little Mario?" I hated to keep asking her the same questions she was asking me, but I didn't know what else to say.

"He's fine, just missing his dad, that's all." She sighed.

"Have you heard from Gucci?" Honestly, I could give less than a fuck about her conniving ass, but curiosity was killing me since she seemingly vanished into thin air.

"No, I haven't. Have you?"

"Nope." I shook my head.

"We're in room 204. Which one are you in?" Nikki asked.

"We're right here in 202." I pointed to the sign on the courtroom door.

"Hey, I have to run, but I'll be praying for Sam. Please do the same for Rio." She patted my shoulder and walked into the other courtroom.

Although we had never been enemies, she and I weren't exactly friends either. Yet and still, this whole ordeal had created an unspoken bond between us. We were both mothers dealing with the wrath of having men in the dope game.

Chapter 92

Nikki

"Do you see Mario?" Anjela asked after we took our seats. There were about ten men in orange jumpsuits sitting near the defendant table. All of them I recognized from the H.O.F. Instantly my stomach did a backflip. Not only were some of these men like family, but it also pained me severely to see some of their mothers, sisters, and wives going through the same torment I was going through. These men were the heads and breadwinners of their families. Without them, these families would surely suffer.

"No, I don't see him." I said, finally processing what my cousin had asked me. She and I were not on good terms yet, but I needed her today. Ms. Claudia didn't need to be in the courtroom in case things went sideways, so I asked her to watch the kids and brought Anj with me instead. We still had to talk about how things went down, but for now I was happy to have someone by my side.

"Damien Davis, bail has been set at one hundred thousand dollars." Judge Kym Louis banged her gavel.

Instinctively I looked over at Sharon, Damien's mother. I knew she didn't have that kind of money, not even 10 percent. My heart ached while watching the tears fall down her eyes. She was a good mother who had worked two jobs to keep her children off the street. However, after being laid off from both places, young Damien took to the streets to keep his family above water. I wanted to go over and console Sharon, but fear kept me planted. I didn't know how she would respond to me, so I decided to catch her another time.

"The court will take a ten-minute recess before the next case is called." Judge Kym banged her gavel once again. All the men sitting near the defendant table stood and were escorted through a side door. They were all chained together by their waists and ankles. The image resembled that of slavery. Although they were responsible for being here, the sight was still unnerving.

"I think we're a few minutes early. Mario is probably up next," Anjela informed me, and I nodded.

"Ms. Nikki." I heard someone say from behind me while tapping my shoulder.

I turned around to see Daysha. She was the girlfriend of Big Red, one of Mario's soldiers. "Hey, Daysha." I smiled. "How are you holding up?"

"They gave Red a thirty-thousand-dollar cash bond, Ms. Nikki." Her eyes filled up with water. "Where am I going to get that kind of money?" That was her subtle way of asking me for it.

"I don't know, sweetheart." I sighed.

"Ms. Nikki, I don't mean to sound rude or anything, but I know you have it. If I could just borrow it to bring Red home, I swear on my kids I'll pay you back." Although the desperation in her eyes tugged at my heartstrings, I couldn't help her even if I wanted to. Not only was I dealing with my own shit, but I also knew that if I helped her, the others would expect the same to be done for them.

"Red should have a rainy-day fund," I reminded her. Hell, it was rule number two in the dope game.

"We don't have a dollar." She looked down at the floor. These young hustlers were out here spending money on frivolous shit like cars, clothes, and shoes they couldn't even pronounce. Everybody wanted to stunt, but nobody wanted to be responsible. If nothing else, this was a lesson learned for all of them.

"Baby girl, I don't have thirty thousand to give you. I'm sorry." With that I turned back around. I hated to be short with her, but my hands were tied.

"Here comes another one." Anjela nudged me just as Joy waltzed her way over to me. She was dressed to the nines in a black pantsuit with a pair of Ferragamo python shoes and a matching handbag. Her Mary J. Blige shades and head wrap looked odd for the courtroom, but she didn't care. Being dramatic was her thing.

"Nikki baby, we need to talk." She removed her shades to reveal the green contact lenses in her eyes.

"What's up, Joy?" I was trying my best not to get irritated. Joy and I never liked each other, but we played nice for the guys.

"I need a few stacks to get Angelo out," she replied casually. "And before you say no, let me tell you why I think it's only fair for you to give it to me." Joy proceeded, "If it weren't for Mario and his mistress—oops, I mean, his wife—none of us would be here." She stated it as a matter of fact.

"Joy, you got five seconds to get the fuck out of my face before this becomes a problem," I calmly explained.

"Nikki baby, I like you, but the truth is the truth. Your man owes us!"

"Mario doesn't owe you a goddamn thing!" I snapped.

"He owes us!" This time she got in my face. Instinctively I balled my fist up.

"Joy, please get up and leave now!" Anjela jumped in.

We were making a spectacle of ourselves, and the courtroom was filled with reporters happily writing everything down. They probably wanted a fight to break out. Be that as it may, I was not about to give them a show.

"The Wallace family owes us!" she hollered, causing an officer to rush toward us.

"What's the problem?"

"Sir, this woman is harassing my cousin. She needs to be escorted out!" Anjela demanded.

"I ain't got to be escorted no damn where!" Joy stood. "I'm leaving, but I will see you again."

"Is that a threat?" I frowned.

"I'll see you again, Nikki!" She put her shades back on just as dramatically as she'd removed them and stormed off.

"You good, cuz?" Anjela asked just as the judge returned. The bailiff called court back into session and then Mario's case. His lawyer stood, but Mario was nowhere in sight.

"Where is he?" I asked while sitting straight up in my seat.

"Mario Wallace, I have received your plea of not guilty. Is this correct?" the judge asked, and I frowned because I still didn't see him.

"That's true, Your Honor."

I heard his voice, then looked over to see his face on a closed-circuit television monitor. My baby looked rough but was still as fine as ever. His eyes were a little weary and his beard was a little longer than it had been the last time I saw him. Although he was in a fucked-up predicament, he still sat tall in the seat where he was cuffed to the table. I wondered if he could see me.

Parish Markel stood and addressed the judge. "At this time, we would like to request that the defendant be released on bail, Your Honor." Parish was the top defense attorney in the entire state of Michigan. With a record of having only three losses in his eighteen-year career, we felt confident in his capabilities. When I met with him the other night, he really impressed me with his strategy.

"Objection, Your Honor!" The prosecutor stood. "Not only is Mr. Wallace a known drug lord, but he is also—"

"Alleged drug lord," Parish interjected.

"He is also a flight risk! A man of his caliber has the means to get out of state like that!" The prosecutor snapped his finger.

"My client has children here and ties to the community," Parish added.

"His wife Gucci Wallace has already fled, Your Honor."

"Mrs. Wallace has nothing to do with my client's case!" Parish shook his head while reminding the courtroom, "As the prosecutor stated, a man of his caliber could be gone like that, right?" Parish mimicked the prosecutor by snapping his finger. "Well, if he were trying to flee, don't you think he would have been gone before the DEA even had time to print up a warrant?"

"Enough!" Judge Kym banged her gavel. "Bail for Mario Wallace has been denied." She banged her gavel once more to call the next case. Just like that, all hopes of Mario coming home were dead.

Hurriedly I stood from my seat and fled the courtroom with tears in my eyes. "Oh, my God," I cried.

"Nikki, it's going to be okay." Anjela was right there by my side.

"No, it's not. Mario is going to prison. He ain't never coming home." My head pounded like a hammer to a nail as I contemplated what was happening. I'd almost lost Rio to death several times, but prison seemed to be the thing that was surely going to take him away for good.

"I can't do forty-five years to life, Anjela." I spoke through my tears. I was crying so hard that snot was streaming down my face. The scene was very embarrassing, but I didn't care. At that moment, my world had come crashing down.

"Ms. Wallace," I heard from behind me. After wiping my nose with the sleeve of my shirt, I turned to see Parish. "I know things looked pretty bad in there, but that's how these things go. I'll submit an appeal tonight. Right now, I need you to come with me though."

"Where?" I sniffed, then wiped my eyes.

"I've pulled some strings with a colleague of mine so that you can see Mr. Wallace in the law-yer's room for a few minutes."

"Really?" I mustered a smile. "Can we do that?" I looked over at Anjela.

"Technically no," Parish replied. "But it'll be okay for just a few minutes. Come on." He nodded for me to follow him.

Quickly I handed Anjela my purse, then hurried to catch up with Parish. That was when I spotted Sam and Mina on the other side of the room. He was uncuffed and dressed in regular clothes. While I was happy that at least someone would make it home to their family tonight, I had to wonder how in the fuck that was possible! Something in the milk wasn't clean.

Chapter 93

Lovely

"Auntie L, are you ready yet?" DeShawna asked for the tenth time in five minutes.

"Yeah, I'm ready." With a smile I opened the door. She had been pacing back and forth the entire time it took me to bathe and get dressed.

"What's the big surprise?" I asked.

"My lips are sealed." She pretended to lock her mouth and throw away the key.

"Well, I have some cookies-and-cream ice cream that says otherwise."

"I'm not telling." She laughed. "And besides, you don't have any ice cream anyways."

"Girl, you are something else." I laughed too.

"Come on." She pulled me down the stairs.

As soon as we entered the living room everyone yelled, "Surprise!"

"Oh, my God!" I smiled. "Nichols? Coco?" Do it and Maine were standing there too, but they weren't the surprise. Seeing Nichols and Coco was a reminder of the things I missed about Detroit.

"Hey, girl!" Coco hugged me tight. "I missed you so much."

"I've missed you too," I replied. Being that I was still a fugitive on the run, I couldn't exactly call or go see her the way I wanted to.

"Hey, baby." Agent Nichols smiled and wrapped her arms around me as well. "I hear you've been having some rough times. Do you want to go somewhere and talk with us?"

"Not right now. Let's just enjoy the moment," I said, before releasing their embrace. "Maine, you did this for me?"

"Yeah." He nodded. "I thought seeing some familiar faces would make you feel better."

"Thank you," I mouthed. "How are my godsons?" I asked Coco.

"Both of them are getting big, girl. Their asses aren't my little babies anymore."

"I can only imagine." Although I smiled, there was a sadness beneath it all. In addition to missing my godchildren grow up, I had also come to the realization that our children wouldn't be close the way she and I always imagined they would be.

"Auntie L, let's open your presents," DeShawna urged.

"I got some presents, too?" I grinned, completely enjoying every moment of this reunion.

"Well, since we missed your last birthday, it's only right." Coco giggled. "Open mine up first."

She handed me a box wrapped in black paper with a pretty silver bow.

"Drumroll please." I made the sound while unwrapping the box to reveal a photo album. The pictures inside chronicled our life together from childhood up until I was arrested. There were pictures of my parents back in the day when things were good and pictures of my sisters, too. Upon stopping on a photo of Tori, I paused. "She would've been eighteen this year."

Ding-dong! The sound of the doorbell broke up the sad moment. Everyone in the room was relieved.

"Oh, that's the pizza I ordered. Lovely, can you get the door?" Maine looked up from the call he was making on his cell phone.

"You stay there, baby. I'll get it," Agent Nichols insisted.

"Make sure you check it before they leave!" I hollered. That was something I did religiously whenever I ordered delivery. There was nothing like sitting down to eat, then realizing your food wasn't right.

Boom! The small explosion completely caught everyone by surprise. Although there was no fire, the smell of smoke and burnt flesh quickly filled the room. "What the fuck was that?" Although I was screaming, I could barely hear myself due to the ringing in my ear. In slow motion I watched as Maine and Do It ran toward the front door. After getting my bearings, I followed suit. That's when I realized what happened.

"Shit!" Maine yelled at the sight of Nichols's headless body in the middle of our foyer. Blood was everywhere.

"Keep Shawnie in there, Coco," Do It instructed.

"Oh, my God!" Never had I seen something so disturbing in all of my life. The explosion had not only blown her head off, but it burst her chest cavity open as well. On cue I threw up.

"Lovely, get back!" Maine hollered before examining the other pizza boxes lying on the floor. He wanted to make sure there were no more live bombs.

"I can't believe this shit!" Had I gone to the door to get the pizza, that would've been me.

"Fuck!" Maine pounded on the floor. "We've been made by the Mexican Mafia!" He looked up at me. I knew then that getting out of here alive would prove to be a struggle.

"This was a warning. We need to get the fuck out of here now." Maine paced the foyer.

"Where are we going to go? We won't get off this island alive." Although I'd directed the statement to Maine, my eyes were fixed on the corpse before me. Seeing Nichols in this state caused pain to rip through my body as I was plagued with death yet again. "How many more people do you think I have to lose before the Lord realizes I've had enough?"

"Lo, this wasn't your fault." Do It took a seat on the floor beside me.

"She was here because of me. She went to the door because of me." I pointed at myself. Guilt was weighing heavy on my chest.

"Everyone needs to go upstairs and pack a few bags." Maine stopped pacing. "When nightfall comes, we'll move." He unbuttoned his shirt and placed it over what was left of Nichols. Then he proceeded down the hallway to his study and closed the door.

Chapter 94

Gucci

"I'm going to blow his muthafucking brains out!" I spat while pacing the living room floor. Aunt Lucy was at work. Rhythm was sitting at the table eating a bowl of Raisin Bran. Although she'd given me the bad news last night, I was still pissed.

"Cousin Gucci, you can't go around killing folks. Let's call the police."

"I told you, where I'm from we get justice in the streets!" I digressed from letting her know that I could very well kill Will and wouldn't think twice. She didn't need to know all of that.

"You are not in Detroit anymore," she reminded me. "Let's just go back down there and talk to him."

"Oh, I'm going to talk to him all right." I nodded. The steam was practically blowing through my nose I was so hot. "Look, I need to get out for a minute. Can I use your car?"

"I'll take you wherever you need to go." She looked at me suspiciously.

"I need to do this alone." I looked her up and down.

"Hell no, you ain't going to use my car to kill Will and have my ass locked up." She shook her head.

"Fuck Will! I'll see him later. Right now, I need to handle some business."

"Where are you going?"

"That place Diamondz we rode past yesterday." I felt like a child having to explain my comings and goings, but it was Rhythm's car, so I had no choice.

"The strip club?" She frowned. "What business you got up there?"

"I need a job." I sighed. Until I could settle this situation with Will, I needed income and I needed it fast.

"I can call my manager and get you in at the general store." Rhythm pulled out her phone.

"Please don't take this the wrong way, but I need some real money. Can I borrow the car or not?"

"Gucci, I can't have my car sitting in the parking lot of the devil's playground." Rhythm took a spoonful of cereal. "What would the church people or my neighbors think?"

"That's your problem. You care too much about what other people think." After grabbing my phone from the wall charger, I headed for the door. Rhythm called after me, but I was done talking, so I left her sitting right there.

***

The walk to Diamondz took a little over thirty-five minutes. When I arrived, the place was mostly empty, which meant it was a good time to talk to the owner.

"Can I help you?" a lady standing behind the bar in a tank top and blue jeans asked.

"Is the owner or manager in yet?"

"Have a seat, and I'll get her for you." The bartender strutted to the back, and I took a seat. The club was decent but had the potential to be even better. Some of the furnishings were old and desperately needed to be updated, like the shaggy red carpet. It had surely seen better days. The dancer on stage was wearing a simple pair of panties and some black heels. Although she was pretty, she looked boring. In Detroit we were used to flashy costumes and state-of-the-art venues. Take my spot the Doll House for instance. It was adorned with leather furniture, mirrors on the ceiling, elevated VIP booths, and rotating poles.

"Hello." A brown-skinned girl with piercings in her dimples approached me. She was covered in tattoos and her hair was black and blue. Nonetheless, she was a cutie.

"You must be Diamond." I stood from the stool. "Nice place," I lied.

"No, I'm Kutthroat Kardashian, the manager. Funky is the owner. Diamond is our daughter."

"Damn, Ms. Kardashian, that's a long-ass name."
I giggled.

"Everyone calls me KK for short." She laughed
too. "When I first named myself, the Kardashian
thing was a gimmick."

"Okay, KK, I feel ya. Well, I'm here to see if
you need any new dancers. I come with plenty of
experience." As a stripper I didn't exactly have a
resume, so she had to take my word for it.

"As a matter of fact, we are. Do you have a caba-
ret license?"

"I do, but I don't have one on me." I'd left my
license at the house when I fled Michigan.

"Baby, I can't have you working on my stage
without proper documentation." KK shook her
head.

"I need this job to get back on my feet. Please just
give me some time to get it sent down here from
Detroit." I was basically pleading.

"It's been real, baby, but I can't hire you." KK
turned to walk away. That's when a big man came
from the office behind her. He was fat, black, and
ugly as ever. However, the swag about the nigga
was unmistakable.

"Did you say you was from Detroit?" He made
his way past KK over to me. "Where did you dance
at?" I didn't miss the way his eyes roamed nearly
every inch of my body.

"I ran the Doll House." I nodded. He didn't need to know I was the owner.

"Okay, okay." He ran a chubby hand down his full beard. "Of course, I'm going to need a private show to see how you work, but I think we can make an exception." He looked back at KK, who had a straight attitude.

"I'm ready whenever you are." I smirked.

"Shit, you can come up to my office right now if you 'bout it."

"Let's go then," I replied, not missing a beat.

"Funky, what you are doing?" KK was pissed. She knew what was about to happen and didn't like it at all.

"What's your name, sweetheart?" Funky asked me, completely ignoring his baby mama.

"Novella," I lied, thinking quick.

"That's different. Where did you come up with that?" he asked as we passed KK.

"When I dance, I tell a story," I adlibbed.

"Well, I can't wait to open your book." Funky led me up the stairs into his office, then locked the door.

The office was a small studio apartment fully equipped with a kitchen, living space, and bathroom. In the middle of the floor was a black leather sofa and ottoman facing a fifty-six-inch television. Below the TV was a cable box and a surround-sound system.

"I'll make myself comfortable while you go change." Funky took a seat on the sofa positioned in front of a pole mounted to the floor. The Polo cologne drifting from his body was a turn-on. I hadn't been this close to a man in a few days.

"I prefer to dance naked." Sensually I removed my bottom and then my T-shirt to completely expose my birthday suit.

"Oh, shit!" Funky sat back farther into the seat, then grabbed the remote to the iPod dock and pressed play. Instantly R. Kelly's song "Imagine That" boomed over the surround-sound speaker system. On cue, I began to do a slow dance. Funky looked like a kid in a candy store watching my breasts shift from side to side. Next, I walked over and positioned myself over the crotch of his jeans and began to grind. I could feel Funky's manhood rising, which enticed me to turn up the heat.

"You like that?" I grabbed his hands and began to caress my ample body with them. Before long he didn't need my guidance. His hands roamed every inch of my body without hesitation. Gently he caressed my nipples. I could feel myself getting more aroused by the second, yet I continued to dance. By the time Trey Songz was singing about neighbors knowing his name, I removed myself from Funky's lap and headed for the pole. I could tell he wasn't ready for me to get up, but he relented and let me do my thing.

Seductively I stroked the pole and made a show making my ass clap. Instinctively Funky reached into his pocket and tossed a few dollars. Just as I began to contort my body into a pole trick, his phone rang. From the expression on his face, I could tell that he wanted to dismiss the call. However, the consistent ringing was annoying us both.

"KK, what's up?" he answered reluctantly. "Give me twenty minutes," he yelled over the music. I continued dancing, completely unbothered by the cock-blocking bitch downstairs. "Girl, I'll be down there in a minute." This time Funky hung up. "I'm sorry, Novella, but we got to wrap this up. My girl is trippin'."

Without a word I started spinning on the pole with my legs open. At the same time, I was stimulating my pussy with the middle and index finger on my right hand. Shit had just gotten real! "I guess you have to go, huh?" I asked before pulling my fingers out and placing them right into my mouth.

"Yeah, I do, but not before I lick that big, fat pussy." He bent down and planted his face deep into my crotch. I was caught off guard but loved the surprise head. It was a bonus in my book.

"Oh, shit!" I moaned as he sucked the piercing through my clit. My pussy was wet and juicy. It didn't matter how big, black, or ugly this mutha-fucka was. At the moment, he had what I needed.

"You like that shit?" He really wasn't looking for an answer, but I gave him one anyway.

"This shit is so good," I moaned.

"Let a nigga slide it in right quick." He was borderline begging. I wasn't really into fucking niggas on the first encounter, but desperate times called for desperate measures. A bitch had needs!

"You got a condom?" My voice was just above a whimper.

"Never leave home without 'em." Funky reached into his pocket and retrieved the black Trojan packet. I knew what that meant and shuddered at the thought.

"Yeah, I'm a big nigga, and my dick is too!" He was cocky but I didn't mind. It was a turn-on.

"Let me be the judge of that." I spread my legs wide and gripped the pole for dear life.

Nothing could've prepared me for the pounding that nigga put down. He fucked me every which way but loose. Within twenty minutes, I'd managed to cum three times before he could even bust once. "Fuck!" I whimpered. I thought I was a monster in the bed, but Funky was a beast! He wasn't the best I'd ever had, but he was definitely a close second or third.

Just when he was about to cum, his cell phone rang, which fucked with his concentration. Reluctantly, he pulled his dick from inside my warm walls. "Look, I'm sorry, but I gotta call this a wrap before KK kicks the door in." He laughed.

"No worries. The pleasure was all mine," I replied with a smirk.

"I'll see your sexy ass tonight. Be here at ten."

Chapter 95

Mina

"Goddamn!" Sam yelled when he walked through the front the door of the building. Inhaling hard, he smiled. "A nigga is happy to be on the outside. You don't know how much you value shit like the clouds, trees, and grass until they are taken away from you." He went on and on like a nigga coming off a real bid.

"I'm glad you're free, baby," I said as we walked down the block. By the time I'd gotten into the courtroom, Sam's case had already been heard. I thought the hearing was at 10:30 a.m., but it was at 8:30 a.m. In addition to being upset for wasting Carla's time, I also thought I'd missed my only opportunity to see Sam. However, to my surprise, we were informed that the charges against him had been dropped by the prosecutor. I didn't know how, and I didn't ask why. All I knew was that my man was home, and this foolishness was behind us.

"Ay, Mina, I'm going to drop you off. Then I gotta go holla at my mans and 'em."

"Sam!" I smacked my lips. "You just got out. Can't that wait until tomorrow? The kids miss you, and so do I," I pouted. "Besides, I need help putting the house back together." I went on to explain how the DEA raided our shit.

"Mina, the house ain't going nowhere. Neither are you and the kids. I got some business to handle. Once it's done, I'll be home."

"What business?" I wanted to know.

"My business!" He shut me down.

"Whatever." Smacking my lips, I unlocked the car.

"What's up with the attitude?" He looked at me sideways while falling into the passenger seat. "I'm the one whose been through a lot these past few days." He sighed.

"A lot?" I frowned. "Nigga, you did a couple of days in the local precinct! Big fucking deal!"

"How much time have you ever done?" He turned toward me as I backed the car out of the parking space.

"It doesn't matter," I snapped. "All I'm saying is your family needs you at home!"

"I'll be home later." He refused to back down. "I told you I need to holla at my mans and 'em." He reclined in the seat.

"Your mans and them, or some fucking bitch?"

"Here you go." Sam shook his head.

"Don't act shocked. After all, it was just a few days ago you told me you fucked Gucci, remember?" By now my blood was boiling. I was livid just recalling the shit to him.

"That was a mistake," Sam insisted.

"A mistake is leaving your goddamn keys in the car," I shouted. "You fucked that bitch with no regard to me or my feelings." On instinct, I hauled off and slapped the dog shit out of him. Instantly I wished I hadn't done that, but I was in a zone. My mother raised me to never put my hands on someone unless they touched me first. Be that as it may, my home training went out the window along with my common sense just thinking about Sam sleeping with Gucci. "Of all people, why her?" I exploded. "What did she do for you that I didn't?"

"Pull over." With a hand to his face, Sam peered out the window.

"I'm not doing shit until you answer me," I demanded. After a few minutes of riding in silence, I sighed. "Why did you come back for me? Why did you propose to me? If you didn't want to be with me exclusively, you should have left me alone."

"Amina, I love you. I swear I do. I made a mistake. On God, that's all it was." His eyes softened as he placed his tattoo-covered hand on my thigh. "Baby, you're my ending and my beginning. Without you and our kids I have nobody. I swear I will never hurt you like that again. I love you."

"Sam, you don't mean that." With the back of my hand, I wiped my face.

"I've killed for you." His eyes met mine, and my heart stopped. He had never spoken of what he'd done for me since the day he did it. "I've killed for you, Mina. If that's not love, then I don't what is."

Sam was right. What he did to my ex was proof that he loved me. However, I didn't appreciate being reminded of it.

Chapter 96

Nikki

"You guys have five minutes," an officer standing outside of a door marked ATTORNEY said. He stood tall and looked stern, like a British soldier.

"She'll be quick." Parish reached into his pocket and handed the officer a business card. Behind the card was a folded Benjamin Franklin. "Go ahead, Nikki. I'll be out here." Parish nodded, and I nervously opened the door.

Mario sat at a small table in the square room with his head down. "Rio," I said while approaching him.

Instantly his head popped up, and he smiled. "Nik, I missed you." He stood from the table and wrapped his massive arms around me. "How's my shorty?" He rubbed my belly.

"We're a little beat up, but we're okay." I wanted to wait until Rio came home to tell him about the accident, but since it didn't look like that was happening anytime soon, I went ahead with it.

"What happened?" He was all ears.

"Is this a safe room?" I asked while roaming the undersized box with my eyes to locate any cameras.

"Yeah, it's safe. It's used for lawyer meetings, so they can't monitor or record. What's up?"

"A car that was watching Gucci's hotel followed us back to the freeway and hit us." I didn't want to upset Rio more than I had already, which was why I purposely recalled the accident with only minor details.

"What?" Mario frowned. "Are my kids okay?"

"Yeah, they're fine. We ran for safety at a nearby house. The man who helped us was murdered though."

"I seen that shit on the news! Did you see the face of the son of a bitch who came after you?" Rio's scowl was bone-chilling.

"No." I shook my head.

"I bet it's the Filipinos. These fuck niggas gon' make me bury some fucking body as soon as I hit the bricks!" Rio hit the table.

"Mario, calm down." I placed my hand on his shoulder. "You don't need any more trouble. Ms. C wouldn't be able to handle it." I smiled.

"How is my mother?" Rio changed the subject.

"She's okay, but it's going to break her heart when I tell her they denied your bail."

"Parish is going to appeal that shit. Tell her don't worry. I'll be home soon." Mario sounded certain.

"I'm not trying to be negative, but what if you don't make bail?" I was a realist. "I need to know what we're up against."

"If they don't grant me bail, then we will push for early trial date."

"Do we really want to do that?" I winced at the thought of the jurors finding Rio guilty.

"Nik, either I'm going to prison or I'm not. It's just that simple." Mario looked down at the ground. "There is no need to beat around the bush, ya know." He took a seat and pulled me down onto his lap.

"Forty-five to life is forever." I laid my head on his shoulder. "Forever is a long time." As a hustler's wife, I always lived with the thoughts of losing my man to the streets by way of death or prison, but when it happened, I still was not prepared.

"Look at me." Mario lifted my face by the chin. "Stop thinking about tomorrow and start living for today." He kissed my lips. "This shit is fucked up! I won't lie about that, but I know it'll all work out in the end. Just trust me."

"Rio—"

"Take this time and put some of your focus back on your writing. Schedule some book events or something. Let me worry about this." He kissed my lips again. "Promise me."

"I promise." Just as I went in to kiss his lips again, there was a bang on the door before Parish and the police officer entered.

"Time is up." The officer walked over to Mario with the cuffs out. I stood from his lap and looked on as Mario was shackled. It was then that I noticed the chains around his feet.

"I'll be home soon. Take care of my kids and my mama."

"I will," I replied while blinking back the tears. I just wanted him to come home with me. It broke my heart to see him like this. "I love you, Rio."

"I'll love you always and forever." He winked, and with that he was gone.

Chapter 97

Lovely

"The vans are outside." Maine walked into the living room wearing a red Polo V-neck and a pair of black joggers. "Coco, Do It, and Shawnie are in the first one. Me and Lovely are in the second one."

"Why can't we all go together?" I asked with a whisper. Shawnie was lying across the sofa with her head on my lap.

"They are after me and you. There is no need to put anyone else in danger," Maine replied solemnly. While I wanted to contest his decision, I knew he had a point. If something happened to my niece, I would never forgive myself.

"Fuck that, bro." Do It stood from the love seat he was sharing with Coco. "Y'all my family. I'm rolling with y'all."

"We appreciate you, but Coco and your daughter need you more." Maine looked down at his watch. "The jet will be at the landing strip in exactly thirty minutes. We need to file out."

"Where are we going?" Coco was terrified out of her mind, and I couldn't blame her. She wasn't used to this.

"I've secured a small villa on Macapule Island. The flight there takes about two hours," Maine explained. He was always on top of shit. Had it not been for the millions he'd managed to stack during his career as a sought-after hit man, we never would've been able to fly all around the world fleeing the situations we always managed to end up in.

"I need to get back to my babies." Coco's leg was trembling.

"The jet is going to drop us off first, and then you will be flown back to Detroit." Maine rested a hand on her shoulder. "Don't worry. I got you."

"Thank you, Maine." Coco stood and wrapped her arms around him.

"Come on, y'all, let's go." After briefly hugging her back, Maine broke the embrace and headed toward the door.

Do It grabbed Shawnie and tossed her over his shoulder. She was still asleep. With one last look around, I grabbed my bag and followed the group. Once outside I inhaled and exhaled deeply to calm my nerves.

"See you on the other side, Lovely." With an uneasy smile, Coco stepped into the unmarked black seven-passenger van parked in front of our door. I didn't reply because her words made me tremble. They were the last words my sister Tonya said to me before she was killed.

"I love you," I shouted, but no one heard me as they had already closed the door.

"Come on, L." Maine urged me to get inside our waiting vehicle.

"I'm scared. Something doesn't feel right," I admitted just as the first van pulled off.

"We just need to get out of here. Once we're at the landing strip, you'll feel better." Maine opened the door to the van.

"I hate leaving Nichols like this. By the time someone finds her, she'll be decomposed." The thought alone was enough to make me grab my stomach.

"I hate to sound rude, but decomposition can't be much worse than the state she's in right now." Maine grabbed my arm. "Let's go. We're like sitting ducks standing out here."

"*No te preocupes voy llegar hasta allí seguro.*" The Mexican driver smiled while looking at me through the rearview. Shortly after that he started the van and pulled away from the house. Something was amiss. I just couldn't put my finger on it.

"Where did you get these vans?" I nudged Maine.

"I ordered them from the airport." He shrugged while peering out the window. He obviously wasn't paying me and my paranoia any mind.

"So why did he tell us not to worry and he would get us there safe?" My Spanish wasn't the best. However, after spending time in the whorehouse with no one but Spanish-speaking individuals, I knew a little something.

"What?" Maine frowned before realizing what was really going on, and by then it was too late.

Out of nowhere two Hispanic men attacked us. They had been hiding in the back row beneath some blankets. "Shit!" Maine tried to pull his piece but was knocked upside the head with the butt of the gun. Blood squirted from his head as he fell into my lap.

"*Agarrar el bitch!*" the driver spat while roughly pulling the van off to the side of the road. By the way the second man in the back seat forcefully wrapped his arms around me, I knew he had instructed them to grab me. "*Mátalo!*"

I'd heard that word enough to know what it meant. "Please don't kill him," I begged while fighting like a wild animal. "Maine, get up please!"

"Shut up." The third man finally decided to speak some English while opening the door and dragging me out of the van.

"*Mátalo,*" the driver shouted again to the man standing by the van.

"Please!" I cried. "Maine, get up." I was screaming at the top of my lungs, but the shit was no use. He was laid out on the seat, unconscious.

"Get inside." The third man forcefully pushed me inside the trunk of an old Pontiac.

"Fuck you!" I spat literally.

"Get in the fucking car!" This time he cocked his pistol and pointed it right between my eyes. Reluctantly, I did as I was told. As soon as he closed the trunk, everything went black, and the sound outside became muffled. Instinctively, I felt around the car for anything I could use as a weapon. It was no use. The trunk was empty.

"*Mátalo ahora!*"

"Noooo," I sobbed while beating on the roof of the truck. "Please get up," I cried. That was when I heard the dreaded sound that ended Maine's life. Pop! Pop! Pop!

Chapter 98

Gucci

"Where are you coming back from this time of night, or should I say morning?" Aunt Lucy stood in her robe blocking the front door.

"Aunt Lucy, I'm grown. Good and grown, might I add." I'd just come in from working my first shift at Diamondz, and a bitch was tired.

"Grown people don't sneak out!"

"I didn't sneak out. I was working." Casually I slid past her.

"Working where?" She frowned. "Especially dressed like that?"

"I got a job at the strip club down the way, and there is nothing wrong with my outfit," I replied while smoothing over the red halter top and mini-skirt I'd purchased after my rendezvous with Funky earlier.

"The strip what?" she hissed. "I know my only niece, my dead sister's daughter, ain't down there taking her clothes off for the devil." She was looking at the ceiling. I guessed she was talking to God.

"Chill, Aunt Lucy. I'm the bartender," I lied. Honestly, I really didn't give a fuck what she thought about how I made my money. Yet and still, I didn't feel like one of her long-ass lectures. It was nearly 3:00 a.m. All I wanted was a hot shower and a comfy place to lay my head.

"Whew!" Aunt Lucy blew out an audible breath. "Girl, bartending at the devil's playground ain't really no better, but I'm so thankful you ain't show-ing folks your cookies." She smiled. "Look, I know you need to get on your feet. Just find something better as soon as you can, baby." She locked the front door, then turned and kissed my forehead. "Good night, Gucci."

"Good night, Aunt Lucy." With a smirk I went over to the fridge and poured myself some iced tea.

"How did it go?" Rhythm entered the kitchen. I hadn't seen or spoken to her since earlier when she wouldn't let me use her car. When I came back from shopping, she was already gone for work.

"See for yourself and tell me what you think." I slid the dance bag off my shoulder and tossed it at her. She set it down on the kitchen table and unzipped it.

"Holy crap!" she exclaimed. "You made all this money?" Her eyes were as wide as saucers.

"One thousand and thirteen dollars to be exact." Honestly, I'd made triple, even quadruple, that on a slow night in Detroit, but this was a good start.

"I cannot believe it, Gucci. It takes me almost a month to get this, and even then, Uncle Sam takes most of it." Rhythm played in the bag of money like a child. "Maybe I need to come up there and get me a bartending job."

"I dance," I whispered. She could be very naive at times.

"Oh." Instantly she released the money like it was on fire.

"Girl, get over yourself." Grabbing the bag, I rolled my eyes, then headed for Rhythm's room.

"There are plenty of decent jobs in the city. You should find one." She followed me.

"I got one thousand and thirteen reasons right here that say this job is just fine." With that I made a sharp right into the bathroom and closed the door. It was the one place I had privacy in this tiny house.

Buzzzzzzzzzzz. Buzzzzzzzzzzzzz. "Hello," I answered while taking a seat on the toilet.

"Hey, Gucci," Nikki whispered into the phone. "I tried calling you earlier."

"I was handling a few things. My bad. What's up?"

"Mario was denied bail today." She sighed.

"What!" I smacked my lips. "Damn."

"He's going to appeal it though. Hopefully, he'll be home soon." I could hear the sadness in Nikki's voice. I felt the same sadness in my heart.

"It'll be okay, girl." I did my best to comfort her about the man we both loved for different reasons. "You and I know he's a lucky son of a bitch." I laughed to lighten the mood.

"You're right. He is a lucky son of a bitch." She laughed back. "Hey, I saw Mina at court today. She asked about you."

"Was Sam denied bail too?" Guilt wouldn't allow me to acknowledge Mina. She was a good friend when I needed one. I knew the way I did her was foul, but it was what it was now. I never cried over spilled milk.

"Surprisingly, no. He was the only one I saw free today."

"Are you sure?" I sat straight up.

"Yup! I even called around to see if I missed someone. Everyone was denied bail except for the low-level soldiers," she explained.

"Then he's a rat, Nikki!" Just saying the words had me hot, but I knew what it was.

"What?" she asked in disbelief.

"He's a slimy-ass rat!" I wanted to hit something but didn't want to wake Aunt Lucy. "Think about it. He was the only one to make bail. That only happens when you snitch!"

"Sam wouldn't do that." She didn't sound confident.

"In the dope game, niggas will sell out their fucking mama. Trust me, I know." Briefly I thought about Cartier and his "loyalty ain't shit but a seven-letter word" speech. "Look, I know you don't want to hear this, but your boy is snitching. You need to tell Mario ASAP. Someone needs to reach out and touch his ass." I knew Nikki would understand me loud and clear.

"I'll look into it, and I'll get back with you." She sighed.

"He is a loose end!" I reiterated. "Tie his ass up!" Click!

Chapter 99

Nikki

"Are you going to eat something, Ms. C?" I looked over to see her staring at the television screen. She'd been in the same spot all morning. Breakfast had been delivered over an hour ago. The grits, cheese eggs, and sausage she ordered was now cold.

"No. I'm not hungry." She finally looked away from the television. "Have you heard from Mario?"

"Not today." I wanted to remind her that she just asked me that twenty minutes ago, but I knew she was in her feelings. Yesterday she cried for nearly two hours when I told her Mario wasn't coming home. My heart broke so bad for her that I hadn't really left any pity for myself. Instead, I'd thrown myself back into writing the follow-up novel to my autobiography. I thought after I penned the first book that would be it, but as I saw now, the life of a hoodwife never ended. "I'm going to take the kids to the pool for a little bit. Would you like to come?"

"No, baby, you go ahead." She sighed. "I'm going to lie back down."

"Okay, get some rest." I looked down at Junior, who was picking at the stitches in his arm. "Stop that."

"Mommy, I want Daddy."

"Daddy will be home soon, Junior." With a smile I started tickling him, and before long, he was over it. "Come on, let's put on your trunks."

As I pulled him toward the bedroom, there was a knock at the door. Instinctively I grabbed the .22 stashed in my purse and headed to see who it was. With so many people mad at Mario and Gucci, I couldn't take any chances.

"Anjie, what are you doing here?" I asked after opening the door.

"Well, hello. It's nice to see you too." She sashayed into the suite and made herself comfortable. The tight ponytail and skirt suit she rocked was a clear indication that she was just leaving court.

"Don't give me that." Casually I slipped the gun back into my purse and zipped it closed. "Me and you aren't exactly besties right now."

"Fine." She grabbed a piece of cold sausage from Ms. Claudia's plate. "Let's talk."

"I was just about to take the kids to the pool. Give me five minutes." I held up five fingers, then took Junior to get dressed.

***

Ten minutes later we walked into the pool area, and Junior took off running. I had to remind him to walk. He obeyed me for all of two seconds before he jumped right in. "Oh, my God, get him," Anj, who was carrying Maria, screamed.

"He's been swimming since he was nine months old." We had a pool at our old house. I wasn't the least bit worried.

"Girl, let's sit on the side and put our feet in so we can be close in case one of us has to dive in." Anj wasn't taking any chances.

"So anyway, what's been up with Carter?"

"I don't know. He left me." Anjela looked down at Maria, who was making spit bubbles.

"What?" I frowned.

"He left me right after they had Mario in custody." She looked as if she wanted to cry but didn't let a tear drop.

"I told you he was only around for the case." Smacking my lips, I continued, "I knew that son of a bitch was grimy. Did you ever divulge our business to him?"

"No!" she snapped. "Ain't no dick that good."

"So, you haven't heard from him since?"

"Girl, the day after we ran into Gucci, he packed his shit and got the fuck out of dodge." She shook her head.

"What about his brother Cartier?"

"I ain't got nothing on him either." She shrugged. "Seems like me and Gucci both got played."

"Mommy, look," Junior shouted. He was trying to do a flip.

"Be careful," I hollered back. "I hate to say it, but I told you, Anj."

"I wanted you to be wrong so bad," she admitted. "I just wanted him to be the one."

"The one is out there. You have to be patient." Although I wanted to gloat a little more, this wasn't the time. Anjela always picked the wrong men because she tried to force love. Anybody who smiled at her or held the door open when she passed by was marriage material in her eyes.

"This might sound silly, but I've always wanted what you had." She looked at me.

"What's that, an ex-husband in jail and a baby daddy who got back with his ex-girlfriend?" I had to laugh to keep from crying. "My shit is fucked up."

"Yeah, your shit is fucked up," Anjela joked. "Seriously though, you and Mario may have had some major ups and downs, but the love you have for one another is timeless. Y'all got that life-or-death kind of love."

Hearing her words caused a tingling sensation in my stomach. "He's been my everything since day one. I don't know what I'm going to do without him."

"Nikki, don't talk like that. This is only temporary. He ain't going nowhere." She slid closer and wrapped her arm around me.

"Mommy, look!" This time Junior was floating backward.

"Good job, baby." I gave him two thumbs-up.

"Speaking of baby." Anjela looked down at Maria. "What are you going to do with this one?"

"I don't know." I shrugged. "Honestly, I haven't thought much about it."

"What if Gucci never comes back?"

"Then I will raise Maria as my own in her absence." It was a no-brainer. If Mario was willing to accept a child I made with another man, why couldn't I raise the one he made with Gucci? "It's no secret that we've never had a real friendship, but Maria is a product of Mario, and that's all that matters." I felt the need to explain it to Anjela, who was looking at me sideways.

"Girlll," she exclaimed. "You need to—" She was cut off by her ringing phone. "Hello. This is she." She turned to look at me. "She's right here. Hold on." Anjela handed me the phone.

"Hello," I said after looking at the call screen. It was Sherri, my book publicist.

"Nikki, I've been trying to reach you. What's up with your number?" Sherri was from New York, and her accent was thick as hell.

"I'm sure you've seen the news about Rio." I sighed, knowing Sherri wasn't going to be thrilled with the recent headlines. "I changed the number and forgot to give it to you."

"Yes, I've seen the news, and I'm glad I found you!" she hollered. "The publisher wants to send you on a big book tour. I'm talking Los Angeles, Las Vegas, Miami, and the like."

"What?" I was shocked. "I thought they may have wanted to drop me with everything that's going on."

"Doll, the fact that your ex-husband is all over the news made your book sales skyrocket!" Sherri was so excited. "This weekend alone you've sold three times the number of books you sold during the initial release. Book venues want you now more than ever!"

"Wow!" I looked from Anjela to Junior.

"What do you say?"

"I don't know." The reality was that I couldn't step away from the kids right now. "There is a lot going on here."

"Please," she begged. "This is the kind of thing that never happens to newbies. If you want to build a solid foundation for yourself and your son, you have to seize the moment!" She paused.

"You're right!" I agreed. "But I can't just pick up and leave right now. I've got two babies and a mother-in-law to look after." From the side of my eye, I could see my cousin mouthing something.

"Bring them with you!" Sherri blurted.

"Are you for real?"

"A change of scenery would probably do everybody some good." Again, she paused. "What do you say?"

"I'll do it!" With a smile I nodded as if she could see me.

"Good! You leave Monday. I'll forward the rest of the details as soon as I get them."

Chapter 100

Mina

"Mina, who the fuck been in here?" I could hear Sam yelling from downstairs. His ass hadn't been home all night, but he had the audacity to check somebody. "Answer me!" he barked.

"Shhhh!" I snapped while walking down the stairs. "Your children are taking a nap. Please don't wake them up."

"Who the fuck been up in here?" He was staring like he was ready to hurt me.

"What?" Nervously I backed up a little. I'd never seen him look so deranged. "Are you talking about this mess?" I pointed to the stuff I hadn't completely cleaned up from yesterday. "I told you the DEA came and—"

Whap! He backhanded me so hard that spit flew from my mouth. Thankfully, it wasn't blood.

"What the fuck is wrong with you?"

"Answer my question." Casually Sam licked his lips and stood there like nothing happened.

"I don't know what you're talking about," I replied while still trying to process what had just happened. Sam had never laid a hand on me before. In fact, he was against domestic violence, which was why he killed my ex-husband, Trey, in the first place.

"There are two wineglasses on the table." He pointed. "One has lip gloss, and the other does not." He raised a brow.

"Jamison came over the other night to check on me and the kids." I felt no need to lie as there was nothing to hide.

"Did you fuck him?" Sam began to chew on his bottom lip.

"What? No!" I shouted quickly. "Sam, what is wrong with you?"

"What's wrong with me?" he asked like I had no right to ask the question. "Oh, I don't know, maybe the fact that my fiancée is in my crib drinking wine with another nigga while I'm locked up has me tripping."

"Nothing happened between us, unlike you and Gucci!" I rebutted.

"That was in the past. We won't keep talking about this." Sam started to walk away.

"Nigga, we are going to keep talking about this until I say we're not!" I was getting just a little sick of his shit!

"Mina, don't walk up on me like that." Sam spun around and put his face into mine. He looked like he was going to hit me again.

"I'm leaving."

"What?" He frowned.

"I thought you was different, but you ain't nothing but a younger version of Trey!"

"Don't compare me to that nigga!" Sam was enraged.

"He cheated and he hit me. So did you." Slowly I walked past him. To my surprise, he didn't follow me looking to fight.

"Mina, I'm sorry," Sam said to my back as I headed up the stairs. "I'm sorry."

"Save it, Sam." This relationship was going nowhere. It was time to get off this train before it was too late.

Ding-dong! The doorbell stopped me in my tracks as I ascended the stairs. Instantly I prayed it wasn't Jamison.

"What up, Nikki?" I could hear Sam. Slowly I turned around to see Nikki standing at the door with bags in hand.

"Hey, Sam. May I come in?"

"Uh, yeah." Sam looked back at me before letting her enter.

"Hey, Nikki." I started back down the stairs to see what she wanted.

"Sorry for just stopping by. I wanted to check on you guys and bring you a few things." I was sure she could feel the tension in the room. "I can come back if it's not a good time."

"Nah, girl. Come on in."

"How are you, Sam?" She eyed him suspiciously. "It's good to see that you got out."

"Feels good to be out." He shifted nervously. "Hey, I got to take a call, but I'll be back down shortly."

"What's up with him?" Nikki asked after Sam was out of earshot.

"Don't get me to lying. The nigga has been acting different since he got out. Come on." I nodded for her to follow me. "Sorry about the mess. The DEA did a number on this place, but we can go into the dining room."

"No need for apologies. I've been there." She laughed. "It'll be weeks before you get it back together."

"I feel so violated," I explained. It felt good to vent to someone familiar with the process. My colleagues at the office wouldn't understand. Besides, I wasn't trying to put them in my business anyway.

"Girl, yes." She set the bags down on the table. "It's a major invasion of privacy."

"They raided my panty drawer and broke a picture frame with my son's picture in it." After pulling out a chair, I took a seat.

"Are you okay?" Nikki stopped removing items from the bags to look at me.

"Everything will be okay." I shrugged. "It's only stuff, right?"

"Mina, are you okay?" she asked again, this time taking a seat and pulling it close to mine.

"No," I admitted. "I never signed up for this. It's a little overwhelming, ya know."

"The minute you decided to date a drug dealer, you signed up for this, boo." Nikki placed a gentle hand over mine. "I wish I could tell you it gets better, but it doesn't. Sure, the money is good. The vacations are lavish, and the benefits are everything, but when the kitchen gets hot, we all end up getting burned." She pulled back and changed the subject. "I was shocked to see that Sam got released when no one else on his level did."

"On his level?" I looked at her, puzzled.

"Everyone in the organization has a 'position,' just like at work." Nikki made air quotes. "At the bottom, you got the lookouts and the corner boys. Near the top you have captains and lieutenants. Sam was a lieutenant," she explained. "None of them were released."

"Really, not a single one?" I was beginning to see her point. Things looked suspicious.

"Mina, do you know if Sam made a deal?" Nikki asked me outright.

"I don't know," I replied truthfully.

"Are you sure?"

"I swear on my son." I raised my hand toward heaven.

"Don't protect him."

"I'm not!" I snapped.

Nikki gently removed her hand from mine. "Did you notice that Sam never asked me about Mario?" She waited for me to process what she'd said. "He's changed. You know it and I do too." She wiped my mouth with her thumb and showed it to me. It was covered in the blood oozing from my lip. "He hit you, right?" She stared at me. "He is not the person you fell in love with."

"I know and I'm leaving him," I admitted, then went on to explain the shit Sam put me through, which included the Gucci situation. "That was my friend."

"Gucci is no one's friend!" Nikki shook her head. "That girl has been out for self since the day I met her."

"It doesn't even matter. I'm done with her and him." I smacked my lips. "As soon as you leave, I'm packing my bag, and I'm leaving."

"Mina, can I ask you a favor?" Nikki slid closer to me. "Sam is up to some shady shit. I need someone on the inside like you to help me find out what it is."

"I can't." I was ready to walk away and be done with this entire lifestyle.

"Look, the H.O.F. is a family. We look out for each other." She looked me over. "Like it or not, you're under Mario's umbrella too, so you're my family, Mina." She paused. "I promise if you do me this one favor, I will protect you."

"Nik, I hope you brought over some of your famous meatloaf, because a nigga is starving!" Sam hollered from the hallway.

"Family don't snitch on family. We can't let Sam hurt our family," Nikki mumbled, but I heard her loud and clear. "Help me and I got you."

"You hear me?" Sam poked his head into the dining room.

"Sorry, little brother. I only brought diapers and formula this time." With a fake smile, Nikki stood from the table. "I'll be out of town for a little while, but as soon as I get back, I'll bring one over especially for you." After grabbing her purse, she turned my way. "I'll talk to you soon."

Chapter 101

Lovely

"Help me please!" I'd been screaming for nearly an hour. Although I could hear the muffled voices of a man and a woman, no one came to my rescue. "Fuck!" Again, I tried to wiggle myself free from the chair I was tied to.

After being forced into the trunk of that car, I was driven to an unknown location. When the trunk opened, I was stuck with some type of needle. It had to be a tranquilizer, because it knocked me on my ass. When I came to, I was blindfolded and bound to a chair.

"Come on, Lovely." I was growing frustrated with myself for not being able to break loose. "Shit!" I must've pulled my wrists and ankles against the plastic ties one too many times. Not only did it hurt like hell, but they'd also started to bleed. "Help me!" I screamed at the top of my lungs.

"You better stop that before something happens." A young woman appeared at the door of the room I was held up in.

"Who's there?" I could only see her silhouette.

"Shh," she whispered before approaching me. "Please don't scream." Her face was thin and dirty. Her body was frail, and her feet were bare.

"Help me get out of here."

"I can't. They will kill us both if you come up missing."

"Who are they?" I wanted to know.

"Here, I brought you some water." She was holding a metal cup.

"I don't want any water. I want to get out of here." Briefly I looked away from the girl and toward the door she'd come from.

"You're not going anywhere. The chair you're sitting in is bolted to the floor." The girl must've been reading my mind.

"If you let me go, I will take you with me."

"I can't!" She shook her head.

"Where am I?"

"I must go." She began to back away just as another person appeared in the doorway. This time it was an older woman.

"*Pasando?*" The woman wanted to know what was going on.

"*No pasa nada, Mama.*" The little girl told her nothing was going on.

"Go back upstairs!" the woman demanded, and she did as she was told.

After she was gone, the gray-haired, overweight woman walked up and stood over me for a moment. "Did you drink some water?" Her teeth were rotten, and her breath smelled.

"Where am I?"

"Did you drink some water?" she repeated.

"Where the fuck am I?" I did the same. Within an instant, she had wrapped her hand around my neck.

"Girl, you're at Mama's house." She gritted her teeth. "In Mama's house, the only person using that kind of language is Mama." With a raised eyebrow, she released her grip on my throat. "Now Mama asked you a question!"

"No, I didn't drink the fucking water," I replied while flinging spit from my mouth into Mama's hair. Part of me wished I hadn't done that, but another part wished she'd just kill me for doing so. I was ready to be put out of my misery.

"You're a bad muchacha I see!" Mama reached into her apron and removed a butcher knife. "Mama don't like bad girls."

"Ahhhhhhh!" I screamed after the old bitch stuck the tip of her knife into my thigh.

"Now look what you made Mama do." She wagged her index finger. "Now tell Mama you're sorry."

"I'm sorry," I mumbled. With a smile she removed her knife, wiped the blood across my jeans,
then placed it back into her apron.

"Mama!" a male's voice called from a distance.

"I'll be back with food and water. In the meantime, don't bleed all over my floor." With a grimace,
Mama turned and walked away.

Chapter 102

Gucci

"You killed it tonight, Novella!"

"Make that money, girl."

'Thanks, y'all." With a smile, I headed down the hallway past Star and Delilah. I'd just come out of the dressing room. It was Friday night, and the place was packed.

"Where exactly are you going?" KK asked after stepping out of her office.

"Home," I replied as a matter of fact.

"This shift isn't over until three a.m." She looked down at her cheap Walmart watch. "It's only one fifteen."

"I made all the money I need to make tonight. I'm going home," I repeated.

"You're not special. If you can't work until the shift is over, then you need not come back." She rolled her eyes. The bitch had it out for me ever since I fucked her man three weeks ago. Although Funky was cool in bed, nobody was checking for his fat ass like that. The shit was old news. KK needed to get over it.

"Bitch, please! You and I both know you can't fire me." With a smirk, I decided to fuck with her. "When Funky hears about it, I'll be back."

"Listen, bitch, I don't know who you think you are, but up in here, you ain't shit!" She pointed her almond-shaped acrylic nail in my face. "I'm the head bitch up in here. Always have been, always will be."

"KK, you ain't shit but a bitch pretending she's the boss." Slinging the bag over my shoulder, I pushed my way past her.

"Don't come back here!" she shouted. "I fucking mean that shit."

"Bye, bitch." I put my middle finger in the air. "I'll see you tomorrow."

"You heard what I fuckin' said," KK hollered back before disappearing into the office like the scared little girl I knew she was. She might have had a big mouth, but she ain't want it with me.

"Everything all right, cuz?" Rhythm asked as I approached the bar. She'd just finished serving a customer.

"I'm Gucci." I laughed, letting her know I was good. "What about you? Do you like the new job?"

"Heck yeah." For two weeks, Rhythm watched me come home night after night with bundles of money. At the start of the second week, I was able to purchase a used Honda and put a deposit down on an apartment. She wanted in on the fast money but wasn't ready to become a dancer. I asked Funky if she could tend the bar for a few nights a week, and he obliged. Rhythm wasn't getting as much money as me, but she was doing well for herself. Naturally, Aunt Lucy didn't know, which meant Rhythm had to sneak in and out of the house like a kid.

"I'm glad you—"

My words were cut short when Will's ass walked into the club wearing a two-piece linen suit and Borsalino cap. The huge rock on his pinky finger was blinding. No doubt he'd melted my necklace down and used the diamond to make his ring.

"This muthafucka got me fucked up!"

"What's wrong, cuz?" Rhythm followed my gaze and immediately tensed up. "Gucci, don't—"

"I'll be right back." Without another word, I reached into my bag and retrieved the .38 Special I'd purchased from one of my customers last week. He said in my profession I needed protection, and I agreed. Back in Detroit I didn't always have to pack heat because I had a team of gorillas ready to go ape shit if I told them to. However, down here I was on my own.

With the gun in hand, I walked right up to that snake and pressed it into his back. A bitch like me couldn't care less that we were in a roomful of people. Yet and still, to my advantage, everyone was watching Lola, a popular dancer on stage, as she stuck a Coke bottle in her coochie. No one was paying me any attention, or so I thought.

"Don't you say a fucking word!" I whispered into his ear. "Head back outside and nobody gets hurt."

"So, you gon' rob me in a roomful of people?" He was cocky until he turned to see my face. That's when he practically pissed himself.

"That's right, nigga." I nodded. "Walk back outside. We need to talk."

After giving it careful consideration, Will gave in to my request. Luckily, no one was outside, which made my plot for revenge that much better.

"Where are we going?" he asked with his hands raised.

"Step behind the club into the alley."

"Take your shit and let me go please." He pulled off the ring and handed it to me.

"Man, I swear on my deceased mother I will shoot you dead right fucking now if you don't keep walking!" I was happy to have my shit back, but this bitch needed to be taught a lesson.

"Okay, I'll go, but please don't hurt me." Will had to have been a capital bitch! A real nigga would have never left the club with me without at least trying to take the gun first.

"Move, nigga!" I cocked the pistol, then nudged his back. He walked behind the club near the dumpsters. The plan was to scare him by hitting him a few times.

"Please don't kill me!" Now his soft ass was crying.

"Shut the fuck up." I raised the gun, then came down hard on his face, striking his ass twice with the butt of the gun. By the time I went to strike him again, the muthafucka collapsed onto the red dirt and didn't move. "Get the fuck up." I kicked him with my shoe. When he still didn't move, I knew that my plan had gone terribly wrong. "Will." This time I kneeled and shook him. He was dead. "Fuck!"

"I knew you were shady. I'm calling the police!" The sound of KK's voice behind me shook me to my core. Why had the nosy bitch followed me outside? The last thing she or I needed was for her to be a witness to the murder I'd just accidentally committed.

"Don't you fucking move." Instantly I pointed the gun toward her.

She looked on nervously. "What are you going to do, kill me too?"

Just as quick as she asked the question, I provided her with an answer. Pow! Pow! Without thinking twice, I hit her with two shots to the lung and chest, killing her instantly.

"Shit! Shit! Shit!" Now I was knee-deep in a bunch of bullshit and needed to get out of there fast. Nevertheless, before I fled the scene, I used my shirt to wipe the gun free of my prints, and then I put the gun into KK's hand. After putting her prints on it, I went over and placed it into Will's hand, where I left it. I needed it to appear like they had killed each other.

Once my composure was controlled, I casually walked over to my car and got inside. Quickly I took a deep breath, started the engine, and pulled off. I hadn't meant for this to happen. Things had gone too far. What was I supposed to do now? Where was I going to go?

Chapter 103

Nikki

"Nikki, this sure has been nice, but I think it's time for me to go home." Ms. Claudia cleared her throat. We were standing in the lobby of the Pendleton hotel in Augusta, Georgia, waiting for the Uber.

"We've only been gone for seven days. You're leaving me already?" So far, the tour had been amazing. All the signings in each city were packed to capacity. Readers from all over the world came to converse with me, and I was elated. Never in my wildest dreams did I think that my words could impact people the way they did.

"I miss bingo and my friends." Ms. C laughed. Honestly though, I thought she was just a little tired of me and needed a break from the kids, which was reasonable.

"I'll be sad to see you go, but I understand." I nodded.

"Are you sure?"

"Yeah, I'll be okay," I assured her. "After we do the event today, I'll book you a flight home."

"There's the car." Ms. C pointed before grabbing Junior's hand and heading to the door. As I bent down to pick up Maria's car seat, the cell phone in my purse starting ringing.

"Hello."

"Nik, it's me," Mario said. For the past few days, he'd been calling me from illegal burner phones. Even behind bars he had the power to break the rules. "Have you heard anything about your boy?"

"No. Mina hasn't gotten back with me." At the suggestion of Gucci, I'd told him about Sam. Needless to say, he was beyond pissed but wanted concrete proof.

"I think I'm going to send some cats to holla at him," Mario huffed.

"Look, there is no need to jump the gun. Let me handle it. When everything is confirmed, I will let you know. In the meantime, just work on getting home." By now I was at the car with Ms. C. Therefore, I switched the conversation up. "Daddy is on the phone, Junior."

"Daddy! Daddy!" My son jumped up and down in the seat. "Hey, Daddy." He took the phone and held it up to his ear like a big boy. "Where you at?"

I didn't know what Mario said because I couldn't hear him. Whatever it was must've satisfied Junior because he kept right on talking. "Let

Grandma talk now." I practically pried the phone away and handed it to Ms. C. While they conversed, I strapped Maria in, and we pulled off.

About thirty-five minutes later we arrived at The Book Hut, a black-owned establishment. Just as I'd suspected, the line was outside the door.

"Hey, doll, don't you look fabulous." Sherri met us at the rear entrance of the building.

"Thanks, girl. You look gorge yourself." I greeted her with a hug after exiting the Uber. Ms. C collected Junior, and I grabbed the car seat before we all headed inside.

"This one is a little different," Sherri explained.

"What do you mean?" So far, all of the book signings had been the same. I smiled for pictures, signed the books, and that was it.

"Well, the owner thought it would be fun to do Q & A with a small group first, then do the book signing afterward." Sherri showed us to the table set up with all of my marketing materials such as a banner, bookmarks, and flyers.

"I guess that's okay." I shrugged.

"Cool! Just have a seat, and I'll bring the line in. Did you want a water or something?"

"No, I'm good." I took a seat. Ms. C and the kids sat at a nearby table.

"Good luck, Mommy." With a smile, my baby gave me the thumbs-up. His little gesture warmed my heart. In the midst of all this negativity, it made me feel good to show my son something positive.

"Okay, guys, we thank you for being here today. Mrs. Wallace is ready for all of your questions, but please only ask one per person so we can get to everyone," Sherri instructed the group of women now sitting in the chairs before me. There were probably about thirty people, give or take a few. Five of them were wearing Black Lives Matter shirts. "Go ahead." Sherri pointed to a young woman sitting in the front.

"Nikki, my name is Kendra, and I too am a hood-wife. My man P-nutt is doing a ten-year bid. He's only been gone for six months, and I'm already lonely." She cleared her throat. "My question is, when is it okay to lie with another man? I mean, we have needs too." Her question was met with a few cheers from those in agreement.

"Kendra, I can't answer that question for you." I smiled. "Everybody's situation is different. You will know when it's time, I'm sure."

"Thank you, Kendra. Next." Sherri pointed at one of the ladies wearing a Black Lives Matter shirt.

"Mrs. Wallace, did you know that by glorifying the term 'hoodwife,' you're admitting your role in the damnation of our youth?" The woman didn't wait for me to respond. "The drugs that your husband sold are just as responsible for killing our people as the police!" Before I had time to rebut, the lady and her small army had pulled out several open jars of red paint and tossed them at me. I hadn't even seen the fucking cans until now. "Mrs. Wallace, the blood of our youth is just as much on your hands as it is on your husband's!"

"Security!" Sherri screamed.

"Mommy!" Junior started screaming, which caused Maria to cry as well.

"Murderer! Murderer!" the ladies chanted while being escorted from the building.

"Nikki, are you okay?" Sherri flew over to where I sat frozen.

I wanted to attack these bitches! I wanted to yell at the top of my lungs that Mario was not my husband and that I was trying to wash my hands free of street shit. However, the bloodred paint covering my body was a clear indication that no matter what I said, the world would always think otherwise.

Chapter 104

Mina

"They are waiting for you in the boardroom, Mina," Kathy, one of the other real estate agents, said as she passed my office.

"I'm on a call, but I'll be there shortly. Take notes for me please," I whispered with my hand over the receiver.

"Hello, are you there?" Jackie, one of my over-bearing clients, asked during my moment of silence.

"Yes, Mrs. King, I'm here," I replied while rolling my eyes. "I heard what you said about raising the sale price of your home from two hundred to two sixty. Honestly, that's a bit steep. The comps in the area are selling between one fifty and one eighty."

"Listen, I'm trying to make more money for the both of us," she snapped. Jackie was a feisty old bitch who was working on my very last nerve.

Buzzzzz. I looked down to see the cell phone buzzing in my lap. It was Sam calling for the fourth time in twenty minutes. Lately he'd been extremely possessive, and I didn't like it one bit. The real reason I hadn't gotten ghost yet was because of my conversation with Nikki. Hell, if the bastard would rat on his own friends, I knew he would drop a dime on me in a heartbeat. Although I really had no part in killing Trey, I was afraid Sam wouldn't see it that way if he ever snitched on me.

"Amina, did you hear me?" Jackie invaded my thoughts.

"Yes, I did. I'll update the listing right now," I replied as Jamison walked into my office.

"Good. I think you'll thank me when—" Click!

"I can't believe you did that." My eyes widened after Jamison pressed the disconnect button.

"I was tired of hearing you talk to her." He laughed. "Come on, let's head to the meeting."

"Thanks for saving me." I sprang from my seat, then grabbed a notepad and pen.

As Jamison and I walked into the hallway, Sam was approaching us. "What the fuck is this?" He stopped in midstride.

"Honey, I didn't know you were in the neighborhood. Is everything okay?" With a smile, I tried to play it off as I hugged him.

"I called your goddamn phone multiple times. Had you picked up, you would've known," he whispered into my ear.

"Sweetheart, you remember Jamison, right?" I backed away from the embrace.

"What's up, man?" Jamison nodded. Sam, on the other hand, said nothing. "I was glad to hear that everything worked out for you," Jamison added.

"What the fuck do you know about my situation?" Sam barked before turning toward me. "Oh, that's right, this is the motherfucker you were sipping my wine with in my house, right?"

"Sam." I tried to calm him down, but it was no use.

"I don't know what's going on here, but—" Jamison tried to interject.

"But nothing, you bitch-ass nigga!" Sam spat. "You want to fuck my woman, don't you?"

"What?" Jamison looked from Sam to me. I was sure he wanted me to stop this circus before it got out of hand, but I couldn't. Sam was showing out, especially now that he had an audience. The meeting my boss Hilda was having had just come to an end. Everyone was now staring at us.

"You probably done already hit that, huh?" Sam continued. "I should whoop your fuckin' ass right now, nigga!"

"This ain't what you want, little boy!" Jamison slapped his chest.

"Oh, my God." I cringed. Now that both were turned up, I knew things were about to explode. However, my boss came just in time.

"Samuel, I like you, but if you don't get off my property right now, I will call the police." Hilda bravely stepped between the men.

"The police?" Sam spat. "Fuck the police!"

"I'm not playing games," she replied calmly. "I know you can't afford any more trouble, so please leave." This time Hilda pointed toward the door.

"Call the police, Hilda." Sam smiled, then looked at me. "I've got a few things I need to talk to them about anyway."

Instantly my heart fell into my panties, then came back up and punched my throat. "I'll get him out of here," I spoke up, totally mortified about the situation.

"Amina." Hilda turned to face me. "Your services here are no longer needed."

"Please, Hilda, I need this job." I couldn't believe this.

"I tried to overlook your situation when it appeared on the news, but now your mess has spilled into my office." She sighed. "I'm sorry, but your affiliation with this ghetto foolishness has no place here, and neither do you." Once again, she pointed at the door.

"I understand." With a halfhearted smile, I nodded.

"Security will bring your belongings outside to your car shortly."

Chapter 105

Lovely

"Mama, please stop!" The more I screamed, the more the woman seemed to enjoy slapping my back with some sort of tree branch. Whap! Whap! "Please!" I screamed again. The last few days had been rough. Mama had whooped my ass more times than I could remember.

"*Suficiente!*" A male's voice from behind the door was telling Mama this was enough. Yet and still, she hit me again. "*Suficiente!*" the man hollered again. Instantly the hairs on my neck raised. His voice didn't sound like the one I was used to hearing; his voice was familiar.

"Mauricio!" I called out. It was Santiago's brother.

"Give us a minute." After dismissing Mama, he came and stood in front of me. I'd known from jump he was behind this whole thing.

"Why didn't you just kill me?" I hollered in agony. The stinging of my skin rocked my body with pain.

"I wanted to, but those weren't the orders." He smirked. "Besides, your nigga ass isn't worth the material they make the bullets with." He laughed. At that moment I wanted to spit in his face, but I didn't have the energy. It was no secret we despised each other.

"What orders?" I grimaced. "Wasn't it you who organized this?" I was confused. The only person who would have exacted revenge on Santiago's behalf would have been his brother.

"*Encantadora.*" On cue, Santiago's ghost appeared in the doorway.

"What the fuck?" I damn near had a massive heart attack as he walked toward me, looking very healthy for a corpse. "I thought you were dead." Relief oozed from my voice shortly before anger took over. "What the hell is going on here?"

"Your boyfriend planned the whole thing." Santiago kneeled before me. "I'm sorry I deceived you, my love, but business is business. He paid me handsomely to pretend to get shot," Santiago explained.

"But you guys sent an explosive bomb to my house. Maine can't be behind this." I rambled on while trying to make sense of the entire situation.

"That wasn't us." Santiago shook his head. "From my understanding, your boyfriend hired a hit man. The explosive was meant for you."

"Fuck!" I spat, then replayed the shit in my head. It was Maine who'd asked me to get the door originally. Had I not passed the task off to Nichols, he would have succeeded with my assassination. "But wait." I paused. "When we were kidnapped from the van, they shot him." Something wasn't adding up.

"He wasn't shot." Mauricio laughed. "The whole thing was staged. He hired someone to kill you and make it look like he was dead."

"What?" A slew of emotions hit me like a Mack truck.

"Sweetheart, when I found out you were being held here with Mama, I used the money your boyfriend paid me to get you back." As Santiago spoke, he pulled a knife from his pocket to cut me free. "Mama is queen of the mafioso. She feeds off torturous punishment. People bring victims to her to pay off their debts," Santiago enlightened me. "The man your boyfriend hired to kill you owed Mama, so he paid her with you."

"But why would Maine play me?" I asked myself more than Santiago.

"Come on, baby. Let me get you home." Santiago tried to lift me off the chair.

"Baby!" The word struck a nerve with me as I figured out why Maine wanted me dead. He needed me out of the way so he could return to Detroit and raise his new baby with his new woman. "Santiago, I need a fake passport and ID."

"You wanna leave me?" He looked heartbroken.

"I told you to leave her here." Mauricio shook his head.

"Please, Santiago." Weakly I turned my back toward him, exposing the blood and rips on my shirt. If need be, I would've gotten naked so he could see the number 42 branded on me by his people. "Haven't I been through enough? I need to go home."

"Okay, I'll get you there. I promise." Santiago nodded his understanding, and it was a deal.

Chapter 106

Nikki

"Hey, it's me. I just wanted to let you know that we landed back in Michigan safely an hour ago. I'll call you later. Thanks again for everything." After leaving the message on Sherri's voicemail, I ended the call, then slipped my cell phone into my purse. I was supposed to be on the road for a few more weeks, but after that bullshit in Augusta I needed a breather. Sherri suggested I take the kids on a mini vacation, but all I wanted was to go home. Besides, I needed to see Mario as well as check in on Mina.

"I'm sorry about what happened to you." Ms. Claudia patted my shoulder.

"It's not your fault," I replied as we pulled up to a stop light. "There are just some ignorant-ass people in the world."

After I was doused with red paint, security had shut down the venue and apprehended the vigilantes. As badly as I wanted to leave right then and there, we had to wait for the police to come to and take our statements. I advised them I wasn't about to press charges, but they considered it a hate crime. Therefore, the State of Georgia would charge them anyway. Even though the publishing house heard about my ordeal and felt bad for me, they weren't trying to cancel any of my upcoming appearances. Sherri was able to work her magic and move some dates around, but I'd have to hit the road again in a few days.

"Have you heard from Mario?"

"No." I shook my head while cutting on the blinker. "After I swing by the house and grab a few things, I'll drop you guys off and make a stop by the attorney's office."

"Have you heard from G-u-c-c-i?" Ms. C spelled her name to throw Junior off. These days he was quite the ear hustler.

"Yeah, she's all right." I decided to keep it short. The less Ms. C knew, the better.

"That's good. I hope this mess blows over soon."

"It will," I assured her.

Fifteen minutes later I pulled onto my block and damn near wrecked the car when I saw the person sitting on my porch. "Baby, who is that?" Ms. C noticed him too.

"A friend," I lied nervously before parking in the driveway. "Give me a second." I didn't need Ms. Claudia getting out and being up in my business. Yet and still, she was all eyes and ears.

"Long time no see." Maine stood from the step and met me on the walkway. He tried to give me a hug, but I had to swerve him for obvious reasons.

"What the hell are you doing here?" While asking the question, I swiftly pulled him back toward the porch, away from the car.

"I been coming over here every day for the past three days hoping to catch you."

"Again I ask, why the hell are you here?" This time I folded my arms.

"I didn't like the way we ended things." Maine peered into my eyes. "I needed to see you again."

"Look, you've got to go." Instinctively, I removed my focus from him and stared at the ground. "I've got too much going on to be dealing with this right now."

"I've seen the news." Maine grabbed my hand. "Let me be here for you, for my baby. You need a real nigga, not some dope dealer. You need a man to provide for you. Let me be that!"

"Maine, please stop." I'm not going to lie. His warm hand felt good up against mine, but I wasn't checking for him like that. My heart belonged elsewhere.

"Whether you like it or not, Mario is going away. You will need somebody to lean on. Let me be that somebody." This time he smiled, exposing his pearly whites.

"You and I will never happen even if Mario does eternity on the inside. Let's not forget about your girl," I reminded him.

"I've handled that part of my life. She is no longer an issue," he replied with a stone-cold glare that gave me chills for some reason. "Nikki, I don't have no family besides the baby in your stomach." He paused. "For the sake of my seed, we need to see if this thing between us works."

"Jermaine, there is nothing between us." Again, I gazed down at the ground.

"Look me in my face and tell me that." Maine bit down on his bottom lip, and I damn near lost it. "Look, I left my contact information in your mailbox." He leaned into my ear and whispered, "Call me when you're done playing games."

As I watched him walk to the cocaine white BMW and drive off, Ms. C practically fell over herself getting out the car. "I know that boy," she hollered.

"Who, him?" I frowned. "Where could you possibly know him from?"

"That's Mario's brother."

"What?" I asked with a chuckle.

"His name is Jermaine, right?"

"Yeah." I nodded slowly.

"That's Mario's older brother. They had the same no-good-ass father, Je'mario Woodson," Ms. C informed me, and I damn near fainted.

Chapter 107

Gucci

"Goddammit!" I hit the steering wheel over and over while speeding down the street. How the fuck had shit gone left just that fuckin' fast? My mind was racing a mile a minute. I needed to get out of Bama like yesterday. Therefore, I decided to grab my shit from Aunt Lucy and lie low.

"Hello?" I answered my cell phone hastily while deciding what my next move was.

"Hey, it's me," Nikki said into the receiver.

"Let me call you back," I whispered while bringing my car to a slow creep. There was an unmarked police car resting in the driveway of my aunt's house. Two things struck me as odd right off the bat. The first was that there was no way the police could've beaten me home from the scene of the crime. The second eerie thing was that the vehicle had Michigan police tags.

After taking a position on the corner, I cut the engine and killed the lights. Silently, I watched as

Aunt Lucy answered the door. She and a man conversed shortly before he handed her a paper then
stepped off the porch. Under the dim streetlights, I
tried to make out the man's face, but it was useless.
All that was recognizable were the three letters on
his hat: DEA.

My phone rang. "Hello?" I answered without
looking at the caller ID.

"Gucci, what in the hell has your ass done now?"
Aunt Lucy snapped. I could see her shadow behind
the living room curtains. Her head was waving
back and forth while her hand flapped in the air.

"I haven't done anything." While lying, I turned
my attention back to the officer, who was now
behind the wheel of his vehicle. He was sitting
in the driveway watching my aunt through the
window just as I was. "What's going on?"

"Some police officer from Detroit just showed
up at my door looking for you. He said there is
a warrant out for your arrest! Are you a fugitive,
girl?"

"No, Aunt Lucy, I ain't no fugitive." I smacked
my lips. "What did you tell him?"

"I told him I ain't seen ya," she stated as a matter
of fact. "Gucci baby, we're family." She calmed
down. "If you're in any kind of trouble, please let
me know so I can help you."

"Thank you." After years of thinking my aunt
didn't like me, it was times like this that made me

tear up. Since being on the streets at 16, I thought it was me and Mario against the world. After losing him, I was all I had, or so I thought.

"I love you the same as I loved your mama." Aunt Lucy laughed. "Even when she did wrong and got into some trouble, I always had her back. I've got yours too. Just come home, and we'll fig-ure this out."

"I'll call you tomorrow, okay?" With that I ended the call. It meant a lot to see that my aunt cared about me, but right now I had bigger fish to fry.

Two minutes after I ended the call, the police officer pulled his vehicle from my aunt's driveway and started down the street, going in the opposite direction. I was right behind him.

"Who are you, and what are you doing here?" I asked aloud as if the officer could hear me. I'd been in the game long enough to know that DPD didn't have the money or the resources to send a bounty hunter all the way to Alabama to get me. There was something shady going on.

"Hello." Quickly I answered the phone again. My shit was blowing up tonight.

"They're dead!" Rhythm screamed into the phone.

"Who?" Although I'd been waiting on the call, my heart still hit my ankles.

"KK and that man from the pawn shop." Rhythm was hyperventilating.

"Oh, my God! Are you serious?" I tried to sound surprised while putting the car in park. The police car had just pulled into a gas station. I was parked far enough away not to be seen but close enough to see him.

"Gucci, please don't . . . don't . . ." Rhythm cried frantically.

"Where are you?" I snapped, instantly growing irritated. I knew what she was about to say, and I didn't need the dumb bitch to say it in front of a whole lot of people.

"I'm in the bathroom at the club. The police have us locked in here for questioning." Rhythm sniffed.

"Don't say shit about me to them! Do you understand?"

"I'm scared," she admitted.

"Did you kill them?" I hollered.

"What? No."

"Then what the fuck are you scared for?" Without another word I ended the call and tossed the phone onto the passenger seat. The walls were closing in on me. I didn't have time for her cry baby ass.

Beeeeeeeep! Jerking my head up, I saw a red Dodge in my rearview. Some lady was trying to pull into the gas station. I was blocking the entry. Normally I would've blown my horn back at her ass, but the last thing I needed was more attention. Therefore, I casually inched my whip up to let her pass.

"Fuck!" That's when I noticed the police car was gone.

Chapter 108

Mina

"Amina, you better get your boy before I call the police and press charges on his ass!" Jamison hollered into the receiver. I was out for my morning run with the ear buds in when he called.

"Slow down." I spoke through strained breath. "What are you talking about? Did something else happen?" By now I was putting the brakes on running and slowed to a steady jog.

"The nigga followed me all day yesterday."

"What do you mean he's been following you?" This didn't make any sense. Sam hadn't mentioned Jamison since the day we left my job. As far as I was concerned it was over.

"He came to my home, then followed me to work. He showed up at my bank while I was there on lunch, and I seen him outside of my daughter's school when I went to pick her up!" Jamison was heated. "I don't know what the problem is, but you better address it before Smith & Wesson do."

"I didn't know any of this was going on, but I'll handle it." Sam and I hadn't spoken since he'd gotten me fired, which was why I had no idea what he'd been up to. "I'll talk to him and call you back tomorrow."

"You better get that nigga, Mina!" Jamison hollered just before hanging up on me.

Instantly I turned around and headed back to the house. Sam was really beginning to piss me off. Something was up with him, and I needed to know what it was ASAP.

As I rounded the corner, Sam was pulling out of the driveway like it was on fire. He went speeding down the street right past me. "What the fuck is going on?" I said to no one in particular as my phone rang again. "Hello?"

"Mina, it's Nikki. How are you?"

"I'm all right, and you?" I knew she wasn't calling me to make small talk, so I cut to the chase. "Hey, now is not a good time. Can I call you back?"

"Mina, have you found anything?" Nikki proceeded as if she hadn't heard me.

"No, I haven't," I replied while putting my key in the door.

"He's hiding something. I need you to find it."

"Nikki—"

"When you find it, please call me?" She didn't hang on for me to reply before she hung up.

As I entered the house, I called Sam's name although I knew he wasn't there. When I didn't hear anything, I made a mad dash toward the basement where his man cave was located. It was where he'd been spending a lot of his time lately.

At first glance, everything seemed normal until I walked over to the ash gray leather recliner. Resting on the seat was a Bible. Sam wasn't a godly man, so immediately my antennae went up. Quickly I grabbed the Holy Book and flipped through a few pages. That's when I spotted a business card for Lieutenant Toby Kaufmann of the narcotics division. Naturally, my stomach did a backflip, yet I tried not to jump to any conclusions. Maybe there was a logical explanation?

Immediately after trying to think of one, the wind was knocked out of me when I looked down to see an old cell phone resting on the coffee table beside the recliner. It wasn't Sam's phone. In fact, it looked like a minute phone from the corner store. My gut told me not to touch it, but curiosity had gotten the best of me. A quick scroll down the call log proved that the lieutenant's phone number was the only one being dialed and the only call being received. Nervously I pressed send and held my breath.

"Samuel my man, please tell me you've got some more good information that could keep Mario Wallace behind bars," Kaufmann said through the receiver.

Instantly I hung the phone up, erased the dialed call, and then dropped it and the Bible like they were hot. Reality had just smacked me in the face. Sam was indeed a snitch.

"What are you doing?" Sam was standing at the top of the stairs, staring me down. I hadn't even heard him come in.

"Are you an informant?" I couldn't beat around the bush since I'd been caught red-handed going through his stuff.

"Mina, they wanted to give me ten to fifteen years," Sam admitted. "I did what I thought I had to do for you and my children."

"We could've fought the case, baby." I tried to sound caring as I walked up to him. Really though, I was nervous as a muthafucka.

"I can't do five let alone fifteen." Sam looked me over.

"What about Mario? He was your friend," I reminded him.

"There ain't no friends in the trap!" Sam barked. "Fuck Mario and the rest of them niggas. My freedom means more to me than theirs."

"You're right, baby." I could tell he was getting turned up, so I wrapped my arms around him and kissed his chest as an attempt to calm him down.

"You can't say shit to nobody!" Sam grabbed my arms tight.

"I won't say anything, I swear."

"Good." Sam smirked. "Because if you do, I'll shoot you dead just like I did Trey, or I might just tell Kaufmann you killed him. Either way, you lose." Sam leaned down and kissed my forehead.

It was right then at that very moment I knew he'd lost his marbles. Sam wasn't the same. It was really time for me to go. The only problem was that he wasn't going to let me walk out the door. The only way I was leaving here was over his dead body, or in a body bag myself. I wasn't trying to die, so I'd have to kill him first!

Chapter 109

Lovely

Thanks to Santiago, I was provided with a new identity and a new lease on life. In addition to the passport and driver's license, he also provided me with $10,000 in cash. It wasn't much considering what I was used to, but it was just enough to do what I needed to do. Although it was sad to say goodbye, we knew being together wasn't in the cards for us. Besides, he knew how badly I wanted to exact revenge on my shady ex-boyfriend. Maine and his baby's mama were officially on my shit list.

"Ms. Walker, your plane should be boarding shortly. Please proceed to gate 27 and enjoy your flight." The pretty young clerk handed back my fake documents. Nervously I retrieved them and headed toward the gate as she'd instructed. My heart was beating so hard I thought people could see it through my shirt.

"Pull it together, L." Quietly I tried to give myself a pep talk, but it was useless. Although the hardest part was over, the fear of being caught had a bitch shaking like a leaf on a tree. Yet and still, I swiftly continued moving through the airport like I hadn't a care in the world.

"Ms. Walker!" a man wearing a blue blazer and gray slacks called from behind me. Although I turned to look at him, I didn't stop. "Tina Walker!" This time he ran up to me. That was when I remembered my alias.

"I'm sorry, were you talking to me?" I played it cool with a smile. He didn't seem so impressed. In fact, he looked angry, which was a red flag in my book. Had I been made? Quickly I surveyed the area for the fastest getaway, but there was none. The nearest door was back by the clerk at the counter I'd just left. I was screwed, or so I thought.

"You left your bag at the counter, Ms. Walker. I practically had to sprint to keep up with you." He huffed and puffed, then handed me the black Hermès bag Santiago had given me. Inside the bag was the majority of my cash and a change of clothes.

"Thank you! I can't believe I left it," I replied, fully relieved. "Can I give you something for your good deed?" Reaching in my pocket, I pulled out a crisp hundred-dollar bill.

He smiled and nodded. "Enjoy your trip."

***

The flight back home was smooth and fast. We even arrived almost thirty minutes early. Words couldn't explain how blessed I felt when the plane landed at the DTW airport. Never in my wildest dreams did I think I would step foot on Detroit soil again, yet there I was. After grabbing the cheapest rental I could get from Avis, I hopped on the freeway and headed straight to the one place I knew I could get answers.

"Welcome to Salon 3K. Do you have an appointment?"

"Is Coco here?" I asked while looking past the flamboyant male receptionist.

"And you are?"

Before I could reply, a familiar face walked into the salon wearing a silk blouse and a pair of Affliction jeans. His short hair was fire engine red, and his rhinestone nails were on fleek.

"Donald, let me call you back!" Semaj, my old stylist and friend, ended the call he was on to hug me. "Lovely Brown, girl, if you ain't a sight for sore eyes." When he pulled back, his eyes were watery. "Last I heard you was dead."

"Nah. Death doesn't become me," I joked. I wanted to tell him that my new name was Tina Walker, but I decided not to interrupt the moment. "Man, I've missed you so much. How are you, boo?"

"Child, I really thought you was dead." He cried some more and squeezed me tight. "What happened to you?"

"It's a long story, but I promise to catch you up one day soon."

"Are you here for good? Where is that fine-ass man of yours? Child, he kept my pockets laced buying shit for you," Semaj rambled on.

"I'm just passing through, and Maine is gone." I swallowed hard. "Hey, can you please get Coco?" I snapped my fingers at the receptionist, who was standing there being nosy.

"Who is up here making all this damn noise?" Coco stepped into the lobby and did a double take. "Lovely? Oh, my God, what are you doing here?" She looked stunned, confused, and happy at the same time.

"Can we go somewhere and talk really quick? It's urgent!"

"Yeah, come on." She pulled my arm toward the back. "Semaj, have a seat. Brittani will be right with you," she said almost as an afterthought before turning her focus to me. "What's up, girl? Are you all right? I got worried when we didn't see y'all at the jet. Do It said Maine probably arranged two planes. You don't look right. Are you okay? Is Maine okay? Is it okay for you to be here?" Coco bombarded me with questions once we were in her supply room with the door shut.

"Maine set the whole thing up!" I snapped.

"Set what up, L?" Coco asked, completely clueless about the shady shit Maine had pulled. Her ignorance was a relief to me, as it was confirmation that she wasn't a part of the plan.

"Girl," I sighed. "The pizza bomb was meant for me."

"What?" Coco's mouth was open so wide I could've counted every filling in her teeth.

"To make a long story short, when the plan to kill me didn't work, he pretended to get killed himself and left me for dead in Mexico."

"Lovely, no." Coco shook her head. "Why would he do something like that? I thought y'all were okay."

"He got Nikki pregnant, Coco!" I kicked the wall. My anger was apparent. Out of nowhere, tears exploded from my sockets. "While finding out my son was fucking dead inside of me, she was probably lying in bed, dreaming of baby names and shit!" I paused. "Why do bad things happen to good people? I'm a good person."

"Lovely, I had no idea this was going on." Coco wrapped her arms around me. "You are a great person. With or without Maine, you will make a great mom one day."

"The doctors told me I couldn't bear any babies, which is why I told Maine to bring me Nikki's baby." Quickly I rubbed a hand across my face. "I guess he didn't like that idea and decided to cut his losses with me. Meanwhile, he's here playing house with her."

"This shit is bananas." Coco was still overwhelmed with the information I'd given her. "What are you going to do?"

"I'm going to kill them both!" With no remorse, I looked my best friend square in the face and told the truth. I had nothing left to lose. Life had turned me into a bitter bitch! If I couldn't be happy, then neither should they.

Chapter 110

Gucci

"Where the fuck are you?" I hollered into the cell phone while pacing the floor of the hotel room I'd occupied for nearly twelve hours. After losing the supposed bounty hunter last night, I rented a room and called Rhythm this morning to bring me the stash of money I'd hidden beneath her bed. The plan was to hit the road ASAP, but she was three hours late.

"I'm coming down the hall now. You said room 403, right?" She sounded like she hadn't a care in the world, which really irritated me to the max. Right away I hung up the phone and opened the room door.

"If you weren't my cousin, I swear on everything I would kick your ass right now."

"Look, you said don't come here if I felt like I was being followed, so I made a few stops." Rhythm smacked her lips and tossed the duffle bag with my money onto the bed. "Gucci, what is going on? First Will and KK turn up dead, and then the police come to Mama's door?" Rhythm shifted her weight to one side, then crossed her arms. "They said you're wanted in some big drug case back in Detroit!"

"I don't know nothing about that," I lied while unzipping my bag to count the money inside.

"Gucci, I don't know about Detroit, but I do know what you did at the club. I can't be involved in nothing like that."

"What did you tell the police when they questioned you?" I looked up from the money.

"I didn't say nothing to them, I swear." She raised her right hand to God.

"Good, because I'm innocent." Again, I lied.

"Okay, you might be innocent here in Alabama, but Detroit is another story. This detective wants you bad!" Rhythm peered into my eyes. "He came back this morning and offered to pay Mama's house off in exchange for your whereabouts. Naturally, she declined, but this is serious, cousin."

"How do you know she declined?" with a raised brow I asked.

"The house was paid off years ago when my father was killed in that accident on the job. Besides, she wouldn't sell you out, and neither would I. Still, you need to tell me what's up." Rhythm took a seat on the bed as her cell phone rang. "It's Mama," she announced. "Hey, yeah, I'm here with her now."

While they conversed, I went into the bathroom to take a shit and collect my thoughts. Not only did I have to worry about where my next location would be, but I had to wonder who this fake-ass bounty hunter was. Why was I so important that he would offer to pay my aunt's house off? The shit wasn't adding up.

"Thanks for bringing the money. I'll be in contact when I touch down in the next town," I said while opening the bathroom door.

"You won't be going anywhere anytime soon." Bayani shifted the gun he was pointing at Rhythm toward me.

"You fuckin' rat!" Although Bayani was about to kill me, I was more pissed with my cousin. "I trusted you, and you bring him straight to me."

"I didn't, Gucci. I swear," she cried.

"Thank your aunt, Gucci." Bayani laughed. "She might not have needed that house paid off, but a hundred thousand dollars in her bank account was another story."

"Damn," I hissed. Just when I thought I could trust my aunt, she did this. "Bayani, before you kill me, please just tell me how you found me." I was trying to stall and think of a way out. However, my options were zero. I'd tossed the gun I used last night in the sewer, which meant I didn't even have a weapon to defend myself.

"I do my research," Bayani replied without offering any more details. "Now I have a question for you. Who goes first?" He looked from me to Rhythm, who began sobbing. She was scared and shaking.

"Let her go! This is between me and you." I tried to move in front of my cousin, but he cocked the gun, stopping me in midstride.

"One more step and you'll definitely be first."

"Run, Gucci!" Rhythm leaped from the bed and tackled Bayani into the wall. She didn't have to repeat herself, because I made a mad dash for the door like a bat straight out of hell. In hindsight I shouldn't have left my cousin, but this was my only opportunity to escape, so I took it.

Pow! Pow! Two shots rang out behind me, but I didn't turn around. Like a breeze I blew down the hallway to the stairwell, taking the stairs in pairs until I reached the lobby. "Oh, my God, she's hurt!" a woman carrying a baby hollered. She was standing at the elevator.

"Call an ambulance!" another guest yelled all while I continued toward the front door. I didn't know who they were referring to, maybe it was Rhythm, but I had to keep going.

"Ma'am, what happened?" the desk clerk called out before I pushed through the double doors and practically fell into the parking lot.

"Where are my fucking keys?" As I looked down to search my pockets, I noticed the blood oozing from the middle of my shirt. "Damn, somebody done got blood on me," I said to myself, completely delusional.

"Ma'am, please come back in. You're hurt pretty bad." The desk clerk tried to usher me inside. That was when I got hot, and everything started spinning. The faces surrounding me in the parking lot were doubled, and a few of them tripled.

"Fuck! He shot me?" I was in utter shock. Shit had never been as real for me as it was in that moment. "Please don't let me die!" I mumbled to the stranger just before everything went black and my body went limp.

Chapter 111

Mina

"Sam," I called from the kitchen where I was standing. While I waited for him to reply, I watched Nikki's name flash on my cell phone for the second time as it rested on the counter. Both babies were sitting on the floor in their car seats with diaper bags beside them. There was one large luggage bag as well. It was mine.

"What's up?" he asked after rounding the corner.

"It's over. I'm leaving, and I'm taking the kids with me." My voice was cool, calm, and collected. I knew the storm was about to come, but I was prepared for the rain.

"The fuck?" he spat. "You ain't going nowhere, especially with my fucking kids!"

Sam inched his way closer to me, and I brandished the butcher knife I'd been clutching behind my back. See, I'd been a weak woman too long in this relationship as well as in my last. From today on, I vowed that I would never let another man treat me like shit on the bottom of his shoe. I vowed that I would never let a man treat me like he owned me! I knew my worth, and I was way more valuable than how I let them treat me.

"You can let me leave voluntarily or involuntarily. The choice is yours." Once again, I waved the knife.

"What the fuck is wrong with you?" Sam hollered. "You think I'm scared of that?" He pretended to laugh.

"Try me if you want to." I gripped the knife tighter.

"Bitch, if you so much as give me a fucking paper cut, I will call the police and tell them our little secret," Sam taunted. He thought he was scaring me, but in fact he was making what I was about to do that much easier.

"If you tell on me, we'll both go to jail," I tried to remind him.

"I get full immunity for my part in any crime I've committed so long as the prosecutor gets to charge somebody." Sam smiled smugly. "I was going to pin the murder on Mario since it's a well-known fact they had beef, but now I guess I'll let you have this one." He reached into his pocket to retrieve the cell phone I'd seen in the basement. "Don't drop the soap."

Before he could punch in the first digit, I charged him full force and started jabbing him with the knife.

"How dare you do me like that?" I slid the knife into his abdomen. "After all I fucking did for you?" Next, I stabbed him in the chest. "Fuck you, Sam!" In tears, I cut him repeatedly until his body got heavy.

Without so much as a gasp, Sam hit the floor hard, almost taking me with him. The color in his body was draining right before my eyes. Blood was everywhere, including on me and the babies. Instantly I began to freak out.

"What have I done?" I screamed. "Sam, I'm sorry. Get up. Please get up." Although killing him sounded like the best way to keep my ass out of prison, it now seemed like I'd just bought a one-way ticket. "Fuck!" I hit the counter with the knife still in hand. "Maybe I can plead self-defense. No, maybe I can say it was a home invasion. No, I'll say I found him like this when me and the kids got home." As I paced the kitchen floor thinking of a way out of this mess, my phone lit up with another call from Nikki.

"Hey, girl." I tried to sound normal.

"I've been calling you all day." She sounded irritated. "Did you find out anything yet?"

"Yeah, in fact I did. You were right. Sam is a rat. I found the contact number for a detective, the cell phone they've been using, and some other stuff," I said.

"Damn, we trusted him!" Nikki hollered.

"I know. He deceived us all." While speaking, I looked down at Sam, who hadn't moved an inch. By now his soul was probably entering the bowels of hell.

"Can you meet me sometime today and bring what you found?"

"Um, it would be better if you come over here. Sam has my car." As shaken up as I was, the lies were flying off my tongue like I'd rehearsed them.

"What if he comes back and catches us?"

"He won't be back anytime soon," I assured her. "Can you come over right now?"

"Believe it or not, I'm actually in your neck of the woods. Give me like ten minutes."

"Perfect."

Ending the call, I inhaled deeply, then grabbed the car seats and headed to the garage. After strapping the babies in, I returned to the kitchen for the diaper bags and my suitcase, which I placed into the trunk. I reentered the house for the last time, then went to unlock the front door. After leaving it slightly ajar, I went back into the kitchen and took one final look at Sam. Quietly I stepped over his body, then went back into the garage.

Inside the car, I put on my sunglasses, opened the garage door, and backed out. A few minutes into the drive, I grabbed my cell phone and called the police.

"911, what's the nature of your emergency?"

"Please come quick. Nikki Wallace is attacking my fiancé with a knife!" I screamed bloody murder. "He's an informant on her husband's case!" I had to get that out there to prove motive.

"What's the address?"

"3898 Hocking Hills Lane. Hurry, she's killing him!"

"Help is on the way. Where are you? Can you get somewhere safe?"

"I'm taking my kids to the car now, and we're leaving. Please get here before she comes after me." Click!

I ended the call and slid the cell phone into my purse, right next to the bloody knife wrapped in a dish towel. Once I found a good place, I would dispose of it, but for now I was satisfied. All I needed was for Nikki to show up at my house, and I would be in the clear. Being grimy wasn't usually my thing, but sacrificing her freedom to save mine was the only option.

Chapter 112

Nikki

Just as I came up on the freeway exit to Mina's house, a call came in from Mrs. Crooks, my neighbor. Although she always had my number, she'd never called me, which was why a red flag went up immediately. "Is everything okay?"

"Nikki, it's your mother-in-law. She had a heart attack." Mrs. Crooks tried to deliver the news as gently as possible.

"What?" I hollered. "Is she okay?" Instantly I turned around and dropped back down on the freeway, heading home.

I'd left Ms. C and the kids there earlier while I handled some business with Parrish. He was working really hard on Mario's case, but the prosecutors and the judge were not making it easy. In fact, it seemed as if they were trying to make an example out of him. Parrish told me that we needed to know what the other side knew, which was why I'd been blowing Mina up all day. To hear that she possibly had the information we needed really made my day. Nonetheless, things would have to be put on pause now. My mother-in-law was my new priority. Although Mario's freedom was at stake, I knew he would have it no other way.

"Mrs. Crooks, answer me. Is she okay?"

"Baby, I really don't know." Mrs. Crooks sighed. "I was sitting here watching the television when I seen the ambulance pull up. By the time I got on my wig and shoes, they had her in the back of the ambulance already. I asked one of the techs what happened, and she said your mother-in-law felt the heart attack coming and called for help. They wanted to call CPS for the kids, but I told them I would take them if it was okay and call you."

"Oh, my God!" I couldn't believe it.

"Look, baby, you go ahead to Providence. These children will be all right until you get back."

"Thank you so much." I ended the conversation and did ninety all the way.

When I got to the hospital, I prayed for the best yet prepared for the worst. "Hello, I'm looking for Claudia Wallace. She was brought here because of a heart attack," I informed the receptionist.

"Okay, what's your relationship to Ms. Wallace?"

"I'm her daughter," I replied.

She searched the computer, then wrote something on a paper and handed it to me. "She's in the emergency room, through those doors." She pointed me in the direction.

"Thanks." With my paper in hand, I flew down the hallway. Once I arrived at the door marked EMERGENCY, I took a moment to calm myself before stepping through. Although I was relieved that she wasn't dead, I still worried about what condition I was about to find her in.

"Excuse me, I'm here for Claudia Wallace."

"May I see your visitor's pass?" the man behind the desk asked, and I handed it over. "She's right behind those doors, to the left. Room 11."

Nervously I approached the room and knocked lightly before entering. "Ms. C? It's me."

"Nikki?" She was lying in the bed with all types of stickers and cords attached to her. It was tough to see my girl like that.

"What happened? You scared me." Dropping my purse, I went over to her bedside and held her hand.

"This thing with Mario is weighing heavy on my heart. I need my baby to come home." As Ms. C talked, a single tear rolled down her face. Seconds later, the monitor started going crazy. Next thing I knew, a doctor and two nurses barged in and kicked me out. They told me that Ms. C had a mild heart attack at my house and that any little thing could trigger another one. They told me to come back tomorrow after she was stabilized but took down my number and promised to call should anything change.

When I arrived at the house, Maine was once again sitting on my porch. "As if today hasn't been stressful enough," I said after getting out of the car.

"Well, hello to you too." He stood to greet me.

"Now is not a good time." I looked over to Mrs. Crooks' house and remembered I had to get the kids.

"Just give me five minutes of your time." When I didn't respond he added, "Please."

"All right, five minutes." I sighed.

"Can we talk inside?" Maine grabbed my hand and led me toward the door, which was unlocked.

"What the hell?" we said in unison.

"Let me go in first and check it out." He lifted his shirt, ready to retrieve the 9 mm handgun tucked into the waist of his slacks.

"It's okay. My mother-in-law had a heart attack, and the EMTs must've left it unlocked." I pushed the door opened and turned on the light. Everything seemed in place except for a gallon of milk sitting open on the counter. I knew Ms. C must've been pouring some just before her crisis.

"Is she okay?" Maine asked, although I was sure he wasn't concerned at all.

"Yes, thank God. So, what's on your mind?" There was no need in dragging this conversation out.

"I'm leaving for good, Nikki." Maine looked me up and down with those bedroom eyes of his. "As much as I wish you'd come with me, I understand that it's not going to happen."

"True." I nodded.

"I realize taking care of a baby by yourself is going to be hard. Therefore, I wanted to leave you with something." He reached into his navy blazer and pulled out an envelope.

"What is it?"

"Open it and you'll see." He handed it to me and watched as I slid my nail into the envelope.

"Oh, my God!" I couldn't believe it. "This is a check for three million dollars. I can't take this." Quickly I handed the check back.

"I assure you it's all clean money." Maine tried to hand it back, but I refused. "Nikki, with Mario out of the picture, you will never be able to care for the children the way you want to. Please take the money. Consider it child support." Maine set the check on the table.

"I'm giving the baby up for adoption," I blurted out.

"What?" He frowned. "When in the hell did you decide that?"

"Remember when you came over here the other day, and my mother-in-law was in the car?"

"Yeah?"

"She told me that you and Mario are brothers." I looked up to see his reaction.

"What?"

"Je'mario is your father's name, right?" I paused.

"Yeah." He nodded, still trying to see where I was going with this.

"Your mother named you Jermaine, and his mother named him Mario. You two are brothers, which changes the game for me entirely. I can't keep this baby."

"You can and you will." As Jermaine spoke, the sound of my basement door creaking caused us both to look in that direction.

"My, my, my, imagine my luck finding both of you in the same place at the same damn time!"

"Lovely, what are you doing here?" Maine turned white, as if he'd just seen a ghost.

"Surprise, motherfucker!" She laughed cynically while brandishing a gun. "Did you think you could get rid of me that easily?"

"Let her go and we'll talk. She has nothing to do with this," Maine demanded.

"Oh, but she has everything to do with this!" the woman shouted. She appeared deranged and looked nothing like the person I'd met at the hospital some months back.

"Put the gun down, Lovely." Maine then pulled out his own weapon.

"So, you're going to kill me now?" Her eyes widened as she pointed her gun at him. "Then again, I guess I shouldn't be too surprised considering you already tried." They were involved in a full-fledged standoff.

"Put the goddamn gun down!" Maine barked.

"Make me," Lovely dared him before turning the gun back on me. "Who lives and who dies, Maine? The choice is yours."

Boom! Boom!

My entire life flashed before my eyes as Maine pulled the trigger, killing his ex-girlfriend right where she stood.

"Shit!" I screamed while watching her body hit the floor. Instantly I wished my eyes could unsee the lifeless shell on the floor, but it was too late.

"Nikki, that could've been you if she'd pulled the trigger. I had to." Maine pleaded his case. "Are you okay?"

"Yeah, I'm fine." I shook my head nervously. "What are we going to do now?"

"Don't worry. I'll clean the mess up and dispose of her body like nothing ever happened," Maine assured me. "Just take the check and get out of here."

"There is one problem though." I was trembling as I spoke.

"What?" He looked puzzled.

"The DEA has my house bugged with listening devices and video surveillance!" I looked into his face, and for the first time, I saw the fear of God in his eyes.

We'd just jumped from the frying pan straight into the fire!